IT WAS THE NIGHTINGALE

HENRY WILLIAMSON

IT WAS THE NIGHTINGALE

'And every stone that lines my lonely way,
Sad tongueless nightingale without a wing,
Seems on the point of rising up to sing
And donning scarlet for its dusty grey!'
From *The Flaming Terrapin,*
by Roy Campbell

ff

FABER & FABER

This edition first published in 2011
by Faber and Faber Ltd
Bloomsbury House, 74–77 Great Russell Street
London WC1B 3DA

A CIP record for this book is available from the British Library

ISBN 978-0-571-27737-7

To
Eric and Kathleen Watkins

CONTENTS

IT WAS THE NIGHTINGALE

PART FIVE
LUCY

Part One

LARK AND NIGHTINGALE

'When Love, who sent, forgot to save,
The young, the beautiful, the brave'

From *The Bride of Albydos*
LORD BYRON

Chapter 1

BÉDÉLIA

They had been married in January, and the winter was glorious
at first, with snow falling to a depth of six to ten inches all over
England; one of those seasons, which occur about every ten
years, when Europe is scoured by winds from the North Cape to
the Mediterranean; when strange birds, with staring eyes and
feathers the hue of frost and fog, are driven far from their sub-
arctic hunting grounds in search of food upon a white continent.

Such a snowfall had covered the West Country from the
end of the month until the beginning of March, bringing hard-
ship to farmers and labourers, death to old people, and joy to
the independent young. But even they were wearied out by the
thaw, which exposed the flattened fields and made every lane
a waterbourne carrying away dead song birds to be scavenged
by the daws and crows.

It had been dark in Valerian Cottage, all wood had long
since become ash in the open hearth, so that the fumes of the
American oil-stove, burning with a blue flame, had penetrated
everywhere within the kitchen and the two small bedrooms.

Now the frosts were gone, the sun shone with heat, celandines
and primroses broke along the hedge-bottoms and banks. By
April all was forgotten, and when the swallows came back, Barley
said, "Let's go and see mother, shall we?"

Irene lived in the south of France, in the foothills of the Pyrenees. They had thought of going in February, to ski on the slopes
above Laruns, but the hard weather had stopped them, while
Phillip had wanted to write his war-book. He had made a sledge
instead, an excuse to put off the start of the book, which had
haunted him ever since she had known him.

Barley realised that it was a part of his life which he could
never share with her, and while accepting this, or rather the fretful

perplexity which came between them whenever he thought about the war, it troubled her. Often at night she heard him sighing, he lying still lest he awaken her; she already awake, for it was as though she could feel his discord even in her sleep, but forbearing to touch him lest she come between him and his world of the dead which awaited resurrection. Mummy had gone through the same thing with Daddy when they lived in India, only with Daddy it had been thoughts of going home to England. Mummy had told her that the only thing to do was to wait for the moods to pass. With Daddy they had never passed, he had grown more and more irritable with Mummy; and now he was dead.

They set out in the third week of April for France; he wanted to see the battlefields of Picardy and Flanders on the way south. Having arranged for dog and cat to be boarded out—Rusty at the Ring of Bells, and Moggy with the Crangs next door—they headed north across Dartmoor on the motor-bicycle, she riding pillion, to the coast of the Severn Sea, to visit Aunt Dora at Lynmouth. They had gone on to Bristol, and so half-way across England to Gaultshire, where he wanted to see once more the woods and fields which he and his cousins had explored in boyhood.

Finding nothing there except change, they went on to the county town, arriving about midday. There was plenty of time; indeed time did not matter; and after a swim in the riverside baths, they had lunch at an inn patronised by farmers, where a good plate of mutton, followed by bread and cheese, could be got for a shilling. Gaultshire, he told her, was a great place for sheep, potatoes, and onions. Vegetables had been scarce, and therefore expensive, in South Devon where they lived; but here there was plenty, the crops had been got in before the hard weather.

Afterwards they wandered down to the cathedral. She saw two groups waiting outside, one of younger men, wearing velour and bowler hats, standing closely together; the other group, apart from the first, of elderly men talking among themselves in twos and threes and fours. They wore dark overcoats with blue velvet collars and silk hats, and appeared to be country gentlemen.

"Who are they, Phillip?"

She found that she was alone; he had turned round and was walking in the opposite direction. What could have happened? Then she remembered that he had gone to prison soon after the war, and so had never returned to any of the regimental reunions or annual dinners of old comrades. This must be something to do with the Gaultshire Regiment.

She went after him, to where he stood by a row of elms bordering the green.

"I don't want to see them!"

"But will it matter, after all this time?"

"I saw the Duke, and Lord Satchville. They'll remember. Satchville knew the name of every officer who passed through the Third battalion."

She asked a policeman what the occasion was.

"Depositing the old Colours of the R'g'ment, ma'm. Beg pardon, sir, haven't I seen you before?"

"It might have been my cousin, officer. He served with the 'Mediators'."

"Yes, sir?"

"Well, we must go to the cathedral, Barley, if we're not to be late. Good-day, officer."

"Good-day, sir."

When the groups had gone into the cathedral they entered by the west door and waited beside one of the massive cast-iron stoves against the wall.

Far away up the nave seated figures were facing the screen, behind which rose the organ loft with its sets of grey pipes. She moved beside him along the south wall, looking at the memorials and the tablets to the dead. They passed a white marble façade with a bronze palm-tree, above which hung a faded Union Jack crossed with a Lancer flag, only fragments of the dull colours of the silks remaining on the webbed frames. Egypt, time of General Gordon.

High above them, in silence and sun-shafts, rose the stone pillars supporting the vaulting of the roof. A bell tolled softly in that remoteness. It ceased, the silence came back. There were several people standing about in the side-aisle; the rows of dark seated figures would hardly notice them, if at all.

They came to a Crimea memorial; another of the Mutiny. She

touched his hand, affected by the very stones of the walls, the
worn Jacobean gravestones paving the floor, with their near-
obliterated names and coat-armour and carved Latin inscriptions. From these came a spirit of tranquillity, of reassurance, of
the essential goodness of man which was the truth of God. All
was well, she thought, with her father. Then looking up at Phillip's
face, she saw him biting his lips to keep back emotion, his eyes
opened wide to clear them of tears as the organ began to play
Bach's *Jesu, Joy of Man's Desiring*.

From an unseen wing of the cruciform church two files of boy
choristers moved into view. They were dressed in white sur-
plices over red cassocks, their hands were folded as they moved
towards the choir stalls followed by the lay clerks. Behind the
choir moved the Dean and members of the Chapter, and after
these old men came the Bishop, flanked by his chaplains, wearing
his mitre and cope of gold brocade. The General with his
G.S.O.s, thought Phillip.

It was a chastening moment when the voices of the choristers
soared up into the contained light of the stone-arched roof. He
felt to be free of himself, to be sharing the feelings, still existing,
of the men and women who had stood there through the centuries
and bowed their heads to the truth of life; as he was now; as they
were then. Life was of the same moment of Truth, from century
to century; the Spirit was from everlasting to everlasting.

In that feeling it was neither strange nor ironic that the Colour
Party marched up the aisle with fixed bayonets, corks on the
points, to deliver the Colour to the Bishop, to receive the Bene-
diction. Then the base of the staff was placed in a sconce on the
wall; there to yield, in dusty Time, he thought, its silks and dyes
to the summer airs which had made them, under God, the Spirit
of flower and winged insect, the Spirit of Evolution, which also
worked through the mind of Man.

They went on to Dover, leaving the Norton there and crossing
by boat to Calais. Looking around before the slow train to Arras
was due in, they passed a garage, and she got into conversation with the motor mechanic who was tuning a *voiturette* in a
shed.

The vehicle was long and narrow, with disc wheels. It had a
twin-cylinder, air-cooled engine driving two belts to the back-axle.

The two seats were placed tandem-fashion, the driver sitting at the back.

"À vendre," said the mechanic, seeing their interest. "Bédélia, c'est bon marque, n'est ce pas? Tres vite!" There followed a conversation in French.

"What's he saying, Barley?"

"He says it won the Grand Prix des Cyclecars in 1920, and is in very good tune. He wants seven thousand francs."

Phillip calculated. "About sixty quid. Too much. I've only got ten fivers on me."

"I've got twenty pounds Mummy sent me."

The mechanic was watching their faces. Then he spoke in French again.

"He says he would like to show you how to drive it. It takes two, one to drive, the other to shift the pulleys."

"But I don't think we can afford it."

"He says there is no obligation to buy, but he would like to show you how it works. It is the same Bédélia driven by M. Bourbeau, the designer, at an average speed of nearly seventy kilometres an hour for nearly four hours, during the Grand Prix at Amiens, when it won the race."

Phillip got into the front seat, which was like a canvas deckchair without the frame. The driver set the throttle, then running round to the back begun to push the cyclecar. Suddenly the engine roared and the mechanic flung himself sideways into the driver's seat behind Phillip.

They rattled up the cobbled street, heading for a road out of the town. From the horn, an affair of several brass whorls, came a series of high notes.

"En avance!" cried the driver, suddenly striking his passenger in the shoulder. Phillip thought this meant he was going open to up, and gripped the sides of the body; but the speed remained as before. The driver struck his shoulder again, while yelling into his ear and jerking about in his seat. Could he be getting into a rage? "Hoop! Hoop!" he cried, pointing over his passenger's shoulder into the cockpit, and making what appeared to be an exaggerated gesture of sawing wood.

"Ah, mon Dieu!" he exclaimed finally in resignation, as he closed the throttle and got out, to explain what was wanted. He pointed to a lever in the cockpit. "Comprennez? Eh bien, regardez-vous maintenant!" He indicated the pulley on the near-side of the engine mainshaft. When he pushed the lever forward and to the left Phillip saw that the outer flange of the pulley opened, so that the belt hung loose upon it. Then going to the other side of the car, the mechanic pointed to the smaller off-side pulley, which was now engaging its belt.

"Regardez!"

He got back in his seat and with a jerk shifted it back, together with the back-axle, this movement taking up the slack of the belt which had been loose while the engine was driving the other pulley.

So that was it—the lever, pulled back and sideways, or forward and sideways, changed over the driving pulleys while the driver took up the belt slack, or loosened it, by moving the floating back-axle.

They started off again. This time the gear was successfully changed while Bédélia rushed over cobbled road to tarmac. They stopped beyond the crest at a buvette, and drank cognac.

"Six mille francs, m'sieur."

"Ex bien, mon vieux!" replied Phillip, spreading his hands like the Frenchman of English newspaper cartoons. "C'est madame ma femme qui est le—la croupier—she has la banque—si vous comprennez?"

"Santé!"

Phillip looked more carefully at Bédélia. The belts were new, the tyres were not worn. It was a lovely horn, tightly curled. No oil dripped from the engine. The magneto looked clean.

From the nettles in the orchard beside the buvette came the notes of a nightingale. "Attendez, monsieur! Le rossignol!" He stared delightedly at the other's face. "Connaissez-vous 'Le Rossignol', par Stravinsky?"

"C'est un auto?"

"Non, c'est un opéra."

The mechanic shrugged his shoulders. They drove back, Phillip at the wheel.

"I've heard the first nightingale, Barley!"

"How lovely. They're always a few days earlier than the English birds. They'll be in full song in the Côte d'Or now."

"Let's buy this 'bus, and go there by road! A thousand miles, what an adventure!"

"Let me do the bargaining."

It was theirs for 5,500 francs. The mechanic filled the tank with *essence*, and put a spare tin of oil in the driver's cockpit, while Barley went to change the fivers into francs. The deal was concluded. One last thought as the mechanic prepared to push them off. What about a driving licence?

"Pfui! En avance! Bonne chance!"

Between trepidation and glee he steered for the high road across the down to Arras. It was tremendous fun down the straight road between poplars. Here he must stop on a slope, and look at Bédélia. Walking round her, examining the brake bands on the rear axle, feeling the tyres. No tool kit, or puncture outfit!

"We'll be able to get some at Arras, Phillip."

Arras! How strange to get anything in Arras!

On down through the poplars lining the road, the engine pulling well on less than half-throttle. The corn in the fields on either side of the road was beginning to shine in the breeze which blew the curls of the adorable head in front.

After an hour's run they came to St. Omer, where she bought sausage, bread, butter, cheese, and a pot of apricot jam, while he went after a bottle of vin ordinaire and one small glass, for of course they must share everything.

They sat on the grass in the Jardin Public, opposite the Place Maréchal Foch.

"I don't recognise anything! But then we arrived at night and saw only the arc-lights in the autumn fog." He sighed; with Barley beside him, the war was faded away almost to nothing. "Have some more wine?"

"Thanks. It's not bad stuff for a franc a bottle."

Marvellous girl, putting away the wine!

At Arras they stayed the night at a small hotel, newly built and decorated, called the Strasbourg. Barley did the bargaining: dinner, petit dejeuner, and room cost 50 francs, about 8/6d.—far too much, they thought, but the English had always been rooked by the peasants.

They walked around the town, still in ruins, and at 10.30 a.m. the next morning made for Cambrai on the straight N 39. The pavé was bumpy with brick-filled shell-craters . . . but where was Bourlon Wood, which had overlooked the Siegfried Stellung in November, 1917? It should have been on the left of the road—a hill one hundred metres high, which the Guards had not taken

and so the break-through had fizzled out. Where was Bourlon
Wood? He looked bewildered, lost.

"I am sure it was on the left of the road! I saw it a hundred
times! The company came out of the line on 30th November, we
had to wear our masks, even the horses—the place was drenched
with lachrymatory and phosgene. That's how I lost the way and
led the company right over there"—he pointed south—"to the
other flank of the salient, and got stellenbosched—kicked out."

"There's a wooded hill over there, Phillip."

She pointed to the right, to where a low long mound a couple
of miles away rose under the midday sun. "It's the only wooded
hill around here, so far as I can see."

"That's not it. It *can't* be!"

A mile down the road, with Cambrai looming near, he stopped
to ask a woman standing in a village partly rebuilt in red brick.
She said it was Raillencourt.

"Ask her if it was called Fontaine before the war."

"She says Fontaine is over there."

"But it couldn't be!"

Again the woman pointed. "She says that's Bourlon Wood."

"But I'm sure it was to the *left* of this road! I saw it many times.
We all did. It was shelled day and night—on the left of the road
as we went up from Graincourt."

"She says Graincourt is beyond the wood, lying off the Bapaume
road."

"Ah, yes! Of course! This is the *Arras* road!" She wondered
why he looked so relieved, as though he had found something he
had lost, and dearly loved. They went on to Cambrai and turned
right at the fork before the town.

"Of course! *This* was the road to Bapaume!"

The wreckage of Bourlon Wood was covered by green scrub.
Far away on the horizon lay the old Somme battlefield, like a
distant sea fretted by waves of wild grass and poles of dead trees.
He longed to be once again in the desolation of that vast area, so
silent, so empty, so—forsaken. Somewhere in the misty distance
were the failed objectives of July the First, that dream-like day of
terror and great heat; and below the horizon of fear was Albert,
and the Golden Virgin.

"It says Albert on the map, Phillip. Would you like to go
there?"

"But there won't be anyone there, now."

She took his hand and they walked into the wood. The forest floor was still rough and cratered, barbed wire among its brambles; half-buried dud shells, yellow gas canisters, faded stick-bombs, rusty screw-pickets—rifle-barrels—shreds of uniform—shattered helmets. There was harshness and distress in the air, the sun had no real kindness. He turned to living flesh for relief from thoughts of the dead, and lay down beside her in an area of sunlight amidst the shade of new leafy growth tenderly covering black and splintered trunks and branches of dead trees. He held her in his arms, at peace before rising on an elbow to regard the beauty in her face. One thought came from his blood into his mind and thence to his will: to make this calm and self-possessed girl pregnant.

"Barley, let's go on south!" he said, after they had lain in the sun. "I don't want to see the battlefields."

Cambrai, shabby and bleak like Arras, was left behind to gay toot-toots of the snail horn, hands waved to children. Onwards to St. Quentin, through the last of the Hindenburg Line country, grave of Gough's Fifth Army in March, 1918. Comrades, I will never forget. Sausage and bread and wine and a sleep in the sun before going on to Laon and thereafter it was all new country as they approached the fabulous Champagne department.

Six hours after leaving Arras they were in Rheims: 142 kilometres in 3 hours running time, and not one miss of either cylinder since leaving Calais. "O Bédélia, Bédélia, she must be christened with the *vin du pays*, a bottle of Veuve Cliquot bought in a wine store!"

After which Bédélia ran south in top gear on full throttle, leaving behind the Chemin des Dames—name inducing compelled thoughts of a hundred bombardments, attacks, and counter-attacks—now but a crest of young tree growth among chalky patches receding behind Barley's curly head. Bédélia rattled and bumped across the plain to the country of the Marne.

Within the hour they were in Châlons. Boys and old men actually fishing there—ah, the *Marne*, a word, a name—he said to Barley's candle-gilt face across the small *table à deux* in the dining-room of the Hotel d'Angleterre—that had the power to raise eighty thousand ghosts of the original B.E.F., ghosts of both dead and living.

"For we were all ghosts, whether in or out of the flesh," he went on, as he raised his sixth glass of vin rosé. "Can 'a necromancer raise from the rose-ash the ghost of the rose'? I shall do it one day soon! Meanwhile let's have another bottle of the ghost of the grape!"

"Vin rosé is fairly strong, you know. I don't want any more, but don't let that stop you. Another half-bottle?"

He sighed. "I'm only in a fume of words, words, words. The necromancer will never raise from the rose-ash the ghost of the rose."

She pondered this remark. Did he think there was a rose essence in the wine.

"I think it's made from a pink grape, isn't it?"

"You don't understand, you are all matter-of-fact."

He drank another half-litre in silence, and when they were in their room, she said, "Did I say something stupid?"

"Not in the least. It was I who was stupid."

"Look at me, Phillip!" She forced him, not unwilling, to stand before her, while she held his shoulders to look into his eyes. "How can I know what you mean, unless what you say comes from your real self? I can only understand you when you feel what you say! If you make yourself clear, in other words! Why should you allow yourself to be hurt, because people don't know what you mean? At first, when you spoke about the necromancer, I didn't remember that it occurred in one of the poems you read in your cottage to me when I first knew you. I do remember, now. It was in *The Mistress of Vision*, wasn't it?" She shook him playfully and said in a quieter voice, "Anyway, you've no need to worry, you *will* one day write a splendid book about your friends in the war. I *know* it. I know also that you feel that time is passing, and you're not working. But it is growing, all the time, in your mind."

He could hardly believe that it was not a dream that he was beside her in deep-feathered softness, sharing the delirious warmth of a girl, all of whose softness was for him: that the dream of love had come true: and most wonderful of all, she wanted him in the same way that he wanted her: all thought between them was a silk gossamer binding them as one person.

"Darling, darling, *darling* Barley, it's too good to be true!"

"Isn't it fun to be friends, as well as married?"

Yet once more he wondered if such bliss could last—to drift into sleep beside her with no more thought than scent was thought to a flower. Deep, deep sleep; to awaken and see the sun shining through the window; and what fun, another day lay before them, on their way to *thalassa!, thalassa!*, the sea of ancient Athens, and the radiance of the Greek poets!

After coffee and rolls and butter they went on their journey, travelling towards the sun above the mountains of the Massif Central. But after a while the sun went in and it rained; it rained harder; it poured down and there was no hood to put up. The belts slipped, the engine went dud, with water in the magneto.

They pushed Bédélia for a mile and came to a garage-shed where a new condenser was fitted to the magneto; very cheaply, he thought, giving the mechanic a *pour boire*. The engine fired at once, the rain ceased to fall, they went on happily through a damp twilight into Chaumont, to leave Bédélia in a side-street barn while Barley looked for a small hotel. It was a relief to him that she decided the price (while he waited below) and all he had to do was to be beckoned upstairs. Safe for one more night! No waiting by the road-side, walking about until dawn: the room, lit by electricity, was a refuge against the darkness of memory. The war was over!

They washed and changed, she collected their clothes to be dried; they went down to a wonderful dinner with a bottle of wine, most of which he drank before going to bed, half-blotto and wonderfully lucky to be safe under a roof with a girl, to watch the trim little female creature undressing quickly and lightly, to see her shape, her gentleness, the small breasts and thin arms and tiny waist and beautifully shaped legs and feet with their high insteps and broad toes; feet which he held one in each hand while determined to make her pregnant. She sighed, she kissed, she nuzzled his throat and cheeks and brow like an animal already enjoying its young.

Again they were on the road early, a clear bright day, the engine running well; through Dijon with its vineyards and rose gardens, stopping to eat their midday meal on a bridge over the Sâone—white wine, cheese, sausage and the usual long loaf of bread. He felt muzzy in the intensely hot sun, and she was sleepy too, so they slept on the river-bank, waking to throw off their clothes and swim naked in the water.

The river turned its course there, the flow had carved a pool at the bend. The water moved gently over a sandy bottom at the verge, and, towards the farther bank, it deepened over a stony pit. While they were swimming to the other side he saw what at first he took to be a water-vole on the bank; but coming nearer, he saw it had a flatter head and curiously small eyes with apparently no nose. It was scarcely seven inches long, with a stub tail, dun brown like its fur. Through the wimpling current he swam, nearer and nearer the animal, which did not move, but opened its mouth in an inaudible mew when the hand of his extended right arm touched the bank. He waited for her to draw level with him, and put a hand on his shoulder to steady herself while treading water.

"I've never seen anything like it."

They got out, and picked up the mite. It was cold, she breathed upon it for warmth, while feebly it sought with its paws to burrow between her fingers.

"It's hungry," she said. "Poor baby."

Phillip, looking down into the water, cried out, "Come here!"

On the stony bottom of the pool lay an animal slowly swaying in the current. It was on its back, it was dark except for a light patch on its throat. As they stared, the body lifted slowly and half turned over; the current checked this movement, and they saw something upon one paw, attached to a chain.

"It's an otter, it's been trapped! The chain is nailed to the top of that sunken post! The weight of the trap has drowned it!"

He swam underwater and hauled at the chain, drawing up the body until its spiky fur showed above the water. It was heavy with the weight of the trap; he released it and sinking down gripped the top of the post, to work it to and fro to loosen it. It was driven too deeply to be shifted.

"What a shame. They trap otters at Laruns, for their fur. I wonder if there are any more cubs?"

"They have them in holes of trees by the river, I think. I wonder how this one got on the bank? It's too small to swim."

"Perhaps she was carrying it to another nest, Phillip." They could find no other cubs, and walked down-river to find a ford.

"We'll get some milk in the next town. I can feed it with my fountain-pen filler."

As soon as they had dressed they went on to Dôle, where

Barley bought some milk and, mixing it with hot water, fed the cub on the rubber squeezer of the pen-filler.

"Good, it's sucking!"

It took three fills of the glass container, then closed its eyes. She put it inside her jumper, next to her collar bone, and seeing an hotel, decided to spend the night there, because of its name, the Pomme d'Or.

Next morning the cub was still alive; with joy they went on south, a new view of mountains immediately before them. They climbed up to Poligny, the engine sharply crackling through the tree-lined streets partly in shadow; and continuing along route 83 they came to Lons-le-Saunier and after filling the pointed cylindrical tank over the engine with *essence*, made for Bourg-en-Bresse, their objective being Lyons—187 kilometres on the map from Dôle. They ran non-stop the last sixty kilometres to find that Lyons was the Birmingham of France, except that it had trees around its great square, and no grime. Even so it was a business town, the hotel they entered for a drink was filled with sallow-faced, podgy men in black coats and trousers, so let's go on to Vienne, he said.

The mountain peaks were ruddy as they rattled down the valley route beside great Rhône whose leaping snow-waters were visible on their right.

"Just fancy, this town is exactly 500 kilometres, 300 miles, from Paris," he said, lying on the hotel bed and reading the Michelin guide, while she pulled off her jumper and put on a silk blouse. After fondling her, he tried to draw her to the bed. She resisted. "I must get some goat's-milk."

"Come back soon, and we'll feed the cub here."

When she did not come back he went to look for her and found her sitting at a table in the *salle à manger*, a young waiter standing beside the table. They were looking at the cub. He saw that the waiter was young, perhaps eighteen, a handsome youth talking excitedly in French. On the table was an open stamp book.

Barley looked up as he came in. "Hullo, old boy, I've been showing Jules 'la petite loutre'." She put the cub back inside her blouse.

"Aren't you coming up to feed it?"

"It's been fed. Jules wants to show me some of his rare French Colonials." She remained seated while Jules continued to look over her shoulder, pointing out this and that stamp, while she turned the pages and appeared to share his interest.

Feeling out of it, Phillip went to the bar and ordered a calvados, swallowing the fiery liquid before going back to the dining-room door. The boy-waiter was now seated beside her, the two blond heads close together. He returned to the bar, drank another calvados, and then walked into the street. It was ten minutes before he returned, to find her waiting for him.

"I didn't order dinner, not knowing how long you'd be."

He seated himself on the other side of the table. Hitherto they had sat side by side.

There were a few local Frenchmen dining in the room, commercial travellers judging by the tucked-in napkins and the absent-minded speed with which they swallowed their food.

Jules gravely examined Barley as he stood awaiting the order. Phillip could not decide. Had she left undone the top button of her V-blouse on purpose?

"Steak for you, with watercress as usual, old boy?"

"What would you like?"

"I think I'd prefer a herb omelette tonight."

"Aren't you hungry?"

"Not very. But you have a steak—you've done all the work."

This wasn't true; she had a blister from changing over the belts, the gradients had varied frequently upon stretches of the journey.

"What wine would you like with your omelette? A Graves? A Chablis?"

"I'll have Vichy water, I think. Where did you get to, just now?"

Was Jules hanging on his answer? *Old* boy—yes, he was that. Was her remark intended to show up his greater age? He gave the order; Jules brought the Vichy bottle, and waited beside her again.

"M'sieur! Du vin?"

"Vin rosé, s'il vous plaît."

He drank silently. The dishes came, expertly placed by Jules. She seemed not to be hungry; she waited, holding her fork as though playing with her food, while he ate the steak and swallowed glasses of wine as though they were water.

"What's the matter, Phillip?"

"Nothing. Why should there be?"

She pretended to eat while she waited for him to finish his steak. Then she said, "D'you mind if I go up now? I've got a bit of a headache. It's the vibration, I think."

"I'm sorry."

"You won't mind my leaving you?"

"Not at all."

He stood up, she left, he sat and ordered a large cognac. Headache—or heartache? But he must not allow imagination to—and yet, in the past, all his forebodings had turned out to be real. Eveline Fairfax—Spica—O for God's sake, not Barley. He finished the bottle and thought to walk into the dark night; but hesitating in the foyer went upstairs to their room, anticipating its emptiness.

She was in bed, only the top of her head visible.

He undressed and washed slowly, and got in his side of the bed, to lie apart from her. At last he could bear it no more, and touched her shoulder with his hand. She patted the back of his fingers, and said, "Go to sleep—you're tired out, you know."

"Don't you want me?" he said at last.

"Of course I want you. But tonight we ought to sleep."

"Is it anything I've done, or said?"

"No, of course not."

He lay awake beside her, suffering. She didn't want him. She was thinking, perhaps dreaming, of the eager youth. He lay still minute after minute, breathing through his mouth to make his breathing inaudible. At last she turned over.

"What *is* the matter, Phillip? I can *hear* you thinking. Tell me, what's the matter?"

He told her.

"Oh darling! How clumsy I am! I am so terribly happy, you see! I feel like—well, like Juliet set free from the vault. I suppose I shouldn't have put 'la petite loutre' there, but Jules was so eager for me to see his collection, and anyway the cub is used to sleeping there. Also I thought that probably Jules had no one to talk to about his stamp album."

"You're not growing tired of me?"

She took him in her arms. "Oh, my poor boy, so you thought you had lost 'Anky'! Never, Phillip, never!—never!—never! I can *never* change towards you, or grow tired, not one smallest fraction of me!" She leaned over him and kissed one eyebrow. "Oh, how could you think that I might ever change? I owe you everything—it was you who first opened my eyes to poetry, and the feeling that 'everything that lives is holy'."

It was his turn to pay tribute. "And I wasn't really alive until I knew you. I could never be my real self with anyone before I knew you."

On the way south they ran into flocks of sheep. The dust of the movement of thousands of lean animals, with long ears and tails, hung on the air. Among the ewes were rams with spiralled horns held well above the flocks.

They sat in Bédélia on the road verge, hearing the *tottle-tonk* of bells, the short clatter of cloven feet in the dust amidst the barking of dogs. Boys with black shaggy hair and dark eyes passed by them, in charge of donkeys which seemed loaded almost to back breaking point. Goats were among the sheep.

"They're going up to the snow-line grass," she told him. "The shepherds call this the 'transhumance'. They live in huts, and eat the flesh of male kids, and drink goat's milk, all the summer."

The long-haired goats looked uneasily about them, uttering plaints of discomfort.

"I always heard that goats and sheep didn't mix."

"They don't as a rule, but they all go up to the mountain pastures together."

"I suppose this summer migration goes on all over Provence?"

"All over Europe, I think, where there are mountains. D'you see the ticks on the ewes' ears?"

"They look like rivets, close together. How do they get them off?"

"They don't, there are too many."

"When are the lambs born?"

"In the autumn, in the lowlands. Some on the way down. The shepherds have to look out for wild boars, and foxes. Lammergeirs, too—eagles."

"In England they usually have their lambs in January, when the ewes are on the turnips. How would you like to be a farmer's wife? I've still got a chance of going in with Uncle Hilary."

"I'd love it! But wouldn't it clash with your writing?"

When the flocks had passed he sat still listening to the sound of bells breaking upon the distant air like the blooms of mountain flowers below the snow-line. "Your word *transhumance* exactly describes it, Barley—the soft bells—cold air in the sunshine, water running from the edge of the snow everywhere—the fritillaries and the gentians pushing through the flat grass—the great empty caves of the valleys below one."

"I was thinking of the Col d'Aubisque just then, too. I was seeing your footsteps as I followed them a year ago—it was a shock when they vanished at the avalanche. I felt awful, I thought I had lost you. It was just a year ago today."

"And at night we both dreamed the same dream about each other! And do you know, Barley, I think I must have shouted to those two peasants, when I had climbed up from below Le Corniche, just about the time you got to the end of my tracks! I shouted out that my companion was dead before I could think. It must have been transference of your feeling to me."

At noon they rested among aromatic bushes growing on a piece of waste land beside the road. The low stems gave a springy couch without injuring the bushes. Near them the scrub had been cleared by a past fire, so that out of reddened stones on the black ground lowly plants were growing. Each flower of the harsh soil was served by butterfly or bee.

"Did you notice that the horns of those rams were like the twists on the heads of Greek pillars? I wonder if their descendants came originally from ancient Greece? Did the Greeks come so far west?"

"The Ionic columns, you mean? Some of the Greeks spread across Italy. It's possible they may have reached here."

"How do you know about the Greeks?"

"Daddy told me."

They knelt to examine the flowers.

"I suppose if this stony soil were dressed with rich sheep dung, the plants and bushes would degenerate, Barley?"

"Yes, they'd grow more leaf and stem than blossom. Like the Romans, they'd grow soft and decadent."

"Did your father tell you that, too?"

"He used to talk to me about farming. He was looking forward to buying a farm in England when he retired from the Bench. He was keen on breeding sheep, and also to improve pastures by breeding new strains."

"He must have been keen on botany, then."

"Yes, he was."

He stared at her, his fond possession. And yet she remained always herself. She was part of him, also apart from him. If there were such things as solar bodies, what spiritualists called astral bodies, she was surely his bright other self. If he should ever lose her...

"I wonder if people like you are born direct and clear, or does it come from a good early training, otherwise schooling?"

"I hated school."

A brown and yellow bee was crawling over the florets of wild thyme. They watched it gathering honey, then he said, "Were you much bothered because your parents didn't hit it off together?"

"I was brought up by my amah, and never heard Mummie and Daddy quarrelling."

"Were they very unhappy?"

"Only sometimes. Their minds didn't think the same way, or rather Mummy's mind didn't see the same things as Daddy's did. He was quick, in both mind and body, and Mummy's slowness used to annoy him. He was older than Mummy, too, about twenty years, I think."

"I really shouldn't be asking inquisitive questions like this."

"Why not? I can tell you things as easily as I can think them to myself."

"Then I really must be a part of you?"

"Have you only just found that out?"

He looked at her face, examining it as though for the first time. "Do you know, Barley, I think that if ever I loved you utterly, so that everything you were, and everything you did, was of the greatest importance to me, I should lose all ambition to write the greatest novel about the war."

"Then I hope you never will, for I don't want to be a piece of blotting paper, old boy!"

"You blot up a part of me already, you young devil!"

"Yes, you old devil!" she laughed, moving out of his reach. Then seeing the shadow of loneliness on his face she crawled towards him and pulled his shoulders towards her, so that they were parallel with her own.

"Look at me, Phillip! Look at me! That's better!" She put an arm round his neck, and kissed each of his eyes in turn. "You think I've changed towards you, don't you? Come on, tell me exactly what you really think!"

"Sometimes I don't know."

"You mean, these last few days?"

"I have sometimes wondered."

"Well, I *have* changed towards you." She held him with her hard young arms. With her cheek against his she repeated, "I have changed towards you, but in one part of me only."

"You mean—physically?"

"Yes."

"I thought you had."

She pushed him back gently and lay on his chest, then lifted her head to kiss him lightly upon his face, planting little kisses while making a sort of humming noise from her diaphragm. "Nice little man!"—kiss kiss kiss—"dear little man!"—kiss kiss kiss—"clever little laddy"—kiss kiss kiss—"he's going to be a daddy!" and then she buried her face against his heart, murmuring, "Now you know, so be kind to me."

Bédélia was moving with its secret shadow along a track through a flat region of reed and water, where pink reflections drew out from flamingos, and distant boats seemed to be sailing above the horns of wild cattle in the marshes.

Here the Rhône had rolled fragments ice-broken from the Alps until its flow was checked by its own rush, so that the river had sought many courses to the sea.

They had arrived at the Camargue—with its strange primitive life of fen-men and water-beasts—wilder and wider and more mysterious than the country of *Dick o' the Fens* and *Bevis,* in those days when, thought Phillip, there had been romance, but little true living, in his life. Now he had got through to that 'other side' which all poets whom life had 'mumbled in its jaws' had dreamed of, but never achieved. How fortunate he was, he thought for the hundredth time, as he listened to nightingales singing among the osiers, and larks above in the sky.

"'If I cannot achieve immortality, at least I can think it'. Like Jefferies, Willie never found true love, otherwise he would have been calm, I think. I'm damned lucky to have found you, Barley."

"What happened to that girl who loved your cousin, Mary someone?"

"Mary Ogilvie? She still lives in her mother's house on the Burrows in North Devon. I ought to go and see her sometime. Poor star-crossed lovers."

"Is that your expression? It's not bad."

"It's Shakespeare's, from *Romeo and Juliet*! You're an uneducated moon-calf!"

"Yes, because you were my tutor, don't forget! Tell me about Juliet."

"She tries to cling to her love, while feeling herself to be on the edge of doom. She tries to keep Romeo just a little longer, when the dawn breaks. 'It was the nightingale, and not the lark, That pierced the fearful hollow of thine ear'; but he replies, 'It was the lark, the herald of the morn, no nightingale'. The mortmain of hate destroyed them. But here we are, alive, listening to lark and nightingale together."

She moved into his arms; he stroked her hair, and kissed her eyebrows; but it was not enough; behind his eyes waited the apparition of magnesium flares and gun-flashes, of toiling men upon the brown, the treeless, the grave-set plain of Flanders——

"Come on, let's get a move on!"

They continued along the track by the shore of a waveless sea, stopping to bathe and swimming apart in order to enjoy coming together again. "Oh! quick, let's get out!" She had seen a fleet of Portuguese men o' war, their single blue sails adrift, their poisonous strings below in the water. The sky was beginning to look sulky; she said the mistral might blow, so they went on to Sète, to wander among the quays of the old port until it was time for dinner.

"I wouldn't mind living here."

"You mean always?"

"Why not?"

"I'm so fond of Devon——" She thought, I want my baby to be born there, where first I saw Phillip, I want to play with my baby on those very same sands of Malandine.

Across a flat plain of stones, through the torrid air with its mirages of shifting dark blue levels, they came to a desert of sand-hills, and beyond the sands was the sea.

A welcome wind blew from the short wash of waves which revealed with every retreat glints of mica in the lapsing sand.

Throwing away their clothes they ran into the sea, then lay upon the shore. He was restless, they walked back to the sandhills, into the intense heat under a motionless air. There they sat down, she letting the cub crawl in her shadow.

He wandered away, and leaning upon an elbow, watched her playing with the cub until his feeling became detached from her, beyond his abiding personal happiness, until he felt himself to be bodiless, a mere consciousness in the timeless elements.

Everything was so still, the sound of the little waves a mere whisper. Yet each moment the sandhills were changing. Every beetle toiling up the hot slope, every touch of gossamer bearing tiny Linyphia, every vibration of wing of sand-wasp and butterfly caused a stir among the grains of sand revealed by a glint, a spill, a change.

Never for an instant did the elements cease to cry their sharp and mindless cries of creation, even on the most still day of summer, under the vast blue silence of the sky.

When the mistral blew, the shape of a dune might be changed in a day, diminishing and streaming away in the coils and re-buffets of the wind until the damper, finer sand of the interior hillock was exposed, to be carved cliff-like, so that roots of the binding grasses hung loose when the wind had blown itself out.

Here the elements of air and sun and water strove to abrade all form, living and dead, in the ceaseless percussion of the sands. Bottles rocked upon the shore of the tideless sea received the blast of grains driven by the wind until the glass was dulled to a beauty like the fathomless light of ocean's floor.

Moving the sand with his fingers, he saw that they had buried the skulls of water birds and the shells of snails; wind and sand wore them thin, they broke, and joined the sand-blast, to help polish newer bones and shells, now lying white, momentarily at peace, under the shimmering sky.

He went back to her, and taking her hand, trudged over the scalding sand, feeling himself to be thoughtless as a gossamer drifting in the air. He was part of her, she of him; they were one in spirit. How vain and unreal was his former conception of love, arising from longing. With her beside him he shed the shuck of experience, to exist within a freedom which, before he had truly known her, had lain always beyond the horizon of life.

With her he felt himself to be of the very air of the shore, of the light of ocean, without body, beyond desire.

Walking on, they came to a lower plain extending to another range of sandhills, where torrid air arose in mirage all around them, where even the skiey whisper of the tideless sea was shut out. Such was the heat upon that dried-up plain that they were forced to put on their *espadrilles*; even then the heat burned through the rope of the soles. In silence they came to wind-ribbed slopes, and ascending to a crest, pale green with marram grasses, met the cool shocks of the breeze moving in through the gaps in the dunes torn by old storms bearing across the sea the yellow dust-clouds of Africa.

The sandy hollows were strewn with the battle-wreckage of air and water—jetsam of rusty tins and bleached corks, litter of pine and cork-tree bark, cast feathers of sea-birds, bottles, sea-coal, shattered lengths of bamboo reeds and roots of olive trees torn from mountain ravines by floods of melted snow.

Beyond, the shore was stony. Unknown wading birds flickered away, to alight and run over the line of pebbles anciently rolled smooth by the Rhône. Among black and brittle bladder-weed the shore-birds would gravely pause to pipe their thin notes, to run on again and pretend to pick up food. Somewhere their young were crouching above the verge of the sea, speckled as sand and gravel. He knew their fears and hopes, and led her away.

He must swim! Leaving her with the cub he ran into the water, to plunge through the translucent shells of waves, to glide with open eyes over blurred sand, and then to jump up, shake water from his eyes before turning on his back, hands behind head, to float there bodiless.

They returned the next morning with a tent; they were the only human beings on miles of shore, their faces gilded by hot, quick-silvery reflections of the sun on the pale green wavelets losing their brief water-shadows as they tinkled on the sand.

He built a fire of sea-wood and grilled a fish, which they ate with their fingers while the engine beats of a coastal steamer came to them, a ship dissolving and disintegrating before their eyes as the medusas of the mirage strove to reduce it to scrap.

Now where was the tent, and their clothes? Where was Bédélia?

"Are you hungry?"

"No."

"I believe the sun feeds us through our skins."

They walked for an hour, and there was Bédélia, apparently uplifted, surrounded by legless black ponies which scampered away into the mirage as they approached.

"I don't want to wear clothes ever again."

"Nor do I."

Cicadas flipped against their legs. Thin and pale in the sky hung a new moon above the Algerian glare of the sun.

She pointed to the sky, where yellow clouds were gathering. "The mistral may be on the way."

"Let it come."

They sat by a driftwood fire and ate biscuits and bananas as the sun followed the moon now upon the rim of the sea. He lay, his dark hair curled with salt, with his head on her lap.

"When does Irene expect us?"

"Oh, any day."

"Won't she be anxious about us?"

"Why should she be?"

A cold wind fanned the flames. The sun was round and red. It was time to leave. They had no light but the moon upon the wastes.

The next day they drove with a view of the high peaks of the Pyrenees. Carcassonne, with its old walled town dark on a hill, was passed; they were making for Pamiers. Before them lay a route of steep ascents with many coiling bends, or *virages*, which so wore the belt of the smaller pulley that they had to change it over at Mas-d'Azil for the climb to St. Girons. The air was cold with patches of snow still unmelted on pastures where sheep grazed upon the subdued grass.

There was a further climb to the Toulouse-Tarbes main road, a steady ascent to St. Gaudens and on to Montrejean—over sixty kilometres from St. Girons. Would Bédélia's belt hold out?

Up again from Montrejean, and on to Lannemezan, which according to the Michelin map was nearly 600 metres high. Could they get there on the belt now frayed and ragged? They took the wrong turning and found themselves on a small stony road, leading with many bends to St. Laurent-de-Neste. She suggested turning back; he went on until the belt-fastener tore loose. He repaired it and fitted a spare link and continued along the twisting route to Bagnères. The engine had plenty of power; up they went in low gear until Bédélia, long and narrow, stuck at a hair-pin bend. They managed to lift round her tail. But how to restart the engine up a slope? It was hopeless.

They lifted the tail round a complete circle and returned the way they had come, spending the night in an otherwise deserted auberge at Bonnemazon, sitting before a wood fire in the dining-room after a dinner of small thin trout and tough mutton. In the morning, back to the main Tarbes road beyond Capern; and from Tarbes along N 117 to Pau, the adventure nearly over, for at the end of the road was Laruns.

It seemed almost the end of the old life together when they stopped at the villa and sat still for a few moments before looking round to see Irene as she came down the garden path to greet them.

"Well, P.M., what do you think of France?"

"A marvellous country, Irene!"

"And how is my brown, brown daughter?"

"Happy, Mummy!"

Hitherto he had thought of France as all one Département du Nord seen in those areas occupied by the British forces. Now he had known a new France—varied, vast, magnificent—mountains, rivers, bridges, cathedrals, meadows, vineyards—France as she had endured for centuries, France now majestic in his mind.

A week later Bédélia, her rear tyres worn to the canvas, was sold —after some hesitation, for they had shared so much with the faithful little 'bus. Still, there was satisfaction in knowing that seven one-thousand-franc notes were folded in his hip pocket, as he sat in the Paris train at Bordeaux, thinking that the blossom of the hawthorn would be white upon the hedgerows when they returned to England. It would be great fun, too, to ride the Norton motor-bike again.

And yet——

As the train ran through the old battlefields she said to him, "Are you sorry we didn't go there, after all?"

"No. It may have been so different from what is in my head."

She took his hand. "When my baby can walk, we'll all come here together, shall we? On our way down to the Camargue?"

She laid the cub, now active and fat, against his neck. "We'll bring 'la loutre', too, shall we? You look after him, and I'll look after Billy! I'm sure it will be Billy!"

At the Dover customs there was nothing to declare. Fortunately Lutra—Phillip had given the cub its Latin name—slept soundly against her heart, so there was no bother about quarantine.

Chapter 2

FRIENDS AND RELATIONS

Their return to Malandine was unexpected; Mrs. Crang had agreed to clean up the cottage, but Phillip had forgotten to send her a postcard. So it was exactly as it had been left.

"Please don't bother, Mrs. Crang. I rather like to see dust over everything."

"My goodness, you'm married now, midear! And you mustn't slape in thaccy bade, you'll get rheumatics! Walter hasn't hoed your garden, and just look at the mores (weeds) growin' up to the cabbages! If only you'd a-sent us a card, us'd had the place all clane for 'ee!"

"Never mind, Mrs. Crang, we can sleep on the floor tonight." Then to Barley, "I'll go and get Rusty."

"My, what a dear l'il kitten you'm got, Miss Barley!"

"It's an otter cub, Mrs. Crang. We found it in France, the mother had been caught in a trap."

"What a shame! 'Tes a bootiful li'l hanimal! Will it bite?"

"No fear, it's quite tame."

"I hope Rusty won't titch'n! Nor Moggy, her's got kittens in your place, her comes in our place ivry day for milk and what us can give'n."

Phillip walked to the Ring of Bells to fetch his dog, who by now was used to master going away. The spaniel no longer ran frantically after motor-bicycles with a low drumming exhaust note; no longer waited half-way up the steep lane for sight of master turning

the corner; no longer climbed upon the church wall at one
particular place, to stare towards the horizon of the land leading
to the sea.

Sometimes Rusty had come down to the cottage, Mrs. Crang
said, to look through the cat-hole and whine before returning up
past the pump and back to his base, the Ring of Bells. Rusty had
almost ceased to grieve, with that deep grief of the single-minded
mammal which has been removed from its natural life and,
through the agencies of food, warmth, and affection, become a
vehicle for extended emotion fixed on one superior object. Rusty
had found relief from mental pain in the affection of the landlord
of the Ring of Bells and his wife; a feeling of safety varied by calls
at the Crang's, where, upon a mat made of scraps of coloured rags,
both wool and cotton, he would stretch himself before the fire, or,
if it were a day of south-west rainy wind, upon the broken armchair
which Crang would give up to "th' ould dawg". Rusty had now
spread his thoughts, usually called up by the sense of smell, the
most powerful agent to influence his mind, over most of the
village: his points of call at which one or another of his hind legs
obligingly gave way, including the foregoing places as well as
a number of garden trash heaps, coign of village shop, Methodist
chapel iron gate, a field of grazing to roll on disguising sheep-
dung if the wind were what fox-hunters called a good-scenting
day, and the blacksmith's shop where once master had gone to
have a piece of iron welded and a rat had run out of a hole in the
wall and into a pile of scrap iron.

Now the spaniel whined on seeing his master, and followed him
half-way to the cottage before standing still. Phillip knew that
Rusty had to thaw out, and went on home.

Barley had waited for his return before introducing the cub to
Moggy. She gave it to Phillip, who let Moggy smell it before
putting it on the table.

"Stand still, and watch."

Moggy leapt upon the table, arched her back and growled.
Then she crept forward cautiously, sniffing. She made as if to
clout with her paw—Barley's hand ready to stop her—while
Phillip spoke to Moggy, stroking her head. Her neck lengthened,
the paw went out, she tapped it, like a kitten in play. The cub
uttered a faint mew, at which the pupils of the cat's eyes were
expanded full. She glanced away, as if to escape; and swearing

softly, jumped off the table and went up the stairs to where her kittens were lying in the dog's basket.

"No good," said Phillip. "She doesn't like its scent."

"Wait!" replied Barley. She crept up the stairs two at a time. Moggy was sitting in the basket beside her kittens. She mewed as though in appeal as Barley lifted two kittens and returned downstairs, to put them on the table beside the cub and rub them gently together before putting them on the floor, the cub between kittens. One, feeling the cold, began to cry. Chirruping reassuringly, Moggy ran down the stairs. She made several attempts to lift it by the scruff, and looking up, clearly asked Barley to carry it up for her. Barley picked up cub and kittens together and sat on the edge of the table; and when Moggy sprang up lightly beside her, rubbed the cat's ear. Moggy crept upon her lap. She put the cub and kittens against Moggy's fur, they snuggled into the warmth. Moggy purred, so did the kittens. Barley pulled one from its teat, and put the cub there. It fed.

There was a whine at the door. Rusty, too fat to squeeze through the cat-hole, stood waiting. Climbing into the arm-chair, the dog went to sleep.

When the year opened into July, Lutra was strong and active, playing with dog, cat, and kittens, racing round the room and pulling at everything with its mouth. The cub loved water, and at first had to be kept from the stream. Barley filled a pail for the cub; it would run to it, slip over one side, slide in and turn over, and emerge from the same place, sleek and spiky-haired.

She bought a large, coffin-shaped galvanised bath, in which the cub, now as long as the cat, rolled and reversed in the water, rocking most of it over the edges. One of its joys was to lie on its back in the bath, when most of the water had been sluiced away, and clutch with stumpy forepaws at the jet poured from a watering-can.

Lutra went with them on the Norton to Malandine sands, starting the journey in the pack on Barley's shoulders, for they were afraid of rabbit gins. Rusty sat as usual on the tank of the motor-bicycle, but halfway there Lutra sinuated out of one corner of the khaki valise, squeezing through until Barley asked Phillip to stop, fearing that the cub would hurt itself by falling on the road.

By now the otter had grown a long tapered tail. Its movements were eager and quick; it raced over the sands in a low rippling movement, sand spurting from behind short legs: suddenly it would stop in full gallop and try to slide, rolling over and over before springing away to make for one or other of its favourite pools, into which to dive.

Underwater its stumpy, rather dumpy shape was transformed to a silent, streamlined tapering from pointed nose to end of tail, smooth as ribbon-weed and as glistening when momentarily its head broke the surface. Sometimes it kicked with all four webbed paws; more often it tucked in its forepaws and kicked with hindlegs together, so that its body moved rather like a loop-caterpillar, drawing itself together for the impulse and then straightening with the thrust.

One night it slipped through the cat-hole and was gone. They spent an unhappy hour calling it all the way down the stream to the sea. At midnight, as they were going to bed, there was the familiar noise of wet fingers drawn down a window pane; and Lutra slid in through the cat-hole, to lollop up the stairs, wet, and belly filled. There was eel-slime on the dun patch of his throat.

"As long as he doesn't get caught in a rabbit gin, I don't mind if he goes wild," said Barley.

As the days went on, they realised that Lutra had nothing to fear from local dogs or cats. Indeed, most cats, once they had crossed its scent, made off rapidly, their hair fluffed out.

There was another couple like themselves living in a cottage in Malandine. They had a young child. One afternoon when the Maddisons went down to the sands Lutra galloped over to see them, for they were doing something near the stream which over-flowed from Malandine Mere, which filled several acres of the shallow valley. When Lutra did not return Phillip strolled over and found him frisking about in a dam made by the couple, while their child slept under a parasol near by.

"We're seeing how high we can build this coffer dam before it bursts!" said the man. "Your otter is doing his best to wash it away, look at him!"

Lutra was rolling on his back, twisting and turning underwater, then dragging himself on his belly over the thin sandy wall.

"May I help you?"

He ran to get clods of sandy grass, to place round the arc of the dam. Lutra enjoyed this, and dragged the grass into the water.

Phillip pulled him out, and told Rusty to see him off. While dog and otter were having a rough and tumble the three managed to rebuild the wall.

"Well, after your kind help, may we offer you tea?" said the mother of the baby, politely. "You are most welcome to share our Thermos and bread-and-butter. Perhaps your wife would care to join us?"

She was tall and fair, and wore a print frock with a large straw sun-hat, complete with blue ribbon tied under her chin. Her face was pale, in contrast to that of her bronzed husband, who was smaller than his wife, and dressed, like Phillip, in shapeless old grey flannel trousers and shirt. It had seemed incongruous that she should have worked so hard on hands and knees, with that hat, more suitable for polite Deauville society (as seen in *The Queen* photographs).

When Barley arrived she said, "Georgie, won't you do the honours?"

"My name is Pole-Cripps, the old pater's rector of Mary-Tout-Saints at Queensbridge, and this is my wife," replied Georgie. "We know who you are, in fact we thought of calling—didn't we, Boo?—but you were here before us, so, as a matter of fact—not to make too fine a point of it—we have been expecting you to call on us! However, why stand on ceremony? Let's all have tea together, how about it? I know you have a kettle hidden in the reeds, as a matter of fact I nearly borrowed it the other day, when you didn't come down, and the old pater came over for the day with the mater. By the way, she got one of your books out of the library, but I haven't read anything of yours yet. I'm doing a course of the Metropolitan School of Journalism, to help eke out my army pension, aren't I, Boo?"

During this speech of introduction Phillip had kept a straight face. However, Georgie—"Everyone calls me that, old bean, so let's drop formality, shall we?"—was so obviously friendly that he felt mean for regarding him as a bit of a joke.

"Please borrow the kettle whenever you want to, Georgie."

"Thanks, Phillip."

They went off to gather dry sticks. Two upright stones supported the kettle blackened during several seasons. Soon it was singing over flames nearly invisible in the strong light of the sun which had burnt three faces to a dark brown. George explained to them that Boo had a delicate skin, which peeled in the sun, that was why she kept her hat on.

"Isn't that right, Boo?"

"Well, Georgie, I don't suppose that it is of any interest——"

After tea they swam together, then lay upon the hot upper sands, the two men rubbing pennies until they gleamed bright, the while Phillip looked up repeatedly to watch the kestrel which usually hovered over the golf links towards late afternoon, its feathers seeming almost blood-coloured in the sun now standing over the cliffs to the west. Thomas Morland had such a bird in one of his books, described as with 'blood-nourished wings'. But they looked red only when the sun was in the south-west, the bird's front to the sun and against a blue eastern sky. Morland was half a townsman, and didn't know; all the great writers' details were exact, 'precisions' as Walter Ramal the poet had said at the Woodford's party in Inverness Terrace when he had met him there. Ramal's country detail in his poems was marvellous, because true.

"In your course of journalism, what sort of things do you write about, George?"

"Oh, anything! I've just done an article on whit-ale, which I'm brewing, by the way. I've got a dozen cyder flagon bottles with screw tops in the cupboard of our sitting room, it's not mature yet, but when it is I'll give you a bottle, and you can tell me what you think of it. It'll be pretty potent, I must warn you, for I've put in all sorts of extras, including eggs, raisins, and some special yeast, haven't I, Boo?"

"You have indeed," said Mrs. Pole-Cripps.

"I used to make it once, but found it rather heady stuff, tangli-legs I think is the local term."

"Oh no, that's scrumpy cyder! But wait till you try mine! I've timed this brew to be mature just before my next medical board. It brings out my rheumatism. I've got a sixty per cent disability pension, and if I can get it increased to a hundred per cent I'll have a chance of commuting to a lump sum, then I plan to set up an Angora Rabbit Farm, don't I, Boo? There's pots and pots of money in Angora hair now, all the old girls in Queensbridge are knitting jumpers with it like hell."

Sometimes at night they went to the Pole-Cripps' cottage, Phillip taking his gramophone. The carpet was rolled back, and they danced, Georgie showing considerable agility despite his sixty per cent disability.

"I've often wondered about the cause of rheumatism, George."

"No doctor knows, old bean! That's the beauty of it! No one can find out how badly you've got it. And I do get it pretty badly at times, don't I, Boo?"

"You certainly do, Georgie."

"It may be living so near the graveyard," he went on enthusiastically. "In the old days they used to say that it's the vapour from the corpses which infects the air. But in my case I'm pretty sure it's inherited rheumatism. The old pater suffers from it, so did his pater before him. Though I'll admit the old devil used to put away two bottles of port every night of his life!"

"I used to know an old sweat in my first convalescent home in early 'fifteen, a ferocious old Liverpool Irishman named O'Casey. He had rheumatism which seemed to become worse whenever matron or the doctor was about. At his medical board in Manchester he almost crawled into the room, leaning heavily on a stick. He must have been cured suddenly, for he came out, while we others were waiting to go in, cursing, upright, and throwing away the stick. They'd passed him fit for service."

"Ah, I know those old scrimshankers! I had a lot of them in my company in the Labour Corps, but they didn't fool me!"

Phillip thought it time to change the subject. "How's the journalism going, George?"

"I've just done an article on Tramps' Signs! They put a chalk circle somewhere near a house where one has called, if it's a dud house, you know, only bread and cheese and an old pair of worn-out boots which they leave in the hedge. An arrowhead for a good square meal, a cross for money, and a double cross if the occupier is a mean old devil likely to set the dog at them. Boo helped me with the facts, didn't you, Boo?"

"Only in a very small way, Georgie." She looked at Phillip. "I had a brother who was one of the first Boy Scouts, and I remember reading about Tramp Signs in *The Scout.*"

So do I, thought Phillip. The difference was that George had got the signs mixed up.

"But the best article so far is one on Drake! I sent it to *The West Country News*, but they wouldn't publish it. They wanted to

know the sources of my information when I said that the story of
Drake playing bowls when the Spanish Armada was on its way,
I mean Drake going on with the game when he heard the news,
was only a yarn, without foundation in fact. I'll tell you why, if
you promise never to say a word! I argued it to myself this way.
You know a south-west gale was supposed to be blowing when he
was playing bowls and the news came? Well, it's simple! Have
you ever walked on the Hoe at Plymouth?"

"Yes, in the summer of 1918."

"What was the weather like, calm?"

"Hot and still."

"Exactly! You help me to prove my point! Have you ever
played bowls? Well then, I have! And the old pater has, too,
often! He agrees with me that you can't play bowls on an exposed
place like the Hoe when the south-west gale is blowing. Drake
wouldn't have been playing during a gale! Simple! But the *West
Country News* were afraid to publish it!"

"Why didn't you suggest the *possibility* of the story of the bowls
being related to another occasion? Then you would have covered
yourself."

"You don't understand, old bean. *The West Country News*, like
everyone else, is out to make money, and most of their money
comes from advertisements. So you see, if they had printed my
article it would have busted the story of Drake's game of bowls;
no one would want to go to Plymouth, Americans especially, and
the hotels and boarding houses would suffer. They'd cease to
advertise in the paper, which might face bankruptcy. So of course
they refused my article!"

George opened a cupboard beside the fireplace, to reveal a
dozen large bottles of whit-ale, with screw-tops, lying on their
sides. He awaited Phillip's praise for his skill.

"Wonderful sight, George!"

"They'll be mature in August, old bean, just in time for my
medical board! You must come over and help me sample them.
I've enquired about the price of hutches for Angoras, and there's
a chap the old pater knows in Queensbridge who is willing to sell
me some of his pedigree stock to start with!"

The Maddisons, a little tired of George's preoccupation with
his own doings—he was an only child—found another beach,

nearer Cornwall, where they went on the Norton, he driving carefully now that she was in her third month of pregnancy.

By now the milky moonlight had ceased to be fretted by the
ventriloquial voices of corncrake and quail in the fields shut
up with dredge-corn and hay. Among the stars pierced by the
church steeple swifts screamed as they dived and turned in space.
Walter Crang declared that the male birds slept on the wing.

Wild roses in the hedges were forming their yellow hips; more
and more visitors were on the sands and by the quay of the town;
and she was saying close to his ear, as they lay in bed at night, "I
feel him kicking, darling."

August 4, 1924. DEATH OF CONRAD was the headline in
The Daily Crusader. Phillip avoided the others on the sands, and
walked alone on the cliffs, his head filled by thoughts of the dead
writer: noble Joseph Conrad, his secret sharer of many winter
nights in the cottage. Now he had crossed the shadow line, having
passed through the heart of his own darkness to—what? At least
to the immortality of men's minds! He felt the loneliness of life
on the broken cliff he called Valhalla, high above the sea, and
hurried home to his love, his love for ever and for ever.

They took up with the Pole-Cripps again, glad to be with them.
"They're both very kind, aren't they?"

"We left you alone, Barley," said Boo, in her modest and
pleasant way, "because we knew that it was a wonderful moment
for you both."

Barley was walking beside her and wheeling the mail-cart in
which lay the Cripps baby asleep, with sun-bonneted head lolling
to one side and shaking to the jolts of the rough road.

"If it sleeps so much in the day-time, won't it keep awake at
night, Boo?"

"My dear, it's a *he*," replied Boo gently, with a sideway smile
at Phillip as much as to say, Isn't she a child? "Oh, please don't
apologise, my dear! It's the most natural thing in the world for a
young girl to call a baby 'it'. Wait until you have your own!"

Barley's cheeks went faintly pink. Boo whispered, "I had my
suspicions, you know! I'm so glad," before continuing in her
smooth voice, "I've never seen a child who sleeps so much as
Maundy does—he's named after George's uncle, did Georgie tell
you? Do forgive me if I'm saying what you know already. Yes,

Uncle Maundy is something to do with the Government. Apparently he has the ear of Lloyd George, and helped him to find people to contribute to the party funds. But I'm perfectly hopeless at politics, I suppose we must have them though. Yes, Maundy's as good as gold, we never get so much as a murmur from him at night, the precious!"

More summer visitors were now appearing on the sands, with jackdaws flying about the rocks waiting for scraps of food. One afternoon George's parents drove over, by taxi, from Queensbridge, and they all had a picnic on the beach. The Reverend Detmold Pole-Cripps was a red-faced man who relaxed from the cure of souls by reading novels of crime and detection. He smoked dried colt's-foot leaves in a large bent pipe because of his asthma, George told Phillip. Mrs. Pole-Cripps looked as though she had started life within the confines of a Midland industrial town. During tea she spoke to Phillip about the novel she had borrowed from the local library.

"I can't say that I approved of it all, Mr. Maddison," she began, in a voice holding a trace of dolefulness, "but I did enjoy the descriptions, which I thought beautiful. But that 'Pauline' of yours, well, I could hardly approve of her, could I? As for the love-scenes, they were hardly what one could call nice, were they? Yes, I read it after Martin Beausire, whose father is a parson in the Diocese of Exeter, as I suppose you know, had given it a review in *The Daily Crusader*. He objected to the slang some of the characters used, but I could allow that, but tell me, Mr. Maddison, *why* did you permit them to bathe, those two I mean, with no clothes on, although it was night-time? His Reverence"—she had referred to her husband like this when introducing Phillip to him—"read it after I'd finished it, for I wanted to be quite sure that I wasn't being unfair to you, you see. Yes, his Reverence has written out a *critique*, for you to think about. Here it is, please put it in your pocket-book and read it only when we have gone."

On starting to read this *critique* as soon as they got back to the cottage, Phillip thought that first impressions were not always the right ones. His Reverence was a dark horse, and knew literature when he saw it!

The *critique* was written on a half-sheet of paper in a tenuous, slanting fist. Barley looked over his arm holding the parson's prose, and when they had finished it both laughed so much that Phillip had to sit down with weakness.

A work of real literature sparkling like a jewel of many facets. A story of the longings of youth in a maze of sophistry and materialism trying to find its feet. A work revealing deep suffering and aspiration, an opal. The inherent poetry glows now like the ray of a ruby, now like the glint of a diamond. It attracts by its sincerity, entrances with its psychology, it inspires by its pilgrimage of a lost soul's search into falsities of the pagan spirit, it intrigues by its interplay of character, it stirs with its pathos, it wins regard by its fortitude, it repels by its pessimism, and nauseates by its utter ignorance of the manifold ways of the Almighty.

The Pole-Cripps' came over to supper one night, Georgie waving a catalogue. His enthusiasm was for a new kind of motor-car which, he said, was designed for country parsons. It was cheap, he declared, with spokeless wheels, solid rubber tyres, two-stroke engine, no gearbox and no diff.

"In place of gears it has friction plates, you see, old bean, like the Ford T-model in the old days. And with no diff to go wrong, it's simple! No repairs! It simply skids round corners, you see!" He went on to say that he was going to try to get the old mater to buy one for the old pater. "I'll tell her that I'll garage it for nothing in my shed. I'll be available then to drive her, free, gratis and for nothing, whenever she wants to go anywhere. Don't you think it a bon idea? After all, old bean, why should she be rooked by a Queensbridge garage when she can have it done for nothing, and have me as unpaid shovver into the bargain?"

Georgie's idea to save their Reverences needless expense materialised one morning when he entered the village in a cloud of blue smoke and a smell of burning oil. The new machine was a box-like affair with a pale-blue all-metal body and dummy radiator.

"Any fool can drive it," he told Phillip, with his usual enthusiasm. "Nothing can go wrong."

"Not even catch fire?"

"Oh, that smoke's absolutely nothing, old bean. All you have to do down these steep hills if the brakes are a bit slow is to shove her in reverse gear. I admit that the friction plates get a bit hot like that, but it won't hurt them."

"Won't they wear out quickly?"
"There's nothing to wear out!"

The holiday season was approaching, and once again Phillip felt it a duty to share his freedom with his mother and sister. It was arranged that Hetty was to come down by herself, a week before the Willoughbys were due. Barley suggested that 'Mother' have a room in Mrs. Tucker's cottage, fifty yards away.

"Don't forget that Mrs. Tucker is an old gossip, so be careful what you tell her, Barley." He meant her pregnancy.

"Her garden is one of the best in the village, so she's all right."

Barley began by praising Mrs. Tucker's flowers, and this led up to her telling Mrs. Tucker how much 'Phillip's mother' was looking forward to spending her fortnight with them.

"I wonder if you have a room to let? Mrs. Maddison loves flowers, she was brought up among the Surrey herb fields, now unfortunately a part of London."

It was arranged; and the good woman, looking at her with a smile, said, "So you'm goin' vor 'ave a babby, be 'ee? You don't mind my saying thaccy, do 'ee now?"

"I don't mind a bit, Mrs. Tucker. I'm interested how anyone found out. Do I look so much bigger?"

"Aw no, 'tes that you'm 'atin' haphazard like! You'm 'atin' blackberries before'm ripe! Then there's that laver you brought back to ait!"

"That black stuff from the rocks? But I was told you all ate it here, fried with green bacon."

"So us do, midear, but you'm 'atin' blackberries too, don't 'ee zee? 'Tes a sure sign!"

Phillip overheard his mother saying to Barley, "It is my dream coming true, dear. My son will have *his* little boy! Aunt Dora, one of my great friends, and I used to talk about Phillip before he was born, and we did so hope he would grow up to love all beautiful things, and to be a fine man."

"Well, it came true. Phillip *is* a fine man, Mother."

"I know he is, dear, and you have helped him more than you will ever know. He is so kind now, and considerate. Too much so at times, perhaps. You know about his trouble after the war, I suppose? Well, Phillip was shielding someone else. It wasn't

Phillip who set fire to that building, but a bad companion who was with him. It doesn't do to be too kind always, you know."

She thought of her own husband Dickie, and how he had suffered as a young man from his father, and again from her father; but while he had the same steadfastness as Phillip, he had given way too early to his own feelings.

Hetty went back to London with what she told herself were perfect memories. Phillip was well and happy, his wife so very calm and practical. If only it were the same with Doris . . . she sighed as she thought of what her daughter had told her: that she could never forget Percy, her cousin who had been killed in the war, whose best friend had been Bob.

"It's no use, Mother. As I've told you before, every time Bob wants to come near me, I see Percy in my mind, and then I can't *bear* Bob." So there had never been complete cohabitation between them—her mind refused any thought nearer the actuality of marriage. It was such a pity; if only Doris could bring herself to have a child, it might perhaps draw the young people together.

The wheels were now insistently audible in the carriage, her spirits were sinking, as the train ran on towards London, at the thought of returning home. Still, trials were sent to test us; she must always trust in God's goodness, and pray to Him to help her husband and her children.

Phillip Maddison, Bob Willoughby, and George Pole-Cripps were walking together ahead of the others on the way to the sands. They stopped before a new bungalow, recently built on a field overlooking the Channel. It was square, red London brick with a pink asbestos roof.

"My God, what a horror!" said Bob.

"I don't know so much," replied George. They walked on until stopped again by a new notice board.

"'Ripe for Development, Apply Mutton & Co, Solicitors, Queensbridge'," quoted Phillip. "Ripe like these thistle seeds blowing away! I suppose land can be bought very cheaply now that farming is depressed."

"That's what my rich uncle said the other day, when he was staying the night with us," said George. "He said it was a shame to spoil the beauty of this coast-line, but if beauty had to be spoiled, he might as well be the first to do it. If I can commute my pension, after getting total disability, buying this land may prove a better investment than Angora rabbits. What do you think, Phillip?"

"Oh, I'm not a business man, George. How's journalism going?"

"I've got a good idea for an article on bell-ringing, which ought to go well at the New Year! I used to be a 'colt', ringing with the team at the old pater's church. My idea is to have six copies of the same article made, then send them out just after Christmas, to six papers. One of them is sure to take it, and it will save time sending the same article back and forth, and so missing the 'bus."

The talk came round to spiritualism; an argument developed and continued on the sands: Phillip in sympathy with Bob, who was devout in his beliefs in life after death and in the power of spiritual healing; George deriding what both said.

"Yes, *you* believe in it, I don't doubt that for a moment, old bean, but what proof have you got? The old pater knows a lot of rogues in his parish, some of them pretend to believe in spiritualism only to get money out of a number of war-widows who haven't been able to get another husband. You ought to hear the old pater on the subject! He doesn't believe a word of it, and says it's against the teachings of Holy Writ."

"I'm not saying that there aren't any f-f—frauds, but I have p-proved that the dead can m-m-materialise," stuttered Bob.

"Belief is a matter of sensibility," said Phillip. "'The fool sees not the same tree that the wise man sees', as William Blake wrote."

"Nor does the fool see the same tree that the dog sees!" chortled George.

The upshot was that Phillip proposed a test.

"Let's have a *séance* tonight in my cottage, and Bob shall show us what he thinks are manifestations."

"Why not in my place?" said George. "Then we can combine it with sampling my whit-ale! It's just mature, and I can guarantee a more substantial kind of spirits if the other kind doesn't turn up!"

Chapter 3

THE ROAD TO EN-DOR

The Pole-Cripps' came over after supper, Georgie waving a catalogue.

His enthusiasm was now for a Home Knitting Machine, on
which his wife could knit a combination of golosh and stocking to
go over a lady's shoes to prevent cold feet when being driven in
winter in an open car. He would breed Angoras, and Boo would
turn them into overboots!

A cold mist had drifted in from the sea, so Phillip lit the driftwood on the hearth. Young Maundy, heir to possible millions
via the Lloyd George Election Fund, lay asleep in his wicker cradle
on one side of the hearth. In another basket on the farther side
lay Rusty, Lutra, Moggy, and the tail of a mouse she had brought
in for her foster-child from whose joyous embraces she was ever
ready to escape by leaping on table, book stand, and if necessary
up trees. But now, filled with herrings, Lutra slept on his back,
legs in air and Moggy across his neck, while Rusty groaned
underneath.

"Half a jiffy, before we start," said George. "I'll just dash
down to my place to see if I've left the fire-guard in front of the
fire."

"We made up a good fire, hoping that you will all come over
afterwards and take coffee with us, and crab sandwiches," said
Boo.

"Don't forget the whit-ale!" called out Georgie from the open
door.

"We mustn't be late," said Doris. "We plan to make an early
start tomorrow, it's such a long way back to Romford." She sat
with impassive face on the settle.

When George returned they sat round the table. A single
candle burned on the book-stand against the wall. Phillip put on
a record of Debussy's *La Mer*. When it stopped he got up, lifted
off the sound box, and sat down again quietly.

Bob Willoughby was staring at the table. He drew a deep
breath, stretched his arms before him, and rested his finger-tips

on the wood. He drew another deep breath and closed his eyes. His body moved back from his arms, which were now taut. His fingers opened, quiveringly. He passed a hand across his face several times before lowering his chin on his chest.

Looking across to George, Phillip saw on his face a childish astonishment. Glancing at Boo next, he saw the same look. Her eyes were upon the medium, and following her gaze he saw that Bob's face was altered. The cheeks were fuller, it seemed that hair had grown on the bare patches above his temples, and the back of his hair, close cut and usually upright, was curly. Was he imagining that Bob now looked like Percy Pickering? Cold shivers passed across his shoulder blades.

"Does anyone notice anything?" whispered Boo.

"I do. His face is altogether different!" said George.

"Others have seen me, too," said Bob, slowly and without stutter. "I am asking to come through you, my friend."

Phillip looked at his sister. She sat with eyes closed, hands folded as though in resignation. The medium gave a deep sigh, and stroked his temples horizontally with long, stiff fingers. His face was haggard.

"Please listen to me," a voice said faintly. "Please talk to me."

Was it Bob's voice? George looked at Phillip. "Do you know who it is?" he whispered.

Phillip put finger to lips.

"Speak to me," came the words from Bob, as though half-strangled. His hands were shaking. His head went to one side; he sighed deeply, twice, then opened his eyes. With arms now limp on the table he remained as though resting.

"How about another go?" suggested George. "After I've looked at my fire?"

"Yes, and with our hands on the table this time, and everyone looking up," said Doris.

"Don't you believe in it, Doris?" asked Boo, when George had left.

"I'd rather not say, if you don't mind."

Boo, surprised at the curt tone of voice, looked across to Phillip. "Do you, Phillip?"

"Well, Boo, I don't see that the idea of vibrations of thought is any more unnatural that the idea of the human voice coming with broadcast wireless waves. One day we may be able to pick up what people said hundreds of years ago. We might even be able to hear the voice of the central figure on the Cross."

Bob nodded slowly to himself.

George came back, noticeably brighter, rubbing his hands together. "I say, old bean," he said to Phillip, "you know I told you that I'd painted the Trojan's mudguards with this new cellulose paint? I reckon it's put fifteen miles an hour on her maximum speed. Hasn't it, Boo?" seeking the accustomed support from his wife. "You timed me, didn't you? I'll tell you how we did it if you like, two days ago, coming back from Exeter. You know that straight bit between——"

"Yes, Georgie," said Boo, as to a child, "but I rather think that perhaps the spirits want to tell us something."

"It won't take a minute, and might help the atmosphere. After all, life is made up of vibrations, and there was plenty in the old 'bus, ha-ha-ha, when you timed me on the straight between the telegraph posts, wasn't there?" He turned to Phillip. "We passed eleven posts in thirty-five seconds, with the wind behind us, I must admit, and as the posts are sixty yards apart, I worked it out at eighty-two point two miles an hour! Although I must admit that Boo's hair-spring was held up, so allow twenty-five per cent fast. I'll show you the first set of figures. Take a look at that, old bean, and tell me what you think."

He selected one of three sheets of paper.

1760 yds   1 mile.

$$\frac{1760}{60} = \frac{176}{6} = 28 \text{ posts per mile. Plus } 25\% = 7 \text{ posts.}$$

$$\text{Total 35 posts @ } \frac{25}{11} \text{ seconds per post} = \frac{35 \times 5 \times 5}{11}$$

$$\frac{175 \times 5}{11} = \frac{875}{11} = \text{say 80 yds per second.}$$

$$\frac{80}{1760} \times \frac{1760}{80} \times \frac{60}{1} \times \frac{60}{1} = \frac{1}{22} \times \frac{60}{1} \times \frac{60}{1} = \frac{1800}{11} = 163\tfrac{4}{11} \text{ m.p.h.}$$

"What's this, Georgie? A message from 'Red Cloud'?"

"Sorry old bean, I've given you the wrong set of figures. Here's the right one."

$$35 \text{ seconds less } 25\% \text{ fast} = \frac{35}{1} \times \frac{\cancel{125}^{\,25\ \ 5}}{\cancel{100}_{\,20\ \ 4}} = \frac{5}{4}$$

$$\frac{35}{1} \times \frac{5}{4} = \frac{175}{4} = 44 \text{ seconds as near as dammit.}$$

"Georgie dear, the spirits may go away if we interrupt the atmosphere."

"Let him get it off his mind," said Bob, quietly.

"Thanks, old bean. Now just take a dekko at this one, will you?"

$$35 \text{ secs., } 25\% \text{ error} = \frac{4}{5} \times \frac{35}{1} = 28 \text{ secs.}$$

$$\frac{\cancel{1760}}{\cancel{600}_{\,15}} \times \frac{\cancel{28}^{\,7}}{\cancel{60}} \times \frac{\cancel{60}}{1} = \frac{1232}{15} = \text{ say } \frac{411}{5} = 5\overline{)411} \atop 82.2 \text{ m.p.h.}$$

Less 25%

= 60 m.p.h.

"Ah, a corrected message from 'Dust Cloud,'" said Phillip. "I don't know how you do it, Georgie."

"Ah, but don't forget the streamlined mudguards! You remember I told you that I had put on some of the new cellulose paint? Well, at first I put it on top of the old paint, and when that curled up I stripped both mudguards to the metal and after I'd painted them again with cellulose it made a tremendous difference to wind-resistance, didn't it, Boo?"

"It certainly appeared to. Now, Georgie, we haven't much time."

They sang *Rock of Ages*, then spread their fingers round the table. Soon it began to quiver. Phillip could see the nails of

George whiten as he pressed. "Ought we to push?" he asked George.

"*I'm* not pushing! I'm trying to keep it down!"

"You're still driving the Trojan," laughed Phillip.

"Let it rise if it wants to, touch lightly," said Bob between his teeth, as the table began to quiver again.

"Its legs aren't very firm at the best of times, so keep your fingers lightly on the wood," Phillip whispered to George.

The table began to creak.

"I know that chap you got to make this table for you, he's a crook," said George. "If you had come to me, I could have put you on to a decent carpenter the old pater knows."

"Georgie dear, we weren't so fortunate as to know Phillip then."

"All the same, he was taken in by the chap who made this table!"

"Have you been drinking some of the whit-ale, by any chance?" asked Phillip.

"You're avoiding the issue! You know it was a dud table!"

"Georgie, if you keep on, you'll drive the spirits away."

"Ha ha, I like that."

"Please keep your finger-tips lightly on the edge of the table," said Bob.

The table began to creak again, then to turn.

"At least you can't accuse me of doing it this time, old bean!" said George as he lifted his hands.

The movement stopped.

"You've broken the circuit," said Phillip.

"*Please*, Georgie! We'll have to stop in a few minutes."

The others sat still, waiting. George put his fingers on the table.

Silence followed.

"I think someone is wanting to speak to us," said Bob in a low voice. He raised his chin, and closed his eyes. "We are ready to hear you speak. Please will you lift the table sideways and tap the leg on the floor once for a 'no', and twice for a 'yes'? Will you first tell us if you are trying to speak?"

The table leg rose up about an inch, went down, and rose again. Phillip saw George's fingers almost clawing the varnished wood towards himself. Not wanting to do the same, he held his fingers lightly, and to his surprise the table rose up on the opposite legs.

"Thank you," said Bob. "Will you tell us if you are an old soldier?"

The table canted twice, away from George.

"Ask a question, Phillip," muttered Bob, who appeared to be wrestling with himself.

"Were you killed on the Somme?"

The table creaked as it canted: Phillip again felt the back of his neck turn icy. Tears stood in his eyes. He smelt again the falsely sweet, sickening smell of a summer battlefield. There was the sound of an explosion, like a distant Mills grenade. Another. A third.

"Oh, my God!" cried Boo, looking frightened. "What can it be?" There was a further muffled report.

George leapt up and ran to the window. "Our cottage is on fire!"

They went to the door and saw a rosy glow coming from the uncurtained lower window.

"It's only the chimney!" cried Phillip, as a lilac flame pierced the darkness above the thatch. "Barley, will you and Bob get all the pails and fill them at the stream? George and I will carry them in. I'll see you by the dipping pool."

Hurrying with George into the sitting-room he heard the roar of the chimney on fire. There followed a wet five minutes, as pail after pail of water was flung into the grate and into the hip bath to soak a blanket for holding over the hearth, to stifle the soot flames in the chimney.

Soon the fire was subdued. George was suggesting a glass of whit-ale when there was an explosion in the cupboard beside the hearth. He opened the cupboard door as a second explosion scattered froth over them.

"Everyone out!" cried Phillip. "A glass splinter can blind you!" They herded into the kitchen, while further reports came from the cupboard.

"It's the heat," said George. "My word, it only shows the strength of the stuff, doesn't it, Boo?" They counted six more explosions, whereupon George said, "All clear! I reckon that's the lot. I'll have to store the next brew in the scullery. Anyway I'll get a new carpet out of the insurance—I'll just chuck a few

cinders over it to scorch the edges of the holes that were there
before! I'll do it now, before the fire gives up the ghost!"

On the way back to the cottage Doris asked Phillip to walk with
her up the lane. They stopped on the high ground, with its western
line of sunset. To the north a steely blue glow arose to the zenith.
Brother and sister looked into the immeasurable cavern of the sky.
He felt tender towards her, she was his younger sister again, brave,
resolute as ever; but lost.

"Phil, will you tell me the truth?"

"I'll try to, Doris. But I'm not infallible."

"Do you think that Bob puts on that face? I mean, they say
that an actor can so think himself into his part, until he *becomes* the
person he is pretending to be. And Bob was Percy's best friend in
the war."

"Yes, I know what you mean. But I honestly *did* see Percy on
his face. The hair wasn't like Bob's. I distinctly saw Percy's
curls."

"What does it *mean*, Phil?"

"I can only tell you what I've heard from other people. Spirits
can be earth-bound, if they arrive on the other side after some
shock, such as violent death. Percy was killed at once. He would
try, if he could, to get to his loved ones. He could only do this by
striving to come through a living medium. Bob was his friend. He
wants to come to you through Bob."

"To live again, perhaps as a child, do you mean?"

Phillip hesitated; he tried to think; no thought would come,
only the words, "Yes, I do!"

Chapter 4

THE LISTING WIND

On a cold day in January, the first anniversary of their marriage,
Phillip awakened and through the open casement window saw
that the grass on the lawn was white with rime. Barley was lying

with her back to him, curled up: an unusual attitude for her. When she turned her head he saw that her eyes looked strained, although she smiled as usual.

"Are you all right, Barley?"

"Oh yes. It's nothing. I'll get up and make the tea."

"No, let me. You rest yourself."

He went downstairs and put the kettle on the Valor Perfection stove, and returning, saw her sitting on the side of the bed.

"I think I'll go downstairs and put my feet up."

He opened the bed for her to return beside him, but she sat still.

"I'll be all right downstairs."

"Is it your time?"

"I don't know."

She seemed so strange, so detached. When she was gone he saw drops of water on the floor and was alarmed. He followed her into the kitchen where she was trying to put on a sand-shoe. The lace broke, she sat up again, still. He made a fire in the hearth, putting on a whole faggot, meanwhile settling her in his armchair with her feet upon a stool. Then wheeling out the Norton he blinded to the midwife's house in Queensbridge. It was a post-war house with three bedrooms. The name on the gate was a little forbidding—PORTO BELLO—so was the midwife, a small woman with a pale, expressionless face, who spoke with a Lancashire accent. Meticulously he gave her a report, and then said, "I'd better go and tell Dr. MacNab."

"No need to bother doctor yet, young mahn. You can go 'ome, everything will be quite all reet." Then seeing that he was un-convinced she repeated that there was nowt to worry about, but if the pains were still coming on by the next morning he could coom and tell her.

He accepted what she had to say against his will, or intuition, and returned to the village. Barley was doing housework, but moving slower than usual. She smiled, saying she was all right. He repeated what the midwife had said.

"Would you mind having only boiled eggs for your lunch, as well as for your breakfast? I meant to go to the shop, but haven't been able to."

"Sit you down yurr, my maid. I am now 'Q' branch. Do you feel like a boiled egg? In case you have any doubt, you don't look like one!"

He boiled two eggs, but she could not eat her egg after capping it, so he finished it. He put the shells into the compost heap, for the garden lacked lime, and lime was essential for vegetables, to form a baby's teeth properly.

"How do you feel now?"

"Much better."

In the afternoon she said she would like to go for a walk across the mushroom field, from where the Channel could be seen, and the tors of Dartmoor with the Cornish hills beyond. Otter and Rusty followed them. Lutra moved in alternate gallops with pauses to stand still. Before they reached the stone-wall at the top of the field Barley said she did not think she could go on any farther.

"Don't let me spoil your walk, I'll go back with Lutra, and keep him and Moggy company, and have tea ready for you when you return."

Phillip's mind had been divided since the morning, and now he was perplexed and near-irritable. He felt the midwife was a fool; yet, he told himself, he must not allow his fears to rule him, and so to interfere in another's job. He must discipline himself: and thus resolved he continued his walk while Rusty ran ahead, nose down to the scents of rabbits. But before reaching the cliffs he turned back abruptly, to the spaniel's disappointment. The midwife was wrong, he knew it.

Opening the cottage door, he saw Barley walking yet more stiffly in the kitchen. Her cheeks were now pale and drawn, her eyes were larger, the irises a fuller black. He knew she was in pain, but she smiled and said, "I'm so sorry I've spoiled your walk. I'll get tea for you."

The cat, seeing the tray, meeow'd and rose on hind legs to touch her hand. Barley put the tray on the table, and sat down. She seemed to have forgotten the tea-tray. She took no notice of the cat. He made the tea, and poured out a cup for her. She smiled her gratitude, looking, he thought, like Irene. He asked, diffidently, if she were in much pain. "It's only sometimes it's a bit bad. But it goes away again."

"Where's Lutra?"

"I put him in the shed."

"I ought to have gone to fetch MacNab."

"Boo says he'll be in the village tonight. She came to see me while you were out for your walk. He's coming with the skittles team." She stopped talking, and after awhile went on. "There's a match in the Ring of Bells—at half—past—six."

Half-past six! It was a long time to go. He kept calm lest he alarm her.

It was dark when he went up the village street. The moon, which only a few nights before had been round and purple-silver above the church tower, would not rise for some hours. He was tense, because greatly anxious. The darkness checked his speed, he had to feel forward, judging the middle of the road by noise of his footfalls reflected from the wall of the cottage on his right, and the sound of the stream entering the culvert under the road on his left. The years of living in the village, much of those years spent in night-wandering in fields and lanes, had taught him to walk by ear more than by sight in the darkness.

Now he had no confidence in his night-sense, but groped his way forward, hands held before him. When the pub door opened he ran forward, using that yellow bit of oil-lamp light before it should be lost. The Ring of Bells was full. The skittles match was between Malandine and Queensbridge. Dr. MacNab was playing for Queensbridge. There was unusual silence in the bar-room.

Dr. MacNab moved his head round slowly to greet the new-comer with a smile. He said gently, "You've arrived at a very important time, Phillip."

"Yes!"

He had left Barley with her feet propped on a stool before the fire, a cup of tea, his third brew since four o'clock, left, like the others, untouched on the table beside her.

He waited for Dr. MacNab to speak, while the doctor continued to watch as the player aimed the swing of the ball on its string suspended from the top of the stick.

"Ah!"

The first ball had 'scatt' only five skittles, leaving four so placed that the player could not get them with his second ball.

"Nine!" cried the umpire.

Dr. MacNab leaned over to Phillip again and whispered, "You're going to be beaten again, you'll see!"

Phillip could wait no longer. "I think Barley is going to have her baby to-night."

Dr. MacNab smiled, without meeting Phillip's eye. "Just watch the play of Billy Chugg now. He'll go out for us this time, you'll see."

Skittles fell with that compact soft-rattling noise which meant a 'floorer'—nine dropped at first ball. They were stood up again. Voices, tobacco fug, paraffin lamp, window shut, landlord and wife and their small grandson leaning over the bar, lurcher dogs moving among heavy boots and legs, rough-shouted talk, pint glasses banged on bar to be refilled, stuffed badger masks, low, yellow-stained ceiling, hot fug which made his eyes smart and his breathing uneasy. They were silent as the stocky little Queensbridge postman bent down to throw the ball again. Skittles fell, a massed shout, many voices, loud laughs, men pushing against Phillip. Twenty-seven, the exact number required to go out! The home team was beaten. He tried to appear easy as he heard Dr. MacNab saying he'd have a glass of mild.

"Have a drink, Phillip?"

"No thanks, really——"

"Do you good. Done any more to that story of Donkin you told me about?"

"Oh, it's got to be rewritten, it's all wrong: too satirical."

Dr. MacNab nodded gravely; and murmured, "Get plenty of hot water, just in case." Then aloud: "Well, here's good luck!" They drank, the tension in Phillip gone for the moment.

On the way back he called at the Pole-Cripps' cottage, to be reassured by Boo, while George offered the use of the Trojan to take them to the midwife's. George was reading *The Fur Trade Journal*. "I say, old bean, you remember what I told you about Angora rabbits? Well, if I can——"

"Another time, Georgie——" said Boo's gentle voice.

He went back to the cottage, seized two pails and hurried to the pump. Then to fill the big cast-iron kettle on the open hearth, light the three burners of the oil-stove, refill one pail and put it on to heat.

Mrs. Crang would be needed. She must wash her hands. Soap, towels. He leapt upstairs and brought down three hand-towels, one each for doctor, midwife Crang, and himself. He put them beside a basin on a wooden box with a new slab of carbolic soap.

Dr. MacNab arrived. He told Barley not to get up, looked at her quizzically before turning to Phillip and saying gently, "There's plenty of time. Better get her to the nursing home. I'll tell the midwife to expect you. Would you like me to send up a taxi?"

"It's good of you, doctor, but I've arranged with George to take us down in his Trojan."

"Ah, that reminds me, I have to give him a certificate for the pension people. We may as well get all we can out of the government, they take enough tax from us, don't they? I'll tell him you'll both be going to Queensbridge."

When the doctor was gone, Phillip was jubilant. All was going to be well. Hearing the doctor's car grinding away from George's cottage he went over and was hardly inside the door when George burst upon him with, "I say, old bean, I must tell you about my bell-ringing articles——"

"Yes, Georgie," said Boo, as to a child, "but I think Phillip rather wants to tell us something."

"That's all right, Phillip, old MacNab's already told us. He says, take her down any time before nine, so there's bags of time. As I was saying, you remember my idea for the bell-ringing articles? Well, I had six copies made and posted them off at the same time, one each to *The Daily Trident, The Daily News, The Daily Chronicle, The Western Morning News, The Daily Telegraph.* The old pater suggested *The Church Times,* as well. My luck was in—they were all accepted!"

"And all published?"

"That's what I mean. Look, I've just had the last cheque—making fourteen guineas in all! Not bad eh, for one article?"

"The same article in each of those papers?"

"Absolutely word for word! Boo typed them out, all top copies, no carbons, didn't you, Boo? So that each copy would look fresh. It was my idea."

"The most brilliant start and finish in journalism!"

"What d'you mean?"

"You'll be on the Black List after this!"

"I should worry! As a matter of fact, I've got a dam' good chance of getting a hundred per cent disability pension, old MacNab says. Then if I can convert it into a lump sum, Boo and I will be able to start that Angora rabbit farm I told you about, remember?"

At nine o'clock Barley walked stiffly, holding an arm each of Phillip and Boo, to the Trojan while Georgie waited with a rug.

Apologising for her slowness in getting into the front seat, Barley was helped in. The driver pulled the starting handle beside the seat and a cloud of blue smoke issued from the exhaust. The friction plates whirred. Clattering noises in the frosty night were amplified from cottage walls.

"You'll see, she'll take Sheepnose in top," prophesied Georgie, wrapped in a British warm, to the collar of which had been added part of an old seal-skin stole once carried by the dowager Mrs. Pole-Cripps, as Boo called her mother-in-law. It was a cold night, stars glittering above bare hedges of the sunken lane lit wanly by the unfocused electric headlights.

The engine conked three-quarters of the way up Sheepnose.

"Curse," muttered the driver. "I can't think why that's happened! I'll go back in reverse and try again."

"Wouldn't it get up in low gear, Georgie?" suggested Boo.

"She won't take a tick, honestly, Boo. The engine was cold. She took it in top this morning like a bird."

"But we're four up now, Georgie. Don't you think——"

Slowly George backed down Sheepnose Hill, while gingerly manipulating the steering wheel. The *équipe* zigzagged more and more until it got stuck into the bank at one place.

"Curse, that's torn it," muttered Georgie. "The reverse gear seems to have gone phut. And I hope to God my new cellulose paint isn't marked!"

He went forward, the friction plates emitting a smell of burning oil. At the bottom of the hill the driver said it was only fair to the old 'bus to take it this time with a rush. This required a further fifty yards of backward movement.

Phillip was inwardly fuming. He could feel that Barley was rigid with pain.

"Might we not have the hill-test another time?" he said distinctly.

Once again Sheepnose Hill was too much for the engine. Georgie, repeating that he couldn't understand what had happened, engaged low gear, and they reached the crest, and so down into the valley beyond.

Coal smoke in layers hung above Queensbridge. At last they were at Porto Bello. Barley was helped out by the midwife and Boo. She walked with slow stiffness into the house.

"Do you think I should go for Dr. MacNab?" Phillip asked Boo. Georgie at once replied for his wife.

"These old girls will get on better alone, old bean. After all, MacNab isn't so hot, you know. There was that case, told to me by the old pater, of Farmer Bill Cane of Sewer who had a pain and old MacNab gave him castor oil, while all the time the poor devil had a rupture! No, take my advice, leave it to the midwife every time! After all, she's a woman."

Phillip went inside, determined to ask for Dr. MacNab. He found Barley being led on a conducted tour around the best room, while its treasures were pointed out—new french-polished draw-leaf table, rexine-covered armchairs and sofa, all looking as though no one ever sat in them.

"You'll send for Dr. MacNab, of course?" he said to the midwife.

"I'll send for the doctor should he be needed, y'ung mahn."

"I'm quite ready to wait, you know, in case you need a messenger!"

"That won't be necessary."

"Are you on the telephone?" He knew that Porto Bello was unconnected. "If not, do use me as a messenger, in case you find the doctor is needed."

"You coom back in th' mornin', y'ung mahn, when you'll be a father."

A coke fire had been banked up in the sitting-room before they left, and here they sat cosily until Georgie began to expatiate on human birth.

"I consider that the pangs of labour are greatly exaggerated. Don't you agree with me, Boo?"

"Well, it all depends on what one means by 'exaggerated', surely?"

"My authority is the old pater, who has visited hundreds of women in the Stews of Queensbridge after confinement. Every old girl, he said, looked cheerful, and said she wouldn't mind going through the same thing again."

"But cases vary, surely, Georgie? Don't you think that women with wide hips find it easier, perhaps, than those with—well, not so wide hips?" Then realising what she had said, she added, "I'll go and fill the kettle for some tea."

The moment she left the room Georgie went to the little book-shelf and took down some bound volumes of *The Bible in Art* which he used to cover his bottles of whit-ale.

"We'll just have a noggin before Boo comes back. Not a word, mind! She knows it's bad for my rheumatism, but I've got plenty more on the way for my next medical board."

There followed, with more whit-ale, an acid argument starting with the miners' threatened strike and ending with the need to abolish, or retain, capital punishment.

"According to the old pater men about to be hanged are always cheerful. I know all 'bout it, ol' bean! The old pater was once Chaplain in Strangeways Prison, Manchester. And I'll tell another thing th' old pater says, and that's that out-of-works are lazy work-dodgers who could find work if it was really needed. To the pure all things are pure, you can't get away from that, you know!"

"Does that also mean that to the rotter all things are rotten, to the crook all things are crooked, to the liar all men are liars?"

"There you go 'gain, ol' be'—dodgin' th' ol' issue, ol' bean!"

"Let's all agree to differ, shall we?" said Boo, brightly.

At 2 a.m., with a headache, he said goodnight, thanked hostess and host, and went to his cottage where he wrote a long letter to his parents, revealing all his hopes of a better world for a new generation. It ran to nearly 5,000 words; and suddenly exhausted, he crept up to bed without undressing, shortly before 5 a.m.

But not to sleep. Black fear was in the room. Try as he might, he could not avoid it. Was it the whit-ale on top of toasted cheese provided by Boo? At 6.45 a.m. he got out of the blankets, and in cold, shrunken moonlight wheeled the Norton into the street and arrived at Porto Bello as the dawn was rising up the eastern sky.

He found the new redbrick house silent and shut. He did not like to knock or ring the bell. He knew her room; it was in the front facing west. The window was open at the top. The concrete sill was not far from the ground. Finding a broken ladder lying against an old wooden wheelbarrow, part of its base decayed, and grey with hoar frost, he set it against the wall and tested the split-larch sides by pushing them against the bricks before starting to climb up. The oak rungs were loose at the top, where the wood at the holes had decayed. He put his weight on the rungs slowly, one foot at a time, bracing himself against the rung breaking. Then, standing on the top rung, while clinging with one hand to the concrete sill, he drew himself upright and with his other hand reached for the top of the sash window, his body curved, for he was holding to the sill while expecting the rung to give way. Fixed thus, with his fingertips he gripped the cross-bar between the panes, and dragged at the window, to bring down the level of the upper bar. It was stiff, and he could not move it. He must go down again, and find something on which to jack the ladder.

"Are you there, Barley?" he said cautiously. When there was no reply, he asked again, louder; while imagining by the continued silence that she was asleep.

He lowered his weight, spreading it between wrists and feet gradually, while a feeling grew that perhaps she was not able to speak. Perhaps she was—— Oh, no, it was his imagination again; they would have sent for him if things had gone wrong.

The idea of disaster grew. It became urgent that he get into the house; and with it as great a dread of knocking at the door, of rousing the old woman, perhaps in dressing-gown over night-dress—for, of course, nothing out of the ordinary had happened, the very quietness of the house showed that all was well, that it was over, and they were now asleep.

Yet fear grew as he half-wheeled, half-carried round the barrow, and set it parallel to the base of the wall, finding that it wobbled a little, so that he went back for some bricks. He found them suddenly heavy, so that he could carry only three together, making three journeys to fetch nine, and very cold they were as he knelt to arrange them to take the weight of the base of the ladder under the decayed bottom boards of the barrow. At last, with bits of broken pink asbestos tiling wedging the space between brick and wood, it was made steady, and up he went again, to hold as before with his left hand and draw down the upper frame of the window with the other. Thus it was safe to pull himself up on the sill and, lowering the frame, to step over into the room.

The first thing he saw was the linoleum floor covered by a dishevelled litter of newspaper sheets; then he saw Barley half sitting up in bed, a pillow behind her, holding a baby in her arms. Her head was leaning to one side. Was she asleep? He crept over the newspapers and spoke to her, to be transfixed with fear when he saw that her lips were grey, her face almost the colour of putty, and that her eyes, which were half closed, did not appear to see him.

"Barley, are you all right?"

Was she asleep? He touched her cheek, but his fingers were cold, he could not tell if her cheek was cold, too. He spoke to her, his mouth close to her ear, "Barley! Are you all right?"

Her eyes opened, she saw him, she looked as though she was trying to smile, but had no strength to open her lips. He was now much afraid, for her eyes had closed again, and the head was leaning on the neck as though all her strength had gone.

He settled the pillow with trembling hands, to make sure that she did not fall sideways out of bed, while noticing that the baby had a red, puckered face and dark hair straggling over the red of its skull.

What in Christ's name had happened? Where was the nurse? Surely it could not be usual? Roused now to direct action through set-aside fear, he went out of the room and knocked on the door adjoining, then on the third door beside the other.

"Will you come at once, please? Will you come, please?"

He waited in silence. Knocked on the near door again. "Will you come at once! I am Mr. Maddison."

Creak of old chain-link mattress, a long wait it seemed, and the door was slightly opened to reveal the Queen Victoria face of the midwife's mother.

"I think my wife is very ill."

"How did you get in, y'ung mahn?"

"Please come at once! I think we ought to get Dr. MacNab!"

"The doctor's got his own work to do, y'ung mahn." She looked at him reprovingly, then she said, "Well, you've got a fine son."

"Has my wife been nursing it all night?"

"Not unless mother'd 'ad a mind to. Baby was crying, and my girl was tired, so I put her to bed. There's nowt t' matter wi' mother or child, y'ung mahn."

"But there is! My wife is unconscious, and very cold!"

He should have got Dr. MacNab himself, the night before. Now it was too late he thought, while the wounds of his mind broke again.

"I'm going to get the doctor at once. Please get some hot-water bottles for your patient immediately! I'll be back as soon as I can!

Dr. MacNab was shaving. Phillip waited until he was dressed, then followed the doctor's car to Porto Bello. He waited below until Dr. MacNab came down to say that it might be as well to get Barley into the Cottage Hospital. He would go home and telephone. "You go and sit with her, Phillip, and keep her cheerful, until nurse brings up a hot-water bottle."

"Is she very ill, doctor?"

"Not as fit as she might be, but she'll pull through."

"When was the baby born, doctor?"

"Mrs. Crump says about one o'clock this morning. Then she put her daughter to bed, apparently, and went to bed herself."

Phillip restrained himself from making any comment on this appalling statement. He felt the terrible rush of time wasting the life of Barley. "Doctor, do forgive me, but she looks so pale! Has she had a haemorrhage?"

"There's been a little bleeding, but she's a strong girl. No need to worry your head, old chap. Go home and have a good breakfast. You must keep up your pecker, you know!"

Phillip went towards Malandine; half-way there he turned back for Queensbridge. There he learned that Dr. MacNab had already telephoned for the ambulance. The ambulance had gone out on a job, and would be sent as soon as it returned. He waited. Ten minutes later it arrived with a scarlet-fever case. It was fumigated. At last he was riding beside the driver. When he got there he was told by the midwife that doctor's orders were that no one was to disturb 'mother'. He went into the bedroom. Barley was lying as though asleep, on her back. He felt that it was his own fault: he had known these people were dud, he had denied his intuition.

The ambulance team was waiting.

"'Mother' must wait here until Dr. MacNab comes," said the midwife. Without a word he went down and called the men up. He waited in the street while they carried the stretcher down. Sitting inside with the nurse he asked if they would give her a blood transfusion.

"The surgeon on duty will do all that is required, I am sure." At the Cottage Hospital he repeated the question to Dr. MacNab. "Well, Phillip, they have the apparatus here, but it is a question of a suitable donor at short notice. But Matron will know. Don't worry, old chap, they'll do everything they can——"

Deathly thoughts possessed him. He saw himself falling down

the cliffs of Valhalla; this time it would be no dream, as in the Pyrenees. He prayed for her to live.

"I realise it's pretty bad, doctor. Can't my blood be used for a transfusion?"

"It's a question of matching groups, old chap. Otherwise clumping will occur."

"They will be quick, won't they? I've seen men after battle——"

"You can be sure they will, Phillip, but these things can't be rushed, you know. There are four blood-groups, and some do not cross-match."

"Forgive my being so persistent, but will you tell them that mine may be the right group? Barley and I think and feel alike, and such traits are in the blood, I think."

"I'll tell the surgeon. Now sit down, and try not to worry. Things are going to be all right."

The surgeon came in with a nurse holding what looked like a watch-glass with blood on it. She put in on the table and with a clean glass in her hand stood by the surgeon as he pricked Phillip's ear lobe. He heard the drops upon the glass. Cotton wool was dabbed on his ear. The glass was then put beside the other glass on the table. The surgeon and the nurse left the room.

"It takes about twenty minutes for the serum to separate from the corpuscles," said Dr. MacNab.

"You mean Barley's?"

"Yes. Then we can see if your red corpuscles will mix with her serum without clumping." He looked out of the window. "It's going to be a fine day, after the frost."

Seagulls were sitting on the chimney pots seen through the window. A jackdaw joined them, and looked through the window. Did the nurses usually put food on the sill? The birds seemed to be expecting something.

A sister came in with two cups of coffee. It was too hot to drink. "I'll bring you some milk, sir," she said to Dr. MacNab.

"Am I keeping you from your round, doctor?"

"Not at all, old chap. I don't start till ten o'clock, anyway." It was eleven minutes past nine. Just before the quarter-hour the surgeon came into the room. He took a bottle from a shelf and with a glass pipette lifted some of it and Phillip saw the drops of clear liquid released upon the watch-glass holding his blood. He stirred it, and added it to the blood in the other glass. He waited a minute, and then looked at the result through a magnifying glass.

"Good," he said to Dr. MacNab. "No appearance of clumping." He turned to Phillip. "Take off your coat, and roll up the sleeve of your left arm."

The nurse dabbed iodine on the skin of the elbow joint, then lit a glass spirit lamp. The surgeon took a wide bore needle and waved it in and out of the pale flame. Then he fixed a short piece of red rubber tubing to the other end. The nurse took a white enamel jug and rinsed it with what seemed to be a solution of Lysol disinfectant.

They seemed to be taking a long time about it. At last the surgeon said, "Sit down in the chair, and hold yourself as loose as you can."

The nurse held his left wrist. Doctor MacNab held his right hand. "You'll be all right, old chap."

"I've seen this done in a Casualty Clearing Station," he said, as brightly as he could, while hearing his own voice croak.

"You've got a fine son," said Dr. MacNab, gently.

The seagulls now appeared to be watching. He closed his eyes. A sharp pain, a greater pain as the needle was pushed into the incision. He heard his blood running into the enamel jug. He felt pale, he floated through regions of hope and despair. A tourniquet was put round his upper arm. He was led away to a couch, and covered by a blanket. He watched the surgeon pouring from the glass bottle a colourless liquid into the enamel jug, and stirring the mixture with a glass rod.

"Everything is going to be all right," said Dr. MacNab, soothingly.

The surgeon and the nurse left the room. Another nurse came in, and sat by his bed. Then Dr. MacNab went away.

In the private ward Barley was lying, with earthenware hot-water bottles covered with red flannel against her feet and her ribs, and a flat rubber bottle wrapped in a towel on her stomach. In her state of collapse, following the haemorrhage which had filled the uterus while in the midwife's bedroom and broken out when she was lifted upon the stretcher, it was impossible to get into the vein at the elbow joint through the skin, so the vein was cut down with a scalpel and exposed. A canula was inserted into the vein, with a yard of rubber tubing attached to the canula. At the other end of the tubing was a glass funnel, with a sterile gauze laid in it to strain the blood as it was poured in from a height. The mixture of Phillip's blood in a solution of sodium citrate passed slowly through the gauze, it moved down slower and slower until it ceased to enter the vein through the canula. The pulse had stopped.

The matron was speaking to Phillip, sitting up on the couch.
"Your wife is asking for you. Now you must be calm, and give her all your assurance, Mr. Maddison. You must be prepared to see a change in her, but above all, she needs your help. So be calm, and trust in God."

He followed her to the private ward, and saw figures by the bed, red rubber pipes and glass-ware, an oxygen cylinder with more pipes and a mask—detached from the head lying back on the pillow, the bloodless lips, the pale sunburn on the hands lying on the counterpane, the eye-lids curiously shrunken, the pale brow, the wan face composed as though beyond resignation, come to a quietude of its own and far away from the Barley he had known in sunlight. He knelt by the bed, biting on his teeth to keep back his thoughts as he took the hand with Spica's ring upon one finger and held it against his unshaven cheek, feeling it to be cold; and leaning over the bed, he stroked the brow, and laid his cheek against her face, and heard the whisper of "I'm—so—sorry——"

He held both her hands, pressing them with his own while willing life into her, his own life to be emptied into her while trying to force all his life into thought to give her strength.

Someone lifted him up from his knees beside the bed, a man in darkness who had come to the end of the world.

The baby, a boy of seven-and-a-half pounds, was left in the Cottage Hospital, and Phillip went back to Malandine to pass the day somehow—walking about, picking up dog and cat and otter in turn, appealing to them as though they were human, climbing to the bedroom to find it exactly as it was before, descending again to see everywhere relics with power to wound anew with their love and tenderness—her small sand-shoes, one with the broken lace; the brown felt hat, with the elastic still sewn to keep it from blowing off, the school hat she had worn at Victoria Station when she had flown to his side from the boat-train; *I am all your friends*; and now she had gone away for ever. No, no! She was in the room, she was with him in his tears, she was bright in the darkness, she was love, telling him he must not grieve, she was watching over him, and his son, their son, who was, did he remember, to be called Willie for she had felt sure the baby would be a boy.

But what had he done? She had asked him, and asked again, to go to see cousin Willie when he was in trouble; and he had demurred—the fatal blank in his nature. She had *known*; he had denied her intuition, as he had denied his own, accepting the unimaginative assurances, based on laziness, of the midwife's mother. He was to blame, not that wooden woman; from a sense of cursed gentility, of bogus good manners, he had denied his clearer vision, and so was entirely to blame for her death.

No, no, her wraith seemed to be saying, you must not blame yourself: or was his mind prompting his own ideas? He closed his eyes and on his knees prayed for simplicity and clearness, saying phrases heard idly in church long ago, among them, *Father, into Thy hands I commend my spirit*.

Mrs. Crang's supper, cooked for him, a plate of baked rabbit with potatoes and sprouts lay on the table; he could not eat it; he gave it to the animals, who between them cleared up all except the sprouts, which he could not throw on the fire, it seemed too unkind, but took out and buried in the freezing compost heap at the bottom of the garden; and walking down to the sea, saw the morning star rising above the crags and pinnacles of Valhalla.

Hetty came down the day before the funeral, and he was glad that his mother was staying with him, for she had loved Barley. She loved the baby, too, and holding it in her arms said, "He is just like you, Phillip, your eyes were very big, too." Then to the baby, "You're going to be a friend to Phillip, aren't you, Sonny?" The use of this name moved him, for Barley had sometimes called him 'Sonny', a name which had always stirred a faint impatience in him when Mother had used it: but now . . .

When his mother was going back, as the train was moving out of the station, and he walked beside the carriage, he was crying voicelessly, *Call me Sonny again, just for once*—but all he said was, "I'll come up soon, and see you again, Mother."

He ordered a small stone of white marble, with her name on it, *Teresa Jane Maddison, aged 19 years,* and below, carved from the stone, a device of reaping hook severing a rose bud from the stem.

George and Boo were invariably kind, always welcoming his visits. George could not do enough for him, giving up his chair by the fire, always cheerful and ready to tell stories about the village people, the old pater, and others; but Phillip did not hear what George was talking about, he shut himself away from the slightly derisive attitude of George towards others—behind their backs. No imaginative life in George, no divining truth—only kindness. He was remorseful when away from George, yet could not bear his presence. Even Boo was a sort of echo of George.

He met friendly faces in the village, for Barley had been liked by everyone; nevertheless he must leave the place, he must go, he must give notice: burn all they had shared and made together in the dark little cottage. He must go away—leave it all—move to another district—but where? Where? He thought of Willie's first cottage beside the disused lime-kiln as a refuge; he must go there; he could not spend another night in Valerian Cottage. He went there on his motorbike, and mooned around only to return again, to find Rusty waiting for him, and Moggy: but no Lutra.

There was a hole dug beside the pig's-house where the otter had been kennel'd, and another hole inside.

"Us zeed'n go!" said Walter Crang. "'A called to 'n, but 'a took no notice. Reckon 'a be zomewhere down the stream, maister!"

He walked down the stream towards the sea, calling and whistling, urging Rusty to pick up the otter's scent, saying repeatedly, "Find Lutra! On to'm, Rusty! Where's Lutra? Find'm, find'm! Good boy, Rusty, find Lutra!"

She had loved Lutra, feeding him first with pen-filler, nursing him against her heart, nourishing the cub back to life, giving him her care, her love—he must find Lutra—someone might kill him——

The night was dark, he walked with hands held out before him; and suddenly, in front somewhere, Rusty barking hysterically, then yelping with pain. What had happened? He ran, coming to the dim line of the stream bank, where he stopped, heard hissing and yikkering, the clank of metal on stone—Lutra in a rabbit gin!

The otter recognised his scent; there followed a period of wild contorted leaping, of blowing and hissing while Lutra bit on steel, leapt into the air and fell short when checked by the chain, to lie there gasping. He pulled off his jacket and threw it over otter and gin, but it was impossible to get the trapped animal to keep quiet. He was bitten through the flesh of his left hand while trying to hold down the head and kneel on the spring, to release the serrated jaws. Abruptly the struggle was over, the otter gone.

He ran back for an electric torch, to search around the area of trodden grass. There were two horny toe-claws near the gin. He followed the course of the stream, and found Lutra's footmarks on a mud scour over which he had passed. He saw blood in the marred print of the off-fore foot.

Below the scour the water ran fast into the reedy mere behind Malandine beach. He whistled and called. Only curlews feeding on sandhoppers along the tide-line answered him as they flew away in fear.

Phillip left for London, to stay with his young cousin Arthur at Cross Aulton in Surrey. They shared a large double brass-and-iron bed in an attic den. When alone during the day he made himself write a story about an African baboon, and then another about a hunted hare. In the evenings Arthur walked with him on the North Downs, Phillip trying to put away his thoughts, to exhaust himself so that he might sleep.

"Father and Mother would be very pleased to let you have the attic room to yourself, Phillip, if you would care to live for a time with us. There's the tennis club, with twenty hard courts, if you care to join. I'd be very pleased to put you up for membership."

While on the Downs he longed for the security of the attic room at night, sharing a pair of divided headphones while listening to dance music from the Savoy Orphean and Havana Bands on the crystal set from 2LO; and later music from France, weak reception but something to hold off the gaping blackness of his mind. After the *Marseillaise* on its worn record at 1 a.m. he was left with the faint crackling of stars and meteorites; and the soft snoring of his cousin. He lay heavy with grief until, feeling the oppression to be unbearable, he got up quietly and went downstairs, put on his trench-coat and in slippers walked down the road and so to the Downs, past the high walls of the lunatic asylum, which did not always shut out screams and cries echoing his own pain in the darkness.

Reaching, beyond the new houses, the thin sward on the chalk, he lay down to let the heavy feeling behind his life fill all his limbs, and by breathing slowly and deeply tried to raise her spirit from the grave, to open the closed eyes of the thin face in the coffin, in imagination going down in the earth to be close to her, to pray to be dead beside her, to become tubercular again as he had been when first he had gone to Devon, and to lie beside her in a gush of his own blood as she had died. This dreadful vision did not last; he knew it for a tissue of grief, to be stripped off; but it recurred until one night in April he heard a nightingale singing. Then his tears broke.

Afterwards he thought, Was it not singing for the honour of life, which was maintained by love? Breathe deeply, slowly, trust in the spirit of poetry, think of the great generations of the dead, of their incurious serenity within the azure of the sky. Remove dark thoughts of defeat by clear thought, accept the light of the sun by day, and the stars by night!

He got up, and cold in every limb, went back to the house, knowing that his duty was to think no more of himself, but of his mother, Irene, his sisters, Bob Willoughby—and the helpless baby. He would go to see Irene, and then to—the battlefields. 'Speak for us, brother, the snows of death are on our brows.'

"I'll come back again, Arthur, if you will still have me. I won't stay so long next time, I know I'm utterly boring."

"No you're not, Phillip. Please come back and live with us. May likes you, so does Topsy. So do I. We'll go for more walks, and I'm sure you will like the tennis club socials."

Once again it was Easter, the *rapide* slowly creeping around Paris: long movement through the night, endure, endure, said the wheels. Life is a spirit, and God is love; endure, endure.

He walked up and down the platform in the sunrise at Bordeaux, up and down while waiting for the slow train for Pau with its wood-burning engine. Then he was sitting in the same yellow-varnished carriage with straight wooden back and hard seat.

Slowly, with much puffing of the forced draught, it drew into Pau. Another wait for an older engine to Gan. At last, at last Arudy; and then his heart seemed to be labouring with the engine hauling the carriages up the valley of the Gave d'Ossau, while he felt upon him the cold turbulence of the snow-waters; and with a shock saw the board of *Laruns*.

On the wooden platform stood Irene, her hair silvered by her ears, smiling as before, but when the smile ceased he saw that her eyes were set as though beyond him, while yet seeing him.

"You must be very tired, P.M."

"Oh no," he said, and stepping out on a left foot that suddenly wasn't there, fell upon the board-walk.

"Oh, poor P.M., isn't that your wounded leg? I should have warned you of the steepness!"

"Just a momentary cramp, Irene."

When he had had tea, she said, "Tell me about my grandson. Is he fair like his mother, or dark like his papa?"

"The hair was dark, but is now becoming fair. And he has his mother's eyes." It was a breaking moment: the pale face in the coffin, the eyes unsunned.

"I am simply longing to see my grandson!"

He sat with Irene through most of the night, playing Tchaikowsky and Grieg and Dvorak on the gramophone, drinking brandy and coffee and eating relays of bread and *saucisson*; he held her in his arms and laid his cheek on her head, comforting her, the ice within melting into tears as at times it seemed that Barley was near, looking directly at him, as though her will-power were being directed into and for him, so that the sense of loss was kept at a distance, as if life were a dream and beyond the dream she was alive and it would be natural to see her walking into the room, when she would never leave him again.

But—the truth was that his weakness, his cursed diffidence had led to, if not directly caused, her death, as it had that of Lily Cornford; and in lesser degree, he had betrayed Willie, Spica, Annabelle, and Sophy. He must have been talking aloud, for he heard Irene saying, "No, no, P.M.! You must not think like that, my dear! It would be the last thing Barley would want. Life must be faced, it must go on, Phillip."

"Oh yes, I can face it, Irene. You are right, of course. But I did feel no real confidence in the doctor, who forgot to tell me, two years ago, for weeks, that I was clear of tubercle. He also diagnosed a rupture as the pains of food poisoning, and gave a local farmer castor oil, which might have led to a broken intestine."

"Did it?"

"Well, no; I was only told that."

"Ah, village tales, P.M.! But to return to the idea of guilt. It is as bad, sometimes, to blame oneself as it is to blame others. Why, I could so easily blame myself because I wasn't with Barley that night. I would have been, but for a wretched tummy upset. No; one must not assume *entire* responsibility when life and death are matters for God to decide! Why, you could blame yourself for living in the heart of the country, and not in London, where she might have had better treatment! On the other hand, it might have made no difference. No, P.M., don't spoil your life by thinking about such things. If there was any blame, it might be attached to that midwife, for going straight to bed and not taking the baby and the cot into her room with her. But again, if she had done so, Barley would not have had the wonderful pleasure of holding her mite in her arms!" and Irene cried again, and it was his turn to comfort her.

He could not rest there, he must go, walk again upon the battle-fields, see once more those places which one day must be re-created as a monument to his friends in the war. The train returned him to Bordeaux, where he dined alone in an empty restaurant, and it was while waiting for the Paris train that realisation of his loss struck him again with such anguish that he hardly knew how to contain his feelings as he walked up and down the station platform without rest until the train from Madrid rolled in under its steaming furnace glare. Having put his pack and staff in one corner of a carriage, he walked up and down again until the express was due to leave.

A small bearded peasant and his wife had taken his seat, after putting his things upon the floor; they sat there impassively; it did not matter; he could lie down upon the floor of the corridor and feel not so alone with the feet of French *matelots* on leave from Bordeaux stepping over his body most of the night.

From Paris he took a slow train to Arras, to seek upon the battlefields the friends of his youth.

Part Two

PILGRIMAGE

'God made the country, and the Devil made the towns.'
Old Saying

Chapter 5

TWO BATTLES

In the village of Roclincourt in Artois there lived a widow woman who kept a new *estaminet* worth 85,000 francs. With pride she told her English guest the value of her new house as she showed him up the stairs of bare poplar boards to his bedroom. He stayed in her home during several nights, after wandering about by himself during most of the daytime.

It was gracious weather, with white cumulus clouds moving high under the blue sky. Cuckoos were calling, larks sang every-where above the cornfields. He carried a map, the names of which were familiar; but when he came to any of the named places he found a strangeness which induced a sort of momentary helpless-ness: they were of a different world: for he had known them only in war.

The hamlet of Roclincourt was a few miles from Arras, on a slope leading north to the villages of Farbus and Vimy. He was glad to be quiet, to walk about slowly in the sunshine which sus-tained his thoughts as he tried to get himself together.

The wheat in the wide fields was beginning to tiller, and the silky reams of the wind moved across the plants from the south and west. One morning he strolled up the long and gradual slope to the northern sky, recalling the story told to him by Colonel Vallum of his Regiment, of Sir Douglas Haig coming from Advanced Third Army Headquarters to Arras on the tenth of April, 1917, and stepping out of his black Rolls-Royce motorcar with the small Union Jack fluttering on the radiator, to ask, *But where is the Vimy Ridge?*

Well, where *was* the Vimy Ridge? Looking east from the Maison Blanche no obvious slope was visible; but when he had walked up the long way to the crest, and was standing on one of the cracked roofs of the reinforced concrete German gun-shelters at the edge of Farbus Wood, immediately there was a view over hundreds of square miles of flat country to the north, where the smoke of industrial towns dissolved the far horizon. Below in the foreground was the wide, sprawling, brick-redness of Lens rebuilt.

Through miles of green plain below, the trench pattern of the northern spur of the Siegfried Stellung was visible in blurred lines of chalky subsoil spread amidst the brown and reclaimed top-soil of the fields.

After wandering among the concrete shelters of the German gun-pits along the edge of the wood, trying to visualise scenes of those far-off days but seeing only a remote face or two, like transfers upon the air, he thought to descend the reverse slope of the Ridge down to Vimy village for some wine, bread, and cheese. With the sensation of remoteness from life still upon him, coupled with a vague resentment of the present, he entered an *estaminet* and had an omelette there with a bottle of red wine that was more an act of communion with his friends of the war than a refreshment. Afterwards he pottered about, looking at old concrete pill-boxes and touching rusty strands of barbed wire.

In one grassy field, revealing its war history by the gentlest undulations where shell-holes had been filled in, the land re-sown with rye-grass and clover, a bull was grazing beside a cow. They grazed quietly and happily nose by nose, less than a yard behind the wire fence at the edge of the sunken road. He stood and watched how their tongues caught and pulled the succulent young grasses. Their noses were apart only by the width of their horns. How content they were! The feeling from those tranquil beasts gave him for a few hours an acceptance of life that was serene behind his fatigue and sadness; but with the sun descending he hurried back to the widow's house as to sanctuary.

His room was bare as before; but in the kitchen there was a warmth and a comforting friendliness. The old woman was wise, gentle and quiet. She was looking after two English gardeners of the local cemeteries, and had done so since the *estaminet* had been rebuilt. There was a gramophone; and newspapers from England arrived regularly. They had their meals in another room, while he ate in the kitchen, at the table that was scrubbed every day and allowed to dry before the new American cloth was relaid upon it.

There was only one picture in the kitchen: the portrait, en-

larged from a snapshot, of the widow woman's only son, a soldier
who had fallen at Verdun. Thin-faced, with fixed eyes and slight
dark moustache, his image stared blankly from the wall. The
mother was proud of her fine new house with its electric light and
central heating (not used yet, for economy), and of her shining
cooking range, porcelain and enamel with a pleasing design of
pale blue birds and pink flowers; but sometimes when she was
telling him how *jolie* was her house her eyes lost their shine and her
sight became unfocused; her voice faltered to silence, and he knew
that she too was lost in her world of wraiths and phantoms.

She was suspended in time, until the voices of the English
gardeners calling "Ma" in the other room gave her new life, and
she shuffled to them swiftly, with food or wine or coffee; her eyes
shone, and she smiled as she watched them, and when she returned
to the kitchen again, he could see that she had gained vitality
once more to feel proud of her fine new house.

After supper the gardeners came into the kitchen for their
evening dance; together they revolved solemnly to the tune of
If You were the Only Girl in the World; then for a change it was
K-K-K-Katie, Beautiful Katie. There were other records of tunes
and foxtrots popular in the war, but those were the favourites.
The old woman and her small grand-daughter looked on happily,
with a neighbour who had come in for a chat.

The widow was a short, red-faced motherly little old person.
She cleaned her poplar floors every day on her knees. Her rooms
held little furniture. The bedroom he slept in had a chair, a bed
of fumed oak, and a pail. She told him she was awaiting *dommage
de guerre* for the rest of her furniture. That, she hoped, would be
fumed oak, *très belle*! He thought that the new house replaced what
before the war had probably been a small pisé-and-thatch *buvette*.

The gardeners told him they were working just off the Arras-
Béthune road, not far from La Maison Blanche. This, explained
one, had been the site of the Canadian Headquarter dugouts
during the battle of Arras in April, 1917. The information excited
him: in a series of caverns deep in the chalk, the generals had
waited while the barrage fire rolled up to the crest of Vimy and
turned the sleet into steam on that morning of April the ninth,
eight years before.

"We're working just now in the British cemetery near there,"
said one.

"That's right," said the other. "You'll find us if you walk up the road past the Labyrinthe to La Targette."

"That's right," added his chum. "You can't miss it, it lies below the German Concentration Graveyard above the Labyrinthe. It looks at its best just now."

The German Concentration Graveyard! So this was where Willie had worked, this the place he had written about in the article which Bloom, in the *Weekly Courier* days, had liked, but not published!

"I'm glad they're looking after them!" he exclaimed, feeling happiness coming over him. "I remember that the German cemeteries always looked very neat and well-tended during the war. So they've planted flowers! Good!"

"I meant it's our little lot, at La Targette, that looks lovely just now."

"Then the German Concentration Graveyard is still as it was?"

"That's right."

Consulting his map, he planned to walk farther that day than La Targette—to Neuville St. Vaast, and beyond. He was specially eager to see the Labyrinthe because it was the scene of some of the fighting described in *Le Feu*, a book which Uncle John had given him with others which had belonged to Willie. Henri Barbusse had put the truth into words, even as he was determined to do, one day.

"Have either of you two chaps read Barbusse?"

The gardeners, both old infantry soldiers, shook their heads. He began to tell them that the French, both white and Colonial troops, had attacked there in blue coats and red trousers, to perish in far greater numbers than the Germans. It was one of the field-fortifications which had to be taken before the assault on the Vimy Ridge was possible. His words aroused no response in the gardeners; the one continued to wind up the gramophone, while the other waited to put the needle in the outer groove of the record.

Apparently he had interrupted a ritual: they seemed to share every action, on the principle of fair-do's all round. Perhaps the one had been winding up the gramophone, the other putting in the needles, for years.

The next morning after breakfast he walked down the road to the Labyrinthe. Arriving there with mounting excitement, longing, and apprehension, he stood in the road below the front position of the field-work, possessed by the feelings of those who once had waited there white-faced, cold, and trembling, to advance into certain death. For it had been a field-work of immense strength, he could see, commanding the Arras-Béthune road. The redoubt, still visible in outline as star-shaped, sloped almost imperceptibly to the eastern horizon. Here wave after wave, in attack after attack by troops from Morocco, wearing the fez—a fragment of red cloth was visible in the grass—had gone forward with French soldiers wearing the *kepi*—straight into the mort-blast of machine-guns hidden under steel and concrete cupolas, some to hang upon the barbed wire until all were shredded to rags fluttering above bone-heaps, wandered over by ants, all to be forgotten in wild grasses by 1916.

Here, out of the massed bloody sweat of a generation the truth had arisen: here, out of the shock of the colossal and prolonged cruelty played with shell, bullet, bayonet and bomb had arisen that flower of the human spirit, a poet upon the battlefield—Barbusse!

Upheld by thoughts of the poet's courage he returned to the road. As he ascended to the crest he perceived abruptly and with dismay a black horizon rising before him. Here the French had concentrated the German dead, upon the position of the invaders' main fortress. Here Willie's footsteps had passed, here his shadow had fallen upon the dusty road—so soon to be lost to the sun, beyond the darkness of death.

Phillip stood still with eyes closed; then, with a sigh, looked about him.

Elsewhere the white subsoil of chalk thrown up by shovel and bombardment had been scattered and plowed under, or in unreclaimed places allowed to cover itself with grass; but on the Labyrinthe the chalk sub-soil had been laid deeply upon the surface in order to create a white wilderness. Yet even the effects of a wide and startling expanse of chalk shone upon by the sun was darkened, as Willie had written in his article, by the massed effect of scores of thousands of tall black crosses, acre after acre of blackness standing under the summer sky; and not even one poppy or charlock growing there.

What ferocious mind had ordered such a revenge on the living, he cried to himself. It could not have been the idea of any man whose body had been used against its will as part of the businessmen's war. Here was hate; here was the crystallized mentality of a declining European civilization: here was the frustration of love that was the Great War. Even the light of the open day was made sinister there: old agonies dimmed the noonday sun.

While he sat by the roadside watching a bumblebee bending a yellow flower of hawkbit, he had a chance to observe the effect upon a German parent, arriving for the first time to seek the place where her little child—for that was how a mother would remember him—was buried. A motor-car stopped on the road below and a woman got out and walked alone through the gates. So cousin Willie had watched a German mother 'beginning a search in the immense silence of charred human hopes'.

She stopped, helpless and appalled, before walking on with lowered head, and pausing to gather her thoughts together, before beginning her search. He got up and went to her. "May I help you, madam?"

"Ach, thank you, thank you, monsieur! My son Carl Kemnitzer—where is he?"

Obviously she had taken him for an official: she produced a card, with her son's particulars. How not to disappoint her? He could not think what to say—waiting there unmoving—until, remembering the war-time inscriptions on German graves he said, "Your son Carl rests with God, m'am."

She looked into his face, hesitated, and wept. He took her hand, and pressed it. Soon they were smiling, almost cheerful. *Nein bitte*, no thank you, she must search for her son alone, she was happy now. He saluted her, and walked on up the road much relieved in spirit, thinking that there must be no more nations, only Europeans, for all mankind was one species upon the earth.

He arrived at La Targette, where the British and French cemeteries lay side by side. There he found the two gardeners working, using little hoes among the plants, kneeling to their work. The spirit arising from the gardens further clarified his mind, for it was of calm loving-kindness. Truly that was God. Flowers which grew in English gardens were to be seen there, some in bloom—columbine, pansy, sweet william, wallflower and campanula.

He looked in the book placed in a green box on a post, for the signatures and remarks of visitors. Many Canadians, Scots and English folk had written their thoughts of the cemetery; the phrase *nice and beautiful* recurred often. The simple head-stones, each carved with a badge and a name, were clean, and the lawns around them weeded and mown. Here was no hate; only the clarity that was love.

Beyond a plashed hawthorn hedge was the French cemetery. Here the white crosses were scrolled with the tricolour, spaced wider; blue, red and white. He felt that the spirits of the slain could breathe here; or rather, the spirit of the living found an easier place for its hopes than in that place up there, the Labyrinthe...

He went on, turning through Neuville St. Vaast and beyond, where the terrain was left wild and desolate. Rank grasses covered the old trenches and the concrete shelters. Willows waved on the ancient parapets, thrice the height of the howitzers which their parent-withies might have helped to camouflage. Reeds had sprung out of old shell-holes stagnating with a brown scum, whence arose the percussive mutter of many frogs.

He came upon an area of the battlefield which was being cleared up. There were many heaps of rusty iron shards piled by a cart-track with barbed-wire pressed into bales as of satanic hay; and farther on there was an immense and rugged pit, several acres in extent, in which bearded men stripped to the waist were working slowly. They had long hair and slanting eyes, were clad in ragged clothes and had the listless, uncaring attitudes of prisoners. A man, apparently their foreman, was standing moodily on a hummock above them.

He greeted him in his feeble French. The man spread his hands as though dumb. He walked around the pit, or quarry, for it was ten to twelve feet below the grass and willows above its perimeter, and was examining a ten-foot pile of shells, the duds of a 1915 offensive, he thought, as he picked one up, when the foreman gave a hoarse cry and violently waved an arm at which Phillip put it down carefully among the other shells.

Later, talking to the gardeners, he was told that the salvage work was being done by Russian labourers, paid a few francs a day. When one pile of duds was large enough a detonator was thrust into the yellow-crusted cylinders, balls, and canisters, and touched off with a time-fuse: away the men would run, to crouch out of sight: and WOMP . . . RUM . . . M . . . M . . . ble! A great slow-billowing mushroom of yellow and black smoke turning the sun brown. Then they would work for another week to prepare the next excitement.

"The weight of iron there, of both exploded and unexploded shells, was greater than the weight of the first eight feet of top-soil," he said—a remark which drew no reply from either of the gardeners. Only later did he realize that they were cut off from England, and existing each in his own thoughts, so they seldom spoke, but lived in dreams of England.

"Can you direct me to La Folie Farm?"

The one addressed did not look up, but pointed with his trowel while pressing into the bed a root-clump of Michaelmas daisies.

Cousin Willie in his article had written of 'a ploughman's mite'—a stick of aspen poplar stuck in the headland of a wheat-field, with a rough cross of the same wood: and the stick had blossomed. Where to look for it? Would it be there, after five years? He walked on, and suddenly it was before him—he might have been led by a spirit guide directly to it. Now a tree two inches thick at the base, and without its cross-piece, there it was and below it lay two bleached leg-bones, a skull, the white cage of the ribs, the arm bones at the ends of which were small white points, the knuckle and finger-bones of human hands. *A plowman has done this act for some unknown German soldier left, perhaps, in the final retreat*—the actual words of Willie, in the news-room of *The Weekly Courier,* five summers before, came to his mind. The skeleton, curved where it had fallen, had lain there during the intervening years, although the field elsewhere had been levelled for cultivation.

"Willie," he said, standing still with eyes closed, "are you near me? Willie, come to me if you can." It was as though a cold wind had moved up his spine; at that moment the leaves of the tree began to tremble, making a bright rustling: yet there was no breeze. Perhaps the warmth of his body had caused a slight movement of air—the aspen was known as the 'trembling poplar'. But was that all? *Willie,* he thought. *Have you now met Barley? Are you both here, behind the sunshine?*

With a wave of the hand towards the aspen, he continued on down the headland of the field. Whole families of women were out in the fine weather, kneeling in line and plucking weeds—

grandmothers, aunts, parents, children, all in dark clothes, kneeling across the rows of wheat-plants, advancing slowly on all fours to pull every weed with their fingers, absorbed in their work. Were these the families Willie had observed, five years before, weeding the field? Such contentment in the sun; such simplicity! They were happy; they were making the earth a better place for men to see and *feel*.

He walked on, coming to other fields, recently levelled, ploughed and cultivated but not yet sown, where peasants were gathering armfuls of docks, pulling up charlock and thistles and laying them in heaps on the headlands. It was pleasant to see them; they were too intent to talk. How easy for a lazy, conceited writer to make them creatures of low mentality, intent only on more money for better crops! They were the strength and sanity of France; they provided the bodies while the towns made the oversharp neuroticism which had resulted in first The Labyrinthe and then the Concentration Graveyard.

The next morning he said goodbye to the widow of Roclincourt, heaved on his pack, took his staff of mountain ash with its iron spike, and set forth again. Where should he go? North to Ypres and the Salient? The thought brought reluctance, as of weight: too much had fallen upon that low-lying area of total destruction, every worm blasted in the bombardments upon village, road, and broken dykes or polders; the thought of the place was too heavy. To the south, and the Somme? That way was easier; he recalled green downland slopes after the 1917 retreat into the Hindenburg Line. He would walk south; he would be on his way home. Home? The thought pierced him: what was home without Barley?

Onwards, through the night if need be; anything but remaining still. If only it would rain, that would be known, that would be a friend. The sky was growing dull, clouds were coming up; let it rain, for God's sake, let the going be hard.

By the evening he had reached Achiet-le-Grand. He was by then wet through and weary. Should he walk through the night, down to Albert and beyond? To Etaples? Achiet when last he had been there was a waste of rubble and cellars; with relief he saw lights in a window, heard music and laughter within. After hesitation, because of his bedraggled appearance, without mackintosh or hat—he was unshaven, too, his hair long and wet—he pushed open the door and entered the *estaminet*. It was part of the new France: a floor of composition made to look like marble; the mirrors behind the bar had the tawdriness of new, factory-made things; the imitation oak panels of the chair-backs were of pressed paper. He asked for a cognac, while assembling himself to enquire about a room for the night.

The bar was lit by a hissing petrol lamp, which hurt the eyes, and by its white light the faces of the young men and women dancing to the blare of an automatic hurdy-gurdy were made the more pale. On the wall a notice was hung:

Grand Anglais Jazz-Balle every
Sunday Night—Wellcome

Although the hot, smoky atmosphere nearly choked him, his melancholy was slightly dispelled by that Wellcome, and he decided to have another cognac. During a break in the demand for drinks some minutes later he managed to edge himself through the crowd to the landlord. His appearance had obviously caused mild amusement among the gang of youths; the long, plus-four knickerbockers were obviously an unfamiliar sight causing unconcealed stares and giggles.

The landlord was suspicious. He asked why he walked in the rain without a coat? Had he been looking for work in Bapaume? It was a shock to hear that name mentioned as a workaday town. Was he like others, seeking more money than could be earned in the brick factories there? What had he got in his pack?

Obviously he was wondering if the stranger had escaped from prison. He asked if he had money for a bed; whereupon Phillip showed him his note-case, taking out the dirty tattered paper-money of the district. It satisfied the *patron*.

"Je suis soldat Anglais, m'sieur—revenu."

"Ah, c'est bon, m'sieu!"

He was invited to drink and dance. In fact, Wellcome to the Grand Anglais Jazz-Balle!

There were Italian plasterers in the throng, who were earning, he learned, from forty to eighty francs a day. While he was speaking to one, a pale thin French youth lurched up, flung down

a hundred-franc note, and yelled for drinks all round. Most of
the men had rum, which cost half a franc a glass—about a penny
in English money. Meanwhile Madame was whispering in his ear
that the benefactor, the son of a millionaire, spent hundreds of
francs in the place most evenings.

The millionaire father was apparently regarded with a mixture
of envy and admiration; when the villagers had returned after the
armistice, she explained, he had bought for ready cash the sites of
many shattered houses as a speculation, hoping that the reparation grants would repay him generously later on. They did,
declared the landlord; for the law fixed the reparation payments at
four times the attested value of each pre-war house. No other
evidence of value was required: you claimed for what you had
had, the total was multiplied by four, and no questions asked.
Now, added the landlord, the speculator was a millionaire, owning
over fifty houses as well as the only butchers' shops in the place—
a flourishing monopoly, buying old cows at four francs a kilo, and
selling bifteck at twelve to sixteen francs a kilo!

The landlord, making the best of all possible worlds, claimed
that he was a great friend of the big man of the village. The son,
he said, was a very nice young chap, very free with his money.
He bought the ancient cows for father, who had acquired some
trout fishing in the Ancre, below Thiepval—did he know Thiepval? The trout fishing was very good below there.

He began to feel that the battle of the Somme might never have
happened. He went upstairs to bed. The moon gleaming in the
east through the open window revealed patches on the ceiling
under the leaking roof. The dancers seemed to be walking about
in the road all night; but at two a.m. the hurdy-gurdy ceased its
blaring jazz; the last unsteady steps and confused voices went away
down the road, and as the moon declined to the west he fell asleep.

In the morning the sun was shining, puddles in the brick-
rubble roads were drying at the edges as he walked about while
coffee was being prepared. After rolls and butter, with apricot
jam, he adjusted his mood of the night before, and saw the suspicions of the landlord as normal, considering that the old battlefield area was over-run by strangers, many of them vagrants seeking
work, about whom stories of robbery with violence were told.

He asked if the *patron* knew of any English cemeteries being
made in the district; and was directed to an area he had known

during the war. He set out gladly, as to an old friend, following
the way he had come, in March 1917, with the transport of 286
Machine Gun Company, when the German Great General Staff
had quit their 'Blood Bath' on the Somme. It had been a
masterly retreat; first they had blown up every cottage and mined
every cross-road, cut down every tree that occluded observation
for their gunners, removed every railway line, put detonators in
some of the porcelain insulators of the thrown telegraph posts,
riddled lengths of corrugated iron with hand-grenades, and gener-
ally destroyed everything that might have been of the slightest use
to the British Fifth Army; and having done this, they walked back
one Saturday night to their *Siegfried Stellung,* which the British
soldier called the Hindenburg Line.

At the time there had been much newspaper talk at home about
the German Corpse Factory, wherein the 'Huns' were said to
have melted down the bodies of their dead to obtain fats for high
explosive. He and his friends in France had regarded it as just
something else in the newspapers, filled with things which were
quite apart from the war; they had known that the story was
a fake, for everywhere in the abandoned country between the
old Somme battlefields and the *Siegfried Stellung* were to be seen
German cemeteries, set with wooden crosses and flower-beds. And
riding around one day, he had seen where British shells, dropping
among the tombs of a cemetery, had revealed long leather boots
and curiously shrunken grey tunics.

There had been many German cemeteries behind their lines of
the 'Blood Bath'. One at Ablaizanville had wrought-iron gates,
and cream-coloured stones and monuments carved with names and
regimental crests. It had caused some wonder and regard for the
enemy in all who passed by, to see the British dead treated with
the same respect as the German dead.

Another spring morning of that early April of 1917, cantering
over the downs, he had come upon a solitary grave in the middle
of a grassy valley: a grave set with a broken-bladed propeller for
headstone, with pansies and violas and mignonette for coverlet;
the three square yards railed off from cattle. *Here rests in God a
brave unknown English flier, who fell in combat, July 1916.*

Now, eight years older almost to the day, he stood and watched
graves in a cemetery he had visited in 1917 being dug up. It was

near a hamlet not far from St. Leger. Here Willie had worked. Was his spirit near in the sunshine? He stood apart, watching the English official waiting beside a French *gendarme*. So they were still transferring the German remains into coffins, each about ten inches wide, to be taken away by lorry. The British remains were being placed in similar coffins, loaded into a second lorry.

"M'sieur, s'il vous plaît, est que c'est vous avez connu un Anglais officiel qui s'appelle William Maddison? Il a travaillé ici quelque années auparavant."

They looked puzzled; they shook heads, and went on with their work.

He began to feel the futility of his task to weigh upon him, while longing grew towards England. He would walk to La Boisselle, see the old front line of the Somme again, then go on down to Albert and take a train to Boulogne.

Walking beside the marshes of the Ancre, set with their burnt and splintered poplar stumps amidst new green growth four and five feet high, he turned east up rising ground to find the wood where the battalions of his brigade had assembled on the night before the attack of July the First. Nightingales had sung there until the beginning of June of that year; perhaps descendants of the birds would be singing there now.

Arrived at the copse, he sat down to rest, and soon afterwards a bird began to sing in the new undergrowth a few yards from him.

It seemed to be hesitating; the same note was repeated among the hazel wands and ashpoles, a note low and plaintive. Next, three high and frail strokes of song and then another pause. Suddenly the green shade around him seemed to shake with the liquid notes of the bird's passion. It was a moving occasion—the woods of his boyhood—Keats' poem—Stravinsky's opera heard from the Dove's Nest at Covent Garden—Barley beside him in the Camargue——

It was right that the villages should be rebuilt; right that the shell-holes be filled, the ground levelled to grow corn once more. The living and the dead were one, united by faith. The nightingale's song was immortal: a symbol of human longing as old as that longing in man for love and immortality. It was poetry, it was truth; and nothing else mattered. The bird's song was perfection: were it a little less so, it would touch all human hearts at once.

He walked on down Railway Road, and at Mill Causeway crossed the marshes and stream of the Ancre, meaning to climb up the slope to the Schwaben Redoubt, and on to Thiepval, and down along the old front line to the Bapaume road, where his platoon had fallen to a man, killed or wounded, on July the First. The battlefield had been left at that place, and he could still see where some of the trenches had been dug in the hillside slopes leading up the high ground and the Schwaben Redoubt.

Here, above Thiepval Wood, like a giant hand of stone severed at the wrist and upheld as a warning, stood the Ulster Division Memorial Tower. The trenches—over which the Orangemen had attacked on that hot summer morning until the enfilade fire from both the south and the north had cut them down—were half-hidden by the long wild grasses of the years, acres of undulating wilderness and silence.

There was nothing to be found on the high ground except an overwhelming feeling of loneliness, whichever way he looked: north to Hebuterne, Beaumont Hamel, and Gommecourt; east to the ridge, failed objective of July the First, with its black stipples of dead tree trunks; south to La Boisselle and Fricourt.

He could go no farther; he hurried away and down to the causeway across the marshy valley, with its charred poplar stumps wherein rusty splinters of shells and rifle bullets were still embedded. A barbed-wire fence enclosed the reeds and rushes on both sides of the causeway; he was about to climb a fence, to seek the position of the German 5.9 howitzer battery which, bestrewn with empty wickerwork shell-cases, had lain there broken and derelict in the winter of 1916, when a voice cried out threateningly, "Que voulez-vous là?"

He turned, and saw an elderly man with a grey moustache and ruddy face carrying a fly-rod.

"Je suis soldat anglais revenu, m'sieur."

"Eh bien, allez-vous-en!"

Seeing the stranger hesitate, he growled in English with a Cockney accent, "This ain't England!" and turning about, walked towards a punt moored to a post by the bank.

That night Phillip lay in bed in another new *estaminet*, thinking that he must learn a fresh way of life before he lost himself in memory, like Uncle John at Rookhurst. The trouble was that he had grafted on himself, during the war, a new personality; he had returned half a stranger to himself, and very nearly an alien to his family. Where was the lost part? Was the war responsible? That shell on Messines Ridge of Hallowe'en, 1914, which had buried him? But did realisation of what had happened help to settle the effect? A madman knowing he was mad: would self-knowledge help to cure him?

Outside in the marshes of the Ancre many frogs were croaking. As the night wore on and he could not sleep he began to believe that the entire valley was permeated with the spirits of the dead, and the ghostly past of himself was being called to join them.

Did one lose a part of oneself, in spirit, as one shed part of the body in normal growth? If not, where was his lost part? Was it still lurking in the marsh, an essence of old emotion? Surely that would only be natural? Memory rules life, or most of it. For years the lost part of himself had lurked in the marsh, seeing wraiths of men in grey with helmets and big boots, wraiths of men in khaki, laden and toiling, wraiths of depressed mules sick with fatigue and mud-rash, walking in long files up to the field-gun batteries, past wraiths of howitzers flashing away with stupendous corkscrewing hisses upwards, wraiths of pallid flares making the night haggard, while bullets whined and fell with short hard splashes in the gleaming swamps of the Ancre.

He could not sleep. Was there a demoniacal influence in the marsh, materialising out of the ceaseless croaking among the stumps of the dead poplars? The perpetual and restless spirits of old wrong and imposed cruelty and hate and despair wandering among the reedy shell-holes, among the broken wheels of guns, and the rusty wire in the long grasses? The young green had grown again, hiding the old bitternesses, but the desolation was still there. The young danced at their Jazz-Balle; the cunning made profit; the money-markets ruled the world as before; the war was still continuing within the crystallised mentalities of human beings; the war had brought no purification to the world, only to those who did not matter any more, the sensitive survivors of a deci-mated generation.

Trains from Lille and Amiens rolled noisily past the window, a star moved across the window space, seeming to look into the room curiously, glimpses of the past came with unavailing sadness.

The dug-outs of Y ravine had subsided, the dry-rotted timbers broke with a touch; the pistons and cylinders and mainshaft of a Morane Parasol rusted in the grasses—the charred fuselage once visible on the ridge above Station Road in December 1916—with rifle barrels and holed helmets and burst *minenwerfer* cases.

Was it all over and done with; or was it, as Willie had declared, all to do again?

The Ancre flowed in its chalky bed, swift and cold as before, gathering its green duckweed into a heaving coat as of mail and drowning the white flowers of the water-crowsfoot. Only one thing of all the Fifth Army's work remained—the wooden military bridge over Mill Causeway. *The Fifth Army?* a voice seemed to be saying, the voice of the wan star, *What you seek is lost forever in ancient sunlight, which arises again as Truth.*

The voice wandered thinner than memory, and was gone with the star under the horizon.

And then, another voice, another face—hovering in the air, looking at him calmly—Barley before the baby had come— looking at him curiously, and with remote tranquility. Was it a projection of his thoughts—or was she really with him in spirit? Would she not be with her baby, if she could materialise? He must return to his son, be mother and father to the little fellow.

Chapter 6

THE SAD GESTURES OF LOVE

Hetty heard the exhaust notes of the motor-bicycle while watering the aspidistra in the front room, and looking out of the window saw him pull up outside. She waved, and hurried to the door.

"Welcome home, my son! When did you cross over?"

"This morning, Mother," as he kissed her. "I've come straight here, I must go to Cross Aulton tonight. I'll return soon."

"At least you'll stay until Father comes home, Phillip? He did so appreciate your postcards from France, and we both followed you on the old trench maps in the drawer of your bedroom. He still speaks of it as 'Phillip's' bedroom, you know. Now come down to the garden room, and I will get you some tea. Sit down in Father's chair, and rest yourself. Was it a good crossing?"

"Not very, Mother."

She hastened to put on the kettle, but stopped on the way to say, "I suppose you haven't heard about the baby while you've been away? I did think of going down to find out, but thought you might think it interfering of me."

"Oh no, of course not, Mother."

He looked tired and very thin. Uppermost in her mind was the thought of her grandson. She nursed a hope that Phillip would come to live at home, now that he got on well with Dickie. Then she would be able to look after the baby. Poor little Billy, he should not be in the hands of strangers.

The french windows were open. She put a plate of bread and butter beside him, knowing that after a sea-voyage he needed plain food.

"Why has Father lopped the elm so much? It looks quite bare."

"He thought the roots might spread too far, and undermine the foundations of the house, Phillip."

Sipping his china tea with a slice of lemon, he said, "I did think of living more or less permanently at Gross Aulton, as a lodger."

"Yes, Uncle Joey told me you seemed to like being there. It's a great deal changed since I knew it." She sighed. "All those new red houses on the Downs——! Ah well, we can't put back the clock, can we? Still, Arthur tells me that the new tennis club is a place of much social activity—and who knows, you might even find someone you might like there."

"No," he said, shaking his head. "I'd never find anyone like Barley again. You loved her, didn't you?"

"We all did, Phillip."

He hid his face with a hand. She wanted to comfort him, to put her arms round him; but knowing his reserve, forebore. To ease her pain she moved to the garden steps, pretending to be looking at her wallflowers.

"Mother, sometimes I feel she is with me, helping me!"

At those words she dared to open her heart. "If it would be

any help dear, I think Father would not object if you left the baby with us for a time."

He knew her intentions when she went on to speak of his sister. "I am afraid she is not very happy, Phillip. I did hope that the coming of her baby would help matters, too."

"Mother, sentiment seems to rule us both. But what mind I have tells me that Doris will never be happy with any man. She is too adamant. I could never have stuck what Bob has had to put up with from her. I know you see it only from Doris's side, you see the effects, not the causes."

"I am only trying to make things better, Phillip."

"I understand you, Mother. I have the same weakness."

"I am thinking of Doris's little one, when it comes, Phillip."

"I know, I know! History must not repeat itself! But who am I to judge Father, or anyone else? I have the same faults, I know. Circumstances bring them out. We are both rather weak sorts, you know. Well, I must be going back to Cross Aulton now." He kissed his mother. "Don't worry, old dear. Try to keep an equal mind in all things."

The sun was over the south-western slope of the Hill, reflecting its rays from the glass turrets of the Crystal Palace when he got astride the Norton.

"Father will be sorry to have missed you. You'll be over again before you go back to Devon, won't you?"

"Yes, Mother, of course I will."

He realised how dear to him his old home was now.

It was good to see the Downs again. They passed an area where hundreds of new houses were being built on what used to be farm and park lands. At first Phillip reacted away from this spreading suburbanisation; but seeing that many an oak and ash and beech—the hedgerow timber of former farms—had been left by the builders of the new Housing Estates, as they were called, he changed his mind about it.

Arthur said, "We're going to make things better than they were in Grandfather's time. Of course Father doesn't like to see things changing, but then I tell him he's old fashioned. I've tried to get him to see that it's a good thing, since it will mean less human unhappiness."

"I expect he, like my mother, remembers the herb fields.

Where are they now? Living in the memories of old people!"

"I don't think people should live in the past, Phillip."

"It's not what men *should* be, Arthur, but what they *are*."

"I don't agree. However, we'll agree to differ, shall we? By the way, I want to see a man at the tennis club, we can get there this way."

They came to an older road of detached Victorian houses, each standing in about an acre of ground. In some a coach-house had been converted to take a motor car.

The new tennis club, presided over by Sir Benjamin Sword, Bart., was the centre of the new social life. They had several distinguished members, declared Arthur, among them the Conservative member of Parliament and his wife and daughters.

There were a score of *en-tout-cas* courts of fine red rubble which made the balls faster than on a lawn, Arthur said, and also play was possible immediately after a shower. There were over a thousand members, and a long waiting list. Phillip thought it was a splendid place, so different from the small one-court club where he had played during half of one season in South Devon. Indeed, as he tried to think of his circumstances now, the old life in Malandine village seemed purposeless; perhaps he should 'learn to submit', in Joseph Conrad's phrase, and return to suburban life. Mother had said that Uncle Joe was quite willing that he should stay with them for as long as he liked.

"We have dancing, or amateur theatricals, or both, every Saturday night, Phillip. By the way, we're having a little dance tonight at home, to celebrate May's engagement to Herbert. Only a gramophone, and ourselves, it will be very quiet."

While he was wiping his boots on the mat Phillip heard his cousin May say to Arthur, "Herbert says he won't be coming tonight."

May was eighteen years of age. Recently she had announced that her name in future would be spelt Mae, after her adored heroine of the silver screen, another *petite brunette* like herself, Mae Murray, who had started her career as that glamour object, a Ziegfeld Folly girl on Broadway.

May, or Mae, her face slightly rouged and a dark whisker-curl pressed on the upper part of each cheek by the discreet application of some of Arthur's Shynecreem, held out a languid hand to her cousin.

To Phillip she was almost a stranger; he had not paid more than half a dozen visits to Uncle Joe Turney's house in his life, and until recently Mae had been at boarding school.

"Hullo, Ma-ee. Is that how you pronounce it?"

"Hullo, Phil-lip. No, it's the same pronunciation."

"I was looking forward to meeting your *fiancé* again."

She gave him a glance; she was not sure that he was not being sarcastic; hitherto he had been reserved towards her.

"So you may be coming to live with us? Aunt Hetty said you might."

"Doesn't Herbert approve of dancing?" asked Arthur.

Mae gave her brother an aloof smile. Turning to Phillip she said, "Jonesy is out tonight, so we're having supper in the kitchen, if you don't mind."

"I like kitchens." Then seeing a motion-picture paper beside her, he said, "Still keen to go on the films? You've done some amateur acting, haven't you?"

She looked at him half defensively, before saying quietly, "Herbert says he won't let me."

"Herbert thinks that all actresses and actors are immoral," explained Arthur. "Excuse me, I'll be back in a jiffy."

He returned with a bottle of sherry and glasses. They drank. Arthur refilled Phillip's glass before hiding the bottle behind the coal-scuttle.

Left alone with Mae, Phillip said, "Will you mind if I ask a rather personal question?" as he drained his glass.

"That was quick!" said Mae.

"Do you really love this chap Herbert?"

She had beautiful grey eyes and long lashes. He felt warm towards her, and saw that she had warmed to him.

"Well, Phillip, I'll try and answer your question. Here is an example. Herbert thinks that a sunset is just ordinary, and tells me that I'm morbid for wanting to look at one and remain quiet, when I am with him. Do you think I am morbid, Phillip?" Her face was a little sad as she smiled.

"Of course you're not morbid! A sunset *is* beautiful. The purpose of life is to create beauty. A sunset can be a glory when one sees it with a kindred spirit, but sad when one sees it alone. One can be alone with another, unless he or she thinks the same as one does."

Mae was looking at him with a kind and gentle gaze. He saw a tear rolling down her cheek, and dabbed it with his handkerchief.

"Cousin dear! First love is nearly always experimental! And when there is doubt——No! There is no doubt in Nature. A wren with a wren, an owl with an owl, a hawk with a hawk, a nightingale with——"

She looked pensive.

"Your intuition is the truth, Mae. Never smother it, as I have done, again and again! Trust it! Don't stifle it, out of loyalty to an idea."

She sighed. "Herbert needs me. Also, he's fearfully jealous. I'll tell you why he isn't coming tonight. It's because you're here."

"Then I'd better go. Is he on the telephone?"

It was her turn to be embarrassed. "I must look at the joint in the oven," she said, leaving the room.

"No need to go," said Arthur. "I don't think Herbert's a genuine religious man. He sneers at poetry, asking what use it is to anyone."

"Poor Mae. She's the steadfast type, like your father and my mother. Life can be pretty awful for such people when they haven't much brain to give their feelings balance."

Arthur felt put off by this remark. "I—I don't think you ought to say such things, Phillip."

"But it's true. They were born like that."

"It's not a very nice thing to say."

"Can't you think with your head?"

Arthur considered this. "Yes, I know what you mean. But I don't like cynicism. Not that you"—he hastened to explain—"are exactly cynical. Anyway, I haven't lost my ideals yet." He looked reflective. "I've got a girl, you know; in fact I'm very nearly engaged to her. There's one thing about her that worries me, to tell the truth. Like some more sherry? I have to hide it, because Herbert doesn't like to see any kind of intoxicant."

"So the man who pinched whisky from the back of the officers' mess cart doesn't approve of others drinking!"

"That was in the war, he's a different man now. Anyway, don't let's talk about Herbert."

Phillip drank his third glass of sherry.

"Men don't change their natures, Arthur. Their habits yes,

but not their natures. May I have another glass? I'll buy you another bottle tomorrow."

Someone was walking up the garden path to the front door. "Here's Father," said Arthur. "He's been down your way this week." Back went the bottle behind the coal-scuttle.

Joseph Turney came into the room, wearing his black hat and dark overcoat. Holding out a hand he said, "Welcome back to Maybury Lodge, Phillip!"

"Thank you, Uncle Joe. Have you had a good week?"

"Oh, not so bad, my boy. Queensbridge is looking its best now. I suppose you'll be thinking of going back soon?"

Joseph Turney, with his large, drooping grey moustaches, grey eyes and mild expression of general kindness, looked smaller than ever to his nephew. His eyes twinkled, and Phillip knew that one of his little-boy jokes was coming.

"You're welcome to stay with us as long as you like, you know, as I told your dear mother. The only condition is that you wash your feet once a month, and change your shirt every six months, ha ha!"

"Ha ha. I would like to stay very much, Uncle, thank you. Of course I'll pay my whack."

"Just as you please, my boy. Make yourself at home."

As soon as he had left the room Arthur said, "I'd like to ask your advice about Gladys, Phillip."

"I'll respect your confidence. What's worrying you?"

"She says when we marry she doesn't want any children."

"Why doesn't she want any?"

"I don't know really."

"Then why not ask her?"

"I have, but she won't give any reason."

"Is she a frigid woman, like Doris?"

"I don't know really," replied Arthur, not liking the question.

"Then why not try her? Doesn't she want to sleep with you?"

Arthur said hurriedly, "She's not that sort of girl, you see. Gladys doesn't care for kissing—she's a serious girl, nothing frivolous about her."

"Then what is your liking for her based upon?"

"As you know, I run the local branch of the Poetry Association. I met her there, as a matter of fact. She was sitting by herself, and looked rather lonely. I spoke to her afterwards, and found that she liked Rupert Brooke. So do I, so we made friends. Then one day I gave her Wilfred Owen's poems."

"What did she think of them?"

"She said they were morbid."

"Which inferred that you were a bit morbid for liking them?"

"Yes, as a matter of fact, I rather fancy she did."

"I've heard that word morbid all my life, Arthur! Nowadays I *run* from people who use that word! Morbid be damned! Are you morbid for seeing the truth, which is compassion, of Owen's verse? Is Mae also morbid, for wanting to be at peace with herself, watching a sunset? You can see the mix-up with Herbert, but are you sure you're not in the same boat yourself? Bob Willoughby and Doris haven't anything in common, so their marriage is a mutual dull ache. To hell with being morbid! It's a word used by fools to maintain their own stupidity. You want to look at causes in human behaviour, not effects only. It's morbid if you like not to want to have a child; but what is the source of that morbidity? Perhaps she heard a woman screaming in childbirth!"

"I—I must ask her——"

"In your case, it's morbid for a man not to want to put the girl he loves, whom he wants to share his life, in the family way. Perhaps she requires an operation?"

Arthur didn't like this turn of the talk. "By the way, Phillip, Aunt Hetty said that Doris had offered to adopt your son."

"Oh, I can't think about it! My brain is a pulp."

"Before we leave the subject, I think I ought to tell you that I have asked Gladys if she would agree to adopt a child."

So that was it! Nobody was going to adopt Billy while he was alive!

"What did she reply?"

"She was against it, I fear. She said that the baby might come of bad stock and turn out to be a criminal, so she couldn't risk it. So I thought of asking her, if it is all the same to you, and Doris doesn't want to adopt your son, if she would consider Billy. After all, your son is my cousin, I suppose."

After a good dinner of roast mutton, with baked potatoes and braised onions, Phillip felt glad to be with his cousins in the sitting-room, the gramophone going and Arthur looking over records. Topsy and Mae wore their glad rags, as the term still prevailed in the suburbs, having arrived there some years after the boy-and-girl dances in Mayfair during the war.

Topsy, Arthur's younger sister, was sixteen years of age and still at school. She was tall and graceful, taking after her mother, and wanted to be a dress designer. She wore clothes, when not at school, which she made for herself with the help of Miss Jones the housekeeper.

During the dancing the front door bell rang. Topsy peeped round the door when Mae went to open it. She looked back and said while screwing up her nose, "It's Herbert! I bet he said he wasn't coming, just to be different!"

Herbert Hukin, dressed in his Sunday best, with tall linen collar in place of his usual (economy) washable celluloid affair, came into the room. After shaking hands all round he turned to Phillip and said, "So you've returned from France. What was it like?"

"Warm in places, with a little rain."

Herbert stared critically at Topsy's dress. It fitted close to her figure, and she wore it with a languid manner, in imitation of an imagined mannequin. Phillip liked Topsy; she had fine even white teeth, like her mother's. At the age of twelve Topsy had asked the dentist to take out her bicuspid teeth, saying she wanted her mouth to look decent when she smiled. Now at sixteen they did look decent; and she often smiled. When Arthur smiled it looked like a grin, for his mouth had retained the crowded front teeth nature had given him to replace those whose roots had dissolved with childhood.

"Rather near the bone, isn't it, that dress?" said Herbert, looking Topsy over.

"What bone?" enquired Topsy, with a smile.

"You know very well what I mean."

"Herbert's private bone, perhaps?" suggested Phillip.

"What d'you mean?" demanded Herbert.

"Well, people talk about having a bone of contention, don't they?"

Phillip wondered how he could make a character like Herbert, in a book, sympathetic. He must have a good side: where or what was it? Was it in admiration of his father that he wore that tallish stiff starched collar and trousers baggy at the knees? How far could unawareness of the feelings of others be related to a strict chapel upbringing? How far was stupidity lack of experience?

Herbert, according to Arthur, had, out of curiosity, bought a copy of his 'Pauline' novel the year before. Herbert had paid five shillings for it, having got 33⅓ per cent off retail price by buying it through the trade, being in his father's printing business. Herbert, having looked through it for what he called 'hot' scenes, had pronounced the book to be decidedly immoral.

Herbert's face was large and square, and his body, as Phillip had observed when the three of them had gone swimming together at the public baths, was entirely white, with flabby muscles; a body altogether too fleshy for a man of thirty. Phillip had not actually disliked Herbert until Herbert had told a story about his cleverness in removing several bottles of whisky from the officers' mess-cart when he had been marching directly behind it in column of route somewhere in Salonica during the war. Herbert had stayed in the ranks, he explained, because he 'had refused a commission'; who had offered Herbert one he had not said. And in telling his story of appropriating the property of those who had been commissioned, Herbert had expected his listeners to share in the self-approval of his cunning. Poor Mae, thought Phillip: no wonder the young girl was already hiding her real self under camouflage as Mae.

"Come on, let's have a fox-trot," said Herbert, trying to pull his *fiancée* off the sofa by one arm. "Put on *Yes, We Have No Bananas*. I like that song."

"Don't pull, you're hurting my arm!" cried Mae.

"Well, come on when you're asked!"

A slow dance of sorts then proceeded round the mahogany table, Herbert pushing Mae before him.

"Aren't you dancing?" he asked Phillip, who was lounging on the sofa.

"Are you?"

The record of *Yes, We Have No Bananas* ran down with a groan.

"Wind it up, Topsy, let's have it again," said Herbert.

"Wind it up yourself," replied Topsy. She gave Phillip a wide smile of white and splendid teeth and threw herself on the sofa beside him and wound her arms round his neck. He kissed her soft lips; Topsy was a darling.

May looked at him with Mae's sorrowful grey eyes. Phillip wondered how Herbert kissed her: probably he gave her an in-sensitive he-man kiss, intense and false as in the films, bending her head back until her neck hurt, while telling himself it was the stuff to give them.

"What's Paris like?" asked Mae, leaning against the edge of the table. "I want to go to Paris," she sighed.

"What for?" asked Herbert.

"Oh, I just do, that's all!"

"What's wrong with London?"

"Oh—London!" exclaimed Mae, as though rehearsing on a stage. "It's a place devoted to Business—and inhabited by people with cramped souls—all hurrying to get more business, and then hurrying to get away from business—with no thoughts of poetry, or beauty, or anything but—money."

"Ever thought where you'd be if it wasn't for Business?" demanded Herbert. "Ever thought of that?" He looked at Phillip and repeated, "What's wrong with London?"

"There are dirty, dreary bits of paper everywhere," said Phillip, imitating Mae's dreamy tone. "There are hard pavements. Orange and banana skins lie all over the place. Whereas Paris is a place of light and gaiety—art and beauty flourish there——"

"I expect it's no better than London, as regards the streets, if the truth be known!"

"Except that there are naked women on the stage," said Phillip.

"Oo, I'd like to be one!" cried Topsy.

Arthur grinned with full display of canines.

"You think you're funny, don't you?" Herbert asked Phillip.

"Oh no, I haven't a sense of humour."

"I can well believe that!"

"Darling cousin of mine," said Topsy. "Can you drink cocoa, or would you prefer tea? Or both? Just say the word, it's Liberty Hall. Come closer, darling cousin Phil, and tell me about Paris. Did you see any lovely clothes?"

Herbert led Mae out of the room.

"I say, I hope I haven't driven him away!" said Phillip, with mock concern.

"Not more than usual," grinned Arthur.

"They've gone down to the summerhouse in the garden," said Topsy.

"That must be where my father used to visit my mother secretly, over thirty years ago! Topsy, don't you ever marry until you find a young man who is *fun* to be with, in ordinary circumstances!"

He held her in his arms, imagining that she was Barley: and then thinking that she had her own sweetness and warmth and gentleness. She was Topsy, she had replaced for the moment the image of Barley. He felt that he loved Topsy, without desire, without longing; content to be with her, to share the moment with her, without demands, but to *be* with her.

"I wonder what Herbert would think if he saw you two now," said Arthur.

"Anything but the truth."

"They're going to be married next year, he's just insured his life for a thousand pounds. His father has promised him a director-ship after two years. I've just given him an intro to the Cremation Society——"

Phillip laughed so much that Topsy said he was shaking her to a jelly.

"Seriously, Phillip, it's the thing of the future. You become a shareholder as well as a beneficiary by paying an annual sub-scription. I am an agent for the Society, which is a non-profit-making concern. It's only a guinea a year. What's the joke?"

"Arthur, you *awful* thing!" cried Topsy. "Fancy talking like that to Phil, at this time!"

"Oh, don't worry about me, darling," said Phillip, stroking her hair. "It's Business. Everything is Business. I met Ronald Harsnop at the Parnassus Club; he dresses his heroes in Thatch's hats, Bonedry's raincoats, and Bashem's boots, in exchange for those goods in real life. Perhaps he'll get on the free list if he mentions Arthur's Crematorium in his next book."

Arthur thought this funny, and laughed loudly. "Seriously, Phillip, I can get you anything you want at a discount of five, ten, or even twelve-and-a-half per cent, through a customer of the firm who is a commission agent. If ever you want a new motor-bike, let me know. You don't want to sell your Norton, I suppose? I wouldn't mind making you an offer, if you did."

"Oh, I couldn't sell my beautiful 'bus, Arthur!"

"You have such soft lips, darling," whispered Topsy, just before her mother came into the room.

Mrs. Joseph Turney was a homoeopathic invalid. She lived out of jars and packets, the contents of which were eaten with vege-tables. She was a beautiful woman with a serene face, who sat

in her own room most of the day and seldom came out for meals.
Miss Jones, an elderly lady housekeeper-cook looked after the
needs of the household, and since both Mae and Topsy helped
her, because they liked her, it was altogether a happy home to be
in. Before living there Phillip had thought of his Uncle Joe as a bit
of a nitwit; now he realised that there was more to a man than
brains. Uncle Joe was kind. He was narrow, but not intolerant.

"I saw your mother today," he said. "She hopes you will go
and see her soon, and wants you to stay there."

During the day, when he was alone with his mother, Phillip
felt a light-hearted freedom about the house; they had the place
to themselves. Doris still lived on the outskirts of London in what
was once an Essex market town, but now rapidly becoming a
London suburb; Elizabeth shared a flat with her friend Nina at
Sydenham. Doris was still forbidden the house by Richard, for
eloping with 'Mr. Willoughby'; so was Elizabeth, for what he considered to be her ill manners toward himself as head of the family.

Both girls were Hetty's constant concern. Doris was not happy
with her husband, although she had at last yielded to the marriage
consummation, with the result that a baby was expected in August.
Hetty had hoped its coming would draw Doris and Bob closer;
she still hoped for such a state, despite her experience; her dream
was of Billy and the new little one growing up together, and
Phillip somehow content in the background with his writing.

In addition to the actual worries about her children and grand-
child, Hetty suffered anxiety on account of Elizabeth's health.
The doctor had, more than once, stressed the point that her only
chance of growing out of her liability to fits was to start her own
life away from home, and—this was most important, he said—
never seeing her father.

But how would Elizabeth be able to manage without her
mother? There were Elizabeth's chronic demands for money to
pay her dress bills. The girl lived to be prettily dressed, and in the
latest styles as they came into suburban shops a year or so after
they had ceased to be fashionable in the best shops of the West
End. When, in the course of time, a fashion got to the factory
girls, Elizabeth became obsessed with the desire for an entirely
new rig-out. At the moment it was Russian boots. Only that
evening there had been a crisis.

"Mother, I *must* have a pair! You must lend me the money! All the other girls at the office are wearing them! Oh you *are* unkind! You are *horrible* sometimes! You know very well that my salary isn't enough to keep me properly!"

"Very well, dear, but this is the *very* last time!"

It was always the *very* last time: but it was better than an 'attack'. Having got the money, Elizabeth hurried away before her awful Father returned. She was down in the High Street before the shops shut, to buy the kind of boots Margot Asquith, whose photographs were constantly in the papers, had been the first to wear, eighteen months before.

Hetty was happy with Phillip. Sometimes they took the morning train to Reynard's Common, and walked over the heath where, in Edwardian days, Hetty had taken the girls, to be joined by Richard and Phillip who had bicycled there. Phillip did not care to go by 'bus, for all around Cutler's Pond was becoming a vast new suburb, pressing upon his spirit as streets and houses pressed upon once-green fields and little cattle-drinking ponds, each with its pair of moorhens and small roach which, in early boyhood, had made part of his life. Devon scenes had superseded those of north-west Kent, now a dark patch on the map; but places, once loved, that have disappeared are as friends who have died, he said, quoting a phrase out of cousin Willie's books by Richard Jefferies.

"'Faces fade as flowers, and there is no consolation'. Honestly, all religion apart, is there any consolation? Beyond feeling that the dead are steadfast?"

"We must live for others, dear. For our children, especially." Phillip and his 'little son' were seldom out of her thoughts.

"I do try to, Mother, only——"

"I know you do, dear. You are a good boy, you always were, really——"

They stopped by a dell in which grew silver birches.

"We had a picnic here once, Mum, I remember. I put a piece of orange peel near a chiffchaff's nest which Father discovered. We had lovely egg-sandwiches and mince pies, and ginger beer. The girls wore floppy hats with ribands round them, and I wore my white cricketing hat, because I'd had sun-stroke at Hayling Island the year before. D'you remember?"

"Oh yes, Phillip! We all had many happy times together, with Father, didn't we? If only they could come again!"

"You know, Mum, I tend to think of those days as always edged by darkness, or fear, but I often wonder if I exaggerate them."

A nightingale began to sing among the green undergrowth. He stopped as though stricken.

"I can't think what to do! I can't see any future, except for my work! I daren't go back to Malandine, and yet—I can never leave it."

"Of course, Phillip, I know exactly how you feel." After walking on together she said, "Has Billy's other grandmother, Mrs. Lushington, any ideas about him, that you know of?"

"Not exactly. I only began to think about it when I was on my way home, one night in the Ancre Valley. When I saw her in the Pyrenees, she did say something about coming to Devon to see Barley's grave. She said she would write and let me know in plenty of time. I haven't heard yet."

"Has she seen the baby, Phillip?"

"No, not yet."

Hetty could not contain her fears. "You won't let Billy go away from you, will you, Phillip? I do think it might be a solution to let Doris take him, for a while, anyway. Looking after two is not much more trouble than looking after one, you know. Why not come over with me to Romford one afternoon, and have a talk with her? Doris is very fond of you, you know!"

He went over with his mother the next day. The Willoughbys' house had an uncared-for look about it. The wallpaper was dark, the paint-work old, both gardens neglected. There was a small glass-house through which one reached the back garden. The shelves of this were empty save for two pots, each containing a plant withered from lack of watering. Patches in the lawn were worn bare.

Doris looked as dingy as the garden. Her hair had lost its lustre, her face was pale, she was getting fat, but that was the baby, he thought. She apologised for the state of the house, saying they hadn't had time to get it in proper order yet. The bathroom had a decayed copper geyser in it, green in places from corrosion by fumes, and under the tap the old enamel paint of the bath was blue where cuprous water had dripped. After Barley's scrupulously neat cottage, it was a horror to Phillip. No, the baby must not be allowed to come to such a place.

He wanted to talk to Bob when he returned from work, so
Hetty went home alone, happy with the thought that her son
might be able to influence Bob away from the man who was, she
thought, leading him astray.

Phillip met this friend with Bob over pints of beer at a pub.
He was the honorary secretary of the local Christian Spiritualist
Church: an earnest, sensitive man. Poor Mother, what prejudices
she had: but of course Uncle Hugh's fate was at the root of her
fears in the direction of 'drink'.

"May I ask a very frank question, Bob?"

"By all means."

"Do you honestly believe that Percy was trying to speak to you,
as a medium, when we had that *séance* in the cottage last August?"

"I am sure of it."

"How did it affect your relationship with Doris?"

"She prayed with our pastor, who told her it was Percy's wish
that she had a child."

"I see."

"B-but," stammered Bob, fingers to mouth. "Afterwards she
told me it was a t-t-trick."

"A conspiracy, in other words?"

"Y-yes."

Bob spoke in a quiet voice with a near-tremulant undertone.
While the three were talking about psychic phenomena, with
references to the books of Conan Doyle and Oliver Lodge, a thin
woman dressed in the uniform of the Salvation Army entered the
bar, carrying copies of *The War Cry*. She spoke to Bob as though
she knew him, and said his father was outside and wanted him to
go to the service.

The public-house stood at a corner of two streets. Phillip heard
cornet music, accompanied by occasional thumps of a big drum.

"I think I'd better go. Would you mind, Phillip, if I leave you
for a bit?"

"No, of course not."

"You see, my father runs the S-Salvation Army b-b-branch
h-here." Again the wry mouth covered by fin-like hand.

"May I come, too? The Salvation Army does splendid work."

There was the usual shrill singing of women, the confident bass
of men's voices, rattle of tambourines, near-strident brass music,
prayers sent up under arc-lights. A convert looking like an old

prize-fighter spoke of how he had found salvation. Phillip thought of Masefield's *Everlasting Mercy*. Another hymn, with the familiar words, *Throw the life-line, there's one more sinner to be saved,* and then he was confronted by a short, stout man who said he was pleased to meet him, adding that he had read his book about Donkin.

"I hope it wasn't a waste of time, sir."

"Not altogether. But what the lad lacked is a positive attitude to life, lack of guts in other words. Write a better one next time!"

"Well, Donkin had a rather bad time as a child, didn't he, Mr. Willoughby? He was struggling to find himself."

"Yes, but the way was open to him, if only he would take it, my friend!"

"But the whole point of the story is that he *is* struggling to find the way, surely?"

"Revelation of the way to salvation lies ready-made for all man, that's my point!"

"But surely you don't despise those who have not yet had the good fortune, like yourself, to find it ready-made?"

"You're a doubting Thomas, my lad! And life's too short for splitting hairs! The way to salvation lies open! Strike up, boys!"

To the *boom-boom-boom* of the big base drum, brass of trombone, cornet and tuba, the procession marched out of step down the street to the next pitch, while Bob, stuttering more than usual, asked Phillip not to take any notice of what his father had said.

"H-he's a f-f-fun-fun-damentalist, y-y-you s-s-see."

"Goodbye, dear cousins! I have loved my stay here. Goodbye, Mae, I wish I wasn't going!" She held her cheek for a kiss. "Goodbye, Topsy darling!" He hugged her and kissed her neck repeatedly. "You are going to be very, very happy," he whispered. "Don't forget to ask me to your wedding!"

He had already said goodbye to his Uncle and Aunt. "Au revoir, Arthur! I'll look forward to your visit. You will give me a few days' notice when you come, won't you? We'll have wonderful walks, all over the moors. I want to follow the rivers, we might even come across my tame otter! It lost two toes in that gin I told you about, and otters are great wanderers. We'll be able to recognise him by his spoor!"

The idea of finding Lutra grew in his mind as he went along the familiar road to Exeter until he began to feel that if he could find the otter he would be able to start a new life: Lutra must be found, and then, with his son for companion, all would be well.

Chapter 7

WATER WANDERER

White clouds were massing in a long and narrow column in the cold high air between warmer hills when he saw the spired church on the high ground above the Channel. Leaving Wakenham at dawn, he had stopped only twice on the way, once for a hurried meal and again for a gallon of petrol and a quart of oil. To reach Valerian Cottage had been his only aim during the long hours on the road, pushing the engine as fast as he dared over bumpy surfaces and around narrow corners of the London–Exeter road. Now, turning off before Claybrough, he descended to the valley of Malandine.

He unlocked the door of his cottage and stood on the lime-ash floor, unwashed and unbrushed as he had left it. An old newspaper lay on the table with an empty cup. His nailed brogues lay uncleaned by the hearth where he had left them. Why had he come?

He took three steps towards the table and sat down, unable to move further. The snowdrops Barley had put in a jar on the shelf were withered and colourless. Dust lay on the table, on the new bee-hive which had stood in the corner for three years, the saddle covering it; dust on the book-shelf, on the arm-chair. The small, closed window let in light grudgingly, revealing a tortoise-shell butterfly lying brittle in death on the wooden ledge.

After a while he got up and moved about the room. The larder door stood open. He remembered his haste in packing his bag, the desperate need to be in London before lighting-up time with no lamp. It hadn't occurred to him, then, to buy a lamp. He must pull himself together: let air into the place. He went into the small larder to open the window. The two shelves within were bare, except for a jam-jar in which a few grains of rice had lain. His eye perceived something on the bottom of the jar.

Looking closer, he saw the corpse of a mouse, flat and light as an old leaf. The mouse had apparently jumped into the jar, nibbled a few grains, and, after seeking a way out of a waterless prison in vain, had died there.

He sat in his chair, eyes closed, with the knowledge that if he sat there all night, and all the next day, and for the rest of his life, it would make no difference to any living person. And then he remembered: he should have called at the Cottage Hospital in Queensbridge.

He went upstairs, to see where a cot could be put in the main bedroom. While he sat in shadow, on the familiar blankets of his bed, he heard a whine below. It was Rusty. After an interval he heard a mournful howl.

"Rusty! Come on up, Rusty!"

There was the noise of prolonged squeezing through the cat-hole, followed by the *tippity-tap* of clawed paws on the bare wooden stairs. At the top, silence.

"Rusty," he said softly, and another wavering hollow cry answered.

"Come on, Rusty!" and with a bubbling sound the dog came sideways into the room, flacking his tongue, his eyes shining. He raised himself laboriously, first on one foot then on another, a third and then a fourth, on the bed beside Phillip. There he filled his lungs with air, breathed out happily, and sat up, looking at his master, the tail-stump knocking Phillip's knee. A voice below.

"Beg pardon, zur, but mis'es zays would 'ee care vor a cup of tay?"

"Dear Walter Crang!"

After tea of toast and eggs in the kitchen with familiar and friendly faces, he felt new life and hope coming upon him. He would clean the cottage on the morrow, and then go to see the baby. Now he must go down to the sands and dedicate himself anew to the elements he had nearly forgotten. So with spaniel straddling the cross-bar above the petrol tank he pushed off for the sea.

The sands were empty. A pair of kestrels called wistfully in the thorn-brake growing down the Valkyrie Rock. After a bathe he stayed there while the tide came in and the flung spray was lilac-coloured in the rays of the sinking sun; he stayed too long, for as the sea darkened a feeling of his own helplessness before Nature, to which he had once trusted, overcame him. What was the life or hope of a man, lacking that human warmth called love, set against the eternity of sea and sky—the cold mindless power of the sea always in motion—surge upon surge of grey rollers breaking and pounding, swirling and receding for ever and for ever? Was any personal life, hope, or memory of more account than the crystal-life within one swirled grain of the immeasurable sands?

"Yes!" he said, loudly. Why had he said that? Or had something said it for him?

For the moment he believed that it was an answer; from his subconscious mind, perhaps, or from some spiritual force, perhaps Willie's.

He thought he would test himself by climbing up the Valkyrie Rock. It was not exactly dangerous, but there was one place by an outcrop of hard quartz where a slip would mean a crash to the rocks below. It was not difficult, if climbed straightly, but if he hesitated at the dangerous turn and looked down in fear, strength would ooze out and enfeeble him. Very well, he would test the *Yes* part of himself. He told himself as he went up that he must not pause to look down at the critical point but go straight on up.

The spaniel behind him whined, he was afraid; but Phillip kept to his determination, refusing the hot thoughts of fear that one part of him wanted to yield to; and in a short time was pulling himself by tufts of grasses over the edge of the cliff. He went on with an almost gay feeling to the lane where, among umbelliferous plants, the Norton was almost entirely hidden. Dog between knees and elbows, he sped up the lane, dust rising behind the open nickel exhaust pipe.

By candlelight he swept out the bedroom, and under the rising moon took out the blankets and shook them, turned the mattress, and worked until midnight, while dog and cat accompanied him up and down stairs and from one room to another. Then, all set to rights, he washed in a pail of cold water and went upstairs, followed by the animals, who settled themselves at the foot of the bed.

Continuing his resolution, or that which had decided for him, he prayed to retain an equal mind, to be calm; and knew that he must live a life of regular habit.

In the morning he went to see the baby. It was lying in a cot under a verandah, kicking both legs together, and when he looked down at it the gentle cooing noises ceased and the small face became as though serious, looking up at him without recognition until the mouth loosened and the head waggled slightly. Was that a smile? A feeling between helplessness and tenderness overcame him; he was afraid when the nurse said he might pick up baby if he were very careful. She showed him how to support its head along his arm.

"Take him, Mr. Maddison," she said, putting the baby in his arms. "I'll leave you for a while. Look, he is smiling at you!"

He held it with great care, and felt the warmth of the fair hair against his cheek; and without knowing what he did put his lips to the skull and not so much kissed it as sent his tender feelings to the innocent head through the touch of his mouth.

After that recognition, through the warmth of a fragile skull, he visited the baby several times a week. From the nurses he received more than one tender glance; but there could never be anyone to take the place of Barley. He wondered if he could ask the Pole-Cripps' to have him, as a sort of paying guest; and thought to ask them later. But somehow he could not bring himself to ask Boo.

His cousin Arthur wrote to say that he had joined the Artists' Rifles and was very keen on physical fitness, and much looking forward to long walks during his holiday the following week.

So began what Phillip later on called the otter's odyssey. They started at the source of the River Exe, Arthur wearing the pack, Rusty sitting astride the tank. Their intention was to follow it down to the sea. Leaving the bike under a beechen hedge behind a gate at evening, they prepared to spend the first night on the moor. There was plenty of shreddings from a recent cutting of beech hedge; they built a fire to grill sausages on forks made of twigs, and boiled stream-water for tea. Then to sleep under the stars. They awoke at dawn, a little chilled, and bathed in a pool, running afterwards to get warm.

That day they tramped for miles over heather, whortleberry,

ling, and cotton-grass upon the high slopes of the moor. In the heat of the sun they threw off their clothes and lay in clear water. To avoid both going back on their tracks Phillip sent Arthur to fetch the motor-bicycle, after planning the rendezvous by a bridge marked on the map.

Thus the days. Their feet were never dry except at night by the fire. They walked across shallows to examine scours, or tongues of sand, looking for the paw-prints of otters.

"There's one-in-a-million chance of finding a seal of three toes instead of five, but you never know your luck. Otters wander a great distance, and there's a sporting chance of finding Lutra. Are you game to go on?"

"Rather! I love this kind of life!"

At Exford they saw otterhounds, and followed them as they went fast down the river. The otter took to land and ran across a meadow. Phillip kept just behind the huntsman, in two minds whether or not to tell him about Lutra. In any case it was too late. After the worry the front paws were cut off and the huntsman showed five toes to each paw.

By the end of eleven days they had walked about two hundred miles, yet had covered only a small portion of the combined length of those streams which drained Exmoor from both sides of the watershed. The walk had been planned to end at Lynmouth, with tea in Aunt Dora's cottage. While they sat down, the faces of two old women, both diminutive, peered round the door of the sitting-room.

"You remember my 'Babies', Phillip? They are still a little shy, but will come to recognise you soon."

When the two men had said goodbye to Aunt Dora, Arthur asked who they were.

"She promised a relation of theirs to look after them for a week-end five years ago."

"You mean the relation didn't come back, but left them on your aunt's hands?"

"Yes."

"Then why didn't she turn them over to the Infirmary or something? One blind and the other obviously dotty! Who pays for their keep?"

"She does."

"I think she should do something about it, Phillip."

"She is doing something about it."

From the high ground of Exmoor the distant tors of Dartmoor lay slate-dim under the sky. They lingered until the sun was going down. Phillip had had a lamp fitted to the Norton, but the carbide in the container was exhausted. Who cared? Arthur, who could run with speed and tenseness, easily outpacing Phillip, was delighted with the difficulties before them: no light, the way uncertain, the only guide for direction being the evening star, a sulphur-yellow globe above the mists. Once, missing direction— the planet Venus lost behind a tall beech hedge—they descended a sled-track over bare rock rapidly, bumpily, ending blindly in a farm-yard. About turn! The problem was to start the engine by pushing up the steep, wet, shaley surface. The engine fired: Phillip vaulted on: Arthur shoved behind while the rider's left foot pressing on the automatic expanding pulley acted as clutch and low gear simultaneously. The engine was revved up, the bike shot forward, and with a laugh Arthur leapt upon the bare steel frame of the carrier. They slid and skidded and plunged sideways, but got to the top somehow to wait for Rusty as the last carrion crow slunk by silently to its roost.

Where were they? Miles out of their way, it seemed, after going up and down lanes with faded sign-posts, or none at all. At long last they climbed to a crest whence a view lay away and below them for many miles, coombes and valleys purple below, woods and fields in darkening light to the glimmering immensity of the sea and lighthouses winking very far away.

"Lundy lights!"

They stood on a bank against which cut ashpoles had been stacked, and gazed in silence. "We've come a dozen miles off course, Arthur."

They stared at the darkening scene below them. At length Arthur spoke. "It's so beautiful, it's almost sad."

"I was just thinking the same thing. I'm awfully glad you came down."

"So am I, Phillip."

They jumped from the bank, and were off again. Phillip opened the throttle. "Tell me if I'm going too fast."

"Go as fast as you like!"

Phillip held the spaniel within his elbows, while the passenger gripped the thin tubular frame as though preparing a hand-

spring, holding himself clear of shocks on the base of the spine
while also balancing with legs hanging loosely on either side of
the rear wheel. It must be painful there, thought Phillip, as he
kept to a speed of about twenty-five m.p.h. over the rock. As they
descended, an unseen cow grazing on the bank above the lane
gave a startled leap and slithered down before them. The back
wheel locked; they swerved and slewed past the cow; wobbled,
rocked, and recovered. Ferns were torn by the brake lever. Great
fun!

They went on, peering into the dimming light, just avoiding a
hedgehog which continued its leisurely crossing of the lane.

It was dark when they descended a smaller moor with its many
narrow forkways and cross-lanes, going down steep hills and
coming unexpectedly to a village with an old pollard elm at its
cross ways. Phillip opened up past the police constable—and
turning sharply left went up and past many thatched cottages—
to find himself at last beside the estuary, throttle opened full-out
along the straight road with blue flames stabbing from the exhaust.
Then on through the old town port, the engine beating like a calm
heart, and the narrow afterglow of sunset upon the high tide under
the bridge.

They bought a tin of carbide, and with a wan light waving in
front set out for the long trek to Okehampton, and a camp near
the head of the Teign before Chagford.

There, shortly after midnight, they made a fire and brewed
cocoa, and munched thick slices of brown bread and cold pats of
butter, and then dossed down beside the embers. And in the
morning they arose in a cold mist and went on to Moreton Hamp-
stead, where they breakfasted on a gammon of bacon each, with
two eggs, sausages, kidneys, and tomatoes. Then it seemed like
the end of the adventure, the world all dull and sleepy.

But later on, at Ashburton, it being market day and the pubs
open from early to late, beer made the world begin again in
interest and delight. And so to the village, and vertical-tail
welcome from Moggy holding the fort—Moggy with five kittens
in Rusty's basket, the second safest place in the cottage, since the
flimsy door leading aloft to the bedrooms had been shut.

That night they lay in bed talking, each in his own room; but
it was a separation; and Phillip helped Arthur to carry the camp-
bed beside his own. They were weary from the cold night on the

moor, and talked drowsily, contentedly, while tawny owls on the church tower hooted with mellow cries one to another under the wreck of the moon declining to far ocean. In the morning, after dreamless sleep, Phillip saw that Arthur's right heel was rubbed raw, for he had been wearing new shoes; he had said nothing about it, for his was the Spartan ideal.

When they had read their letters, Arthur said, "Father was in Exeter, last night. He'll be in Queensbridge today, and wonders if we'll have time to see him."

"Well, I must do an article today, Arthur. Also I must look through Massingham's book sent to me by the *Outlook,* and post off a review. But why don't you go on the Norton? You'll make my apologies, won't you?"

Phillip sent off his work by the midday post, and replied to his letters. His cousin returned in the afternoon, looking subdued.

"How did you find Uncle?"

"Oh, very well. He sent you his kind regards, by the way. He's gone on to Plymouth."

There was something on Arthur's mind. While they were walking along Malandine sands Phillip asked if he was worried.

"Not particularly."

"Anything I can do to help?"

"Well, I may as well tell you. Father, as you know, is a bit old-fashioned. And many of the firm's customers are solicitors, of course."

"Whatever are you driving at?"

"I hardly like to tell you. It may be nothing, after all." At last he said, "Apparently there's some talk about the nursing home, where your baby was born."

"Well?"

"Father heard something—it's probably only talk—of what you are supposed to have said about the midwife and her mother."

"Both the old girl *and* her daughter went to bed and left Barley to look after the baby, from one-thirty a.m. until I found her sitting up in bed six hours later! In that time she had had the hæmorrhage!"

"I don't doubt it, Phillip. But the point Father made was that, if I am to take over his territory when he retires, I can't be too careful where customers are concerned."

Phillip went straight to Porto Bello.

The midwife's mother stood in the doorway, looking at him accusingly.

"Well, y'ung mahn, what have you to say for yourself?"

"If I did say anything which upset you both, then I am very sorry, but I don't remember saying anything to you on that morning."

"But you told young Mr. Pole-Cripps, the Vicar's son, didn't you, that your poor wife died through neglect while in this house?"

"I'm not responsible for what Mr. Cripps says, surely?"

"But you told y'ung Mr. Pole-Cripps, didn't you?"

"I don't remember, but I may have done."

"My daughter, Ah'll have you know," went on the grim little woman, "is a licensed midwife, and very upset by what people have said! What's more, Ah've taken her to see Mr. Wigfull about it, and he's going to write you a lawyer's letter. Ah'm leavin' it to Mr. Wigfull, so it's no good saying anything 'ere, y'ung mahn!"

He walked down to see Mr. Wigfull, who was out. The clerk asked him if he would like to see Mr. Thistlethwaite.

"Ah, we meet again!" said Mr. Thistlethwaite, shaking hands.

He got up and closed the door.

"Now I know very well how you feel, and it would be unkind of me not to try to help you. If you will consider making an offer to compensate them for what they have suffered in the matter, I will be prepared to pass on that offer to them."

"But I, too, have suffered from their neglect! They both went to bed, leaving my wife sitting up to nurse a crying infant!"

"It would be very hard to prove neglect on their part, you know. Dr. MacNab, I understand, issued a certificate of death due to natural causes. Furthermore, I understand that it was a most unusual type of hæmorrhage, and one that could not be detected, as it was an interior bleeding, showing no outward sign. Also, both the good women are prepared to swear, in court if necessary, that their patient asked to be allowed to nurse the crying infant. In fact, she suggested that the midwife should have a rest, and lie down. So it would not be easy to establish the contrary in court, in view of what mother and daughter say."

Phillip replied bitterly, "Don't worry, Mr. Thistlethwaite, I would never sue anyone for anything!"

"I think that is the proper way to look at it." Mr. Thistlethwaite pushed over an ash-tray. "I well remember your magnanimous attitude, if I am allowed to call in that, in the matter of Mrs. Nunn and that tennis-club affair three years ago. You were misled, if I may say so, by the wrong advice on that occasion. Now strictly between ourselves, I'm not taking up a partnership with Wigfull. In fact I'm leaving here very shortly, and setting up on my own in Dorset. Shakesbury to be exact. But that's between ourselves, of course. Now about this 'Porto Bello' business. I take it that we are both men of the world. My suggestion to you is to give the old girl a tenner, to shut her mouth! Well, what do you think?"

"I think Queensbridge is a dreadful place!"

"So do I, old man, but we don't have to stay here! Now look here, I give you my word that I'm trying to help you. After all, the midwife has lost money on her room, you know."

"Yes, I understand that, Mr. Thistlethwaite."

"Good. Now may I say how very very sorry I was to hear of your recent sad loss. I do assure you that my two old girls, too, were deeply upset. They may be a couple of fuddy-duddies, but they've always done their best according to their lights, and as I said, Dr. MacNab's certificate clears them of any blame They're quite poor people, and can't afford, really, the loss of profits due to the non-use of their only accouchement room, which was, I understand, engaged for ten days. A pound a day is not exorbitant."

"Of course I don't want anyone to be the loser for anything he or she has done for me. So I'll offer seven guineas."

"Spoken like a gentleman!" said Mr. Thistlethwaite, rising to hold out his hand. "You'll send along your cheque, then?"

"I'll write it out now!"

Having done this, Phillip said, "I do realise that my previous hard feelings about 'Porto Bello' were based on ignorance of all the circumstances. I had no idea that—that—their patient had suggested that the nurse should lie down——"

"It's not unusual, you know, for the mother to want to hold her baby in her arms. There was, I understand, a crib beside the bed——"

"Yes, I saw that." He steadied his voice. "I'll go round and thank them for letting me know the truth." He said after a pause, "She was generosity itself. I see it all now."

"I like you," exclaimed Thistlethwaite. "You're North Country

by your name, I fancy. By the way, didn't you once have a tame
otter? I thought so. Someone was saying in the Club here that
it got caught in a rabbit gin, and lost two of the toes on one of its
front feet—pads I think is the correct expression. I ask because
I was out with a pal of mine last week, following the otter hounds
beside the Taw in North Devon, and they spoored one below the
bank with a maimed front pad. It got away, let me add! I told
someone afterwards about your tame beastie, and he said it was
quite possible for it to have got up the Avon here to the moor,
and then gone down the other side of the watershed, otters being
nomads. I thought I'd tell you if I saw you, and now this gives
me my opportunity."

"Mr. Thistlethwaite, I am doubly glad I came to see you!
Good luck to your new practice in Dorset! I'm going to North
Devon to live! I feel I shall be able to write there!"

Cousin Willie's cottage at Speering Folliot had remained empty
after his death; the day was fine, he would collect Arthur and go
across the moor at once.

He returned that evening the new tenant of Scur Cottage.

He made up his mind to burn the furniture, together with
all Barley's things, before he left; but when the time came he
packed everything into his trunk while awaiting the van. Even
the broken lace was taken with the sand-shoes, for she had broken
it.

> Scur Cottage
> Speering Folliot
> N. Devon.
> Date unknown. You never date
> your letters; I think I know why,
> now. Don't worry.

Dear Mother

Please note my new address. This is Willie's old cottage. About
your letter—I am sorry I can't make up my mind about Doris taking
the baby. Nor about anyone coming here for holidays. The baby
is still at the Cottage Hospital. No, he won't be christened until you
come down. I cannot say when that will be. I am sorry about being
inhospitable, but will write later——

He had written variations of this letter during the Sunday and
Monday, each version being scrapped. He had eaten nothing

since his arrival two days before. It was now the late afternoon. Soon the farmer who tilled four of the splatts in the Great Field would be passing down the lane with his horse and butt, after collecting sea-weed from the shores of the Crow shingle tongue.

He heard the clang of the falling bar of the double doors leading to his yard, followed by the rattle of butt wheels on the dry stones within.

Phillip sat in his armchair. He wore his trench coat. The kitchen door was open. He had sat there for two days, while the cries and sounds of the hamlet had floated in. He was filled by a strange comfort, a calm detachment from all life, a sensation of ease beyond the body. He floated in a vacuum, occasionally drinking water; and went to bed while the sun was still in the sky, to lie between army blankets, still with the feeling of Nirvana; to get up when the sun shone in his window and take his rest in the armchair once more, deliciously void of life.

The baker's horse and van was approaching. It stopped. The single loaf, left there on the Saturday, was still on the table. The baker's boy's iron-shod boots struck upon the sett-stoned path.

"Nothing today, thanks."

"Nice day again! Thankin' yew!"

The boy went out again, prepared to close the door behind him. Almost anxiously Phillip cried, "No, leave it open!"

His eyes closed, he drifted, lapped in warmth.

Beyond the edge of consciousness light footfalls, as of small feet on tip-toe, came nearer, slower and slower. With eyes closed, he could sense the boy peering round the door-jamb to see if he were still there. He heard the boy creeping back.

"'A be still sittin' thur, Mum. 'A didden move!"

Then the boy was running past, crying, "Thur be my daddy! My daddy's corned whoam, Mis'r Mass'n!"

"Lucky boy!"

He felt the poignancy of the child's happiness. The labourer clumped past, holding the hand of the child. The two went into their cottage next door. He heard the loving words to small daughter and baby. Then came the noises of sluicing, swish of water thrown over the garden wall, scrape of chairs drawn up on lime-ash floor, talk in low voices. The family was having tea.

He could not remember ever before having remained so still in contentment, floating on a temperature of between 100° and

101° F. Influenza was about; he had felt bad on the first night of his arrival, and gone to bed in his day clothes, to awaken with a strange feeling of comfort, a warmth and sensation of being levitated, floating upon the material illusion of life. Or was it possession by the spirit of Willie? He lay in contentment; then with a start realised that the weight of grief had lifted from him. He felt that Barley was in the room, smiling at him, wanting him to know that all was well; then it seemed that his cousin's spirit had brought her there, to help him. How much was this his own inducement, how much arose from memory, this feeling of the presence of the dead?

He lay in the chair while a parallelogram of westering sun moved across the worn lime-ash floor. A late cuckoo was calling from the elms, a faltering voice beginning to crack.

Hearing footfalls, he pulled himself out of the chair. From the window he saw Mules the postman alighting from his bicycle.

Dear Mules, he had known Willie. He stood in the doorway, watching him wheeling his red machine to the side of the road, placing it carefully against the garden wall before walking forward in his slightly deprecatory manner, not so much a walk as placing one foot before the other, a loose motion which set swinging each arm and leg independently of its fellows. Even his head bobbed, as though in rehearsal of a profoundly courteous but equally shy greeting.

He felt desire to meet gentle motion with gentle motion in the sunshine, and with streaming eyes floated forward to meet Mules through the curiously unreal afternoon.

Mules appeared to be existing in an identical fourth dimension with himself, as with brown canvas post-bag slung on shoulder of blue serge tunic he stood there; and then, enclosed within these startlingly clear colours his form began to bob, to undulate, to move a hesitant hand in rehearsal of touching peak of cap.

Overwhelming gratitude arose at sight of the dear fellow with his shy upward glance and smile; sudden tears enclosed his eyes. Whatever was Mules saying?

"I'm sure I be very plaised to hear the noos. Zillah read it on th' paper, Zillah did, read it like—the noos—on the paper," said the postman softly, almost coyly. "Us wondered if you'd be bringin' of'n yurr now. Zillah and my wife would be very

plaised vor look after th' li'l fellow, very plaised like, Zillah and
my wife would be to look after you and young maister, beggin'
your pardon, zur," while touching Phillip reassuringly with a
forefinger.

"I'm afraid I am very dull, I don't quite understand, Muley
dear."

"'Tes all on th' paper! Di'n 'ee zee th' paper, surenuff? 'Tes
all thur about young maister, the babby, surely you zeed'n?"

"I haven't seen a paper for ages. What is it?"

Mules spoke very gently, "Have 'ee not, surenuff? Yes, 'tes on
the Gaz-at-ee this week, my wife's sister to Queensbridge sent it
to my wife. 'Tes your li'l boy, you know, 'tes young maister, he
won a prize for being the best babby at the Flower Show. 'Tes all
on th' paper! I'll show 'ee if you come along home with me,
zur."

"Won a prize for being the best baby? Are you joking?"

"Oh no, zur, it be true—true like—'tes on th' Gaz-at-ee."

He managed to look Phillip in the face, a quick glance before
looking away again. The gentle look returned, this time without
falter. "You look a proper weary man, proper weary man you
look, midear. But 'tes true what I be tellin' 'ee. My wife saith
her and Zillah would take care of the babby for 'ee, if you'm a
mind to't. Poor little maister, without a mother, poor li'l babby.
That's right."

His mind seemed to dream, then to hover back. "Your li'l cat,
too, I zeed her sittin' on th' wall, homely already her be, homely
like. Your old dog, he followed me home. Just like pore ole Billjohn, Mr. Willie's span'll. 'Tes true. 'A knoweth, I fancy. Your
dog—your span'll—'a did, surenuff, just like ole Billjohn, your
cousin Mr. William's span'll Billjohn, do 'ee mind he? 'A used
to come down to our place, us was very plaized vor see th' poor
old dog, just as us be plaized vor see Rusty."

Mules glanced around, then lowered his voice. "Us would be
very plaized vor you to come too, if you'm a mind to. Only don't
'ee come if you'm not in a mind to come, like. And don't 'ee tell
no-one what I zaid, wull 'ee? There be some what'd take the
bread out of a man's mouth!"

Phillip looked steadily at the slightly foxy face and said softly,
"I used to look after mules in the army, they were lovely animals,
very gentle and hard-working."

"Aw, you'm a funny man, midear, a funny man, zur, beggin' your pardon." A hand came out to touch him, the hand hesitated, then rested on Phillip's arm. "You come to our place," said Mules quietly, without nervousness. "You look a proper tired man, midear. Zillah and my wife won't zee 'ee wrong. Us'd like vor look after the li'l old babby, tew. Us would!"

A hand was put in the bag, a letter taken out. "Oh my, I was very nearly forgettin' this yurr letter comed for 'ee, I hope 'tes good news, I do, surenuff."

Phillip glanced at the unfamiliar writing, and put the envelope in his pocket. The postman said as he turned away, "You'll come vor zee little maister's photograph up on th' Gaz-at-ee, won't 'ee? Zillah and my wife would be disappointed if you don't come vor see it. 'Tes a bootiful boy, smilin' away like anything up on th' paper." He touched Phillip's hand. "My dear zoul, you be hot, your hand be proper hot! Be'ee feelin' a-right, zur? Many people be complainin' of this yurr Roosian 'fluenza what be goin' about. Plaize vor take care of yourself, midear. You'm so thin as a rasher of wind, a proper starved man you look. Us wouldn't like vor zee 'ee go down through not takin' proper care, you know that. Many people were sorry vor zee Mr. William go down. I mind the time when I zaid these very words to your cousin, I do. Us was standin' in this very same place just like you and I be now. I mind zayin' the selfsame words to 'n." He patted Phillip's hand once again. "Come you now to my wife's place. My wife an' Zillah wull look after 'ee praper, us wull."

"I'll come along very shortly, and thank you, thank you very much."

Phillip in the Mules' parlour, drinking cup after cup of weak hot tea with lemon and honey in it, felt blissful. The baby's photograph in the *South Hams Gazette*, together with the enthusiasm of Mrs. Mules and her daughter in offering to have him as a lodger had been crowned by exaltation when, upon opening the letter Mules had brought, he saw the signature of *Mary Ogilvie* and read that he was invited to Wildernesse.

He kept the full reading of the letter, as a reserve against the possible return of the blank of loneliness, until he was safe under blankets in his cottage bedroom, friendly candle shining in the night.

Wildernesse
Barnstaple
Devon
Tuesday

Dear Phillip

Mother heard that you were here, and asks me to say that we shall be most pleased to see you any time that you feel like coming out to us. I need hardly say how glad I am at the thought of your being in Willie's old cottage. It is strange that you should be there, and yet not really so. Whenever he mentioned your name in the old days, it was always with such happiness. I know how very fond he was of you, and you of him.

It is getting on for two years since that time, Phillip, but it still seems like last week to me. Do come as soon as you can. The children, Ronnie and Pam, are at school now, and my sister Jean has a job at Minehead looking after polo ponies. My cousin Lucy from Dorset is staying near Bideford, she will be here next week (on Monday) when the otterhounds are coming to the Duckponds, so if we don't see each other before then, perhaps we can meet there, and you will come back to tea here afterwards?

He read it many times before blowing out the candle, and trying to settle to sleep, with many sighs.

Part Three

AT THE MULES'

Chapter Eight

LIBELLULA

Phillip put off a reply to Mary Ogilvie's letter until he returned from a journey by train, accompanied by Mrs. Mules and Zillah, to fetch the baby.

Billy was immediately at home as, strapped in the tall chair that had been Phillip's, he sat in the Mules' kitchen, rattling an enamel mug on the tray before throwing it on the floor; whereupon Zillah picked it up and the game was repeated. The energetic and noisy Zillah never tired of playing the mug game with him, although Phillip once suggested that it might end in the baby learning to throw everything about when he grew up. At this Zillah became immediately possessive. "Whose baby be it? 'Tes I who looks after him, you know!"

She teased the baby, then reproved him when he cried out in a pet: but Phillip did not like to interfere. Soon he was having his meals alone, sitting at the circular table in the parlour, while repeated laughter came from the kitchen.

Having failed to compose a satisfactory reply to Mary Ogilvie's letter, he decided to walk to the house on Sunday afternoon; but determination failed when he saw Mrs. Ogilvie and her uncle, Mr. Sufford Chychester, gardening beside the lawn. He tried to write a letter for Mules to deliver on his bicycle early the next morning, but failed again. What must Mary think of him? Finally he wrote a brief note saying that he was looking forward to seeing her and her cousin at the Duckponds. After more indecision on the day he walked there and arrived during the luncheon interval. Mary came to meet him with a smile of welcome.

"I am so very glad you could come! How are you? Do you know my cousin, Lucy Copleston?"

"How do you do."

"How do you do."

"Uncle Suff is over there. Would you like to talk to him?"

"Yes, Mary, I should."

Hardly had the acquaintance been renewed with apparent heartiness on the old man's part when a hound ran past gulping the remains of a pork pie. Mary laughed and touched the arm of her great-uncle to call attention to the sight. "Ha, you rogue!" exclaimed Mr. Chychester, genially, giving Phillip a comradely glance as the hound barged past his thin legs.

Thereafter Phillip began to feel easier as hounds, having drawn blank all the morning, left for the stream which fed the Duck-ponds. He found himself walking with Mary's cousin beside a small mill-pond, round the edges of which dragonflies were darting and hovering.

"Do you know the various kinds, Miss Copleston?"

"Only that there is usually a blue one in our water-garden tub, that my father calls 'Libellula'."

"What a beautiful name—Libellula! Too good for the harsh, prehensile life of a dragonfly!"

When she said nothing more, he felt blank. They were now walking past brambles and alders which almost choked the small stream.

"Mary said you live in Dorset, Miss Copleston."

"Yes, we are on the edge of Cranborne Chase."

"I suppose you don't know Colham? It's a bit north of you, I fancy."

"It's not far from where we live."

"My cousin, who knew Mary, used to live there."

"Yes," she said.

They crossed another meadow. "Did Mary tell you about Willie?"

"Yes," she nodded.

"Are you staying long in Devon?"

"Until next Monday."

Hounds were speaking in the undergrowth adjoining a rushy depression. There were cries and whip-cracks. *Gor'n leave it! Leave it!*

With relief he heard that hounds, marking at a holt where a bitch and cubs were laid up, had been taken off the line.

"There's a meet tomorrow at Meeth Bridge," he said. "Will you be going?"

She blushed at his question. What a strangely sensitive girl she
was, he thought, as he told her about his tame otter, which had
been seen along the Taw. "Is Meeth Bridge on that river?"

"Oh no, the Torridge."

"Thank heaven for that!"

It was a day without a kill, for which he was thankful; and
afterwards a dozen or so men and women drove to Wildernesse
for tea. He enjoyed himself, and as he was leaving Mary said,
"Phillip, I shan't be able to come out tomorrow, but Lucy is
going, and there'll be a lift from Bideford, if you don't want to
go all the way on your motor-bicycle."

At the Meeth meet he found himself, by invitation, among the
fortunate ones by the Master's car at luncheon, drinking cyder
drawn from the keg on the Trojan's running board, and eating
crab sandwiches and cherry cake offered him by the Master's lady
herself.

Sweet country hospitality, he thought, as he walked beside Lucy
along the banks of the upper Torridge. He had discovered by now
that she knew all about wild birds and flowers, and liked nothing
so much as being out in the woods and fields by herself. Whenever
she could, she told him, she slept out of doors beside a camp
fire.

They met again the following day, and the next day. Soon she
would be going home, and he would be seeing her no more.
Meanwhile everything they saw together must be cherished, as he
walked by her side for many miles in the hot sun above the valleys
through which flowed the pale amber waters of Dartmoor in their
descent to the sea. Yes, the wonderful time would soon be over,
he thought as he sat in the midst of tobacco smoke and cheery
talk outside an inn at midday, and again at tea when hounds had
gone back in the van to kennels. For the hunting he did not care,
but he wanted to learn the technique of hunting otters in the
waters of brook and mill-leat, weir-pool and runner; for the idea
of a book about Lutra's life was growing in his mind.

On the penultimate day of the Joint Week he saw to his dismay
that Lucy was accompanied by two older people, whom he
imagined to be her uncle and aunt. They had not been out before.
Should he go up to her, and say good-morning? Or wait for her
uncle to invite him to join them? He shrank from the thought of

attaching himself to them, and kept away until, alarmed that they
might consider him rude—after all, Lucy must have spoken to
them about him—he went towards them, prepared to remove his
cap and say good-morning. Before he reached them, her uncle
began to talk to someone else, together with his wife: he hesitated
whether or not to turn away: but it would be obvious if he did, so
he kept on his course, and lifting cap, bent his head as he passed
the group, and said, "Good-morning, Lucy!"

Immediately her cheeks flushed; he walked on past them, feeling
that he had been presumptuous by addressing her by her Christian
name on what must appear to be so short an acquaintance;
and pretended that he was on his way to look at the hounds
sitting by the road verge under the eye of huntsman and kennel
boy.

Soon the field moved off to draw the banks of a weir-pool. He
walked by himself, keeping well away from Lucy and her people,
and staring at the water as though greatly interested in what he
saw there: hounds clustering about the roots of a sycamore tree
growing on the banks, obviously an otter holt. Then hounds were
taken away, and a man with an iron bar began to thump the
ground above the waterside roots.

The pool was long and deep. The otter holt apparently went
back far under the roots, which resisted penetration by the bar, so
a terrier was put in. From underground came the faint noises of
barking. The terrier crept out, shivering. Another, with bigger
head, was put in. Within a minute there was a cry from the bank of
Bubbles-a-vent! and looking into the water Phillip saw the chain of
small air-bubbles rising, section by section, upon the surface, as the
otter swam underwater to the opposite bank.

The otter crossed again, re-entered the underwater entrance of
the holt; was driven out once more, and went upstream, individual
hounds swimming and giving tongue as they lapped the scent on
the water. People were running, it was exciting; for Phillip, a
cause of disquiet. Supposing the otter were Lutra? The chase went
under a stone bridge, and to the throat of the pool, where it was
shallow. There a massed clamour broke out; the pace of pursuit
increased upon the stones by the edge of the river. Suddenly he
saw the otter galloping across a bank of flat stones called shillets.
The horn rang out with long notes and uniformed men jumped
down into the shallows. to form a stickle across the shillets and

so bar the way back to deep water. But the otter went on upstream, and when last seen was swimming under a wide bridge that crossed the road.

Phillip listened to men saying that it was unusual for an otter to take a direct line like that for more than a mile upstream, away from the deep holding of a weir-pool. By its size and shape of head it was a dog, they said. Phillip recalled how Lutra had run before him over fields and by the sea, like a dog hunting before his master.

On the right bank above the bridge was a mill. The wheel was not working, it was the sawyers' dinner hour. He heard the Master say that the otter might be lying in the water under one of the flood-piled heaps of branches lodged against the cut-waters of the bridge.

"We'll give him a breather while we eat our sandwiches."

Motor-cars, which had followed on the road rising through oakwoods above the meadows, had now returned to the bridge.

Sitting on the parapet, Phillip began to feel more and more depressed as he watched, from a distance, the group of friends about the Master's Trojan. He had not been invited by the Master's wife to help himself. Was it because of Lucy? Or had her uncle and aunt heard the rumours from South Devon? He sat a hundred yards from the Master's car, while laughter and talk floated to him through vacant sunshine.

The Master's wife, a florid lady wearing a floppy, summery hat and a pink gown with a pattern of roses, was looking round. He stared up into the sky; then, feeling that he was perhaps conspicuous by remaining away, strolled back to the near end of the bridge, which had about thirty yards of parapet, and leaned over the northern end, watching the huntsman looking about him on the stones at the river-verge below.

He saw him stooping over what perhaps were the tracks of an otter's feet on the mud beside the stones. The huntsman then looked up under an arch, below which lay the bed of the flume from the mill-wheel hidden in the darkness of the tunnel. The huntsman crept up the tunnel, and soon returned under the arch. Climbing up the bank, he went to the Master and touched his hat.

Phillip waited until Lucy and her party had moved away; then crossing the bridge, he slid down the track in the grass beyond the end of the parapet and stood beside the river, seeing in the mud under the bank the track of the otter's pads. One seal, beside the mark of dragging rudder, was imperfect. Peering low over the scour of mud, with beating heart, he saw what he had dreaded, but not believed he would see: every fourth seal held the print of three claws instead of five. He remained bending down, appalled, until he felt strong enough to climb up again.

The huntsman, waiting above, said cheerfully, "I fancy the otter is lying up on the water-wheel, sir. We'll soon know when they start up again after lunch."

Phillip waited: unable to tell his fears to the Master: unable to leave the scene.

Four hours later the otter was lying in a long shallow pool some miles below the bridge. When the hatch had been raised to allow the weights of water from the leat above to fill the wooden troughs of the wheel, the trundling had flung off the otter. It was seen going down into the river with the renewed gush of water. There it rested and looked up at the faces lining the bridge above. It stared at Phillip, who recognised Lutra as the hounds splashed baying into the water.

O why had he not spoken to the Master, he cried again and again within himself as he sat on the bank of the long shallow pool half a mile below the weir and watched hounds swimming, one occasionally baying, in the scarcely moving water. It was too late now.

The otter had shown what was called good sport after entering the river from the flume. Given two minutes law, it had gone down, down with the current, emerging at the stony shallows to gallop amidst its own splashings over thin, rapid streams running between banks of stones and gravel, to enter deeper, slower water beyond, there to swim submerged for fifty yards or so, as revealed by the bubbles-a-vent, from one bank to the other bank, finally to hide among the thick pointed leaves of flag-lilies until disturbed by hounds. Then down, down, down again—under oaks and alders and ash trees on the banks of the long weir-pool until it came to the sycamore holt above the weir.

It had been driven by a terrier from that underwater fastness and made straight for the weir, crawling out to shake itself, to look around on the concrete barrier as though seeking the face of its master; then over the weir in sunlight, in water just covering its

dark brown body sleek to shapelessness, to be tossed in the turmoil
below and then down the rapid current, the beginning of one of the
best salmon beats on the river.

Down, down, down in the fast water it went, hounds racing after
it, following by scent which they appeared to lap as they ran. Men
and women followed, Phillip ahead, just behind the huntsman.
Constantly the horn sounded, huntsman running hard, scooping
with his grey pot hat to urge on his hounds.

Three hundred yards above the tide-head, with its mud-stained
rushes, the otter vanished. There followed searchings under the
banks, patiently, for the afternoon was hot. Below, at the tail of
the pool, across the breaking wavelets of a stony ridge stood a
stickle—a line—of men and women with water over their boots
and shoes, waiting to turn back the quarry with crossed poles should
it try to get down to the tide-head.

Phillip saw, with some relief, that Lucy was not among them.

Then he saw her, sitting a couple of yards back from the bank,
beside Mr. Sufford Chychester.

The Master walked down to the line of men and women standing
on the flat stones which made the stickle of breaking fast water.
Phillip followed. He heard the Master saying that the otter was
probably lying up in the reeds somewhere. Tom the huntsman
would find it, when it might make for the stickle in an attempt
to get down to salt water.

The Master looked at his watch. "It's high water at Bideford
Bridge now," he said. "If the otter gets through hounds won't be
able to follow him, for as you know tide-water carries no scent."

Phillip made up his mind to go into the water and rescue Lutra
if he went down to the stickle and found his way barred.

Across the pool ripples flickered with the sun now in the western
arc of the sky. Look-outs on the bank were leaning on their poles.
Patiently the huntsman moved with his hounds, covering every
yard of both banks, below which grew flag-lilies, musk, watercress,
and other plants. Was the musk scent overlaying the scent of the
otter? he heard someone say; and the reply that surely musk scent
ended, all over the world, in 1914?

"Wasn't it only the garden varieties of Muscari?"

In the centre of the pool lay a dark length of sodden branch,
left there by a past flood. A dragonfly was hovering over the pool,

dropping eggs around the length of the branch. They would hatch, and the prehensile underwater nymphs would hunt the frailer nymphs and creepers of the ephemeral flies—the innocent beauties of the river, who lived but a day, with mouths sealed against feeding or drinking, hatching to arise into air for love, and so to find—death.

He watched the blue dragonfly hovering. It lit on the water, then flew up as though alarmed. He saw ripples spreading away, delicately. From what? Staring, he saw the thin nostrils of the otter, and when the dragonfly alighted on them he saw the scratch of its whiskers. He saw that Lucy had seen the otter too, betrayed by its sneeze. The nostrils were half an inch above the surface. Lutra was hanging down in the water, one paw holding, below the surface, to the sodden branch.

Phillip saw that Lucy's cheeks had flushed, that her eyes were downheld. Mr. Chychester had been looking at the water, too, but he had not connected the ripples with the alarm of the dragonfly, which was now darting over the water, perhaps seeking flies to eat while waiting to drop more eggs. It hovered near the branch; it flew low; it settled. There was the sound of a sneeze again, the shake of a head.

Mr. Chychester saw it this time. Phillip heard him say, "Ah!" then he was getting to his feet with difficulty.

He removed and held aloft his grey hat.

"Bubbles-a-vent!"

"O faithless Libellula!" said Phillip aloud, hoping that Lucy would hear.

The otter was hemmed in. It swam across, was turned back, to swim underwater again and again, in shorter and shorter journeys, always betrayed by the chain of bubbles rising in straight line along the surface. It swam about the pool, slower and slower. The time came when it could swim hardly more than a yard without rising to breathe and rest. The huntsman was now in the water to his waist, softly speaking to hounds by name. They were confused, they hunted by scent, which was all about them: even when Lutra was lying, head out of water, looking at them from less than a yard away.

"He's dead beat," said the Master.

Hearing these words Phillip slid down the bank and waded close to the huntsman.

"Don't move, sir," said Tom, respectfully. "Let hounds hunt him, sir."

"I think this may be my escaped otter!"

How feeble his voice sounded—the wind-risp of a dry reed.

"Lutra! Lu-Lu-Lu!"

At the sound of the voice Lutra stared up at his face. The otter's mouth opened, as though in appeal.

"This *is* my escaped tame otter!"

"Stand still, please, sir," replied the huntsman. "I don't want my hounds to riot. Stand still, please, sir."

Phillip knew the danger of hounds rioting: if he tried to pick up the otter he might be attacked, dragged down, and killed. He did not care. Lutra sank down; a hound, pounding slowly and heavily by, its stern flinging drops of water in arcs, saw the head look up again and with a plunging leap chopped at it. Baying loudly, hounds massed for the worry.

Phillip groped with his hands and grasped Lutra's hind legs, dropping them as a hound leapt upon him. Lutra came into shallow water, following him as he waded to the stony edge of the river.

"It's my tame otter! Make way, make way!" he cried to the figures across the stickle. Pushing through, he kept an open place for Lutra to slip past him. On the fast stream the brown body was carried away into the deeper water of the tide-head.

Hounds were swimming aimlessly in the pool, others baying about the broken stickle. The huntsman was talking to the Master. The look-out from the bank below, hurrying upriver to the uniformed figures, said that the head of the otter, its mouth open, was going down with the tide.

There remained for Phillip a duty almost as hard to face as his act of interference in the water. He went to the Master to apologise.

That gentleman listened to what he said with great courtesy, and then replied, "I am glad that we did not kill your otter, Maddison."

"Thank you, sir. I feel greatly ashamed for not having spoken to you about it at Mill Bridge."

The Master saw that his hands were trembling. Mildly he went on, "As it happened it turned out better than it might have done."

"Yes, Master. I blame myself entirely."

"I am happy that no harm was done to you," said the Master,

kindly, as he leant on his pole taller than himself: a ground ash, three parts covered by silver rings on which were engraved places and dates of old kills, with zodiacal sign of dog or bitch on each. He wore a dark blue jacket with a yellow waistcoat and white breeches, with coarse blue worsted stockings and a labourer's heavy boots. The yellow hair of his head and drooping moustaches was turning white; gold-framed spectacles sat on his nose, adding to a mild and amiable expression.

Raising his cap, Phillip set off up-river; his motor-bicycle had been left at Mill Bridge. Through the hedge of the next meadow he glanced back, and saw Lucy with her uncle and other friends moving away in the distance. It was her last day; she was going home that evening; he had disgraced himself; if hounds had worried him it would have reacted badly for the Hunt, whose guest he had been; never, never, never again would he mix with people; he was no good.

But the incident did not, as he had imagined in his black mood, mark him as an outsider, or a 'mere humanitarian', at least in the eyes of the Master, who wrote him a brief note saying that he accepted his apology, and regarded his action for what it was, a rash but brave act made without regard for personal safety. He hoped that he would come out with them regularly, to instruct him (the Master) when he considered that he had seen the spoor of his tame otter, 'and so allow us to give him law to follow his own devices'.

The search for Lutra now became a major aim of Phillip's life. Not only did he attend every meet of the home pack, but studied also the lists of meets of the Dartmoor pack and the Quantock pack in local papers; he travelled far on the Norton, bumping down sunken lanes and up unmade rocky tracks to higher fields whence to search for distant dark figures under riverside oaks and alders, the familiar otter-hunters wearing grey bowler hats and uniform jackets of navy blue serge with white breeches. Always aloof, peering and listening, often envious of laughter and friendship; sometimes at the end of a long day near to despair; ever rehearsing the moment when he would save Lutra as it left water for the land, the last refuge of an otter; or lay in a pool with no strength to run, able to swim only a few strokes underwater before rising to lie still once more and watch the faces of big white, black, and tan hounds so near, their baying so loud upon the final moment of being overborne, seized, lifted, dragged and torn from life.

One morning on the banks of the Taw a brown-faced athletic man came up to him as though in a hurry and cried, "How are you! I met you in the *Crusader* office before you went to the Pyrenees with Rowley Meek and Bevan Swann."

"Of course! You are Martin Beausire!"

"What are you doing in my country?" demanded the other, his face assuming blankness at the evident delight in Phillip's face. "Now tell me, you know much more about these things than I do, are we going to find an otter today?" He looked around, apparently needing no reply, for the next moment he said, "My God, I see we've been invaded by the portly pole-carriers of Sussex, where for my sins I am living now. The entire whisky trade appears to have followed me—and I've travelled two hundred miles to avoid them!"

This address, beginning with what seemed enthusiasm, ended with a growl at the sight of several bulky men, all dressed alike, coming nearer. With a muttered 'Don't go away', Beausire strode off with pressure upon large muscular calves below dark blue running shorts worn with a thick white jersey with the letters O U A C woven across the chest.

Phillip wondered what reason Beausire had for avoiding the group of 'portly pole carriers' as he disappeared among the crowd of waiting people; then to his surprise he heard Beausire's sudden cackling laughter on the river-bank, and there he was, addressing first one then another of the Sussex 'invaders' with loud geniality. There were a half-dozen of them, all looking the same, with big heads and bodies; thick-necked men with rolls of fat visible whenever a head, crowned by a size 8 or possibly 8½ grey bowler, was turned. The pot hat of the local hunt was grey, too, but with a more curly brim; the hats of the Sussex men had wide level brims which emphasised the thickness of the Dun-whiddle family head.

"'Whisky' Dunwhiddles," remarked Beausire, returning to Phillip's side. "Four brothers and two cousins. I wrote an article about them in my paper, and they objected to being called 'the portly pole-carriers of Sussex'. But if they aren't that, what in God's name are they?"

"Perhaps it was the word 'port' they object to, if they are whisky."

"You have a point there," conceded Beausire over his shoulder, as he hurried away to talk to someone else.

During the luncheon interval Phillip saw him standing on the bonnet of an immensely long touring Bugatti drawn up beside the road—which followed the river at that place—under the shade of oak trees. Apparently this very expensive motor car belonged to the clan, for the six were sitting around it, eating. From his stance on the bonnet Beausire was addressing them while gnawing what looked to be the leg of a cold turkey.

"You're the sort of people who should be hanged from the nearest lamp-post!" he was saying, genially. "You are the natural patrons of the Arts, Big Business having replaced every country house in England," as he gnawed the drumstick bare before hurling it away and bending down to take another from the plate offered by the uniformed chauffeur. While stripping this of flesh with rapid bites he saw Phillip, and with a wave of the bone said rapidly to the company; "D'you know Phillip Maddison's work? May I present him—General Dunwhiddle—Colonel Dunwhiddle—Major Dunwhiddle—Captain Dunwhiddle—Lieutenant Dunwhiddle— Private Dunwhiddle—this is Captain Maddison who is Nimrod, W. H. Hudson, and Surtees all rolled into one. Now I've got to write my blasted article. See you all later!" as he jumped off the bonnet.

The Sussex Scotsmen were kind, quietly-spoken. He was offered food and drink, but declined, while wondering what to say after such a sporadic introduction.

"Got your pipe?" asked one, offering a cloth bag of John Cotton tobacco.

"I don't smoke, thank you, sir."

"Breezy chap, Beausire," said a second.

"Yes."

"Not much water," said a third.

"No."

The cloth bag of John Cotton was passed round from pipe to pipe, each one thick-bowled and charred at the top. Phillip noted that the two fattest wore celluloid collars, apparently against the sweats of walking: an odd detail, since, according to jokes in *Punch*, only those fancying ready-made bow-ties wore such things.

He made an excuse to follow Beausire, finding him sitting on a
fallen tree, writing rapidly on pink sheets of paper.

"I must get this on the London train," he said, without looking
up. "It slows down through Morchard Road Station, where I've
arranged to give it to the guard. Can you take me there on your
stink-bike? When? Now, of course, you blasted ass! Haven't you
been in Fleet Street? We'll be there and back by the time hounds
cast off again. Don't talk."

He scribbled fast.

"My bike is two miles down the river, I'm afraid."

"The Dunwhiddles' motor will be going back to Umberleigh
soon, we'll get a lift," said Beausire, still writing furiously. After a
few minutes he stood up. "Why aren't you ready?" he demanded,
to Phillip, who was sitting down.

"Oh, by the way, a motor-bike is a bit bumpy, you know——"
said Phillip, getting to his feet.

"Good God, d'you think I don't know that? What d'you
suppose I've been doing all my life, sitting in a bath chair?"

Beausire thrust his copy into an envelope, drew the gummed
flap through his mouth, and said in a rapid mutter, "If I can go
down the Cresta Run backwards with a drunken brakesman from
the House of Lords on top of me at midnight at seventy miles an
hour d'you think I can't sit on the back of your stinking machine
on a tarred road? Come on, you gazing genius!" He took
Phillip's arm and led him back to the Dunwhiddles smoking in a
row as they sat among plants of wild garlic beside the drawn-up
grand-tourisme Bugatti.

"If your shover is going back to Umberleigh, would you mind
giving us a lift there, Jumbo?"

Beausire rapidly swallowed a glass of Dunwhiddle whisky before
jumping in.

That evening Phillip took him to Exeter, where his parents were
staying at the Malmesbury Arms. As soon as they arrived in the
drawing-room Beausire took up a length of galley proof and lay
full length on a sofa with eyes shut and mouth open, apparently
in collapse. His mother drew Phillip aside to explain that her son
undertook far too much while living under stress, due to 'that
wretched girl Ursula'.

"Have you met Martin's wife?" she enquired.

"Well—I have a very bad memory, I'm afraid——"

"Well, if you haven't met Ursula you haven't missed much, I can assure you! There were two colonel's daughters, you see, and Martin chose the wrong one. My son is a genius, and Ursula fails utterly to understand him. Martin is the most generous man alive, and so everyone imposes on him."

Mrs. Beausire said this in a quiet, deep voice coming from considerable strength of will. She was a stout woman of the same stocky, powerful build as Martin, who was, she went on to tell him, her only child. She asked no questions about Phillip: her entire concern appeared to be for her son, who, she said, had far too many so-called friends, all of whom had sought his acquaintance solely for the purpose of furthering their own interests.

"They use him, then invariably they abuse him."

Beausire's father came in later. He was a tall modest man with a face as pale and thin as his wife's was florid. His parson's clothes were old. Around his straw-hat was a faded black band. He was quiet and gentle, his frequent smiles revealed teeth the same colour as his yellowing celluloid collar and old straw hat. Phillip stayed to dinner, which Martin ate vigorously, having recovered from exhaustion.

The next day, there being no meet of otterhounds, Phillip met Martin at Barnstaple and took him on the Norton to the north coast of Exmoor. They left the machine in a hedge, and set out to climb a pyramid-shaped hill which Martin said was the Little Hangman.

"I was in Fleet Street five years ago," said Phillip, as they climbed the zigzag path up to the summit, with views over the Severn Sea to Wales. "I didn't much care for the work."

"Who does? I wouldn't stay a day if my novels sold."

"I thought you were a best-seller!"

"Good God no—my novels don't pay for the cost of typing. So I have to compromise between grubbing for a living and trying to write what I want to write. You must have had tremendous guts to get out when you did, and chuck everything for writing. But wait till you're married, then God help you, my lad."

Phillip had not spoken about the death of his wife.

"What exactly do you do on your paper, Martin?"

"Office boy, combined with Book Critic, Dramatic Critic, Film Critic, Leader Writer, and the daily Society Column, most of which I write myself."

"Isn't it a bit of a strain sometimes?"

"Not if I can get away like this into God's clean air where nobody talks about London. What's that bird?"

"A stonechat."

"What does it do?"

"Insectivorous, builds low in a bramble, makes an alarm cry like two pebbles chatted together. By the way, have you come across the novels of Scott Fitzgerald, an American?"

Beausuire did not reply, but taking the lead, set a faster pace up through the heather. The sun was hot, Phillip kept close behind him.

When they stopped to look back he could see that Beausire was trying to conceal heavy breathing, just as he himself was.

"Evidently you don't read my book reviews. Now tell me. what's the gull up there making that noise? What kind is it?"

"A greater black-backed gull. Rather rare down here. By Jove, there's a raven! The black-back's after it! I expect both have seen some carrion on the rocks below. They're rivals, in a way. The black-back can swallow whole a half-grown rabbit."

They watched until both birds were out of sight below the cliff edge, then walked on.

"What do you think of Scott Fitzgerald?"

"I think he's good, but must we talk of authors up here?"

The Little Hangman was left behind, they climbed to the summit of the Great Hangman and stopped to look over the sea, a milky azure in the morning sun. The Welsh mountains were blue on the horizon below a chain of white-bubbled clouds.

Onwards down the reverse slopes of the hill, where, passing a cairn, Beausire stopped to throw a sixpenny piece among the grey stones.

"Why do you do that?"

"Don't you know that the pixies must be propitiated, otherwise they'll lead one astray in a fog? You're supposed to know all about this country."

"I haven't heard that the pixies have migrated from Dartmoor," laughed Phillip. "But they may have, now that the chars-à-bancs have arrived. What do you think of Dikran Michaelis, the Armenian writer?"

"You should take my job in London, you are interested in books and authors while I, a poor damned hack, want only to hear about birds and flowers! Well, come on, what else do you want to know, get it off your chest, then we can both, for a few hours, live in the sunshine. What do I think of Dikran? He's every other inch a gentleman, and his writing is not so much brilliant as brilliantine. Does that satisfy you?"

"I'm sorry. Of course I know how you feel. Only I never meet anyone who is interested in books in Devon."

"Don't I know it! I was born and bred in this country, and lived much as your Donkin lived in your first novel. All authors go through hell before they find their feet, and when they do, it's another species of hell." When Phillip looked sympathetically at him, Beausire growled, "Don't take any notice of my bear-with-a-sore-head attitude. I was an usher for too many years, and dashed myself against the rock of the average public school intelligence again and again with about as much effect as one of those waves down there. When John Masefield's *Everlasting Mercy* filled an entire number of Austin Harrison's *English Review* I read it to my class at Milborne, and after the fifteenth 'bloody' three of the senior boys stood up and asked permission to see the Head Master."

"Good lord, why?"

"They objected to what they called the 'obscene language'. That's all that Masefield meant to them—one of the purest poets this country has bred in all its literary history! All literary London was talking about *The Everlasting Mercy*, which sold eighty thousand copies of that number of *The English Review*. Even prizefighters in East End pubs were reading it. But public school prefects, with their own cults of pederasty, had to object—and that after a war in which poets like Rupert Brooke, Wilfred Owen, Julian Grenfell, Charles Sorley, Francis Ledwidge—who as you know was a Dublin dustman before the war—Isaac Rosenberg, and a host of others—including George Butterfield the composer of *The Shropshire Lad* songs—gave their lives. England that was good died with them. Today I'm trying to get readers of a daily newspaper owned by the Uncrowned King of Glasgow to read decent stuff, to realise what England is, through its solitary great writers who burn the midnight oil alone, as they always have—but not one reader cares a hoot about prose or poetry, all they read my blasted stuff for is to see what moronic actress lunched in the

Savoy yesterday, what horse is going to win the Derby, what titled woman has run off with whose husband. Tomorrow I'll be back among it all, in a room facing a north wall so sunless that no pigeon ever sits on the sill outside, a room not much bigger than a cupboard, so I'd be most grateful if you would not talk so much next time, and more particularly if you would refrain from asking me questions about Fleet Street."

Martin strode on faster than before, while Phillip followed, determined to show him that what Martin could do, he could do; but with no more words.

Chapter 9

A FLOWER-LIKE GIRL

He said goodbye that evening at the Malmesbury Arms, and re-turned along the winding road beside the river to Speering Folliot. He felt his life to be blank again, after so much activity; and a letter from his mother, awaiting him, raised again the problem of what to do with the baby. He could not leave Billy with the Mules', kind and considerate as they were, for ever. Perhaps, as Mother proposed, he should let his sister Doris adopt him? Billy in that sad, neglected house in Romford? Oh no! Every time he saw Billy, happy in the postman's kitchen, he knew that he could not let him go. And Billy seemed to like him, for some odd reason. He could talk now—well, almost.

"Dada! Dada!"

Wide-mouthed smile, one tooth coming through—tears and cries until Phillip rubbed the gum, then smiling, smiling, smiling—Billy on the floor crawling to meet him, arms held out . . . the same feeling, only brought to the point of desperation, that Lutra had had for him, surrounded by enemies it could not understand —who had no idea of what they truly did—gay women not cruel in themselves—neither they nor their men had the blood-lust that some critics of hunting declared—they merely had no imagination to realize what death meant to a so-called lower creature. Even so, was not all truth but relative, with no validity beyond the consciousness of each living creature? Otters slew fish for sport, men slew otters for sport—or to keep them from becoming too numerous lest they eat the fish wanted for food by men. It was the natural scheme of things—all species were full of a sense of fun in killing, little tigers burning bright, in the forests of the night.

He met Mary in the village, and the talk turned to otters, and so to the otter hunt ball being held in the Albert Hall of the town next month. He said, "I suppose you wouldn't like to come with me, Mary? I'm afraid I don't know anyone else to ask, to make a party, otherwise I would ask you all to dine with me first at the Imperial."

"I'll be away then, Phillip. I'm going to stay with some of my father's cousins in Scotland. But if you want a partner, why not ask Lucy? She will be coming for a brief visit in two days' time. She hopes to find a camping site for her Girl Guides on the high ground over there somewhere"—she pointed to the north—"near the bay, and sheltered, with an empty barn for her girls to go in when it's raining. I suppose you don't know of a farmer who would give leave for a troop of Guides for a fortnight? They'd want butter, milk, and eggs, and usually the farmer's wife is glad to see the girls——"

"I think I know the very place, Mary! Shall I take you to it—perhaps this afternoon?"

"Why not wait until Lucy comes, and take her?"

"Well—to be truthful, I wondered if I had offended her by calling her by her Christian name, Mary."

"So *that* was it! And Lucy's been wondering why you had dropped her!"

"I——? Drop Lucy? I *liked* being with her!"

"She liked you, too, Phillip. Come to tea the day after to-morrow, and tell her about the site."

Lucy met him at the door when he called at Wildernesse on the appointed day. He saw suddenly how beautiful she was when a blush came upon her cheeks. She told him that she was going to spend the next day and night with her aunt and uncle at Bideford, but might she come over by 'bus the following day, and see the camp site?

The visit was arranged for a Thursday, when Lucy would come to luncheon with him in his cottage at one o'clock.

On the Thursday he waited, with Mrs. Mules and Zillah in their best clothes, the circular mahogany sitting-room table laid with clean cloth and bowl of flowers, until a quarter to two; and when Lucy did not arrive, he ate his omelette alone. When she had not appeared by three o'clock he decided that she would not be coming; and closing D. H. Lawrence's *Sons and Lovers*, which seemed to him not to be of the first clarity of genius—the author was somehow immoiled within himself, like Julian Warbeck, though in a different way—he returned to his cottage with dog and cat—Moggy so slow, running to him and then stopping, always lagging behind, while Rusty went on ahead like a scout.

His cottage door was open; it was seldom closed from one week to another; and to his surprise and happiness the strains of *Destiny Waltz* were coming from the kitchen. And there was Lucy, sitting at the table beside the open Decca trench-gramophone, her lips parted, her head moving slightly as she smiled.

"Hullo," she murmured, standing up.

Her voice was almost inaudible, lost in the colour rising in her oval face. She wore a pink cotton frock with short sleeves, and a hat whose brim made her eyes seem to shine darkly in the room. *Destiny Waltz*, the record worn out in 1917 and not played for the past eight years, scratched on.

"I'm fearfully sorry! I've been waiting for you in Mules' cottage! I have my grub there! Please forgive me—I forgot to tell you——"

"I've been quite happy," she smiled.

"But have you had any lunch?"

"I bought a banana and an apple on my way here, and ate them walking beside the estuary."

"Let me cook you some eggs and bacon?"

"No thanks, really."

"Let's make some tea?"

"I'd like some tea, but only if it's no bother."

"Oh, no bother at all, really." He went to the empty larder. "Well, when I said 'no bother', I should have said 'no milk'!"

"I like tea just plain."

"I'm afraid there's no sugar, either."

"I don't take sugar, thank you." Her cheeks were now their normal colour.

"Heavens, I'm frightfully sorry, but there's no tea, either! But there's water. It's very good water."

"I like water," she said.

"We dip it from a well behind the cottage."

"Ours at home comes from a well, too."

Carrying two mugs and an earthenware pitcher, he went with her to the well. One neighbour watched from a small back window, another from a second window.

"It has quite a different taste from our water," she said.

"It's iron-stone water here."

"Ours is chalk, I think. And it has shrimps in it, and ammonites."

"How fortunate! Shrimps in your tea! But it shows the water is pure."

"Pa wants to get a trout to put in the well, to eat the shrimps. But I like shrimps." She blushed again. He thought of fresh-water shrimps, the larger male carrying the smaller female in its arms as they flipped about a stream: but said, "What is an ammonite? I thought it was a Biblical tribe."

"It's a prehistoric fossil, I believe."

Their thirst slaked, they went back to the cottage. Should he ask her if she wanted to wash her hands? There was nowhere for a guest to go; the privy, with its walls of cob, had collapsed during the previous winter; and the landlord had not yet had a new one built. He must make some excuse to leave her on the walk to the camping site. He played the two records of César Franck's *Violin Sonata in A minor*, and then they set out.

It was a long climb to the fields above. The site was another two miles after the high ground had been reached. They passed through a village of lime-washed cob and thatch, and so to fields overlooking the sea.

On the banks of the sunken lanes grew many wild flowers. They played a game of taking turns to guess a plant pointed out by one another. The score was even, with six guesses each, when they came to a colony of rare plants, previously identified by Phillip from Johns' *Flowers of the Field*. Could she name it? Perhaps the scent would help?

While she sniffed inaudibly he regarded her curve of cheek, and set of waist where she bent down to touch the miniature yellow-thistle flower. Her legs were a pleasing shape, too; indeed, he could hardly believe his good luck. With added joy he realised that she had a delicate sensibility: she made no attempt to pluck the flower, but barely touched it with the tip of one finger. She is a green-corn spirit, he thought, she is more delicate than Barley. In a way she was like his mother, gentle in thought to all she beheld; but without the sadness of Mother.

"I can't think what the darling is," the soft voice murmured, as the finger-tip caressed the miniature cardoon of yellow. "I don't know!" she said, with a small laugh.

"Well, I oughtn't to count this one, as I looked it up only the other day. It's Ploughman's Spikenard. Can you smell the aromatic oil? I wonder if Jesus smelled it when his feet were anointed by Mary Magdalene?"

She blushed again, her lashes hid her eyes. Then she was smiling, her head moving slightly as she contemplated him. "Ploughman's Spikenard—what a lovely name."

"Do you know Francis Thompson's poetry?"

"A little. Mary showed me her book once, which your cousin had given her."

"Thompson fell in love with a girl who didn't understand him —or perhaps she understood him too well! She probably thought him a half-man! 'Like to a box of spikenard, I broke my heart about your feet, That you did love me.' I suppose, biologically speaking, a woman has no real use for a poet when he is obsessed by his vision of harmony and beauty."

Lucy did not reply, but looked upon the ground. She did not know what to reply, and felt stupid. What could she say? No thought came.

"Very few writers or poets know the feeling. D. H. Lawrence touches that feeling sometimes—but he's engaged in clearing away the effects of his writhen childhood—like these wind-blown thorns you see here——I'm afraid I'm not really being very clear."

Lucy was stroking the spaniel, her face still averted. "Rusty," she said in an almost inaudible voice. Then, looking up, "Have you written many books? Someone was asking the other day what it was you wrote."

"Oh, I write magazine stories about birds and animals."

"How lovely!" With a hesitant smile on her lips, "I used to write and edit a 'Nature Magazine', for the Boys." She was blushing again, smiling at him with her grey eyes set with long lashes. "It was read only among ourselves, of course."

"How many brothers have you?"

"I have three."

"Do you still keep a nature diary?"

"Yes."

"So do I!"

She stroked the spaniel, who was overjoyed at his good fortune. She looked up. "I'll put Ploughman's Spikenard into my diary when I get back!"

They went on down the lane, past the high walls of a manor garden, with farm premises beyond. Calling at the farmhouse, he explained what was wanted.

"This is Miss Copleston, the Guide Mistress of the Shakesbury Girl Guides."

"How d'you do, Miss!"

Phillip felt pride as she asked about water, supply of milk, and if there were a building into which her guides might go in wet weather.

The farmer was a newcomer, having bought the land and buildings from the former owner, a gentleman who had sold the manor and gone to Kenya Colony, believing England to be finished.

The farmer was cautious, non-committal. Yes, he might be able to supply milk. Yes, he might have a barn, perhaps. He couldn't say for sure. Yes, he might sell some firing for camp fires. He would talk with his wife first. Yes, he would let the gentleman know, when he called next.

Lucy said when they were alone again that the fields were high, and exposed to winds; but soon they spoke no more of the site. Should they return to the cottage, or walk over the down to the Burrows?

"I'd like to show you a new way, but it is a bit longer."

"I love walking!"

"We go up Sky Lane, and down to a post-office, where we can buy cheese and biscuits. It's a jolly walk along the shore, or we cross the sandhills, to the lighthouse. There's a ferry then, to Appledore. But how stupid of me! Of course, you must know it well."

"I'd love to go there again! One sees no one, only birds."

"Perhaps we should call at the cottage—won't you be thirsty?"

"I think I can manage."

"But it's three miles before we get to the post-office, then four miles round the coast to the lighthouse."

"I'm not a very thirsty person," she said, and whispered "Rusty —Rusty," to hide her happy feelings—patting the head of the dog resting its head on her knee.

They set off about five o'clock of that afternoon of sunshine and high cirrus clouds. Down a red sunken lane through a valley, to stop by a pollard ash with a bee's nest in it, pointed out as one of his 'secrets' to be shared with her; and round a bend in the lane, a quarry hung with ivy where a pair of grey wagtails had a second nest. After inspecting this they turned off the lane and up a farm track and so on to the farmyard, to be challenged by the cattle dog on guard with mincing minatory steps and fluffed-up tail.

"The farmer is rather grumpy," he said. "I hope we don't meet him, as this isn't really a right-of-way. Rusty—heel!"

Rusty stood still, rolling his eyes and whining and not daring to cower lest he be seized across the neck. Taking no notice of the two dogs—"Hackled master and cringing mastered," he re-marked—he led Lucy past a circular building wherein was fixed a cumbrous wooden cage of vast proportions, explaining that a horse in winter moved round and round, driving a shaft, the cogged end of which turned a turnip-slicing machine.

After peering for signs of owls in the round house, they con-tinued up a narrow track which became steeper, stonier, and more enclosed by thorn and bramble as they climbed. Water trickled down among the stones of its bed, nourishing plants of brook-lime and forget-me-not. The track was sunken between steep banks, a stony way now almost entirely choked by umbelli-ferous plants. They stepped slowly upwards, into the sky it seemed, he leading, Lucy in her cotton frock following, spaniel panting behind.

"There are vipers here, we must be careful. Foxes, too. In the evening one sees literally hundreds of rabbits. If we'd come here in April, we'd have seen the windflowers—lovely white anemones like stars—tinged with pink as they die. But I expect you know them?"

"Yes," she said happily. He thought she was like a little child, with her small face and gently smiling lips; she was all innocence. He, too, felt to be his innocent self.

"We mustn't look back until we get to the top. There's a fine surprise in store!"

They toiled up, he holding her hand, her eyes almost closed. "We're nearly there."

He led her to the top, and still holding her hand, stopped.

"Now look!"

Together they looked over the country they had walked through, lying away below their feet as hundreds of fields, with the manor house distantly among trees; and nearer, to the east, a grey Norman church tower among diminutive elms. Amidst the irregular strips and shapes of hundreds of grassy fields, each within its thick dividing banks, were occasional plots of corn beginning to turn into the hues of high summer; for the cuckoo was already silent. Here in the high air he had often walked with Rusty, alone with the songs of pipits and larks.

A chain of swifts passed in the sky, and he thought of Barley, and her question years ago in South Devon—*Do they beat first one wing, then the other?* What would she think of him now? Or were all her thoughts, if her spirit still remained near the earth, for her child?

They walked, apart now, to the crest of the hill, coming to a small and narrow gate of grey weathered oak covered with greyer lichens in a gap of the hedge grown tall with many ash-plants. The gateway led to a stony field of poor oats, from where was visible the far wide tract of the Burrows, and the Atlantic lying away to the west and vanishing in summer's heat.

"I'll be back in a minute."

He climbed over, and went down the outside of the hedge bordering the track they had come up. He wanted to think. What was he doing? Gould she take the place of Barley? With Barley he had always felt *clear*; but not innocent. He wasn't innocent, except when writing—sometimes. If he did not feel *clear* with Lucy, would it not be fatal to go on?

He returned to where she stood by the gateway, and seeing her gentle smile led her by the hand among the low, rabbit-gnawn stalks of the oats. They stood in the breeze from the sea, watching the hawks hanging along the ridgeway. Her hand lay almost inert in his hand. After a while he pretended to be looking for a plant among the thin oat stalks, and let go her hand. The faint thread of pain which had entered him when they had been looking at the Ploughman's Spikenard returned and settled to an ache of negation. Here he was, one moment overjoyed to be with her; the next, overcome by feelings of mortification, pretending to look for a plant.

He got up and ran down the steep field, pushing through a rabbit-tunnelled bank of furze and blackthorn; and jumping off, continued to run down towards a round pond made to hold water. There he sat down, waiting for her to come to him, and the more he wanted to turn and wave to her, the more he sat still, his chest held on his drawn-up knees, as though trying to hide himself in the knot of his compressed body. He thought how, as a very little child, he had sometimes refused to kiss his mother goodnight, thus to hurt himself by hurting her. Denied a good-night kiss, Mother would be sad, and after leaving him alone for an interval she would steal back to his bedroom; but by then he was fast in a self-fixture of unhappiness, and would not reply. Left alone again, feelings of anguish and remorse would spread over him, he would weep silently on the pillow, and yet remain despairingly obstinate when she returned once more. Yes, that was himself at three or four years of age; but after he had known Barley, the natural girl delighting in natural love, surely the kink had been removed in him? Was there a connection between loving a mother deeply, too deeply, as D. H. Lawrence had done—*Sons and Lovers* was obviously based on the facts of his own early life—and losing a wife one had loved with all one's being? Was he back where he had started?

Almost silently Lucy came to where he was sitting, and sat down near him, speaking softly to the spaniel who was panting, with sandy elongated tongue, beside her.

"Did you enjoy your run down the hill?" she asked, gently. "You looked so happy. I found a late robin's nest, with young ones, among the ferns in the hedge up there. Such darlings."

"I have a nestling, too," he said. "A baby son."

"Yes, Mary told me," she replied, smiling unsteadily at him. All the afternoon he had looked so lost, so worried; and now he seemed happy at last.

They came to the road, and the post-office shop on the other side. There they drank ginger beer from earthenware bottles and bought biscuits, chocolate, and Canary bananas for their journey across the sandhills. He felt that he knew her now. Spirals of joy arose in him, uncoiling in desire to sing and jump about: the spaniel's front paws were lifted up and he was made to dance, to swallow a trickle of ginger beer; and afterwards a saucer of water in preparation for the long trail across the estuarial flats to the white lighthouse beside the estuary where Willie had had the life choked out of him because of a dream. Like Barley, who had dreamed of the baby in her arms, patient unto death. He thought too, of Ralph Hodgson's *Song of Honour*, which Julian Warbeck had first told him about; and he thought, I must make my life in that spirit, with Lucy.

At first it seemed to him that everything Willie had dreamed and hoped in the last spring of his life was being transferred to him. Was he a medium for other people's feelings or thoughts? Was that the weakness of the true artist—never a man of character, but only a sensitised instrument for receiving the feelings of others? Was it more than that, a sort of possession by others, beyond impersonation? Here he was, walking with this flower-like girl over a tract of sandy country, possibly following the very same way where Willie had walked with Mary, while being told by her that every kind of English wildflower grew on the Burrows, just as Lucy was telling him now. Would the end be the same for Lucy, as for Mary? For it was not the drowning that had taken Willie from Mary; the break had happened before that, many times. Perhaps if Mary had been a stronger character, like Barley, then Willie . . .

His thoughts appalled him; was he leading Lucy into the same dilemma?

"What a pity the flowers are over, they are so beautiful in the spring," she was saying.

"Yes," he said.

The petals had fallen: the wildflower air of spring was now the radiant heat of young summer arising from the bronze mosses and glinting grains of loose sand. The time that Willie had entered there, as in a dream of tenderness and renewal was passed with the wild-sweet cries of lapwing and the high songs of larks above a green place which Phillip knew from reading Willie's diary—a passage, known by heart, describing marsh helleborine and whitlow grass, heart's-ease and celandine, dove's-foot crane's-bill, and 'that pink dewdrop of flower, the bog pimpernel'. If only his own heart and mind could re-create, out of Time, that first walk of Mary and Willie upon the Burrows, and all that year now lost in ancient sunlight, that spring of tenderness and renewal of plant-life in beauty—yellow-wort and ladies' bedstraw, sea-rocket, horned poppy, and wild thyme—for a novel about Willie! But—'never a bone the less dry for all the tears'. Willie was gone; the flowers he had seen were dust, the earth had trundled over six hundred times on its axis through space, night succeeding day, since that September night.

Would Lucy understand such 'immortal longings'; or would they be 'morbid thoughts?' How deep were Mary and she in friendship? Did Lucy feel as Mary once had felt?

"Did Mary tell you much about Willie?"

"A little," she said, and could not look at him for tenderness, having divined how much he had loved his cousin.

They walked on, side by side, and after a while he glanced at her and she shared the glance, their fingers touched, he held her hand naturally, thoughtlessly, it was as though Spring had come again, and all the lost beauty of wild flowers and the thoughts they had given Willie were resurrected through her presence beside him.

They passed over the mossy pans and came to the sandhills. Taking off their shoes they climbed barefoot up the loose slopes, the soles of their feet burned by the sand that spilled away under each tread. He was thinking, Barley, Barley, like this we walked upon the hot sands of the Camargue.

Reaching the crest of the chain of foot-hills they found the sea-breeze stirring the marram grasses, and saw the sea beyond, crinkled in the heat ascending, so that the white lines of breaking summer waves seemed to be a mirage in the lower sky. They played a game of follow-my-leader along the peaks of the sand-hills, running at a slow loping pace, arms extended like wings, continuing without pause even when a sudden precipice opened before their feet. It was a wonderful feeling to stand still at the moment of poise, of being buoyed by the wind, to feel oneself a bird about to fly—and then to drop down a sudden cliff of sand, to feel oneself as Ariel until legs sunk into the loose sands ten feet below.

And playing thus they reached the Valley of Winds, a place of great heat and silence, a veritable plain of the dead, an ossuary of bleached bones of rabbits and shells of snails, which must be crossed before coming to the sea whose crinkling blue was fused into the Atlantic azure.

He lingered behind her on the cool shore, to see with what grace she walked; and hastening to be beside her, was delighted by what he now knew to be her serenity. What a lovely girl she was, smiling and natural beside him. She was a Shakespearian heroine in quality, with the simplicity of naturalness. He wondered again, as they sat by a fire, what age she was, thinking that she was about twenty.

She had mentioned her father and her brothers, but never her mother. As they gathered more wood for the fire, which was now embers over which hovered sodium flames pale yellow in the sunshine, he said, "When these are burned, I think perhaps we'd better be moving on. I know well the feelings of a mother about her daughter staying out late."

"My mother is dead."

A pipit fluttered into the hollow where they sat, and alighted among the grasses. The sun would soon be resting on the rim of ocean. "She died when I was seventeen, during the war."

He calculated that, if her mother had died in 1918, she would now be twenty-four.

In silence he covered the embers of the fire with sand, and turned east along the shore of the estuary, where heavy waves were pounding the shingle. The wind blew fresh; the sun was burnishing the horizon; the light was bright gold, and very clear. Across the water the pebble ridge of Westward Ho! was distinct and grey. Windows of the houses on the hill beyond seemed to be on fire.

"Isn't it beautiful here?"

"Yes."

"Are you happy?"

"Yes."

"I am happy, too."

He picked up stone after stone and hurled them as far as he could into the waves. They walked now with the sun behind them, along the shore of the estuary. Everything was beautiful: every wet stone, every wave sweeping grey and aslant the pebbly shore;

the buoys marking the fairway; pink white clouds remote in the sky; their long halo'd shadows moving before them on the strand. Their feet crunched on wet shingle, past the black iron tide-ball at the top of its post; past the white wooden lighthouse rising out of the dunes; and as the sun's rim rested on the lilac heave of ocean they came to the narrow shingle-tongue of Crow, set with wooden mooring posts of gravel barges.

He tied his handkerchief to his stick, set it in the sand, and sat down beside her.

The lower half of the sun was now quenched in blinding fume upon the waters; the crescent moon revealed a point of light above its horn. The wind was dropping; the fume of spray was clearing; the fairway buoys were no longer leaning and wallowing. He waved his banner towards Appledore while they sat side by side in the sand, the spaniel between them, turning its gaze upon first one face then the other—his own feeling to be thin and brown with sharp, pointed features; Lucy's gently curved, her expression innocent as motherless Eve's when first she sat beside Adam. But no, he thought, with feelings that descended with the going-down of the sun, he was no natural Adam. Like his features, his mind had become too sharp; a mind stripped of normal flesh, like something hanging on the wire entanglements of the past, deathlessly, crying that by clarity alone could human un-understanding, the conditioner of all wars great and small, be removed forever from the mind of man.

The image felt upon his face was seen by Lucy, who after one glance became as though subdued; he felt it; he turned to her and said, "I must tell you, Lucy! I feel as though I am possessed by Willie! Do you see any difference in me?"

"I thought so, just now. You looked very anxious—sort of lost." She longed to say, You looked such a poor one, but forebore. I am a medium, he thought, I am an instrument of the dead.

The handkerchief fluttered on the stick. No boat came. He imagined the salmon-boat crews sitting in the inns, or resting in their cottage parlours. The top of the sun was now under the rim of the west. A green twilight held sky and water. Light suddenly flashed from the white tower.

"One would think that the idea of a lighthouse, when first suggested, would be welcomed by all men. But it wasn't."

She looked puzzled.

"To many land-dwellers on this coast a wrecked ship meant a lot of loot."

She sat quietly beside him, her eyes reflective. The spaniel, tired, was curled asleep in a hole it had dug in the sand. The air was quiet, except for the wash of wavelets receding aslant the shore.

"Ah, there's a boat putting out!"

They watched the small triangular sail, preceded by its wavering streaming image, crossing the wide lagoon of the Pool.

They sailed across as the water was beginning to move gently to the west, and in ten minutes were among lively bare-foot children playing and shouting. A hawker was selling fruit on a barrow. He bought three pounds of strawberries. Farther on stood the remembered black omnibus, with wooden forms for seats and an iron railing fixed above its sides to prevent passengers from falling off: the converted lorry in which Willie, Julian, and he had arrived there during the January of 1923.

They sat in the back seat, pulling strawberries off stalks with their teeth. He held out a particularly luscious strawberry for her to bite. She took it in her hand, saying, "Thank you." Then it was her turn to take a large berry from the bag; and after inspecting it, give it to him, saying, "Here's a nice one." Her upbringing, of course; but he felt slight disappointment that she hadn't held it for him to bite.

Lights were twinkling along Bideford quay when they got down from the bus, and set out to walk on the road above the tidal river gleaming below trees and rocks amidst muddy banks, until they came to the white gates of a drive on the right of the road. There he stopped, and before she could ask him in out of politeness—it was getting on for ten o'clock—he said, "Well, goodbye, and thank you for coming. I'll write what the farmer decides about the field. Oh, may I have your home address?"

He wrote it in his notebook, and saying, "Goodbye," was about to turn away when she said, "Won't you come in, I'm sure they're not all gone to bed——"

"Well, it's awfully late, thanks very much, and it will take some hours to walk back."

"I am sure we can fix you up with a bed for the night, if you're tired——"

He wanted to stay; he hesitated, while the thin thread of negation returned; and the foolish thought of the mouth-rejected
strawberry. Of course people of her sort didn't behave like that,
in public anyway; usually they never ate outdoors, in public——

"I think I ought to go back, thank you. Well, goodbye."

"Goodbye," the soft voice came through the dusk, and then he
was walking back beside the river, a weary dog at his heels. The
pubs in Appledore were closed, but not all the lights in the cottages
were out. He knocked at one, and after direction to someone in
Irsha Court, and a promise to pay five shillings, followed a bulky
form to the sands below the quay.

Midnight was striking as he clambered over the gunwale of a
salmon boat and was rowed to the Shrarshook, long and dark in
the half-ebb. There he waited for the water to lapse on the lighthouse side, imagining himself to be Willie waiting for boats
which never came on the *flowing* tide that late September night
of that fatal year, 1923. Supposing the tide didn't go all the way
out, but flowed back, unexpectedly, due to a distant earthquake;
and history repeated itself?

He thrust away the thought; it persisted. Was Willie beside
him? At the idea he felt reassured, that his cousin's spirit would
help him. He waited calmly in the noises of lapsing water, and
after half an hour or so began to pick his way among the pools
glimmering in starlight to the loose shingle of the shore. He
climbed a sandhill, and setting direction by the lighthouse over
his shoulder, set off for the hill down which he had run from Lucy
that afternoon.

The stars which had been at the zenith when he had gone down
to the quay at midnight had moved into the western hemisphere
when at length he got to the summit of the tangled track by which
they had earlier crossed the ridgeway. He realised that he had
come far out of his way. Too weary to move, he lay on his back
upon the bare rock, while the stars appeared to swim about the
sky. After a rest he sat up, forcing himself upon his feet despite the
heavy feeling in arms and legs; and turning round, descended to
the road. The spaniel was very tired; he lay and whined when
Phillip moved on. He was carried the couple of miles home, head
hanging over his master's shoulder. They arrived at the cottage as
cocks were crowing and the silhouette of the church tower was

sharp in cold eastern light. He carried Rusty upstairs and put him on his bed, to the purrings of Moggy.

Too tired to remove even his shoes, he lay down and slept.

Chapter 10

COUNTRY TALK

The farmer, he wrote to Lucy, was agreeable about the camping site for her Guides. She replied saying she was looking forward to coming in the second half of August, and thanking him for arranging it and for giving her such a splendid day. She felt rather guilty for allowing him to return so late at night after their walk, and hoped that he was none the worse for it.

Phillip was now writing regularly in the morning. He took Billy to the sands every fine afternoon, carrying him in the pack on his back like a papoose. Rusty came too, perched on the tank.

"Mind you don't go sparking, Mr. Maddison! I don't want my boy killed, you know!" said Zillah.

"That's right," added Mules. "Zillah, her loveth li'l Billy, proper li'l chap, dear li'l boy." He giggled as though with some secret thought.

Zillah was a tall girl about eighteen years of age, with long and lustrous auburn hair. She sang in the church choir, where her voice, which had a shrill harshness within the confines of the low-ceiling'd kitchen, sounded surprisingly clear and pure.

Nowadays he had his supper with the family in the kitchen. He was usually on the defensive, assuming a fire-cracker personality to dissemble his real feelings. They were obviously curious about what Zillah once referred to as his young lady, challenging him on that occasion to deny that he had one.

"I have several friends, men and women, and treat them all alike."

"I bet!" cried Zillah.

He replied often nonsensically; good-natured scorn and repres-

sive ridicule became the attitude of mother and daughter to most
of the things he said. Mules acted as soother and peacemaker,
with the frequent comment, "You'm a funny man, Mis'r Mass'on.
What things you do zay, you'm a funny man, you be!" after
Zillah's excited treble had rung out with her usual half-laughing
challenge of, "It's a dirty lie, Mis'r Mass'on, what you be telling
us! Tidden true, you know, is it? Us knows better than that old
flim-flam you'm always telling!"

"Well, it is possible that the original of 'walking on water' was
the equivalent of our 'walking on air', to express spiritual happiness——"

Mrs. Mules, arms across wide bosom, would rock a little in her
chair at the top of the table and chant with a subdued excitement
akin to Zillah's, "Tidden true, you know! I won't have what
you'm telling! The high-up people knaw what they be doing,
don't you know that? They'm eddicated, you see, that is it!"

"Also, the Jacobean translation of the New Testament at times
takes poetic tales to be literal, not spiritual, truths."

"My wife be right, zur," Mules affirmed gently. "My wife hath
been in service with high-up people, my wife hath. She was cook
to Mr. Wigfull the lawyer in to Queensbridge, do 'ee know that?"
His voice was now very quiet and respectful. "Mr. Wigfull, the
lawyer. 'A knoweth everything about everybody, Mr. Wigfull did,
a local praicher 'a were, next to the parson in the church. 'Tes
true as I be sitting yurr. It be!"

"Yes!" burst out Mrs. Mules, memory reanimating her to
produce words in a series of little gasps.

"You see, Miss'us had a parrot too once—and Polly knew more
than you would think Polly would have the sense to knaw! I tell
'ee, this be true—not made up flim-flam like you'm telling! Mrs.
Wigfull—her came into my kitchen one day, and she sot down on a
chair—and un-beknown to Miss'us one of the maids had stood
down a dish of butter on it—and as Miss'us stood up agen with a
cry, Polly Parrot calleth out, 'Missis's arse! Missis's arse!', for
Polly knew, you see, what had happened! And that's as true as I'm
sittin' yurr! 'Missis's arse. Missis' arse!' Polly called out!"

"That's right," murmured Mules, standing behind his wife's
chair. "That be true, zur. My wife's quite honest. My wife wouldn't
tell a lie to save her zoul, noomye! And my wife hath known
high-up people. High like. High."

"Well, it depends on what you mean by 'high', Muley dear."

He continued, slightly parodying Mrs. Mules' way of speaking, "I came across Mr. Wigfull in Queensbridge, and he was certainly 'high'! Wigfull! Wigfull of what? As you know, a wig is made of wool, a lawyer's wig anyway. So what can it be full of? Fleas?"

"What be you chatterin' about now?" cried Mrs. Mules. "My dear zoul, what be 'ee about? Tes high-up people, don't you zee, what us be talkin' about now! That be the name—Wigfull, you see —Mr. Wigfull, the lawyer to Queensbridge!"

"I meant 'high' in the sense of having been dead for some time, like a pheasant before it goeth into the oven."

"That's right," Mules hastened to explain, "that's what'm be. Highups. What us calls yurrabout highups. Highup like."

"How did they get to be high up? By crawling? And high up what, Muley dear?"

"Aw, you'm pretending you don't knaw what a highup person be!" cried Mrs. Mules. "Do you zee any green in my eye?"

"Ah, now I know what you mean! They climb as high as they can, like those village chaps on the green cliffs after gulls' eggs!"

"Aw, tidden no sense what you'm telling'! First it be wigs, then it be fessans, now it be gulls' eggs!"

Patiently Mules tried to explain. "High-ups, that's right. High-up Tories they be. Conservatives like."

"They all vote Tory!" cried Zillah. "Now do you understand, Mis'r Mass'n?"

"That's right!" murmured Mules. "Tories they be. Tories. Unionists, like."

"Stories? Do all high-ups write stories? Wigs full of stories— or fleas?"

"You'm talkin' like a proper mazed man!" cried Mrs. Mules. "And mind 'ee don't upset the babby, rinning about like you be on that noisy ole motor-bike of yours!"

"Yes, you look out you don't hurt the baby, Mis'r Mass'n! Or you'll hear from me! They say in the village you'm riskin' the little dear's life, sparking about so fast as you du!"

"Zillah be right, you know," said Mules, soothingly.

"Who says that?"

"Aw, don't 'e say nought, Zillah, don't 'ee say a word, for goodness' sake."

"It be Miss Seek, the churchwarden, if you want to know, 'Mis'r Masson'!"

"Ah, the lady who proposed to have cousin Willie prosecuted for blasphemy!"

"Don't you say 'twas Zillah what zaid zo, will you, zur? Tidden no business of ours. I don't know reely, 'tes only what I've heard, you see. Heard-like, while I was paring th' grass i' th' churchyard. 'Tes only what I heard. Zo plaize don't zay I said zo, wull 'ee?"

"They said your cousin was a Communist," declared Zillah.

"Aw, 'tidden no odds what some people zay!" cried Mrs. Mules. "They'm always talking about this and that, don't 'ee zee? Talk goes away light."

"That's right!" Mules said, gently. "Mother, her be quite right, you knaw! Mother be honest, you knaw, without a word of a lie. Her was cook to Mr. Wigfull, a proper gen'l'man. Wigfull. Wigfull, like."

"Don't you go about saying nought about Miss Seek, mind!" cried Zillah.

"I don't even know her. Anyway, what is a Communist?"

"A Red!" said Zillah.

"Muley has a red head, so have you—are you Communists?"

"Us ban't what your cousin Willie was! He was a proper Bolshy!"

"Don't you go 'bout zaying Feyther be a Communist, now!" said Mrs. Mules.

"By 'red' I meant a joke, Mrs. Mules. Not 'red' in politics, but red in hair and bicycle! William the Conqueror had red hair, the finest colour in the world."

"A joke be half a lie!" challenged the bright-eyed Zillah. "Ban't it Mis'r Mass'n?"

"I wish I knew," he replied, taking up *The Manchester Guardian Weekly*.

"'Tes all this yurr studying of books, you'm always studying of books, studying, reading of books like! You be a funny man, he-he, 'red hair', that's right, 'red hair'. Poor old Muley, you say I be, poor old red-haired Muley, poor old gravedigger I be."

"I love you, dear Muley, Your hair is so warm, And if I don't rag you, You'll do me no harm."

"Don't you cheek Feyther!" challenged Zillah. "Or I'll scatt 'ee, I will."

"Then I'll scatt 'ee, Zillah!"

"Go on, try it!"

It was innocent fun, they were kind and gentle people; he ragged about and played the fool to avoid his inner difference, and despair that he was betraying Barley. Zillah had a serious side, he realised, when she called at his cottage for his washing one evening after choir-practice.

"Would you like me to clear up this mess?" she asked, in a quiet voice.

He looked up and saw she was puffing nervously at a cigarette.

"Yes, it's a proper muddle, isn't it?"

"When that young lady comes down with her Girl Guides, what will she think of Mother and me, to let you keep your place like this?"

"Oh, I'll clear it up before then, Zillah. Anyway, I don't expect she'll come here. She'll be fully occupied with her Guides. Just a moment, I'll get my light cotton breeches. Do you think your mother would wash them for me?"

"Yes, that will be all right. You won't be late for supper, will you? Mother doesn't like having to put it back in the oven."

"I'll be over at eight sharp." He looked up, and saw her looking at him seriously. "I won't be late," he said, "I promise."

"Mother worries when the food is spoiled, you see."

He missed Lucy, and the idea to see her grew until he could think of nothing else. Without telling anyone he set off early the next afternoon. The weather was fine, the motor-bike ran fast along the curving road to Exeter and beyond, rushing up the hill outside Honiton to the high ground of Dorset with the sun behind the rider. Over the downs and past the heaths with their pine trees and soaring kestrels, through forest land with views of the sea until he turned inland for Shakesbury.

After some searching and enquiry he discovered the house down a turning off the road. As he slowed by the gate, he saw a long and narrow cycle-car standing close against the bank. It had a body like the fuselage of a two-seater aircraft. Dismounting, he touched the fins of the air-cooled engine. They were cold. He peered through the hedge. Which gate should he enter by? There were two: the first consisted of double doors, over which he peered,

seeing an empty yard; the other, of iron and painted white, led
to the front door a score of yards down the lane.

He decided to try the double doors. Pushing one open the first
thing he saw was a canoe lying in a shed among empty flower pots.
Beyond outbuildings were the walls and roof of the house. He
waited. Shouldn't he have written to say he was coming? What
would they think of him, barging in like this? Then feeling that
he was about to invite his own dissolution, he went down the lane,
opened the iron gate, walked up to the little glass-covered porch
before the inner door, and pulled the bell-handle. A fat black
spider ran agitatedly out of the wire-hole, but no bell-tinkle
followed.

Having watched the spider well away to safety, he tapped discreetly on the glass door. No one came. He tapped again. There
being no reply, he opened the outer door and stepped into the glass
porch. Spiders' webs nearly covering the panes were thick with
blue and green fly-shells. Several walking sticks, some bored by
the death-watch beetle, stood in an upright drain-pipe in one corner, with an umbrella whose faded cover was green with age. He
rapped sharply on the inner door, which was open. A noise behind
caused him to turn. He saw the bespectacled face of a young man
disappearing behind the open door of a potting-shed down the
garden path. He waited, then knocked on the door again; and
looking round, saw the same face disappearing in exactly the same
place. He determined to knock once more, and if nobody came
this time he would go away.

While he waited he heard a noise as of stealthy footfalls and
whispering coming down the dim passage in front of him.

"Anyone in?"

There was no reply. He was about to leave when he heard footfalls coming down the stairs. The next moment the face of Lucy
showed genuine surprise, followed by warmth and pleasure. She
came forward with blushing cheeks and said in her soft voice,
"Hullo."

"How do you do," he said.

"Won't you come in? My brothers are about somewhere."

"I think one must be in the potting shed."

"Oh, that's Tim. He's fixing up a model electric-light plant
for Pa to watch a spider at night by."

Smiling now, she led him through a room, which at a glance

seemed to be full of animal-skulls and portraits of men and women of a bygone age, and into another room.

"Won't you sit down. I'll tell Pa you're here. He's gardening."

"Oh, please don't! I can't stop very long, really!" He sat down on the sofa, the covering of which was worn. It was broken in one corner.

"I think you'd be more comfortable in this corner—it's rather dumpy at that end," she said.

"I was looking at the cycle-car outside."

"Oh yes, that's the Tamp!" She laughed softly. "You have to be very careful at corners, else it turns over!"

He noticed many small paper-covered boys' adventure stories lying on the table and the floor. There were several Wild West magazines, and issues of *The Model Engineer*.

"Pa and the boys are keen on engineering," she said.

"What does the model electric-light plant run on?"

"Oh, steam I think."

"Won't the spider be disturbed by it all?"

"Oh, it's only an idea of Tim's! He made the generator himself, you see, and Ernest made the steam-engine, so they're keen to see it working."

How lovely she was, sitting opposite him, with her grey eyes and vivid colouring, her friendliness and naturalness.

At that moment the figure of an old man moved past the open window, a shapeless tweed hat on the back of his grey head. There was no collar on his shirt. His ancient tweed jacket hung loose from thin shoulders. When he came into the room, Phillip saw that he wore a very old pair of navvy's corduroy trousers, worn thin above the left knee as though he had spent much time sitting with crossed legs, while his tweed jacket was frayed above the pockets, indicating that he spent more time standing about with his hands on his hips.

"Hullo, hullo," he said, with uplifted chin and direct glance of kind grey eyes. "I've been gardening. Nothing but confounded weeds in our garden. As fast as one patch is cleared, the beastly things grow up again. You fond of gardening?"

"My seeds never come up, sir."

These words produced laughter, in which Phillip joined. Then, feeling it was a propitious moment to leave, he looked at the watch on his wrist, and pretended to surprise. "Heavens, it's six o'clock! Well, I must be going. Goodbye, sir."

"Goodbye to ye."

"Must you go?" said Lucy, outside the iron gate. He hesitated, and pretended interest in the cycle-car. "Is it yours?"

"Oh no, my brothers are going to sell it for a friend, who has gone back to Africa."

"I see. Well, I suppose I should be going back now."

"Must you go?"

"I don't *have* to! Only I don't want to be in the way!"

"Oh, but you won't be."

She led him through the wooden gates by the canoe and into the neglected garden.

Soon with a cloth he was drying and polishing knives and forks, while she washed up. When the job was done they went down the lane, and getting over a stone wall entered a wood above a river. This was one of her favourite walks, she said, as they sat down under a tree.

On returning to the house, he was invited to stay to supper. Soon he was feeling entirely at home, sitting at the table among them, the spaniel lying on the floor. So quiet, so friendly, so free— could any young men anywhere else in the world be so nice, an old gentleman be so merry, so natural, so courteously indifferent about the world in general, never bothering about things outside his house and garden? A tremendous admiration grew in Phillip for him, and he told himself he was indeed fortunate to have met with such a family.

For supper Lucy had cut a plate of bloater-paste sandwiches. A silver kettle stood on the table, heated by a spirit flame. Everyone made his own coffee, by pouring a tablespoonful of brown liquid out of a bottle, filling the cup with hot water, adding sugar and milk and leaving the next person to fill the kettle and put it on the stand to boil. Likewise with the sandwiches: no formality of helping someone else first; hands stretched out to take.

"Everyone pleases himself here," declared Mr. Copleston; and, as far as Phillip could see, pleased everyone else as well.

However, the last sandwich left on the plate was subject to ceremony. Four pairs of male eyes looked at it. "Odd man out!" said the youngest brother, who wore spectacles like the eldest. Immediately four coins were tossed into the air. By a process of elimination the sandwich was won. Without a word the winner was about to put out a hand to take it went the youngest brother exclaimed, "By Jove, wait a moment, I say! Our guest didn't toss odd-man-out!" Five coins were then tossed. Four of the losers laughed as it was grabbed and immediately eaten.

"If you don't take what you want in this house, you won't get anything," remarked the old man.

Phillip was looking forward to the washing up, to be alone once more with Lucy. This presented no difficulties, for as soon as anyone had finished eating he left the table, leaving Lucy to do the clearing-away. The table-cloth, she said, was left where it was, for breakfast. The salt cellars and pepper pots were also left.

He went happily with her into the scullery. The work seemed to be finished almost as soon as it was begun, and it was time to join the others in the sitting-room, where four grown men were sitting in silence, all reading. Only the youngest, who sat beside a pile of bound volumes of *The Model Engineer*, moved to make a place for the newcomers on the sofa. Phillip sank into the broken corner, content to sit beside his pretty girl.

After awhile he became interested in what the others were reading. Mr. Copleston, sitting in the only armchair, which had partly burst away from its frame, was intent on a small paper-backed booklet meticulously fixed on a brass-and-mahogany reading stand beside him. The youngest brother, solemn of face, was examining the blueprint of a wireless set. The middle boy, who was fair and good-looking, sat back in a creaking wicker affair and smoked reflectively.

"I say," said Tim, the youngest boy, in a soft whisper, to Phillip. "Must you really go back to Devon tonight? You can stop here if you like, you know. Please do, if you'd like to. We'd love to have you, really. There's a hammock outside in the veranda. Or you could have the chalet on the lawn if you like."

Phillip thanked him, and after awhile he and Lucy went outside, where they could talk the easier. It was decided that he should stay the night in the chalet, one side of which was open to the air.

He wanted to wear his best Indian cavalry drill breeches, washed, for when Lucy arrived with her Guides. They had been made by his London tailor, Mr. Kerr, in the autumn of 1918, when Phillip had been ordered to India, but the posting had been stopped owing to the Armistice.

When he arrived back he saw that Mrs. Mules had *boiled* his breeches. Giving them to him, with his other washing, neatly folded, she exclaimed before he could open his mouth, "I know what you be looking at, but 'tidden no good you saying naught! 'Tes what you asked Zillah for me to do! You told 'r I must boil'm, so I boiled 'm! And there you be, you see, 'tes no good you saying naught about it! I've done my best vor 'ee! You axed Zillah for me to boil'm in the furnace, an' I boiled 'm, and so you see it be no good you telling me they'm zamzawed, because I knows they'm zamzawed, see!"

Before Phillip could utter a word, Mules broke in, bobbing his carroty head with, "I'm sure my wife's been very kind to 'ee, very kind to 'ee. My wife hath always done her best to plaize ivryone, ivryone my wife hath; ivryone, like."

Phillip looked at the buckskin strappings. They were shrivelled, and had drawn the cotton cloth. Seeing him looking at them, Zillah cried in her ringing treble, "'Tes no use your saying anything, Mr. Maddison! Us knows all about you, and why you wanted to smarten up, so don't you say naught, for we won't believe it, see?"

He looked at his bill for the baby's board and his own. By a simple error in rural arithmetic the past week had been reckoned as eight days. He knew the Mules to be scrupulously honest and particular; it was merely a slip in calculation.

"Tes no gude you lookin' like that!" said Mrs. Mules. "You told Zillah I was to boil'm, so I boiled'm! You can't get over that, not with all your nonsense!"

"Are you sure I didn't tell Zillah that I wanted them fried? And while Jehovah worked to a seven-day plan, why does this village apparently work eight days in a week?"

But it was no good arguing. He went back to his cottage; and later in the afternoon went to see Mules, who was digging a grave in the churchyard, and made a man-to-man appeal on this question: "Are there eight days in a week, or are there seven? Would you just answer that chronological query?"

Perhaps Mules thought he was swearing; for with Christian humility appropriate to the place they were standing in he said, while tapping the thigh-bone of a previous tenant of the grave upon the handle of his shovel:

"My wife hath been very kind to 'ee, zur. Very kind my wife hath been. My wife hath done her best for 'ee, Mis'r Masson. I'm sure you know my wife hath."

"Your wife hath, I know. But will you please look at this piece of paper. I paid my bill exactly a week ago. Under the solar system, to which mankind endeavours to adapt itself in this vale of tears, there are seven days in a week——"

"Us have looked after 'ee proper, us don't mind what us does for 'ee, us'll do aught for the babby, Mis'r Masson, and for your Rusty old dog tew—*he-he*. I shouldn't by rights be laffin' in th' church-yard, should I? Don't 'ee tell his Reverence, will 'ee? There be Rusty, dear old dog, Rusty, surenuff, Rusty—dear li'l ole dog, dear ole Moggy, too. Moggy cometh often and my wife doth look after Moggy, when you'm gone, gone away, like."

"Yes, I know, I agree, I couldn't find nicer or kinder people anywhere; but just tell me this, Are there seven days in a week, or are there eight, my dear old wimbling machine?"

"I'm sure us does all us can for 'ee, all us can, my wife doth." *Tap tap* of the bone on the handle of the shovel. "When be 'ee goin' vor 'ave th' babby christened, zur? Tidden right, you know, people be zaying it ban't right. There was your cousin, beggin' your pardon, zur, there was Mis'r Will'um, you know what became of he, don't 'ee? Twas God's punishment, I did hear someone zay. Only don't 'ee tell anyone I told 'ee, wull 'ee?"

"Muley, my dear," Phillip said, as quietly as the gravedigger had spoken. "Do you not understand that a man may care for truth for its own sake? Do you remember what my cousin Willie said? The village thought that he was 'mazed'—but the village lives in a world actuated by suspicion, mental fear, distrust of self and therefore of neighbour. That is what my cousin was up against."

"I'm sure my wife hath always bin very kind to both of 'ee, very kind my wife hath bin, my wife," murmured the grave-digger.

Phillip amended the bill to seven days, and left it with the money under a saucer on the kitchen table.

At supper that night both daughter and mother blamed him for the underhand way he had altered the bill in pencil, instead of having the *honesty* to speak openly to them about it. His lips parted, but both women told him not to dare to say anything further. "Proper old praicher you be!" cried the daughter. "Us heard all about 'ee praiching to feyther in the grave 'a was digging!"

"Yes," he said, "I was quite wrong. I asked you to roast, boil and fry my breeches; and there are eight days in a week!"

Within a few minutes they were all laughing together, and in the excitement Rusty stole the Mules' cat's supper.

Later Phillip said, "Now I know why the Romans, who built straight roads, never came to Devon. They conked out, defeated by the Dumnonians, or Damnonians as they later became. They chucked in their hand at Exeter! And after that the Damns settled down for life as Dumms."

Lucy arrived with her Girl Guides, together with an older woman Ginny, who was in charge of younger girls, the Brownies. When they were settled in the camp Phillip called there with baby and spaniel, both of whom immediately became favourites. This visit was known by the time he arrived back at the Mules' cottage, and he realised the underlying resentment after he had told Mrs. Mules how his new friend thought Billy was a wonderful child.

"Pshaw! 'Er's set 'er cap at 'ee," said Mrs. Mules. "Can't 'ee zee that? 'Er don't want Billy, so much as 'er wants 'ee, but if you think——" Mrs. Mules was getting excited—"If you think 'er'll look after Billy better than us can, then why don't 'ee get 'er vor come and take on the job? I seen many like that in my time—as soon as baby be born they'm after folks like us to be wet nurses, just to save their own figures and go out into Society agen, and can't be bothered to feed their own babbies! Don't tell me! Why, any young leddy wanting a man will make a fuss over his babby, if he be a widower, and for why? To catch 'n, that be why!"

"Anyhow, she said that Billy had been very well looked after."

"There, you zee!" Mrs. Mules cried. "No one can zay us don't do our best to look after 'n, noomye!"

"Of course not, Mrs. Mules."

"You can 'Missis Mules' me, if you'm a mind to, but I'm telling 'ee to look out for yourself, my dear man! You'll be catched before 'ee knaws it, yesmye, you'll find yourself catched!"

"That's right, zur," murmured Mules, "My wife be quite honest."

He determined not to be affected by these remarks, while feeling that he was entirely responsible for the growth of familiarity. No reserve, as Mother had often told him.

Seeing his face, Mules chipped in, "Us be very fond of 'ee, zur, don't 'ee zee. Us wouldn't like vor 'ee to come to no harm. Harm, like. There be all sorts about today!" he giggled. "Zome high-up ladies do paint their faces, and wear short skirts, so I do hear!" This bold statement was followed by Mules bending almost double with subdued hilarity. "Mrs. Wigfull, 'er paints her face, zo I did hear zom'n zay, he-he-he."

"Have a fag, my dear old Wimbling Machine!" cried Phillip, offering his case. "You and I are above the gossip of the sergeants' cookhouse."

"Now don't you teach Feyther bad ways, Mis'r Mass'n!" cried Zillah. "We've read your book you know! We all know it was you, called yourself Donkin, didn't you, and that 'Pauline', who was she really? The fast thing!" She fired again. "Tes all lies, anyway, I reckon!"

Mules took the cigarette, and held it wobblingly to the match offered by Phillip.

"Well, I'll be off now, Mrs. Mules. Thanks for my sandwiches. I don't know when I'll be back."

"They say in the village that you're taking the Girl Guide mistress on the back of your bike!" Zillah challenged him.

"Only as far as Bideford, to visit her relations."

"I know—Commander and Mrs. Gilbert!" said Zillah. "Can you deny it?"

"My," said Mules, gingerly puffing, and blowing smoke through a round hole of his lips. "You be goin' up, you'm goin' among the high-ups, like. I'm sure I be very glad to hear it." He puffed gingerly at his cigarette: it was the first time he had smoked.

"Have a good time!" cried Zillah, as Phillip got up to go. "Us'll mind your son and heir for you, Mis'r Mass'n. Now don't go too fast, and have an upset with your passenger, will you?"

Mules took another delicate puff of the cigarette held at right angles between two fingers. "My, ban't you be goin' up! What times us be livin' in!"

"And don't 'ee forget that you've got another leddy and gentleman comin' vor zee 'ee, will 'ee? They'm comin' tomorrow, mind, so don't 'ee get hitched up with no young leddy an' forget all about Mr. and Mrs. Beausire," Mrs. Mules reminded him.

Martin Beausire had written to ask Phillip if he would find him lodgings, with a private sitting-room, for his wife and himself, for the next fortnight. Mrs. Mules had agreed to take them, and Phillip had already sent a postcard to tell Beausire this at his Fleet Street address.

Chapter 11

TOWN TALK

Martin Beausire was not on the fast midday train from Waterloo. Phillip went for a walk around the Great Field while waiting for the afternoon train. No Martin and wife. Later, having postponed his supper, he went to meet the nine-thirty p.m.; to return once again and apologise for the non-appearance of his guests.

"What sort of people be'm?" asked Mrs. Mules. "My dear man, I've a-had the cockerel ins and outs of the bodley since lunchtime!"

"Mr. Beausire is a very busy man, Mrs. Mules."

"So be I a very busy woman, my dear man!"

"And don't you forget it!" cried Zillah.

"That be true," put in Mules. "My wife be very honest, very honest, like."

No letter arrived the next day. At the end of the week Phillip insisted on paying for the lodgings. Then came a scrawled note saying that Martin and wife were coming on Saturday and reminding Phillip to have a taxi for him at the station.

There was only one in the village, a Chevrolet open tourer. It rained on the Friday night and all Saturday morning. Phillip went to see if there was a hood on the Chev and volunteered to repair the celluloid curtains with bits of an old hood, which he stuck across the holes with rubber solution. It was better than nothing. Once again he was waiting for the Waterloo train, in vain; and again in the afternoon. Then a telegram came saying that Martin was arriving at Victoria Road Station in Barnstaple, which was the

Great Western Railway terminus, at 7.18 p.m. Thither he went in the rattling pre-war taxi.

Martin's first words on getting out of the carriage with two heavy suitcases were, "The most ghastly journey! We might have been two characters in 'Outward Bound'. Look at your blasted weather!" The platform roof was gushing water from a squall. Phillip made to take his bags. "I'll manage these, my lad. Take the heavy one from Fiona. The latch is broken, so be careful, there are five hundred books inside."

Phillip took the bag from the very young and slender woman in a green cloche hat matching her eyes. "You don't know my wife, do you? This is Phillip Maddison. Come on." Wrapped in a heavy overcoat, Martin led the way to the barrier. "Is this the only taxi you could get?" he growled, glancing at the sagging hood of the Chevrolet.

"It's the only taxi in Speering Folliot, Martin."

"Then why didn't you get one in this town? There's Grinlings in the Square, and Pedler's."

"It's not far to go."

"Come on, girl, don't stand there as though this is a fashion show," he said to Fiona, who had hesitated. "There's no need to freeze to death." To Phillip he said, "I hope you've had the sense to order fires to be lit in both our sitting-room and bedroom! This blasted English weather," he moaned, trying to look through the small space left in the celluloid curtain on his side of the back seat. "What's this?" He pulled at the black material stuck on with rubber solution and it came away on his fingers.

"It wasn't very secure, rubber solution won't stick on celluloid, I'm afraid, Martin."

"You don't need to tell me that." He flapped his hand, shook it violently, the tacky black cloth stuck to his cheek.

"Let me sit where you are," suggested Phillip, removing the material. "The rain will beat against the curtain as we go beside the estuary." Martin moved up against Fiona. "Why are we waiting here?" he asked, unhappily.

"Aiy Aiy, I'll get'n started," said the driver. "My Gor', I 'opes it will spark! Tes a turrible drop o' rain us'v had last twenty-vour hours, zur."

Fortunately the engine started. Martin made further observations as they left the station yard.

"Your railway supplies the bloodiest food in Europe. The General Manager deserves to be drowned in a bath of his own Brown Windsor soup!"

"Isn't that a soap?"

"Soap or soup, the taste is the same."

"How's Fleet Street getting along?" asked Phillip, stopping the inrush of wind and water with the near side of his trench-coat.

"Good God," muttered Martin. "Here I am, having just managed to crawl for my life out of that stinking sewer, that cesspit which deals in the direct by-products of the creeping paralysis of our so-called civilisation—and the first thing I hear after arriving in Glorious Devon is, 'How's Fleet Street getting along?'" A paroxysm of coughing stopped further words.

Phillip looked at the supposed Mrs. Beausire, remembering that Beausire's mother had spoken of Martin's wife as *Ursula*. "It will soon clear up! This country is like that, grey and wet and suddenly open blue and shining!"

Martin's mouth was open, his eyes half-closed. He held up a hand for silence. After hesitation, an enormous sneeze shook him.

"There you are!" he turned to Fiona. "Why the hell didn't you bring my aspirin bottle?"

"I did, Martin. It's in my suitcase." She made as if to lift it from under her feet but Martin cried, "Don't open the damned thing here, for God's sake!" as there came a thunderous flapping of the hood. They were now going along the estuary road.

"It's the south-west gale," explained Phillip.

"Good God, do you think I thought it was an April shower?" said Martin.

"I can taste the salt!" cried Fiona, her eyes shining. "How lovely!" She seemed to Phillip to be extraordinarily young, with fair bobbed hair and a slim figure. She turned greenish eyes upon him. "I hope it will soon clear up, as you said. Martin is tremendously looking forward to walking under your guidance. He wants to write a book about walking in Devon while he is down here, and has waited for simply ages to talk with you."

"As long as he doesn't ask me about the human rat-runs of the publishing world," growled Martin. "If I hear one word about Fleet Street or the Stock Exchange I shall get out and take the next train back." Wrapping the collar of his greatcoat round his neck he appeared to go to sleep.

Zillah soon had a fire going in the sitting-room, where a clean laundered cloth was spread on the circular mahogany table, with the supper things and a bowl of flowers. Phillip sat there until the guests came down from upstairs.

"No fireplace in the bedroom," grumbled Martin. "Fifi, get them to put in hot-water bottles." He turned to Phillip. "Cold pork and cold prunes, is that the best you could do?"

Phillip felt like saying that if he had come a week earlier there would have been a cockerel of six pounds including the bones for him to gnaw. Zillah came to the defence.

"We didn't know when you were coming, you see, Mr. Beausire, else we would have had the roast duck ready. It's no good you blaming Mr. Maddison! When you didn't come at five o'clock, Mother didn't like to put it in the oven in case it got zamzawed like the cockerel Mr. Maddison ordered for you last week. It isn't his fault at all!" she cried in a voice slightly higher than usual in her nervousness before these London visitors. She fired another shot: "Last time you wrote and said you were coming you didn't turn up, you know!"

"Oh, I expect it was my making a mistake in the date," said Phillip. "You know how unreliable I am about letting you know when *I'm* coming back, Zillah!"

"Well, you're all here now, that's the main thing!" the young girl announced. "I'll bring along the soup. It's Mother's special soup, so mind you like it!"

Fiona whispered to Phillip, "What a perfectly sweet baby asleep in the cradle in the kitchen! Who's is it, the girl's?"

"It's mine."

"But, Martin, you didn't tell me that Phillip had a baby! What is it, a boy or a girl, Phillip?"

"A boy. Please don't say anything about it to the Mules."

They sat at table, Martin with back to the fire, writing a letter. Zillah brought in three plates of soup, Martin went on writing rapidly with a thick black fountain pen. Then putting it down, he tasted the soup. "My God, it's Brown Windsor!"

"That's where you're mistaken," said Zillah, entering unexpectedly. "It's Mother's special soup. I hope you like it, there's giblets in it."

"It tastes like mulligatawny to me," said Fiona.

"There's some of that in it, but that's not all," replied Zillah. "Mr. Maddison likes it, don't you, Mis'r Mass'n?"

"Beautiful soup, Zillah. If Mr. Beausire doesn't want his, I'll eat it for him." But Martin, having put aside his writing, was already sucking his down.

"Anyone like another helping?" enquired Zillah, coming in later.

"Would I not," said Martin, in a clipped, donnish voice, as he took the dark-blue writing paper pad to dash off another line before looking up to say, "What's that at the window?"

A black and white face, with staring green eyes, was looking through the lower panes of the casement.

"That's Moggy, Mr. Maddison's cat," said Zillah, arriving with the soup tureen. "She always comes in at the window. I expect Rusty will be here in a minute. Rusty's Mr. Maddison's spaniel," she explained. "Ever such a dear old dog. So's Moggy a dear little cat. They go through a hole in Mr. Maddison's door, they always know when he comes back, and wait for him in there. That's more than we do, sometimes!" she cried, turning her head as she went out to give Phillip a soft glance, which Fiona noticed.

"I believe Zillah's the mother of the baby!" she whispered to Phillip.

"Why not ask her?" suggested Martin, writing away.

"Yes, why not?" said Phillip, "and earn half-a-crown from *The People*."

Although he had grumbled at the idea of cold pork, Martin soon ate his helping, and pushing aside his plate, continued the letter writing. How crowded his brain must be, thought Phillip: he must live under pressure the whole time.

Having finished the letter, Martin said to Fiona, "Bed, Fifi my love," arid led the way to the kitchen. Phillip, sitting by the fire, was relieved to hear his jovial voice, amidst laughter, for a couple of minutes before their footfalls went up the stairs.

When they were in the bedroom, Zillah slipped in to say to Phillip, "I thought you told us Mr. Beausire had two daughters!"

"That's what he told me."

"Now he's just told us that it's his wife's nineteenth birthday! Funny goings on, if you ask me! She seems so shy, Mother says. Of him, I mean. 'Tidden right, you know, to pretend you'm married if you're not," mixing school-lesson English with her

native Devon dialect. "*Is* it, 'Mr. Donkin'? Yes, it's you in that
book you wrote, I know it, and you can't deny it. Can you?
You and your 'Pauline'! Wasn't she someone you knew at Folkestone? Admit it, now! Tell the truth and shame the devil! Come
on, Mis'r Mass'n!"

There was a bump overhead. "My lor', I hope Mr. Beausire's
not bangin' his young leddy about! I'd give any man a thumping
big bang if he tried any tricks on me, Mis'r Mass'n! Don't you go
treating *your* young leddy like that, will you?"

She came close, creamy cheeks and vivid red hair, teasing him.
Her face was so young and pretty that he kissed her. "S-sh!" she
whispered, looking round. "Don't let Mother or Dad hear you,
or they'll wonder what we'm up to, all alone in here." She
skipped out of the room.

Martin had left the writing pad face down on the sofa beside
his attaché case. Phillip thought it best to put the pad in the case,
and picking it up, saw in one glance the first words written in the
large, sprawling hand. Looking no further, he pressed the lock
buttons and slipped the pad inside.

Zillah returned. "Anything I can get for you, Mis'r Mass'n?"

"No thanks, Zillah. I think I'll go to bed. Good-night!"

He left thinking that if he hadn't seen the beginning of Martin's
letter he might have kissed Zillah again: thank heaven he hadn't,
in the circumstances.

In the morning the sun was shining. Martin was almost a
different man.

"We've had breakfast. We want to get out as soon as we can!"

"I imagined you'd be sleeping late. Still, I can do without
breakfast. Where do you want to go?"

"It's your country, you lead on and we'll follow." Martin
delved into his attaché case, took out a stamped addressed envelope and put it in his pocket.

"Where's the post office?"

"Mules will take it." As Phillip had anticipated, Martin wanted
to post it elsewhere.

"Shall we be going near a village?"

"Yes, at Broccombe. By the way, there's our otter hunt ball
next week. Would you and Fiona care to come as my guests?"

The association of the words *hunt ball* had a distinct effect on

Beausire: he spoke like a gentleman. "My dear Phillip, it's most kind of you, but we've both got to go back on Sunday." He became himself again. "Hell! Back to that stinking little office, half as big as an early Victorian lavatory, literally no room to turn round in, the boy coming up every afternoon at four p.m. with a cup of cold tea half-swimming in the saucer with smuts and drowning flies. Let's get out while we can, for God's sake!" as Fiona joined them. "Where are you taking us, my lord?"

"Up over the fields to the high ground and round the coast to Broccombe, if that will suit you."

The walk was at first enjoyable. Then it formed into the previous pattern: Martin continually asking questions about country matters, Phillip supplying the answers until he grew weary of Martin's search for information and lagged behind for Fiona to catch up to him.

It was now Fiona's turn to seek information.

"Tell me, Phillip," she began, while Martin tore alone into the morning. "Is your partner at the otter ball the Girl Guide mistress that the Muleses told me about before breakfast?"

"I haven't had any breakfast, so I can't really say."

"The Muleses say that you are interested in her, and that she's a foreigner. Does she speak English?"

"A few words, now and again."

"Where is the camp?"

"Beyond those pine trees on the horizon."

"She's been here before, so Zillah said."

"She came with me to view the site."

"Are you having an *affaire* with her? Why don't you answer, Phillip? There's no harm in having an *affaire*, is there?" persisted Fiona.

"It depends on all sorts of things, I suppose."

"What do you mean by that?"

He walked on faster, then lagged for her to catch up, having recalled to mind Martin's opening sentence in the letter he had written at the supper table the night before. *Dear Ursula, I am down here alone with Phillip, being bored blue*——

"How old is this girl, Phillip?"

"Oh, extremely old, like good port. You know, any port in a storm."

"What is her name?"

"Lucy."

"That doesn't sound like a foreign name to me."

Martin obviously had keen hearing, for he shouted over his shoulder, "'Foreigner' is a local name for anyone living a mile or two away. I told you that, coming down in the train!" He waited for them. "Both you and I are 'foreigners' to any Devon village chawbacon."

"Where does Lucy come from, Devon?" continued Fiona.

"Her people live in Dorset, I think."

"What do they do?"

"They're gipsies, always on the move."

"Are you joking?"

"I mean, of course, when they're not 'in residence'."

"What's that bird flying over there, a goose?" demanded Martin, as they walked on, more or less in line.

"That's a heron."

"I thought herons lived by water?"

"They fish in water, but not while in the air."

"Of course I know that, you ass, but what's it doing here?"

"Well, what are we doing here?"

"But we're not fishing, are we?" said Fiona.

"Nor is the heron."

"If you can be serious for a moment, Fifi, I'd like to hear from Phillip why the heron is up here on the moor, with no water about so far as I can see."

"It's probably flying from the Fuddicombe reservoir to the Speering Folliot duck-ponds, Martin."

"But why, Phillip?" asked Fiona, her eyes opened wide.

"To catch fish to eat, obviously," said Martin.

"There are rainbow trout in the duck-ponds."

Noises of cawing floated down. "Why are those crows flying after the heron?"

"Oh, just chivvying it away from their territory, Martin."

"But *do* crows own land, Phillip?" asked Fiona.

"Of course they do," replied Martin. "Everything owns land, or water."

"Fish, particularly lobsters, are very religious, Fiona."

"How do you mean?"

"Well, Victor Hugo in one of his novels speaks of the lobster as 'the cardinal of the sea', doesn't he?"

"Did you know that, Poogs?" she said to Martin.

"Of course I knew it. Everyone knows it."

"But why 'cardinal'?"

"Because it's red. You've eaten lobster, you ought to know."

"The point is that it's not red in the sea. It's blue, except for the tips of its feelers," explained Phillip.

"Then why call it a cardinal, that's what I don't understand?"

"Why do you wear a green hat, when your lips are red?" asked Phillip.

"But I'm not a lobster! And I still don't understand why, if a lobster is blue when in the sea, it is called a cardinal."

"A literary floater," said Martin.

"But surely lobsters live on the *bottom* of the sea? Tell me, Phillip, I really *do* want to know!"

"There are many theories why the lobster's feeler tips are red. Some say to attract fish, others that the red draws light through the water to renew sensitivity, possibly smell, or perhaps sense of touch while actually not touching, like wireless waves. All I know is that they are red at the tips. Victor Hugo made a slip when he called a lobster 'the cardinal of the sea'. That's all."

Martin strode on ahead, visualising the scene of the next chapter of his novel, wherein the hero, misunderstood and married to a famous titled Society beauty, would go to Devon with his secretary, who was in love with him. The hero's sense of correct behaviour and good form—Eton and Balliol—forbade him even to think of platonic love with the young woman; so they slept in separate cottages.

Martin Beausire had been educated at a small public school for the sons of middle-class parents. He wrote his biennial novels in the train to and from Fleet Street; everything he did, everyone he met, was *pot pourri* for him. His aristocratic heroes existed, invariably lonely, in a world of *nouveau riche* cads, poor bounders, and middle-class thrusters.

Having digested the cardinal of the sea, Fiona thirsted for more human information.

"Where exactly in Dorset do Lucy's people live, Phillip?"

"Near Shakesbury."

"What is her name?" demanded Martin. "Copleston? That's one of our West Country family names," he explained to Fiona. "It goes back to the Conquest. The Saxon Booscers were here before them, of course, Cruwys' *Wessex Worthies* mentions that we were hereditary food-tasters to the Saxon kings. Beowulf the Booscer was given an earldom by Ethelred the Unready."

"Poor chap, he deserved his title, always having to eat zamzawed food!" cried Phillip.

Ignoring what he considered to be a Cockney exhibition of bad taste, Martin took another line. "Shakesbury! Good God, that brings back memories! I used to hunt the hare all over that country when I was an usher at Milborne," he went on, his voice sounding terse under a stiff upper lip. "Before that swine Markton sacked me for saying I was condoning pederasty because I pleaded with him not to sack three boys for taking the usual adolescent interest in their own anatomy and its prospects."

"What is pederasty, Poogs?" asked Fiona.

"Sodomy."

"But I'm no wiser now, Poogs."

"You don't need to be."

"Wasn't Milborne the scene of *Warp and Woof* by——" began Phillip.

"If you want to talk about books and authors, talk to Fifi, she knows nothing about either," Martin replied, as he strode on ahead.

"Tell me more about Lucy, Phillip. Is she very pretty? How does she do her hair?"

"In ringlets."

"But that's very old-fashioned, surely?"

"It's the fashion down here."

"Are you serious?"

"You should see the grocer's wife, from Monday to Saturday. She regularly tears up her bedding in order to tie up her hair, which is about the same texture and quality as an Exmoor pony's mane, into hundreds of little blobs. She does this in order to look smart in church on Sunday."

"But I can't believe that *Lucy* wears her hair in ringlets!"

"Either that or an Eton crop."

"But that's the very latest West End fashion!"

"Not down here. Ever since Cromwell forbade Christmas puddings, the basins have been used, with sheep-shears, to crop hair."

Martin's cackling laughter arose in front. Phillip felt himself to be almost a wit.

"Do tell me," went on Fiona. "What colour are Lucy's eyes?"

"My God!" yelled Martin. "Never in all my life so far, which has been spent almost exclusively among half-wits, have I had to listen to such utterly footling questions! Here we are in God's own country and all you can talk about is human hair!" He proceeded at five m.p.h. to increase his distance from Fifi.

"When Martin's not out in the open air, and the sun, he is never really himself," she explained.

"But he *is* in the open air and the sun!"

"What I mean is that he was very depressed when he arrived yesterday, because it might rain all the time. But to be serious for a moment. Is Lucy's hair *really* Eton cropped?"

Martin stopped. He pointed into the sky. "What's that bird?"

"A buzzard."

"What does it do?"

"Pounces on rabbits and rats. It's a hawk, one of the short-winged species."

"Its wings look long to me."

"Does it take the farmers' hens?" asked Fiona.

"No, but it will sometimes wait on walled hedges to take rats which come after the corn for the farmers' hens. Hello, I can see the Guides' campfire smoke! They're behind that wall, out of the south-west wind."

"I can't wait to see Lucy!" said Fiona.

Phillip was glad that Martin seemed to like Lucy; he was proud, too, of her bearing and her beauty. Martin seemed to be an entirely different man as he laughed and talked with a genially impersonal air. Just before they went on, Fiona invited Lucy to supper that night at the Mules' cottage.

"Phillip will fetch you, I'm sure, on his motor-cycle, and bring you back here afterwards, won't you, Phillip?"

"I feel we would interrupt Martin's work. He's really fearfully busy," he said to Lucy.

"I'd love to come, but I really think I should remain here with the Brownies," replied Lucy, blushing. "There are only two of us to look after the camp."

"Well, my dear," said Martin, patting her hand between his hands, "I am glad to meet a young woman with a sense of duty.

It's been most pleasant meeting you. Perhaps we'll meet again some other time."

"But why, Phillip," asked Fiona, when they were over the skyline, "didn't you want Lucy to come tonight? It would have made a nice foursome."

It was now Phillip's turn to walk on by himself.

Martin continued his quest for country detail after supper that night when he asked Phillip to read some of his short stories.

"Oh, they're pretty bad, Martin. After all, I wrote them a long time ago. Won't you let us hear what *you've* written while staying here? I am sure it would be extremely interesting."

"My work is not of the slightest interest to anybody, including myself. Yours, on the contrary, is. You are the only really dedicated writer I know, and must have plenty of guts to have broken away to face comparative poverty. And, since I've come two hundred odd miles especially to see you and to hear all you have to say, I'd like to hear your stories now."

He settled himself comfortably in the only armchair in the room, feet to fire.

Phillip read a story about a raven. Martin was enthusiastic. "That's your line of country! Why don't you publish your stories in one volume? They would go like stink. Read some more. Of course we'll wait while you go to your cottage! I could sit up all night listening to you on nature and the countryside, and I wouldn't say that to any other man or woman on earth."

When Phillip reappeared, Martin was snoring.

"Shall we wake him up, Fifi?"

"Why wake me up when I'm not asleep?" demanded Martin, opening an eye. "But before you start, let me change my position. There's a draught from the window."

He lifted his stockinged feet upon Fifi's lap. Delighted by this show of stability and affection in her first love-affair, Fifi began to massage them.

"For God's sake leave my feet alone!" growled Beausire. "I want to listen to Phillip, not tortured to death by your tickling. Get on with your reading, you prize genius!"

It was midnight when Phillip ended the fifth story, about a heron. His reading had been interrupted by occasional snores;

but whenever he had stopped Martin had cried, "Go on! Why the hell d'you keep stopping?"

"Because you were snoring, Martin."

"I never snore, you prize Ass!" and settling back with eyes closed, Martin began to snore again, deeply and consistently.

"He *is* asleep now, at any rate," whispered Phillip, putting down his manuscript.

"Don't be a bloody ass!" murmured Martin, half opening one eye. "Go on reading. What happened in the end to Old Grock the raven?"

"I finished the raven story three hours ago, Martin. Honestly, you've been asleep."

"On the contrary, I've listened first to the story of the raven, then the buzzard, followed by the crippled ex-soldier and the otter, and then Old Wog, or whatever his blasted name is, who emptied his crop of eels, snakes, toads, newts, and rats into the crops of his young, and we left him flying off to catch some more. I want to know what happened to him."

"That was the heron's story, and it's finished."

"Of course it's finished! Old Bog or Old Wog the heron is finished, like any other bloody fool who catches the 8.15 down to Brighton at night and the 8.58 to Fleet Street again the next morning until he becomes a corpse long before he dies. Old Sog or Old Tog or Wog or Jog or whatever his name is is finished, of course we know that, but what I want to know is, what happened to Old Crock in your first story? It ended in the air."

"Yes, it did. Old Krog flew away to a better land, after crying his eyes out because North Devon had become a land of portly pole carriers from Sussex."

"Then why the hell didn't you say so before?"

Martin yawned like an old dog showing a mouthful of irregular teeth. He stood up. "Bed, Fifi, my love! Goodnight, you blue-eyed Nog!" he said, hugging Phillip with one muscular arm. "And thank you for reading. Your stories really are first class. I really am most grateful to be allowed to hear them. Don't be late tomorrow, we leave here at 8.15 a.m. precisely, to go to Hartland. I want to see as much of you and your country as I can." He turned to Fifi. "We love our old Phillip, don't we, Fifikins, God knows why we do, but we do, don't we, my precious?"

as, still holding Phillip, he hugged Fifikins with the other arm and kissed her on the cheek.

"Before I say goodnight and sweet dreams, Phillip, *do* tell me why you wouldn't let Lucy come back with us tonight," said Fifi.

"Sh-sh!" as he pointed to the half-open door.

"But I don't understand! Surely the Muleses know about her?"

"Sh-sh! Please, Mrs. Beausire!"

"Do *you* know why?" she said, turning to Martin.

"I've not the slightest idea."

A smile broke over Fifi's face. "Ah, *I* know!" She touched the end of Phillip's nose with a finger, and whispered, "It's because of Zillah! Why, I believe you're a dark horse after all!" Her clear eyes became puzzled. "But *why* Zillah—when you can have Lucy? She is so lovely! And such a sweet person! Why don't you let her see Billy? My dear, if you really want her, all you have to do is to put that adorable baby in her arms!"

"Goodnight, you great big beautiful doll," said Phillip, kissing her on the cheek.

On the last evening, after supper—they had spent the day, by Chevrolet, at Hartland—Martin set about writing his weekly article, 'From the Cottager's Study', for a syndicate of provincial newspapers. The heavy portmanteau was opened and five or six dozen books laid on the table. Then various book-pages torn from *The Observer, The Sunday Times, The Saturday Review, The Outlook, The New Statesman, The Manchester Guardian Weekly, The Weekly Westminster Gazette* were spread on the floor about his feet. He took a book from the table and mused upon a page or two before turning them over faster until he almost struck them. *Flip-flip-flip*—he appeared to Phillip to be musing rather than reading, while his tongue was slightly protruded and curled against his upper lip as though it had an irritation upon the tip. *Flop*—the book was dropped on the floor, while reviews by other critics were examined. An average apparently having been struck, Martin made a critical cottage pie. An hour and a half passed in which a dozen reviews were written. "Bed, Fifi!"

"What do you do with all these books, Martin? Keep them?"

"Good God no! Where's your bookseller in Barnstaple?"

"There's one up Cross Street."

"Martin gets half-price for the best ones," said Fifi. "But the one's he's marked he uses for lecturing, don't you, Poogs?"

"Do you ever stop talking," growled Martin. "Our train leaves at eleven tomorrow morning. You did order the taxicab to come early, as I asked you, I suppose, Phillip?"

"Yes, Martin. It will arrive outside at ten o'clock sharp. That will give you bags of time to dispose of the books——"

But Martin was already thumping upstairs to bed.

Phillip saw them off at the junction. Martin's face seemed leaner as he stood by the open carriage door.

"I'll see you again?" he said between his teeth. "Don't heed my gruffness—we both love you. Come and see us at Worthing. Bring your adorable Lucy with you." He jumped in as the whistle blew, and sitting down in a far corner, opened a paper.

Phillip stood on the platform, watching the guard's van round the curve of the line. Dear Martin, dear Fifi.

He walked to the end of the deserted platform, and made up his mind to ask Lucy Copleston to be his wife.

For the dance Lucy had been invited to join the Master's house party, and to his surprise Phillip received an invitation as well. A score of guests, most of them young people, assembled to dine in the tall room, once the refectory of a monastery. Footmen, wearing livery for the occasion, stood against the walls panelled in dark oak to the ceiling; faces glowed in the flames of branched candelabra on the long table.

Afterwards they were driven, in several motors, to the Assembly Rooms in the town a dozen miles away.

The hour after midnight seemed to pass very swiftly, both on account of the champagne he had drunk and because he seemed to have been talking, as he and Lucy sat at the top of some stairs, about everything except what he wanted to say.

At the end of an hour he was exhausted, and talking wildly; while Lucy sat there with pale face, unable to help a mood that was, by its very nature of exhaustion, not to be helped by words. At last he arrived at the unadorned point with, "Lucy, would it be awful if I said to you, 'Will you marry me?'"

She replied, "Yes, didn't you know already?"

"That it would be awful for you?" he laughed.

"Oh, I didn't mean it that way!"

"Will you marry me?"

"Yes."

She looked pale.

"Thank you," he said.

They sat unmoving for a few moments. "Shall we go and have a drink?"

She said, "Yes, certainly." She, too, was exhausted; she waited while he finished his whisky and ginger ale, and said she would see him in the ballroom in a few minutes.

"Oh, I've left my bag on the stairs!"

"I'll fetch it."

He hurried away. Where they had sat were a young man and woman, arms round one another's neck, kissing. Lucky young people, not to be in love! They moved politely apart. He apologised for his presence, saying that his partner had left something there. Recovering the bag, he took it to her, thinking that he had not yet kissed her. Had he acted from his head only, and not from his heart?

While she was away he drank more whisky, and on her return took her to the supper room and gave her some food. They both cheered up; he danced with her, while happiness began to flow in to fill the vacuum of the past hours.

"Don't tell anyone, will you?"

"No, my dear, I won't."

"You called me 'my dear'!"

She looked at him steadily. "Well, aren't you my 'dear'?"

"Am I?"

"I only hope you won't be disappointed in me. I'm not clever at all, you know."

"Nor am I. I'm often a terrible fool!"

"We'll be just ourselves, won't we?"

"Not *all* the time!" he laughed.

Too soon *The Post-Horn Gallop* sent them racing with others round the floor. The dance was over!

"I wish it were just starting!"

"It's been lovely!"

The next day, saying goodbye to the family at Arleigh, he set off with Lucy to her camp. She rode behind him on a cushion strapped to the carrier. They avoided the main area of the village by taking a side-lane which came to the Great Field, where he stopped to tell her that the villagers thought him a little mad. Unknown to him, Lucy had absorbed his mood, which he had cast off in the telling of it; and when they arrived at his cottage she walked past the open doors of the neighbours unspeaking, her eyes on the ground. He left her in his kitchen with the gramophone while he went to enquire if Mrs. Mules would prepare an omelette for two.

That excellent woman at once asked who it was, and he said, "Miss Copleston, who is a Mistress of the Dorset Girl Guides."

"Tidden true!" cried Zillah, with sparkling eyes. "I reckon you're the Guide, Mr. Mass'n. Tell the truth and shame the devil, is it the same young lady?"

"Yes, it is," he replied sharply, in his nervousness. "Do you mind?"

"I don't trouble who it is!"

"Right, we'll be down at one o'clock."

"And mind you see that she turns up this time!"

The feeling of constraint remained when he returned with Lucy down the lane to the gravedigger's cottage. Dreading possible remarks, he did not introduce her to either woman. It was therefore an uneasy meal, served almost in silence by Zillah, while Lucy kept her eyes upon the table.

Afterwards he took her to his cottage, and going round the back way for a word with his neighbour—"Don't you think my friend is lovely?" he found Zillah already there.

"Copleston—well, us don't think her's much cop, her didn't say good morning like a proper young leddy would!"

This was both hurtful and humiliating, and he tried to explain that his guest was shy.

"Shy!" said his neighbour. "What—be 'er too shy to say good morning? 'Er thinks 'er's too grand for us, I reckon!"

It was useless to try to explain: he realized afterwards that he should have taken Lucy to see them then and there; but at the time felt hurt that they had so misjudged her. This led him to say to Lucy that "some people in the village are a bit narrow-minded". Then he said, "If perhaps you could say 'Good-morning' to them——" and then was startled when she stopped, with reddening cheeks, and broke into tears.

"Lucy, please forgive me! It is every bit my fault!"

"I have let you down," she wept, her head turned away.

"No, I was stupid and nervous! Of course, I should have introduced you in the first place. Really, it is all my fault."

He was startled and dismayed by her tears, for she had told him that she had cried only once in her life, when her mother had died.

He walked beside her, while thoughts of his own failure made him numb, and apart from her. Lucy was similarly unhappy. In her modesty she had no feelings of superiority to the Mules, who had thought that she had scorned them as servants, and so beneath her. She should have said good-morning to them, she knew, but had waited for a lead from Phillip, because she was his guest. Now she felt that she had behaved badly, and had spoiled it all for him.

They walked back to the camp, seldom speaking. There they said goodbye, Lucy to walk on with feelings of grief at her own stupidity, Phillip to return, damning himself for having ruined her holiday.

That evening he went back to the camp, and found the site empty. He had forgotten that it was their last day. What must she think of him?

After a sleepless night he filled his pack, settled Moggy on top of his shirts, and with Rusty on the tank, set off for Dorset.

Part Four

DOWN CLOSE

'Oh, we don't bother about anything here.'
Saying of Adrian Copleston, Esquire

Chapter 12

PA AND THE BOYS

During the days that followed he never ceased to wonder at the happy feeling in the house above the river. He told himself again and again that he was very lucky to find himself the friend of the kind of family he had thought never to exist outside a picaresque novel. In that house, where Lucy looked after three grown-up brothers and an old father there was an ease and a kindness, an absence of fuss and social convention that were entirely new in his life. He learned from Lucy that they had very little money; and the unconcern about this seemed to him to be ideal. This was, if not Liberty Hall, at least Liberty Lodge. Meals were at no regular times. If one brother were absent, the others tossed Odd Man Out for his portion. If the absent one came in late, Lucy would drop whatever she was doing, and either cook something for him or cut bloater-paste sandwiches to be served with a cup of Bivouac coffee—the dark liquid from the bottle with the label of a kilted soldier in parade dress sipping a cup beside a camp fire. How poor they were he could not decide: certainly the house was full of objects and portraits denoting a different past.

He began to wonder if he could be of help to them. This feeling came to him on the fourth day of his stay, when as lunch-time approached he discovered Lucy in the dark larder, with Bukbuk the cat and four growing kittens mewing about her feet, while she gazed at the shelves, and after awhile said, "Bother, I don't know what to give them. There just isn't anything. Bukbuk has eaten the rest of the cold mutton. Oh dear, and she's been at the rabbit pie, too."

On the shelves, beside innumerable empty bottles and jam-pots, were two large cold potatoes on a plate; scraps of pastry around the dish of rabbit pie; the crater of a Stilton cheese within a blue-and-white Wedgwood cover; half a loaf of bread, and some mildewed crusts in a box.

"Bother," she repeated. "I don't know *what* they can have for lunch. There's bloater paste, but they are going to have that for supper. Oh well, I suppose they'll have to have potato soup."

"Give me just ten minutes!"

He ran to the Norton, and leaping on, went into the town to return with several pork pies, a bottle of sherry, a Dundee cake, and four pounds of tomatoes.

Lucy had told him that the dining-room was being converted into an office (for what he did not ask) and so meals were taken in Mr. Copleston's study, a small room with scaling blue colour-wash on the walls and filled with books to the ceiling against one wall, while along another stood a cupboard with guns behind glass, cabinets of shells, coins, and birds'-eggs. The third wall held family portraits and faded photographs, swords in cases, horned heads, and other relics of a sporting past.

By the window stood Mr. Copleston's desk, with blotting pad almost covered with ink, paperweights, a spring balance, a brass duck's head with ruby eye holding down bills, and a tray of faded pens.

On the round table, still covered by the table cloth, Phillip set pork pies and tomatoes, while Lucy pulled lettuces from the garden and washed them under the rotary pump. Phillip found some Waterford wine-glasses and polished them, afterwards setting them on the table. Lucy brought in a silver tray engraved with coat-armour, holding cream jug and sugar bowl; and after lighting the spirit flame under the kettle on the stand she went outside to beat a gong which hung near fox masks mounted on oaken shields along the passage wall, while Phillip examined sporting prints dating from the eighteenth century. Among them were engravings of a garrison hunt in Ireland; and the portrait of a young man with side-whiskers and sensitive face, who was, Lucy had said, her mother's father. Cobwebs linked them. The stair-carpet was more earth than carpet, with several rents in it, and no wonder, for the Boys thumped up and down in nailed boots and shoes.

The gong sounded gently. They waited for a few moments, while he stroked her cheek with the back of his fingers. "Perhaps Pa didn't hear," she said, taking his hand. "He's a bit deaf."

Phillip went to where Mr. Copleston was digging. "Lucy says lunch, sir!"

"Eh, lunch? Good idea!" He stretched his back. "One gets too beastly stiff, nowadays," he muttered. Phillip followed him into the room. "Ha!" The old gentleman eyed the food. "Pork pies!" He sniffed appreciatively. "H'm," he looked at the sherry, then at Phillip, with a genial look in his grey eyes. "Your doing, I suppose? Well, no objections from me! I'll go and wash my hands."

Phillip went to the door of the workshop, seeing the Boys at treadle lathes, apparently turning some brass parts. "Lucy says 'Lunch'!"

The treadling ceased.

"Ah, lunch!" Ernest, the eldest, spoke as though to himself. He surveyed a slide-rule critically, and went on making notes on a piece of paper beside a blueprint.

"That's absolutely splendid news!" exclaimed Tim. "Lunch, by Jove, Fiennes!"

Fiennes, fair of hair—his two brothers were dark, like Lucy— said nothing as he threw a file on the bench and left the workshop.

Phillip returned to Lucy. They waited happily while Pa came slowly down the stairs and seated himself in the chair at the head of the table. Phillip held Lucy's chair for her, and then sat down beside her. Meanwhile Pa had been scrutinising the label on the bottle of sherry.

"Won't do much work afterwards if I have too much of that," he said, with a knowing look at Phillip.

Ernest came very quietly into the room. He was tall and be-spectacled, with a sallow face, and still wore his dungaree jacket. He took his place without a word, then after staring at the pies, exclaimed "Ha!" with quiet satisfaction.

Fiennes came in next. He too said "Ha!" then added, "Pork pies, I see! Well, I'm hungry." Finally came Tim, who exclaimed "By Jove!" enthusiastically. "Pork pies! Well, well, well! Jolly decent of you," he smiled at Phillip, and sitting down, exclaimed "Ha!" to the sherry bottle.

"Long time since a bottle was opened in this house," said Mr. Copleston. "May I offer you some of your own wine?"

"Thank you, sir. I'm afraid I haven't a corkscrew."

"Corkscrew, corkscrew," muttered Ernest, with a preoccupied air. "Now where have I seen a corkscrew. H'm, there *was* one in the workshop somewhere. But someone took it."

"That corkscrew, by Jove, yes," said Tim, who looked to be about twenty years old. "I had it to try to get the bell-pull wire out of the wall. Now where did I leave the dashed thing?"

They sat still, as though ruminating, while Bukbuk, the small grey cat, came into the room with arching tail, followed by four kittens with similarly arching tails. While those around the table remained still, the cat with a chirrup leapt upon the edge of Lucy's chair and stared at a hole in the cloth about six inches away from its nose. Was this some ritual? For the faces around the table-cloth were watching the cat with anticipation.

"Bukbuk," said Ernest.

At this labial sound the cat put its head on one side, delicately lifted a front leg over the cloth, and with curl of paw tried to draw the hole towards it. It made several hesitant attempts to do this, before withdrawing the paw, and, looking at Lucy, opened its mouth to mew inaudibly. At that everyone laughed.

"You see," explained Tim to Phillip, "Bukbuk is very fond of currants, and when we have any we put one on the table-cloth for her to take. A year ago, when she was a kitten, she mistook that hole for a currant, and whenever she sees that hole now she thinks of a currant." They all laughed again.

"Pork pie, anyone?" asked Mr. Copleston, knife and fork poised. He looked at Phillip.

"Thank you, sir."

"Sherry," said Ernest, with sudden quiet forcefulness, staring before him. "I—want—sherry!"

"By Jove, yes," cried Tim. "Now where *did* I leave that dashed corkscrew?"

"Yes, where?" demanded Ernest. Phillip had observed a faded photograph of Ernest on the fireplace shelf: Ernest at three years wearing large straw hat, black button boots, white socks, sailor suit with skirt: Ernest with bashful reluctance facing photographer. Lucy had told Phillip that Ernest had so hated his public school near Shoreham in Sussex that he had run away several times, each time arriving home without a word of explanation, or of questioning from Pa, who thought that Ernest had come home for the holidays.

"Corkscrew wanted," said Fiennes firmly, sitting still.

"Ha, yes," replied Tim. "Now where the blinking blazes *did* I see that cursed corkscrew?"

Nobody left the table. At last Mr. Copleston, having apportioned the pies, opened a drawer in the gun-cupboard behind his chair and took out a nickel-silver whistle. He unscrewed it across the middle, and flicked one end. Screwing the sections together again, there was a corkscrew.

After putting a little wine in his own glass, he went round the table, filling the other glasses before his own.

"I say!" exclaimed Tim, "we ought to drink to the New Gas Engine!"

"Ah!" said Fiennes. Ernest was already sipping his sherry.

"We're going to get an oil engine to work the lathes," explained Tim to Phillip. "With a little dynamo, for electric light in the workshop. It will make a great difference when we are working an all-night session."

"To the New Gas Engine," said Phillip, raising his glass. Only Tim responded to this toast.

Phillip noticed that the top half of the window, which was open, was covered by a wire-netting frame. Seeing him looking at it Mr. Copleston said, "A confounded robin used to come in and take the food on our plates, but when his relations arrived as well and the little beggar spent the entire meal in chivvying them out again we thought it time to keep out the lot!"

After lunch Phillip washed up with Lucy in the scullery, then she took him to see the workshop, where Moggy had taken up her quarters inside a straw skep. Within the wooden building were many rows and shelves of tools—many kinds of saw, chisel, drill, hammer, gauge, plane and set-square. There was a mahogany cabinet containing a hundred and more steel bits for woodwork fixed on the wall behind what Tim had explained was a very fine Holtzappfel lathe for turning ivory, woodwork, and metal.

"This is Pa's lathe," explained Tim. "It is a marvellous example of engineering. Among other things, it can turn three hollow ivory balls, one inside the other!"

"It looks a wonderful piece of machinery. I haven't seen one like that before."

"There were only about ten in England. Pa bought it when a young man. It cost six hundred pounds."

Lucy told Phillip that the Boys were making parts of sac-machines for an East Anglian firm, which sold them to "little men" who, having seen advertisements in various magazines, bought the sac-machines together with all the materials for making batteries in their spare time, and then sold back the batteries to the East Anglian firm.

"Sometimes the Boys get rush orders and then they work all night. I don't know what Tim would have done if he hadn't thought of answering an advertisement in *The Model Engineer*."

She went on to say that Ernest and Fiennes had been in the Merchant Service, as wireless operators, but when the shipping slump came they returned home.

"Did Tim run away from school, like Ernest?"

"Well, not exactly that, but he did spend the last year at Shakesbury grammar school playing truant, setting off in the morning on his bicycle and coming back at night. The headmaster thought he had left, I suppose. He spent his time reading engineering books out of the public library, I believe. Anyway, he didn't like school very much. Then Ernest and Fiennes apprenticed him to an ironmonger, but all Tim had to do for months and months was to weigh up small packets of nails, so after six months of that he didn't go back any more."

"Well, I hope they are doing well making sac-machines."

"Oh yes, not too badly, you know. The new oil engine will save treadling, which is a bit tiring, especially when they work all day and night and then the next day as well, to try and get the orders done to time."

"How much would it cost them to install an oil engine?"

"About sixty pounds. They're trying to save up for one now."

After watching the Boys hard at it, Phillip thought that he must certainly do some work himself. He had already scoured the scullery floor, now for the walls and ceiling. He would prepare them for distempering, then buy brush and materials. It would be a surprise for Lucy, who was away decorating the church with her father. He brushed and scraped the ceiling, then the walls, including the iron pipes and handle of the pump, washed and polished the windows; and looking in the larder, decided to tackle that while he was about it. The job would take two days in all.

The kittens of Bukbuk were playing in there; he lifted them out with his foot after noticing the messes in the corner and on the shelves. Some of these deposits were old and covered with mildew. The perforated zinc window was overgrown with ivy which made the place dark and airless. The ivy must go, at least round the window frame.

Lucy came back and said, "How lovely!" While she was upstairs changing her clothes before going for a walk by the river he went into the dining-room to look at the books, as he had been invited to do. There was Kipling's *Plain Tales from the Hills*; a Railway Edition, in green paper covers, of *Wee Willie Winkie*; P. H. Gosse's books on the sea-shore, with hand-coloured plates, also Goldsmith's *Birds of Britain,* and others on British Fishes. Ah, a first edition of Pickwick Papers! He remembered reading in *The Times Literary Supplement* that this was valuable only in the original fortnightly parts—a pity. It was bound in tooled leather, with the bookplate of Pa's father. Most of the books had this bookplate stuck inside the covers, with the family coat-armour and the engraved names of *Adrian Ernest Fiennes Copleston,* with what appeared to be his original address, *Hernbrook House, Oxon.* There was a set of Sowerby's *Wild Flowers,* with tinted wood-cuts, each volume uniform, bound in calf, tooled with gold leaf; a first edition of *Treasure Island,* one of a set of Stevenson; some first editions of Thomas Hardy; many novels by William Black; all Surtees' first editions. The books on birds, which he looked at eagerly, were massive, with plates of eggs, many coloured by hand; three volumes on British conchology, with engravings also hand-coloured.

On one wall was a portrait of Lucy's grandfather, a tall, dark young man with large brown eyes, in the uniform of the Royal Navy.

"Pa was one of a large family," said Lucy, coming beside him. "I don't know all of them. Pa and Mamma were so happy they kept to themselves, and didn't bother about relations." Like we shall be, she thought happily to herself, as they wandered down to the river.

"I wish I had known your mother, Lucy."

He learned that she had spent her last years in the chalet on the lawn, ill with consumption. Lucy had been at school near Oxford, when Sister Agnes had told her the news of her mother's death. She had returned home at once, deciding not to go back to school, but to stay at home to look after them. She and Tim used to go for walks together, while playing a game of imagining fine meals they were eating. That was in 1917, when German submarines were sinking many British ships. Most of Pa's money was in

Russian bonds, said Lucy, and when the revolution came they lost it. Ernest and Fiennes were away then. Ernest had been round the world twice, and had been torpedoed three times; but he never spoke about it.

"What was the favourite meal you and Tim used to eat in imagination, you poor starved creature?" he said, putting his arm round her and laying his cheek against hers.

"Usually sausages and mashed potatoes," she replied, laughing. He determined to go into the town immediately after tea and get several pounds of sausages for supper.

They came to the oak tree where usually they sat on the afternoon walks. It grew out of a steep slope above the river. They agreed to bring a kettle there, and hide it, to make tea every afternoon. There was an old nest of a heron in the top of the oak above them. He made plans to climb there in the following spring; he had never found a heron's nest, he said.

"Perhaps we can tame a young heron, and train it to catch eels!"

The oak tree became a friend to be visited every afternoon by the river. Phillip borrowed from the workshop an iron bar, and spent many hours digging a cave under the roots of the tree, playing a game of make-believe, two castaways hiding from the world.

The cave was never finished; and after a fortnight he went back to North Devon, to find that only one letter had arrived during his absence, and that Billy was as well as ever.

He forestalled any complaints or questions from Mrs. Mules and Zillah about his absence by saying at once that he would pay for the two weeks he had been away. But layers of thought about this absence, day upon day, had raised a monument in Mrs. Mules' mind.

"My dear zoul, us nivver knowed when you'd be in mind to return or not, do 'ee zee? Us'v kep' the room for 'ee when us might 'v let'n to someone else, you knaw! So us ban't over-chargin' 'ee, mind!"

"Of course you aren't. That's why I offered to pay for the time I've been away."

Mrs. Mules began to explain again that she was not overcharging.

"I think five shillings a week is most moderate, Mrs. Mules. Anything happened in the village while I've been away? What about my paying for food as well? After all, you must have kept the fire in the bodley ready to cook a duck, or a cockerel, or a hedgehog."

"'Tes all very well vor make a joke of you not comin' back as you zaid you would, but don't 'ee zee——"

Remembering the character of Mr. Padge in *The Diary of A Nobody* who stuck to the only armchair in the Pooter household, preferring comfort to the Pooter supper, Phillip said, "That's right!" to all Mrs. Mules said. Martin Beausire had declared that talk with Mrs. Mules was like trying to talk to a perpetual gramophone record, while Mules' style of talk was like the same gramophone record sticking in the same place for three revolutions until it passed on to further inanities.

While Mules kept repeating, over his wife's shoulder, during her pauses for breath, "That's right! My wife be quite honest!" Phillip opened his letter. It was from his sister Doris, asking him if he had made up his mind yet about her adopting Billy; her baby had been born, a son; she was still in the nursing home, but had heard of a good nurse; would he agree to share the wages if she engaged the nurse before anyone else engaged her. Would he please let her know immediately?

He sent her a telegram with congratulations, ending *letter follows*; then dropping his work, wheeled out the Norton and made for Down Close.

"Shall we get married fairly soon, Lucy?"

"Yes! Then I can look after Billy!"

"I'm down to my last ten pounds in the bank!"

"Oh well," she replied, "I don't expect we've got even that much!"

They agreed to keep the secret for the time being. Lucy said that two of her mother's old friends would like to meet him, and would he care to spend the week-end at Ruddle Stones, their home. "You've already met 'Mister', haven't you? Mrs. Smith asked me to take you to see her."

"'Mister'? Oh yes, quite a nice old chap."

'Mister' had arrived to see the Boys, during Phillip's first visit, on an ancient two-stroke motor-bicycle which he called The Onion. The Onion was always breaking down, he complained.

The wheezy engine, puffing out oily smoke, somehow seemed to fit the tall, thin, huddled figure that perched upon it. 'Mister' himself was wheezy, being asthmatical; he was plaintive, appealingly human.

Lucy told Phillip that he had never done any work, and since the war his income was so reduced that his home could only be maintained by the taking-in of what he and his wife called Pee Gees.

Mrs. à Court Smith was a squat, dark woman with remotely inquisitive eyes. Hardly had they arrived for the week-end when 'Mister', asking Phillip to look round the garden with him, began to ask questions in a roundabout way.

At last he said, "My wife and I are very fond of Lucy, you know. Between ourselves, we have wondered if there is anything between you two."

At first Phillip remained unresponsive, but 'Mister' appeared to be so friendly that at last he told him, in confidence, that he and Lucy were engaged, mentioning that they were keeping it strictly to themselves for the time being.

"We hope to be married before very long, 'Mister'!"

"Oh. What about Pa?"

"Pa?"

"Haven't you asked for his permission?"

"Well, you see, I want to write a book on an otter that I have long planned; and when that's a success—as I feel it will be—then I shall go to Pa and tell him."

Very soon after hearing this, 'Mister' left him. To Phillip's surprise he saw, as he wandered in the garden, the old fellow talking to his wife through the open french windows. They glanced in his direction as he sat alone on the lawn. He knew what that meant, and was prepared when 'Mister' rejoined him, and said, "Now you know, old fellow, I think it only right to tell you that my wife and I feel a great responsibility towards Lucy who comes of a very good family! We both consider that you ought to ask her father's permission before things go any further!"

"Well, as I told you, when I gave you my confidence, 'Mister', Lucy and I rather thought we'd wait until my book was a success."

"That's all very well, my dear fellow—but as one of her mother's oldest friends, I—well—dash it all, it isn't cricket! If her mother were alive she'd jolly well have been after you for your intentions long before this, don't you know!"

'Mister' at the moment seemed to be more like his wife than himself, thought Phillip.

"Well, I'll talk to Lucy about your good intentions."

"Eh? What? Oh yes—Jolly decent of you, I'm sure, Phillip! I knew you had the right stuff in you, don't you know."

Lunch was ready before he could speak to Lucy, who was working in the kitchen. It was a constricted meal; he found himself sitting on his hands, with hunched back, wondering what to say; stammering at times; laconically answering the veiled and lethargic questions of Mrs. à Court Smith.

Afterwards Lucy and he went for a walk, and he told her what 'Mister' had said. Lucy seemed unable to decide, which added to his perplexity; with the result that he made up his mind abruptly to go at once and tell Pa.

"If he refuses, I'll have to leave here at once. I'll come back and tell you."

She reassured him as he left, seen off by 'Mister' ruefully comparing the Norton with his own creeping Onion.

Fiennes was cooking in the kitchen when Phillip arrived, a new cookery book open on the table.

"Hullo, when's Lu coming back? I'm bored with basting and garnishing. How long should a duck stay in an oven with a crack across the top and a hole in the back of the flue? The book says, 'Stick a fork in and see——'"

"The duck, or the oven?"

"Both probably."

"Well, if you stick a fork in, you'll see if the juice comes out red or not. I say, where's Pa?"

"He's in the garden."

Phillip drew a deep breath. "I say, Fiennes, I'm going to ask him about Lucy."

"Good," said Fiennes, scrutinising a jab in the bird. "It's gravy coming out. If he asks you about the duck, say it'll be ready in half an hour."

"Yes. Well, he's in the garden, you say?"

"Somewhere about."

Phillip went into the garden. Mr. Copleston was bedding out plants.

"Ah, hullo, hullo! Coming back tonight?"

"I hope so!"

"Ah yes, I thought you wouldn't want to stay long with that idiot 'Mister'! Well, it won't be too soon to have our cook back again, I can tell you. I don't know what we should do without Lucy."

This was fearful. "What are those plants, sir?"

"Hey? Oh these, they're Chinese wallflowers. Yellow little beggars, but a change."

"I wonder if I might——"

"Hey?" The grey-bearded face looked up into his. The mouth was open, the lips slightly blue. He was over seventy. Who would look after him when Lucy——? Phillip's determination weakened. He could not hurt him: he knew what Pa had been through. How could he take away Lucy from this lonely old chap? And so poor, too. No: Pa needed Lucy.

She had told him that Pa had lived in a larger house with servants to look after them, a base from which he and his wife had gone together to Ireland, Scotland, London, and Italy. Pa, she said, had been twelve years older than Mama, he was always very devoted and considerate, they were sufficient to one another.

What about you children? Phillip had asked. "Well, Nannie looked after us when we were small, and later there was a governess."

"Didn't you miss your parents?"

"No, I don't think so. We were sufficient to one another, I suppose. Fiennes and Ernest being bigger, went about together, while Tim and I were friends. Then we went away to school, but there were always the holidays to look forward to."

How well he knew the old fellow's feelings after his wife's death, knowing that wherever he went, whatever he did, there would always be the same hollow feeling, the same aching weight. Sitting alone, hour after hour, day after day, without purpose. They seldom saw Pa, Lucy had said, after her mother's death. He spoke rarely, he looked old and sad. Then one evening Tim had dared to invite Pa to their room for a game of Ludo, and to their surprise Pa had come. He came the next night and the next, and they all played games together.

"Later we took him exploring, and Pa loved it. After a week or two he thought nothing of walking twelve and fifteen miles a day with us. His whole life was altered."

"Yes," Phillip had said. "I can understand."

Lucy had seen tears in his eyes, she had longed desperately to comfort him, but he had seemed to want to be alone, like Pa. To conceal her feelings, she had shown him a photograph of her mother.

"You are exactly like her," he said. "She has the same serene and sensitive face. Thank you for letting me see her."

Lucy sometimes thought that she would never be able to take Barley's place in Phillip's heart; but being deeply reticent about her feelings, she had said nothing; and Phillip had mistaken this for absence of feeling.

Now, he thought, he was about to break up the happy life of a courteous old country gentleman and his children, living where no angry voice, no unhappy cry, was ever heard. He thought, too, of his old home, of his parents and sisters; and the strangled, inner feeling, which he had never felt when with Barley, repossessed him.

"I wonder where I can get some Chinese wallflowers for my garden, sir."

"Oh, they're quite common nowadays, I fancy. Has Lucy come back?"

"She's still at 'Mister's'."

"H'm."

Pa and 'Mister' had once been great friends; but something had happened, Lucy had told Phillip, over some money, she believed.

Pause.

"Well, I think I'll be going back now, sir."

"You leaving for Devon?"

"Yes, sir."

"Well, you'll be back some time, I expect?"

"Oh yes, sir, if I may! Thank you!" He returned to the kitchen.

"Did he ask you about this confounded bird?" asked Fiennes. "All the heat of this blasted stove goes out of that crack at the back! Listen to it roaring!"

"Yes. No, I mean. Nothing about the duck. I say, Fiennes, what shall I do? I mean——"

"Do? What do you mean, *do*?"

"I mean, about Lucy. After all, she keeps the place going, doesn't she?"

"Oh, haven't you asked him?"

"No, I didn't like to, really."

"Well, go to him and say, 'I love your daughter, I want to marry her, and damn well mean to do it'."

"No, be serious, Fiennes!"

"I am serious! That's what you mean, isn't it?"

"Yes."

"Then go back and say what you mean! You're an author, you ought to know what to say."

Phillip went back, made some remark about the Chinese wall-flowers, returned to the kitchen, where the duck was now out on the table; but unable to face Fiennes, sought once more the old gentleman stooping with trowel over another box of plants.

"Hullo, not gone yet?" was his encouraging remark.

"I've come to say the duck will soon be ready, Fiennes says."

"Hey? Oh, the duck. Ha, I've been looking forward to that! I've got precious few teeth left, but what I have got will do! No time to bed-out another box of these," he added half to himself.

"I don't think it will rain, at least I hope not!"

"Hey?" he cried, standing upright and leaning back. "H'm, one doesn't grow any younger. Get dashed stiff bending down! Oh well, I don't care!" he said brightly, with a genial glance of his eyes.

Phillip pretended to be deeply interested in the box of wall-flowers: noting almost painfully that it was old, partly dry-rotten, red potsherds over the draining holes, fibrous rootlets holding to gravel. Then he heard his voice saying, "I want to ask you something about Lucy, sir."

"What's that?"

"Sir, Lucy and I love each other, and would you please consider giving your consent to our engagement?"

Fear came into the eyes looking up into his: the look passed instantly. Pa slowly straightened his back, then, moving his feet away from the wooden box, he turned to Phillip and held out his hand, smiling, and said in a voice appropriately hearty, "I congratulate you! I must say I thought something was in the wind! H'm." He felt for his cigarette case and holder—a gunmetal case, Phillip noticed—took out an Empire-tobacco cigarette, fitted it carefully into a cherry-wood holder and lit it. Phillip thought fervently that he would buy him a gold cigarette case for a Christ-

mas present. Pa puffed, and then said, "Well, I suppose I've got
to do the heavy parent, and ask you about your means?"

Fortified by his humorous attitude, Phillip replied, "At the
moment I have only my pen, but as regards my financial status,
my agent tells me that in a year or two I shall have several
thousands a year."

"Ha! Well, that's more than I shall ever have!" and with that
Mr. Copleston went on with his work.

Phillip hurried away, appalled by his rashness in thus fore-
casting his future 'financial status'. Would Pa think 'his agent'
meant 'land agent'? Well, he might very well inherit Rookhurst one day—Uncle Hilary had bought about a thousand acres
—so it was not altogether untrue.

Jubilantly he told Fiennes what Pa had said, and Fiennes
replied, "Do you or don't you want to stay to lunch?"

"Thanks all the same, but I've had lunch."

It was already nearly four o'clock, so he hurried back to Ruddle
Stones.

He found Lucy in the à Court Smiths' scullery washing up cups
and plates, for both cook and maid had gone to a wedding—not
their own, for the respective fathers of their infants were already
married. Mrs. à Court Smith wasn't at all conventional about
such things, Lucy told Phillip.

"Good for her."

"Oh yes, she's very kind, really, only she's rather extravagant,
and can't manage very well. She always orders the best food, so
they are usually rather hard up," said Lucy. "Even Pee Gees
make no difference."

Taking the drying-up cloth from her, he screwed it up and
kicked it on to the scullery table, then kissed her.

"I knew Pa wouldn't mind. He likes you, he says you're a good
worker!"

"So you've guessed?"

"Well, your face was like a small, happy boy's when you came
in just now!"

Her own face had the rich hue of a peach on a sunlit wall, her
warm responding sweetness made him say, for the first time, "I
love you, Lu. You are a turtle dove, the gentlest, kindest, and
most innocent of birds. But I am a phoenix."

Shyly she whispered that they would be like Pa and Mamma,

always happy because they were together. "We won't bother about silly people, will we, when we are married?"

In the warmth of believing that when he was married it would be like Barley come again he clasped her small head, stroking it, his lips upon her hair, feeling as when first he had felt the warmth of his son's fragile head on his cheek.

"Oh, my God! I quite forgot to tell Pa about my first marriage!"

"He knows already."

"Did you tell him?"

"No. I think it was either Aunt Connie or Aunt Jo, who wrote to him."

Chapter 13

ANNIVERSARY

The next day he and Lucy went to Devon, she to stay with Aunt Connie and her Ogilvie cousins at Wildernesse, he to his cottage to try to work.

It was near the equinox; much rain fell on the Wednesday, opening day of Barnstaple Fair; again on Thursday; but on the Friday, when the highest tide of the year moved into the estuary, the rain had cleared. They had been invited to spend the night with Uncle Biff and Aunt Jo—Commander and Mrs. Gilbert— at Bideford, and thought to spend the day on the Burrows, and cross over the estuary in the afternoon.

The sky was wholly overcast when he called at Wildernesse on the Friday morning.

"Do be careful, won't you, dears?" said Mary, as Phillip and Lucy set out. "There will be a fairly big fresh coming down both rivers, but at noon the tide will be out, and you should be able to get a boat then from Appledore without any difficulty."

She and Phillip looked at one another: it was the second anniversary of Willie's death.

As they walked hand in hand through the passes of the sand-hills rain began to fall steadily. They were wet through long before they reached the Valley of Winds, and the rain was coming down so heavily that he decided it would be hopeless to expect anyone across a mile of rock and water to see a signal; so they turned north and looked for the cattle shippon in the grazing marsh below the sea-wall, said once to be a chapel, in which to shelter.

The sky at midday was darker than at twilight. Their shoes squelched, their clothes heavy with water. At last they were under cover in the shippon; now for a fire. He went across the marsh to collect driftwood below the sea-wall. The wood was sodden and heavy; he cut off chips with his knife and kindled them by feeding the yellow sodium flames and fanning the sullen embers for half an hour or so, until the fire gave out warmth. He removed coat, shirt, and shoes, and stood by the flames to dry his trousers.

The kettle boiled, they drank hot tea, sitting round the fire.

"You must dry your clothes, too. Why not take off your jacket and skirt?"

She did so, hanging coat and skirt among the rafters, moving boylike with bare feet and legs, in home-made bodice and dark knickers, her hair hanging to her waist.

The fire was smoky, for the high tide of early morning had borne away most of the old jetsam, and the only fuel was sea-logged wood. The inside of the shippon became brown with smoke; outside rain fell darkly.

"We may have to stop here all night. I'll go and get all the fuel I can, Lu. The tide will now be up fairly high under the sea-wall, with lots of flotsam brought down by the river."

He came back dragging two tree-branches, one old and easily broken. Sections were put on the fire, while the harder branch burned across its middle. Then back to the sea-wall. The estuary was flooded with wide rocking brown water, the full spate pushed against the tide.

He waited to see if the strong muddy waters would flood over the top. The wind, inert with falling rain, fortunately was still. If the south-west started to blow, the inrolling waves would pile higher the spates coming down from Dartmoor and Exmoor, the marsh would be flooded, and they would have to run for their lives to the sandhills. How ironic if that happened on the anniversary of Willie's death.

He kept watch on the wall, walking up and down to keep warm.

The sea came to within a foot of the top of the wall; the rain continued to fall straight and heavy. He hastened away to report; then ran back to the wall. A vast dun lake, topped by foam amidst black limbs of trees and an occasional drowned sheep, bore water-logged pleasure boats (torn from their moorings above Barnstaple bridge) moving seawards. They were safe!

They ate the last of their food, followed by a long and happy silence as they stared into the embers of their fire, before leaving the shippon. It was already dark when they reached Crow Shingle Spit; his shouts, and flares of burning newspaper, brought no flash of lantern or answering hail. What to do? Ah, the lighthouse keeper! They trudged down the shingle and asked the keeper if he would telephone for a ferry boat. The keeper said he would try; but warned that there was a big tide going down, and the wind was rising. Did they still want a boat?

"I think we ought to cross, thank you."

Half an hour later they saw in the near-darkness a salmon boat coming aslant the tide swirling down very fast with the pressure of the combined spates of the Two Rivers. The single lug-sail was reefed to its highest cords. One of the crew of two said they had had a difficult time to cross.

"The tide be holding the Pool buoy flat, Gor'darn, th' water be ripping auver it! Us dursen't go back between Crow and Shrarshook, 'tis a proper hurly-burly there!"

The roaring of the waters almost leaping seaward was growing louder every moment. Phillip began to feel apprehensive. Should he take Lucy back to the Ogilvies? Not a star was to be seen, the lights on the quay of Appledore were blurred. Every moment the sea-ward race of the tide was increasing.

"How fast is the tide?"

"I reckon ten knot, mebbe more. Gor'darn, us can't remain yurr much longer!"

"We'll cross."

He helped Lucy over the gunwale and sat on a thwart beside her, their feet in bilge-water. One man pushed off and clambered aboard.

The wind was rising with the lessening of rain, blowing strongly from the sea. The boat surged forward against the tide, driving its bows almost under. He saw, with a stab of fear, that they were moving slowly backwards. From behind could be heard the growling of the Hurly-burlies, rocks over which, in white undulations, the ebb was leaping.

"Do 'ee mind coming aft a bit," asked the man at the tiller. "'Twill drave under else."

He saw that water was lipping over the bows. The mast creaked with the weight of wind in the sail. He shifted to the back of the boat, remarking, "An extra lot of water coming down tonight, I fancy."

"Aiy," said the other man, also in a matter-of-fact voice. "Us thought one time us wouldn't get across. Us tried to make Point o' Crow, but the tide be rinning too strong tonight."

Lucy and Phillip sat quietly on the back thwart, holding hands. The boat appeared to be surging ahead; yet when he looked to the left the shore seemed to be sliding forward. The lighthouse was also moving forwards.

"Gor'darn, us won't make it!" said the man at the tiller, suddenly. "Us'll be down to the 'urly-burlies in a minute! Take a pull at the sweeps, Jimmy."

The other man slowly put first one sweep then the other sweep through the thole-pins, and began to pull. The shore ceased to slide forward: the puller of sweeps grunted; the thole-pins squeaked. At last they were gaining slowly. Yes, they were definitely gaining, getting farther each moment from the roar behind them.

It took several minutes to return to the place of embarkation. At Point of Crow the boat swung about as its nose pushed into the backwash of the swilling tide. Sweeps were shipped; cigarettes lit. They sailed very close inshore, carried forward fast by the backwash, then swung into the main thrust of the Taw tide and across to the opposite shore where black rocks seemed to hurtle past on the port bow. The lights of Instow came nearer and larger. Soon the noise of agitated water arose ahead. This was The String, where the ebb of Taw from Barnstaple clashed directly with ebb of Torridge from Bideford. The choppy, agitated water, dancing and jerking in the darkness, seemed thick to enter, confusing to their boat's shape. They swung about amidst water leaping in a thousand jets, each with its splashing sound: but the water was comparatively level, tide holding tide and leaving a luminous ribbon of froth to wander irregularly seawards in the midst of petty agitation. The noise of the tides in conflict filled Phillip with dread, and when the boat swung round, its rudder momentarily useless, he took Lucy's other hand, fearing the worst: a repetition of cousin Willie's fate.

"Isn't it lovely?" she whispered.

He felt apart from her; he smothered the feeling. How could she know his thoughts?

Now the bows of the boat were pushing into the press of the opposing tide; and the Torridge ebb was too strong, they moved backwards, rocking, faster than they had crossed. And suddenly, all was calm. They were in an eddy taking them into the Pool, where the conjoined tides of Taw and Torridge were racing at possibly twelve knots to the open sea. Christ, he thought, it is going to happen after all, and my thoughts of Willie were foreknowledge? What was the helmsman doing? Was he drunk? Stiff with fear?

It looked as though they were, after all, to be carried down in the whirls and hollows of the tide, past the Lighthouse, to the swamping white water of the South Tail; but this was Phillip's inexperience, the men knew what they were doing. Soon the boat was in the offshore backwash, a riband of water going the opposite way to the main ebb, and coming easily to the quay below *The Royal George*.

How quiet it was there!

"Thank you very much. How much do I owe you, please?" The usual charge was a shilling a head, and he thought five shillings would be fair.

"Ten shilling it's worth, sir. Dirty night, too."

He gave them his last note, while wondering where he could cash a cheque on the morrow.

They walked side by side down the sett-stoned street, dark and narrow between fishermen's cottages lit by an occasional gaunt gas-lamp.

"It's been lovely, Pip!"

"Do you know, Lu, I almost feel that I've no right to be here."

She thought that he was worried about being late, and said, "Oh, I don't suppose Aunt Jo will mind in the very least!"

They found Commander Gilbert waiting by the fire in the hall.

He was polite but curt, and apologised for his wife having gone to bed; then led them into the dining-room and to a plate of sandwiches.

Phillip saw that it was nearly midnight.

"I must apologise to you, sir."

He told Commander Gilbert about the rain, and the eventual telephoning for a boat from the lighthouse; and as he spoke, he realised that he had forgotten to suggest to Lucy to ring up her aunt to tell her that they would be late. The Commander showed them where coffee was being kept hot under a spirit flame. As soon as they had finished, he led the way to Phillip's room upstairs, said he hoped he would find all he wanted in his bedroom, gave him goodnight, and went away.

After breakfast Mrs. Gilbert took Phillip to see the gardens, where men were at work bedding out, sweeping paths, and edging lawns. He thought she was going to ask him about himself, but it turned out that she wanted to speak about Lucy's brothers.

"I hear that they intend to sell their reversions," she said. "Have you any idea of how they intend to go about it?"

"I really have no idea, Mrs. Gilbert. I have heard that they are thinking of erecting some sort of engineering works in their garden."

"How can they possibly know about engineering? What is Adrian doing to allow them ever to think of such things?"

Later, Commander Gilbert had a word with him in the smoking room.

"Ernest and Fiennes stayed here recently," he said. "Ernest said not one word to me or to his aunt, indeed when she came into this room he continued to sit still, making no attempt to get up when he saw her. As for Fiennes, all he did was to smoke his pipe in my wife's drawing-room, as though it were a public house. He also remained seated when my wife went there to write a letter. What is the matter with them, haven't they any idea of manners? One has heard of young people in London behaving oddly, even with downright insolence, to their parents and others, but one hardly expects that sort of behaviour from one's nephews."

"The Boys seem to have an unworldly approach to life, Commander Gilbert. It's an innocent sort of household altogether, at Down Close."

"I should not call it innocence." The Commander was annoyed. "I should call it something else. After all, one does expect people of our class to know what manners are. And when they had gone home we had not one word of thanks from either of them."

"They've been extremely busy, often working all through the night."

"No doubt it's good of you to find excuses for them, Maddison, but damn it, among people of—of—our sort, such conduct is inexcusable!"

The scullery walls at Down Close were distempered, the ceiling was white, the larder shelves were clean. Pa had shot Bukbuk's kittens, "the only shooting I get nowadays!"—and having returned the Purdey to the gun case, imperturbably continued his work in the lichened orchard of renewing the zinc labels which Tim, years before, had taken to make battery wet-cells.

Fiennes and Tim treadled away in the workshop, Ernest pored over blueprints that arrived from a monthly advertisement in *The Model Engineer*, which cost £9 every issue, Phillip had found out. Inventors wrote in, asking for models to be made—every kind of machine and gadget. Plans and sketches arrived by almost every post, to be examined, discussed—and set aside while Ernest continued to work at his selected model.

The one he was working on had already occupied Ernest more than ninety hours. Phillip asked Lucy what he would get for all that work.

"Oh, I don't think Ernest charges very much. The 'little men' haven't any money, usually."

"Does he quote a price?"

"Oh, no. You see, the models always take much longer than he thinks they will. So he usually charges about ten shillings."

The Boys were late with deliveries of sac-machines for the firm of Scotland-Roberts (Fakenham) Ltd. And daily frantic letters in red ink arrived from Mr. Scotland-Roberts at that East Anglian town, demanding that orders sent weeks, months before, be dispatched forthwith.

"I'm a bit overdue in my work, too. I must go to London and see my agent, Lu. I think I'll go tomorrow." But tomorrow was tomorrow, and tomorrow; while Phillip went on with paint brush, distemper pail, and putty knife.

"I've had a letter from Granny, Pip. She wants to meet you. Do you think you can spare the time to see her?"

"Of course, of course! Ought we to arrive on the Norton?"

"I don't see why not. Grannie doesn't fuss, like Aunt Jo." She added, "Although Aunt Jo is a dear."

"It was all my fault. Mrs. Gilbert must have thought badly of me, bringing you there after midnight!"

"But you couldn't help the weather, could you? Anyway, what does it matter?"

"I still think it might look a bit strange, arriving on a motor-bike at your Grannie's."

"Oh, I am sure Grannie won't mind. But if you would rather go in the Tamp, the Boys will lend it, I'm sure."

No, not in that canoe on wheels, not after Bédélia——

"Well, thank you very much, but I'm not a very good driver, and it looks as though it might turn over at the slightest accidental flick of the wheel. Are you sure that it won't matter if we go on the bike?"

"No, of course not! I love the dear old Norton!"

Mrs. Chychester lived in Belville Cottage, not far from the gates of her old home, Tarrant, a Palladian-styled building standing amidst trees on a hill west of the town. Lucy had told Phillip that Tarrant had been sold on account of some trouble through an uncle, Grannie's younger son. Thereupon Grannie had gone to live in the late butler's cottage, at the invitation of Ennis, her lady's-maid, who was seventy, and ten years younger than Grannie. Ennis had been the butler's wife. When the butler had died he had left the cottage to Ennis; but really, said Lucy, the cottage had not been his to bequeath. It was Grannie's cottage. Of course Grannie had not told Ennis this, but had secured it for her in her own Will.

"Now Grannie lives there with Ennis and Martha, the under-cook from Tarrant."

Belville Cottage was meticulously clean, with copper kettles and pans polished on the shelves along the walls of the lower room, an oak dresser with china, an oak table and chairs—these, he under-stood, belonged to Ennis. Upstairs was Grannie's own room, con-taining a few of her cherished belongings, including the campaign clock that had accompanied her husband throughout the Crimean War, and later, with the regiment in India.

Ennis, otherwise Mrs. Rawlings, received them at the door. She was tall and stately in mid-Victorian bodice and skirt from which the bustle had been removed, the embodiment of simple dignity. Mrs. Rawlings had accompanied her lady for more than half a century in her travels over half the world with the regiment. Mrs. Rawlings had a complete set of the paper-backed sixpenny Railway Books which she had bought in India when the young Mr. Kipling was beginning to be talked about, not always favourably, in the hill-stations; he was considered to be a half-and-half person, not exactly a gentleman, for he went to the bazaars and talked among the natives as though he were one of them. That had been towards the end of the Colonel's soldiering, when he was about to be retired, to return home to spend his days as a country gentleman. Mrs. Rawlings had held Lucy's mother in her arms; she had nursed Lucy herself, not as a duty of course, but as a privilege. She knew all the grandchildren, and their many cousins, and had seen them all grow up; to the young men she was always 'Mrs. Rawlings'; to the daughters and grand-daughters, she was 'Ennis', which may have been either her maiden name, or her name before she was married.

"Hullo, Ennis," said Lucy, happily.

"Good afternoon, Miss Lucy, good afternoon, Sir," replied Mrs. Rawlings, with a slight curtsy to each in turn. "Mrs. Chychester is in her room. She is much better than she has been lately. Her cold is nearly gone, I am most thankful to say. What do you think of our garden?"

The little square of garden was formal as herself: lobelias, geraniums, and arabis with other plants arranged within small beds of correct earthen slope, and set with a minute border of clipped box. Not a weed was to be seen. The coconut mat behind the oaken threshold of the door seemed not to have a fibre out of place.

After praising the flowers, the two visitors went up the stairs to Mrs. Chychester's room. She had seen them arrive from the window, but had drawn back to greet them as they climbed the stairs.

"My dearest Lucy, what a happy surprise for me! How well you look, my dear!" She took her grand-daughter's hands lightly, drawing her to be kissed gently on the cheek. "And this is Phil!" as she turned to him and clasped his hand between hers, and it seemed natural that he should incline his head and touch the back of her hand with his lips. "Now come and sit down, draw up the chair, my dear Phil, and tell me about your work—I hear such good account of your country essays——"

From the first glance at Mrs. Chychester's face and sound of her voice, Phillip had felt at ease; he could be nearly all of himself in her presence; more so than with Pa—in fact, he could be only about one-tenth of himself with Mr. Copleston. But now, with Mrs. Chychester, he could talk freely. Was it because her father had been an architect, as she told him—a soldier turned architect. "A square peg in a round hole, dear Phil, he was never really happy when in uniform, but with sketch book and pencil, he was the dearest of fathers."

After tea Mrs. Chychester said, "Do smoke, won't you—have you your pipe? I do so miss the scent of tobacco, you know!" When the Navy Cut was burning well, having been first rolled on the palm, the old lady gave him an ivory paper-cutter, the handle carved in the likeness of an eagle about to tear a snake which was coiled round the bird's body; open beak menacing open fangs. She said she had had it more than half a century, and she would be so glad to think of him having it on his desk, as a small token of her regard and affection for one who henceforward would be taking care of her dear Margaret's girl. Would he accept it as a mark of her esteem? She spoke with so soft and charming a voice that he found himself wanting to say that he wished he could take care of her, too; he stammered a phrase of conventional thanks and added that as all his grandparents were dead, might he call her Grannie?

"Indeed you are to be my new grandson, my dear," she replied. "And I do not know of another so kind and considerate to go through life with dear Lucy." Did her voice tremble ever so slightly as she spoke? He could not be sure, for he felt the tears coming to his eyes, and thinking to blow his nose, noticed with dismay that he had no handkerchief in the breast-pocket of his jacket, as was the correct thing.

As they were about to say goodbye, the door opened inaudibly and Mrs. Rawlings glided into the room with something in her hands. It was a folder of tissue paper, and some light blue silk riband.

"Ah, Ennis, how thoughtful of you," she murmured, as Mrs. Rawlings took the ivory paper-knife and discreetly, a few feet away, wrapped it with care and tied the blue riband with a neat bow, before giving it back to Mrs. Chychester.

"With my love, dear Phil," she smiled, her faded grey eyes looking into his as she took his hand, patted it, and gave him a light kiss on the cheek. "You will forgive an old woman for not coming to your wedding, won't you? I shall be thinking of you on the day. And be sure that my thoughts will follow you to London tomorrow, on your adventure to work hard and win further successes. Now do come and tell me about it, won't you, when you return at Christmas? Good night, Lucy dear, you look so well and happy."

Mrs. Chychester went to the door, and stood there with a smile as they went downstairs, to be shown out by Mrs. Rawlings, who remarked confidentially that Grannie was not so well as she would have liked, but it was nothing to worry about. Martha came from the kitchen, with her face of a young girl, though she must have been nearly forty; curtseying to Lucy, and pressing something into her hands, a wedding present he thought, as he pretended not to see, for Martha looked shy. Mrs. Rawlings came to the little green-painted gate, and as he got astride the Norton, praying that the engine would fire as soon as he paddled off, with Lucy perched on the carrier, down the road. It fired beautifully; and on the pilot jet they went slowly and almost silently down the lane past the demesne walls of Tarrant Park.

In bed that night, lying in the chalet, he meditated upon this experience of meeting a lady of a past generation. Was her graciousness more than the effect of good manners practised since before she could walk in the nursery, in the school-room, and later with her governess abroad; or were hers the natural manners of a clear nature reinforced by training? Was human nature perfectible, under a balanced economic system? That seemed to be the problem that Willie thought he had solved.

While the wind moved in the branches of the trees beyond the little lawn, he sought to find some fixed truth in human nature, other than that aspiration and emotion of the mind which saw the poetic truth of life; and considering this now in relation to Mrs. Chychester, he wondered how much of the balance of her character was made by environment, and how much of it was born in her.

Mrs. Chychester was what was called an early Victorian—by popular literary accounts she should have been a woman of frustration and unnaturalness. Or was that phenomenon only of the aspiring middle-class commercial and professional families: of the rise of the Victorian and Edwardian middle-class, coincident with the growth of factories and slums in a dark period of England's history when the influence and stability of the landlords were waning, and the power or money of the nation was being transferred, through trade, to a class which outwardly imitated the landed families but lacked their traits of responsibility and obligation?

He thought again of Willie—he saw his cousin's life suddenly in perspective. He must write the last novel of Donkin's short life. He could not write it where he was; he must go to London in the morning. It was as though Willie was urging him to write it for him. *Speak for us, brother; the snows of death are on our brows.*

Chapter 14

TURMOIL

On a dull and rainy London evening Phillip drew up his chair to the green baize table, uncapped his pen, wrote the words *Chapter 1*, paused, lit a cigarette in a sudden mood of excited satisfaction, pushed back the chair, and began to pace the floor of the room. It was a thrilling moment; he felt that the breath of creation had come upon him, its servant. Then he closed his eyes and tried to think of Willie.

In one corner of the otherwise empty room were his camp-bed and sleeping-bag, and an army hold-all. A coal fire burned in the grate. Every footfall was magnified with echoes in the empty house. Uncle Hugh had died in the very place where now he sat, alone with what spirits of love and hope. His footfalls resounded on the floorboards; the vibration gave him power. When he listened, silence fell as dust; and the peculiar stuttering flap of coal-flames came intermittently from the hearth.

He sat down, and began to write in the green-covered book, bought with two others for a shilling each at a stationer's shop in Ludgate Circus. Now he was moving away from the ancient hopes and torments of Gran'pa and Hugh Turney, Uncle Charley and all who had been in the room, to the wraith of cousin Willie in the silence of sandhills and the snow, while frost held earth and water in its thrall; shadowy figures were moving about a house remotely holding the dull growl of the winter sea. But he knew little about the figures with his conscious mind; he only knew they were there. The place was ghostly for him, the figures insubstantial, save that of one, to whom went his reawakened love.

What she would do, how appear, he did not know; he was trusting himself to the spirit of creation, which caused a strange dissolution within. He did not know what he would be writing on the page a moment before it happened. Trusting himself to the imaginative flow, in the secrecy of the empty house, he wrote steadily, light replacing shadow, living creatures the still figures, sunshine the candlelight of the empty room.

At midnight he put down his pen, arose stiffly, and regarded a sandy tom-cat that had entered through a broken window, and after yowling about the empty corridors, had come to sit by the embers of his fire.

"Zippy! Poor old Zippy——"

There were irruptions in the state of dream.

"You see, Phillip, I bought back Gran'pa's house for a special reason. Your father does not understand, but that does not matter any more." Spoken sadly, with resignation.

The house had been sold a year or two ago to a childless couple who had lived in two of the rooms only; they had moved away, put the place up for sale, and Hetty had—on what, according to Richard was one of her foolish impulses—bought it back for the same price for which she had sold it.

"Are you sure I am not interrupting you, Phillip?"

"No, Mother. All is fish in my net."

"But you won't tell anyone what I am saying, will you, dear?"

"My mouth is sealed."

Her face brightened. "You see, Phillip, I begin to feel that I have not many more years to live, and I want to see my children, and their children, happy. When Elizabeth and Doris come to live next door, how can that possibly interfere with your father's life, as he insists?"

"Why, is Doris leaving Bob?"

"Phillip, he has threatened her! He has actually struck her! And while she was nursing her baby, too! Can you understand that?"

"Oh, yes. Doris is very stupid and obstinate at times."

"Elizabeth went over one evening, and soon came back. She thinks that Bob is going insane."

"Mother, can't you understand that Doris, *and* Elizabeth, both in the same room with Bob, both disliking him, can cause a break-down of manners?"

"Ah, but it is the little one I think of, Phillip my son!"

"Of course—so does everyone else, including Bob, Hetty my mother! However, I'll try to explain your point of view to Richard Maddison."

"Do be careful what you say, won't you, dear?"

Phillip said to his father, "I suppose that Mother feels lonely during the day, and it's rather a journey to go across London to see Doris at Romford, and be back in time for your home-coming——"

"And pray, why is it necessary that she has continually to be gallivanting about to see Mrs. Willoughby? Whose fault is it that she has made such a disastrous marriage? Who connived at it, who encouraged the secret marriage, and helped to arrange it? Now your mother proposes to make the house next door into two flats, and no doubt will become the servant, in due course, of her two daughters, while neglecting her duties in this house!"

"Mother and Doris are good friends, apart from the fact of being parent and daughter, Father——"

"Can you say the same thing about your mother and Elizabeth? She continually uses your mother for her own selfish purposes! She is a little bully, too, the way she gets money repeatedly from her! And now, if you please, your mother proposes to set up Elizabeth in a flat next door, together with Mrs. Willoughby for whom, apparently, she is to provide a home, apart from her husband! Why, bless my soul, has she not heard of such things as Conspiracy, and Alienation of Affection? A wife's legal position is with her husband, unless she can show cause otherwise—in which case she is entitled to ask for a legal separation; and in this case, on what grounds, pray? It's a case of 'marry in haste and repent in leisure', if you ask me, Phillip."

"Yes, I understand how you feel, Father. Human life is very much like rookery life, I sometimes think."

"What's that got to do with it, pray?"

"Well, I only meant it as a joke, Father. You know how the established rooks sometimes drive off the young birds——"

"I don't see what that has got to do with what I was saying, but then you are a nature writer, aren't you? Well, I'm off to the moving pictures down in the High Street, to see Blanche Sweet in *Anna Christie*, for the second time. There's drama for you!"

"Yes, Eugene O'Neill is a real writer, Father. All great drama exalts us in our loneliness."

"If you want my opinion, most people are lonely, Phillip. Well, I'll see you when I get back, if you're still here."

"I shall probably be next door, writing, Father, but good-night in case I don't see you."

Phillip sat with his mother over a cup of tea in the kitchen.

"What has *really* happened about Bob Willoughby? Can you give me hard facts, rather than opinions, Mother?"

"Doris is very unhappy, dear."

"I know that; but what about Bob? Do you realize his point of view?"

"I realize that he is being led astray by a so-called friend of his."

"Why 'led astray', Mother? Men aren't 'led astray'! They go the way they want to go. It's like the old Fleet Street joke —a man spent his life in the West End of London trying to find a 'well-known man about town' of the evening newspapers gossip columns. The search wore him out, for he never found one, and when he dropped dead in Piccadilly, all the evening newspapers printed, 'Well-known man about town drops dead'."

Hetty laughed. "By the way, dear, Julian Warbeck called here this morning to ask if you were home again."

"Oh, no! What did you tell him?"

"I said you were in London, and I would tell you that he called."

"Then he knows I am here? Oh, hell and the devil! Couldn't you have said I wasn't staying here?"

"He asked before I had time to think, I'm afraid, dear."

"Well, don't tell him I'm next door, whatever you do!"

"Certainly not, Phillip. Now tell me about your little son. Have you had a photograph taken yet?"

"No, Mother—I sent you the newspaper cutting, didn't I?"

"Yes, Phillip. Will you let me pay for a proper photograph? I would so like to have one. I haven't seen him since—since that winter day when I came down to you, dear!"

Her voice trembled. She saw again Phillip, so pale and upright at the funeral; the sleet on his bare head, as he stood to attention, his jaws clenched like his hands, which later almost tore at the frozen earth to drop the first soil on the lowered coffin.

"Well, my dear son, I must now sew some buttons on your father's shirts. Don't work too hard, will you?"

"Mother, I want to finish my book before Christmas, for a very good reason. I'll tell you in confidence, if you promise to keep the secret to yourself. I'm going to be married again in the spring. But you won't tell either of the girls, will you? Or Father? Yes, of course she loves Billy, otherwise it wouldn't be any good. Now, Mother dear, I don't want to talk about it, otherwise I shan't be able to write. Yes, you'll see Lucy before we're married, of course you will. Now I really must think about my story!"

"Yes, dear, of course, naturally! Kiss me, my dear son! I'm so very, very happy for you!"

Fire made up, fresh candle stuck on guttering stump, chair settled firm on wooden floor: against memory of the vanished lives of his grandparents, uncles and aunts—who were not characters in the story, that was for time ahead—the scenes of the book created themselves, as a plant grows out of soil composed of ruinous tissues. Every evening he went to the gate, tip-toeing down the darkness of the porch to let himself in at the front door, stealthily, feeling, as he shut it silently behind him, that he was a conspirator in a world beyond life and death. Evening moved into night, which carried him onwards with his story in the silence of the house disturbed only by the soft padding of the cat, his own footfalls, the stealthy noises of the fire. The packet of candles grew smaller, shadows flickered on the walls as he got up, speaking aloud with excitement of the life arising before him.

This imaginary life grew with a reality that was more vivid than life beyond the empty house. During the day, in London and elsewhere, he avoided familiar faces and walked alone, taking his meals in coffee house or restaurant as fancy settled. He was happy to be alone, he avoided re-entry into the world of chance acquaintance; even Mrs. Neville, once his *confidante*, was avoided. He had nothing to say to her, after a brief visit.

One night, as he shut the gate on leaving, a form detached itself from the hedge and came forward to greet him in a rough, scornful voice which made him, as always on hearing it, flinch a little before fortifying himself against its abrasion. He had not seen Julian Warbeck for two years. Julian's hands were thrust into the pockets of his overcoat. Phillip knew by his tone of voice that Julian had been drinking.

"Well, Maître, how goes it? Still like a spider getting thinner and thinner as it pulls gossamer after gossamer from its spinnerets, to launch itself into an air of flaccid dream?"

"I'm just going for a walk. On the Hill. But I warn you that I'm a very dull dog nowadays."

"Why only nowadays? No, don't take any notice of what I say. Honestly, I'm extremely glad to see you again! I've read all your books. Gossamers, I think you used to define your poetic inspiration? But you aren't that kind of spider, old boy. You'll never rise into that air which nourishes true poets. You're a reporter of talent—sometimes—— Otherwise you're a wall spider, grabbing what passes. But seriously, old boy, I'm very glad to see you again."

"How did you know I was here?"

"'I have my methods, Watson'!"

Phillip could tolerate the image of Julian absent, for then he could see the authentic Julian, void of that scorn which was of his own exacerbating self-doubt and therefore unhappiness.

He had heard about Julian from his literary agent, Anders Norse: how Julian was deteriorating, a seedy sponger upon his old father; a haunter of Fleet Street pubs where journalists and writers foregathered, some to turn their backs upon his entry.

In the light of a street-lamp, as they left the north side of the Hill, Phillip saw that Julian's boots were down-at-heel. His face was more puffy than when he had known him before. Walking down to the High Street, he caught a 'bus going towards London, followed by Julian: to get off at the next stop because Julian's loud voice and manner were drawing attention. They walked along the Old Kent Road, stopping at various pubs; at every visit becoming more remote from each other. Phillip strode on, followed by Julian, until he came to Blackfriars Bridge. On the Embankment Julian became so derisive that to escape the torment of his presence Phillip jumped on a motor-bus that had slowed down to pick him up, and jerked the cord twice for the driver to go on. Julian ran after the bus, but was soon winded. Phillip saw him ramming his hat over his eyes, before the hunched figure strode away into the night.

The next evening he was unable to write; he spent the time prowling about the empty rooms, cursing Julian's wraith and lamenting the dereliction of his poetic talent, while dreading to hear a resounding hollow bang on the door which would entirely dissipate the vision of the manor house by the sea, of imagined figures washing plates in the scullery; while outside lay ice and snow, under a keening wind which brought the wild geese to the estuary; and in another room an old grey-bearded man took down his 10-bore fowling gun.

Such fancy was for the night only; by day he wrote short stories, despite the knowledge the last seven he had sent to Anders remained unsold. The chief English magazines, together with the high-paying U.S.A. editors, had rejected them. One was about a bob-tailed fox which, during two seasons, a certain pack could never kill. It had been told to Phillip by a retired huntsman who kept a pub in the South Hams. Another was an account of the last run of a pack of harriers on Dartmoor, and their destruction by the Master, officially for sheep-worrying; but, it was said, because they had worried and eaten an escaped convict. There were others, most of them arising from what he had heard at night, while sitting in various inns. One had been written in a couple of days following delivery by post of a crude pen-and-ink sketch from the United States, sent by a poor student, of baboons sitting on rocks in South Africa. Having written a story, he had posted it with the sketch to the artist who had hopes of a career as an illustrator of magazine stories, and was working his way through a mid-Western college. It was a poor bit of work, and Phillip was not surprised when the story was rejected.

Nevertheless, he considered that the editors were missing something when they turned down his later, and better, short stories.

Looking at printed stories in American and English magazines, comparing them critically and with detachment for excitement, colour and originality with his own rejected stories, he had given a few contemptuous snorts and realised that his stuff had no hope with such editors; or perhaps such a magazine public. The English magazines, particularly, printed feeble, false, conventional stuff, and were obviously so out of touch with the rise of modern feeling, that surely they could not last for many years. Even so, he must earn some money; he had less than five pounds in the bank.

He went to see Anders Norse in the Adelphi, who suggested that he call on the editor who, having accepted half a dozen of his earlier yarns, had rejected the later 'more realistic' stories.

"Well, the later ones are more truthful, you know, Anders."

"Why not go and see Teddy Dock, Phillip? You'll find him a very nice person. Right! I'll give him a ring that you'll go round straight away."

"Ah," Mr. Dock began earnestly, "the very young fellow I want to see! Come in and sit down! Now tell me—when am I going to have some more good stories from you?"

He was a kindly man, his manner was encouraging. Phillip told him that he was going to be married. Mr. Dock listened carefully; and then, pursing his lips, he said, "Now look here, Maddison, I am really concerned about you! You say your writings earn for you what must be little more than the wages of an agricultural labourer. A man with your ability ought to have a big reputation, which means a big public. Yet you are wasting your powers of perception, your sense of narrative, your faculty of observation on—what? On *animal* stories! No no, hear me out, wait a minute! I know I am right, man! Take those stories of an otter your agent sent me—how many people are interested, frankly, in the rather humdrum details of an otter's life? Besides, your otter is not a very pleasant creature, judging solely by what you have written! And again, the animal-story public is a very small and limited one. Now take my advice, and write about human beings! There must be romances in the country where you live! Write stories which please the average man and woman, that take them out of their surroundings—romantic, clean stories about human life. Now just a moment! I know what you are going to say. Now don't be offended——"

"I'm not offended. Do please say exactly what you think——"

"Very well, I will, Maddison! Don't write about sordid things! That little story your agent sent me about a mouse, for instance! It was well-written, I admit, but aren't you aware of a misplacement of your talents in writing such a thing? Why bother to do it at all?"

. . . Donkin observing the skeleton of the mouse in the jam-jar, amidst a few grains of rice, on the larder shelf: Donkin fully aware that *all* living was based on the dead—moths flying down to lay their eggs, the grubs consuming fur and skin, spiders descending delicately on their life-lines to climb up again with fragments for their egg-nests: all patient removal and use of the dead until only the little bones were left; shadows in the eye-sockets of the fragile white skull; yellow bones of tiny paws, lying so silent and quiet, so peaceful behind the bubble-flawed glass, after the hours of jumping up the walls of a waterless prison; even as Donkin's own mind, after . . .

"Now I am telling you exactly what I think, mind! You're not offended, are you?" went on Mr. Dock.

"No, not at all."

"Very well, you have no sense of humour! Now take that story of the hare being hunted in Surrey. Why harrow people's feelings unnecessarily? Frankly, I can't see any point in it!"

. . . hare in a chalky field near Cross Aulton dragging stiff limbs, straining for its life from beagles in a wheat-field whose green blades were not yet shining with the late winter sunshine. A heavy City man running slowly past, white stock round thick and ruddy neck, yelling at hounds with excitement. The great vein of his neck swelled. So were the eyes of the hare as it limped into a garden of one of the new houses of the new road made through the cornfield. A thin froth on the sportsman's heavy lower lip which soon would be pressed against the rim of a large glass of whisky-and-soda, this Saturday morning sportsman of the City of London.

Donkin, a stranger come among them, stood apart observing the scene and all it implied; hating nothing, despising nothing, but looking at these things as they happened: looking at the truth: and trying afterwards to convey it in words . . .

Almost pleadingly, Teddy Dock was saying, "People don't want to be made melancholy, my dear boy. There is enough sadness, God knows, in the world already. And it is my opinion—and I know I am right!—that a kink in you prevents you from writing as you ought to write! Something in you has checked your life, your youthful exuberance. What is it? Or is it just perversity? I know! You say to yourself scornfully, 'The public—Why should I write for clods!' Well, why do you not say something?"

. . . le Labyrinthe was made in the town long before the soldiers were burrowing into the chalk of Artois and the rats and grubs and worms were burrowing into the soldiers to make the soil for the corn which will belong to the financial forces of the towns which will send another generation into the earth. Donkin praying, *I would to God that the green-corn spirit of truth rise from the clods. Streets, houses, pavements, the pressure of city work, the pressure overlaying the green spirit of earth, will finally kill the truth if there is no clarity.*

"Find some joy in life, man! Get out of your moodiness! Look on the bright side!"

"I don't think of people as clods," he replied, dreading lest the editor think him scornful of his friendly intentions. "I honestly do try to write as I see and feel things. May I read you what I wrote in the train coming up today? It may explain things better."

"Just as you like."

"'My words are part of me, both my spoken and my written words. A man sees with his two eyes, and he sees the world, the moving shapes, the people in the streets, the sun and the sky, everything—he sees the changing and ever-moving world as one immense hollow, filled with what his senses perceive, a hollow existing above and around and below the orbits of his two eyes. Every man perceives a world in the hollow fixed to his open eyes. And that world, his world, fades as his senses fade; and when they fade forever, where is his world?

"'Is one man's world the same as another man's world? How can it be? There are seven million people in London, there are seven million worlds. There are many unhappy people who are unhappy because they strive to enter the world of the beloved, to mingle in spirit in that other world, to change that world into their own world—that world into which others can never wholly enter. Even the mother is no more in her son's world when once he has awakened to himself.'"

When he had ceased reading, Mr. Dock stared at him across the desk with intentness and perplexity. After a pause, his expression cleared, and a light came into his eyes.

"I see! You've gone all highbrow! That explains it! What a pity! I was prepared to back you against any other writer whose stuff I print—but you've gone highbrow, Maddison!"

After another puzzled look at the young man before him, Mr. Dock went on, "Very well, here's something else for you to consider, though I suggest it without much hope. You tell me you must have money before you can marry. Then write the kind of stories that people want to read!" The editor's manner changed. "You *can* do it *if* you want to; but you *don't* want to! Am I right? Of course I am right! My dear boy, I am quite upset about it— it is absolutely a case of leaving your talents buried! Do you know, and I say this in all seriousness, you *could* be another Kipling? That astonishes you, doesn't it? But you won't be, as you are going on! And shall I tell you why? It is because you have a kink! Now go away and think things over. Write good, clean, healthy stories about human life! People will always want to read about romance, despite all fads, fashions, cubism, and all this Vorticist nonsense. Now go to it!"

After shaking his hand and thanking Mr. Dock, Phillip went along a corridor, passing a boy who had been waiting to go into the editor's room with a cup of dark brown, half-cold tea, some of it slopped into the saucer. He remembered Martin Beausire: how welcome his face would be!

He wandered through Covent Garden market, among broken cabbage leaves and dropped flowers, thinking of a small oval face, of dark hair over shoulders in the early morning when Lucy had come across the lawn shyly to kiss him on the cheek or forehead as he lay in bed in the chalet. He longed for her clasp and warmth—waiting for him, far away from this glittering Strand.

One day, one day, they would know! A *kink*, had he? So they had said, nearly all of them, from boyhood up: morbid!—perverse!—slack-twisted!—egotistical! One day—their children perhaps—would see with new eyes.

The flow of unknown people, each with a world that would break like a bubble when its owner was earth again, was going—where? Abraded by the dark and deadly pressures of urban life to another Concentration Graveyard in a few years' time? Aroused by internecine financial forces, as Willie had prophesied, to counter the spirit of revenge, of blood calling to blood? If only the dead could speak: but the dead did speak: and their spokesman was Christ. But did the meek inherit the earth? Other than the white chalk of the Concentration Graveyard?

He thought to go into the crypt of St. Martin-in-the-Fields, where perhaps he would see Dick Sheppard; but Martin Beausire, who knew him, had said that he was ill with asthma . . . the effect of death and derision in his life? *For love of God seems dying*, Wilfred Owen had written—not ironically, for there was no irony on the battlefield; only iron and flesh. No, he could not bother Dick Sheppard, with nothing in his hands.

He crossed Trafalgar Square, meaning to call at his publisher's office in Pall Mall. Outside the door he hesitated. Would he be welcome, with five books, all failures? He went up the stairs, and was taken into the inner office, where the manager, a young man, courteously arose from a desk to greet him. While he was talking to him an older man wearing a morning coat, high stiff collar with cravat, and spats over his boots came in and was introduced as Sir Godber Hollins. Phillip remembered him from J. D. Woodford's party in Inverness Terrace on the night before he went down to Devon, nearly five years ago now. After a cursory greeting Sir Godber pressed a bell, and a woman secretary hurried in.

"Bring the Sales Book, will you?"

Sir Godber laid the ledger on the marble shelf above the fire and flipped the pages; studied a page for a few moments, then turning to his manager asked if they had got the American rights. No? Then why not?

"They were reserved by Mr. Maddison's agent, Sir Godber."

The publisher turned away and began to pace the room, his hands under his coat-tails. Abruptly he turned to Phillip.

"Can you come back another day? I am due at the House shortly, and want to speak to my manager on urgent business."

Phillip left at once, followed out of the room by the manager, who, fumbling in his pocket, produced a crumpled packet of Gold Flake cigarettes and shook out a cigarette, saying, "Have a gasper? Don't take any notice of the old boy, there's a division in the House tonight, and he's the Party Whip, you know."

"I quite understand. Sorry about my poor sales. I'm writing a book now which I think will sell."

"Good for you. You had some good reviews, they ought to get you some journalism. Up for long? Call in again when you're passing, won't you?"

Phillip ran down the stairs, and saw outside a yellow Rolls-Royce drawing up. Once it had belonged to the famous sportsman and coal-owner, Lord Lonsdale. Out got a slim dark man whom he recognised as the famous Armenian writer of romantic stories, Dikran Michaelis. After hesitation he went to Michaelis.

"May I say how much I like *The London Idyll*, and all your short stories? I'm a writer, too—of sorts."

"You look as though you've seen Christ crucified," replied the small dark man. "Come and have a drink in the long bar at the pub round the corner." They drove to the Carlton. "Tell me about yourself. Whisky? What are you writing now?"

"I'm writing a novel about a man called Donkin who saw Christ crucified."

"You were a soldier in the Guards?"

"I served in the First Brigade beside the Grenadiers and the Coldstream at First Ypres."

When they had finished their drinks Dikran Michaelis said, "I'm going to Victoria Station to meet the boat-train. Can I give you a lift, if you're going that way?"

"Thank you, I wanted to go to that station, as it happens."

"To meet someone?"

"I've already met her. She used to go back to her school in Paris from there."

The other asked no more questions.

"You must have hundreds of friends," said Phillip.

"I have none. People despise me, they think of me as the Armenian Cad who dodged the war, fakes all his characters, remains 'every other inch a gentleman', and whose books are 'not so much brilliant as brilliantine'."

"I know how you feel, for I feel exactly the same. We forget the nine and ninety, and think only of the one lost sheep."

"You are at least English, or shall I say British? I am a damned outsider! Oh yes, I am!"

"So am I! All artists in England feel they're outsiders, whatever class they come from. I'm a suburbanite, camouflaged as half a countryman."

They drew up in the crescent outside the station.

"Thanks for the lift. Don't believe that your stuff isn't good, for it is," Phillip said. "It has feeling, and sensibility. Please keep on writing!"

He raised his hat, and saying goodnight, walked away into the station, and hid himself at the suburban end, intending to wait there until all the arrivals at the boat-train platform had left.

Faces of City workers passed in stream, most of them set dully in the fatigue of bodies which were tired because they were not used naturally. These were the weary City workers pressing home to their suburbs. He looked at the face of every girl that passed, seeking a look of Barley. Most of the faces were pale, the lips pale. Then a girl went by with a calm, self-possessed walk, beautifully dressed, poising herself apart from the City-worker-rush. He followed her to the Arrival Board before which she stood, coolly inspecting it, while he remained a few yards away; apparently finding what she sought, she turned casually and gave him a glance, at which he felt himself to be integrating once more, though he was still feeling hollow. She sauntered away, and he moved to the board, wondering if she were waiting for the next Dover train. An idea for a romantic story began to arise in his mind. He imagined the beginning: bright bustle of station, beautiful girl waiting for handsome, strong, bronzed, clean Englishman to arrive, dressed in immaculate Savile Row evening clothes, 'faultless Lincoln Bennett' silk hat, ebony stick with gold top, and 'monocle'. Just come from the Great Open Spaces (via Paris) after Big Game Shooting to cure a broken heart.

The hero arrived, with stiff upper lip and unfathomable blue eyes. The beautiful girl smiled. What then? Ah, they were being watched by a thin, somewhat morbid artist from the Café Royal; member of impoverished British aristocracy. His threadbare clothes were well brushed by ancient retainer living in Shepherd's Market. Dikran Michaelis had done it already.

Why were so many of the literary critics derisive about his work? His reputation had fallen among beeves: the sharp Armenian goat herded among dull British beeves.

When he looked round, the girl was gone. So was the story.
So much for the idea of writing romantically about men and
women for Mr. Dock. And now for some food, lord he was hungry,
and then back for some serious work. He must not break his habit
of writing in the evening. But the face of Mr. Dock persisted; he
writhed away from its stupidity; cursed it, washed it away with
two large whisky-sodas, when satire replaced desperation.

After eggs and bacon at the buffet, hope came back to him as
he sat in the train and thought of the estuary and the sandhills
which he would revisit in spirit later that night. His tin of hand-
made Gold Flake cigarettes; a cup of char out of the kettle;
sitting by the fire until the small hours of the morning. He wondered with secret excitement what would happen that night. The
book was writing itself, no need to strive to imagine into the future:
he had only to trust the inspiration which always came from
outside himself.

"Hullo, you're home early!" said Hetty, gay with relief.
"There's a letter for you, my son."

He took it with him to the 'Gartenfeste', his old name for the
room next door when he had left the army in what seemed now
to be another world.

Lucy's letters were tender but simple. This letter was a reply
to one enclosing, from *The Daily Crusader*, a series of articles on
Arnold Bennett written by his wife: an appeal, it was said in Fleet
Street, by the wife to get her husband back. A.B. had gone off.
The articles were of much interest to Phillip, who had seen himself
in them. They disclosed that Bennett was meticulous and easily
upset, easily disbalanced by the writer of the articles. Phillip had
sent them on to Lucy, asking her to read them carefully, "because
I am exactly the same sort of creature".

Lucy's reply chilled him.

> Bother old Arnold Bennett! What has he got to do with you and
> me? We will be different, won't we, dear?

Phillip paced the bare boards, in doubt and disquiet. He talked
to his idea of Lucy. "I asked you to read the articles as a barrister
reads a brief! Or as a sailor studies the chart of a rocky coast!
And all you say is, 'We will be different, won't we, dear?' for all
the world as though you are my mother over again! I tell you that

only if both of us can see things plainly, both cause and effect, can we be happy!" O God, was it to be Father and Mother all over again? Poor Lucy: ought he to break it off? Was he changing his nature, becoming like Father? Ought he to go on with the engagement? It would mean a return of the darkness for him; but what mattered was Lucy. Poor innocent Lucy, without a mother, yet so cheerful, kind, and willing to help anyone in trouble. But pity was a snare; a poor substitute for compassion.

Yes, Lucy was right; it was up to him so to discipline himself that he kept his sensibility inside a routine, or code. Now to work. The novel must be finished by Christmas! Then he would be returning to the friendliest people he had ever known, outside Irene and Barley; a home of warmth and kindliness. Had Wildernesse House seemed to Willie as Down Close seemed to him now?

Now he, the necromancer, must raise from the rose-ash the ghost of the rose: Willie to be transmuted to Donkin: Donkin risen from the grave to live in the eternity of sea and air and sunlight, to be found by others as truth, perhaps for the rest of their lives. Mr. Teddy Dock, bless you for your good intentions! Now I beg to be excused; my way lies, not with docks and thistles, but with the goodly grain and the sun-hazed sleeper.

> The sleep-flower hangs in the wheat its head
> Heavy with dreams, as that with bread
> The goodly grain and the sun-hazed sleeper
> The reaper reaps, and Time the reaper. . .

It was cold in the garden room, the frost had come, bringing yellow London fog and the dull reports of detonators upon suburban railway lines. He sat there, writing fast, until the red sun of dawn hazed the ice-flowers on the eastern windows.

Chapter 15

THE WORKS

It was already dark when he arrived at Shakesbury station, but as he gave up his ticket to the porter at the barrier he saw Lucy's face in the lamplight, framed in the grey felt hat, smiling towards him. Tim stood by her, a mild benevolence on his face.

"I'm frightfully glad to see you," he said earnestly. "What fun we'll have, now you've come!"

Lucy was smiling gently, "He's come, too," she said, looking to beside the taxi-driver's seat where sat Rusty, beating a tail-stump. He felt he had come to his ultimate happiness when he found Moggy curled up on a cushion in the chalet, beside his bed.

"She's such a good little cat. I hope you don't mind that we went over to fetch her. Tim and I went in the Tamp. We saw Billy. He's a darling!"

After tea Lucy and Phillip retired to the scullery to be alone with an accumulation of cups, plates, and cooking pots. He washed up as usual, then taking the cloth from her kissed her on both cheeks. Her warm sweetness made him say, "Well, if it's to be 'bother old Arnold Bennett', then I must train myself to be a normal, healthy person. The trouble is I've tried to reform before, and never seem to have succeeded. It's my kink, I suppose, as the editor of Pa's favourite magazine told me."

"Oh, Pa reads anything and everything, then forgets it all immediately," replied Lucy. "Anyway, I like you as you are, so don't let my silly remark bother you any more, will you?"

He had brought a present for each of his new relations-to-be; a pair of leather motoring gloves for Ernest, a scarf for Fiennes, a pair of woollen stockings for Tim, an anthology of W. H. Hudson's writings for Lucy; and for Pa a book, *The Impatience of a Parson*, by the Rev. R. L. Sheppard, priest of St. Martin-in-the-Fields who was beginning to be known and loved for his broadcast services.

While he and Lucy were getting supper he said to her, "Dick Sheppard is a clear man, who lives in the spirit of Jesus."

He had bought the book for Mr. Copleston, knowing that he was a devout Churchman, vicar's warden of the little Norman church in the hamlet. Lucy had told him how Pa had repaired and restored some of the old woodwork; they always decorated the font and pulpit for Easter, Harvest Thanksgiving and Christmas Day.

As a foretaste of Pa's delight at receiving the book, at supper Phillip said casually, "What do you think of Dick Sheppard, sir? I went to the crypt of St. Martin-in-the-Fields while I was in

London, hoping to meet him, but he isn't well, he suffers from asthma, brought on by frustration."

"Hey? Oh, Dick Sheppard! I've no use for the fellow."

This was a shock. Later, sitting in Pa's chair (the only comfortable one in the room) while Pa was having a bath, he glanced idly at the copy of *The Church Times*, which 'Mister' had brought over. 'Mister's' wife, Lucy had told him, took the paper for its advertisements for paying guests. In the current number was a literary criticism disparaging the very book he had bought for Pa's present.

He would send the book to Mother; she would appreciate it. But what could he give Pa? The shops were now shut. A copy of Housman's *Last Poems*, which he had bought for himself? No, not that, Pa would prefer a detective story. Ah, cigarettes! He had a tin-box of a hundred hand-made Gold Flakes: but had smoked two in the train. Could he put two ordinary Gold Flakes among them? Borrow them from Tim, and trust that Pa would not detect them with the others?

After supper of bloater-paste sandwiches, with Bivouac coffee, and healths drunk in sherry, the family played their usual games of rummy, snap, and Mah Jong. Phillip did not care much for Mah Jong, so he listened, marvelling, to voices and music from far away in the ether through the head-phones of the wireless set Ernest had made. It was romantic to hear, far out across the dark sea and distant fields and forests, the Morse of ships like the high piping of birds migrating through Arctic zones where icebergs clashed and jarred, and whales spouted in lonely seas glowing with Northern Lights; and moving the dials, to bring in the plainsong chants of priests in some remote monastery or cathedral at Midnight Mass. How Mother would smile her child-like smile as her spirit was set free.

The morning joviality around the breakfast table dissipated his vague thoughts of the dismissal of Dick Sheppard; and afterwards they went to church, sitting among half a dozen other people of the hamlet while the vicar, who came from two miles away, conducted the service. Mr. Copleston, looking unusually serious in his suit of early Edwardian cut, with high lapels to the jacket, took round the collection bag. After the final hymn to the tune of the harmonium they filed out into the crisp air, and so back to a meal of scraps; the main feast, with turkey, pudding, Stilton cheese, nuts, mince-pies, crackers and port-wine was to be eaten in the evening.

This was followed by games—ludo, draughts, and Mah Jong —during which Ernest went upstairs to get the 'prizes', from a large box of chocolates, Ingpan and Bounderbury's best, which Mrs. à Court Smith had given him for a Christmas present. The box was taken from its hiding place under Ernest's bed, and each person was invited to make one selection, after which the box went back under Ernest's bed, where it remained until emptied by the owner while lying in bed and reading, night after night, one of his presents—*Stories of Horror and Mystery*.

When the others had gone to bed Phillip walked alone under the stars, thinking of that Christmas night in the wood below Wytschaete, the perforated jam-tins filled with glowing charcoal, the frosty moonlight, the miracle of silence over the battlefield broken only by distant singing from the German trenches. He thought of the lonely Christmas his parents must be having, and returned exhausted, longing to be with Lucy as he lay alone in the chalet.

There was a party on Boxing Day at the house of the Squire. Thirty guests for dinner in a lofty panelled room lit by silver candelabra; merriment and laughter at the long table; hide-and-seek in the great warren of the upstairs rooms; rushing down corridors and landings where statues, armour, and other objects were likely to crash dreadfully as one fled away from capture or in pursuit of other players. He felt happy to be in such free-and-easy company, proud of Lucy's beauty, reassured by Mr. Copleston's handsome and distinguished demeanour. How foolish he had been to feel depressed because the old gentleman had merely indicated that his taste in spiritual and literary matters was his own!

After the New Year there was the Hunt Ball of the local pack. The Boys did not dance, also they were having what Tim called "an all-night session" in the Workshop. Phillip took Lucy in the borrowed Tamplin. It was the first car he had driven since Bédélia in France. The roads were icy; the tyres of the car were narrow; the burners of the acetylene headlights sooted up, causing the light to be weak and uncertain; he was nervous of the long and flimsy wheelbase, which so easily could overturn into ditch or hedge along the narrow, winding road to Shakesbury. They left for the dance not having had dinner, after a sandwich lunch and scarcely any tea; supper would not be until midnight. It had been his idea to go alone, and not in a party with some of her friends. As they drove slowly through the frosty night he knew that he should have taken her first to dinner at the Royal Hotel, and gone to the dance happy and fortified instead of hollow and doubtful. In his low physical state the misery underlying the privileged, gay assembly was apparent to him—the unemployed in the coal fields of Wales, and the general sense of frustration among the workers already talking of a General Strike.

On the way home in the early hours of the morning he stopped the Tamp by a coppice and began to talk of how he had failed Willie at the crisis of his life, even as he had let down Barley by not acting on what he had felt all along—the utter incompetence of both doctor and midwife. "I shall no doubt behave in exactly the same way to you, neither one thing nor the other, but a half-and-half person in all I do or don't do. I even allowed your very natural and kind reassurance to me, that Arnold Bennett remark, to stop the writing of my book."

Lucy sat quietly beside him, and when he said he was sorry she put her arms round him and told him not to worry. They drove home, had some hot milk, and the ghosts temporarily departed.

The next evening, determined to make his life orderly and regular in habit, he went on with his book from where it had been broken off before Christmas. Mr. Copleston had allowed the use of his library (for some reason the dining-room which had been about to be an office was now the dining-room again) and while he and others sat at night in the far room, reading or playing games, Phillip retired to the other end of the house, and sat in a small space surrounded by shelves of books; cabinets of eggs, shells, coins; guns, swords, daggers, animal heads and other relics of a full life about the world. There was a model railway-engine, to scale, in copper, brass, and iron, which Pa and 'Mister' had made in days before their friendship had become commonplace and then void. There was a walnut cabinet of drawers filled with trays of salmon and sea-trout flies, many eaten by moths. There was a glass-covered case of fossils and geological specimens. Among the prints on the walls was one of Pa's old home, with its lake, deer park, and house of half a hundred rooms.

By now he had an idea of the declining fortunes of the family. Pa, being a younger son, had inherited nothing from his father; but from an Aunt had come the Oxfordshire mansion, together with a dozen farms comprising the estate of two thousand acres; but the inheritance was subject to various charges, which, in the decline of agricultural values in the later decades of the nineteenth century, could not be met without reinvestment of capital produced from the sale of some of the land. Grandpapa, said Lucy, had been rather extravagant, and when he had died Pa had had to sell the rest of the estate with the land and the house, to pay his debts. Even so, he had been able to live as a country gentleman until the war of 1914–18.

"Ah," said Phillip. "I remember Aunt Dora telling me that Napoleon, when he was captured in 1815, made a prophesy. He said, 'Britain will rue the day, in a hundred years' time, that she refused to work with my system. For there will arise a nation, Prussia, who will challenge the British sea-power for the second time.' Napoleon was only a year out, Lulu, for 1914 was ninety-nine years after that prophecy! Do you remember telling me that the greater part of Pa's money was invested in Russian bonds?"

What a story, he thought, as with imagination stirred and flowing freely he prowled about the room staring, under the large hanging oil-lamp, at the relics of a bygone age, finally to sit down at the oak table to continue his story of the family in the house by the sea.

But nothing would come. He got up from the table, glancing half-seeing at the books, at the birds' eggs—Mr. Copleston had said he might look at them, "if you care to do so"—and crouched down by the hearth to alter the coals in the fire. Anything but write. He could not write in that room; it was stored with too diverse a life; it was too rich with the past; there was too much for present distillation by the imagination. So he sat at the table again, feelings of frustration growing in him.

Was it because too many voices were speaking from the past? Or was it because Pa, trying to read Dostoevski's *The Brothers Karamazov*, which he had lent him, had put it aside remarking that it was "the most frightful nonsense"? It was a copy of the Everyman edition; Phillip had not yet read it himself, but only of it, in a magazine called *The New Horizon*, where Wallington Christie had declared it to be a book of deep spiritual significance.

It was so with other books; half-hesitant attempts to discuss them had met with no response among his new friends, except Tim, the youngest, who was always ready to listen, but had little to say beyond occasional exclamations such as, "By Jove, I must read that!" "Yes, of course I see what you mean," and once, "Absolute confounded ass!"—this last referring to the reviewer of Keats' poems in *The Edinburgh Review*, who, said Phillip, had "advised Keats to go back to the gallipots". Phillip liked Tim, an attentive and willing younger brother; and yet, even as they talked together alone, in kitchen, workshop, or the potting shed, he felt himself becoming weary, and a suggestion of impatience came into his manner. After all, Tim's life had been so different from his own. But was that the only reason?

In the sitting-room at night among the others, Phillip had ceased to utter the thoughts that held him. References to Shakespeare, Tolstoi, Barbusse, Bernard Shaw—whose play *Saint Joan* he had seen in London, and been deeply impressed by its balance and interpretative fairness to all the characters—watching the scenes on the stage with wonder and emotion, while ideas for his own work clarified in flash on flash—references to these writers induced monosyllabic utterances of "Ah", or "H'm". From the mental habit of transposing himself so that he might see from the eyes of others (a process started on Christmas Day of 1914) he saw himself, if not as a bore, at least as one who interrupted the settled ways and thoughts of the family. This did not upset him unduly: but it was the cause of evening retirement to the library.

One night as he sat in that musty room his thoughts wandered to the sky of the snow-fields above the Pic de Ger; the azure sky above the peaks with their immense loneliness; the sudden deep blue of the gentians growing out of the grey grass where the snow had melted, the clear blue air far above ordinary human life, the clear and deep blue eyes of integrity, of beauty that was truth, a clarity he would never find again, far surpassing the tenderness of a charitable woman. With the feeling almost of levitation he felt the room to be full of the dust of things, of life outworn, of the spirit uncreated; and as he got up from the chair with a stifled groan, to seek Lucy with whom to plead for understanding, he saw the door opening, and she was standing there, a little hesitatingly.

"Come in, please come in!"

"You look tired, dear," she said gently, closing the door behind her. He longed for her to put her arms round him and clasp him to her breast. "Don't write too long, will you? I came to say goodnight. I think I'll go to bed, but I didn't mean to disturb you."

"Oh no, really, you're not disturbing me."

"Well, goodnight, dear."

Still standing there, he said goodnight to Lucy. She looked at him with a tremulous smile. He hoped she would kiss him; but he knew his mood was forbidding. "Goodnight," he said, almost formally, and with another half-glance, she was gone.

It was the first evening since his return that they had not kissed each other goodnight.

Rusty was watching from the worn rug before the fire, and seeing Phillip take his stick from beside the door, jumped up, wagging his tail. Any time during the day or night Rusty was ready for a walk. Phillip felt like walking all night, to tire himself out, to reduce his mind to nothing. What was he doing there? What would happen to that gentle trusting girl if he married her? Had they anything in common, she and her family and himself, except a knowledge of the names of birds and some wildflowers? Would she be hurt if he went away, and stayed away for weeks, even months, to write? But would he be able to remain alone, ever again?

He went out of the hall door and down the little weedy path to the iron gate and so into the lane; and, crossing the river over the old hump-backed bridge, stared at the stars shaking in the moving waters below. He walked up the hill, and along the crest of the down, the short grass rimed and the rising moon a swelling gourd in the east. He returned by other lanes that led down to the valley, and finding direction by the moon above, reached the hump-backed bridge. It was two o'clock in the morning, the Christmas truce was over, the dull flat reports of rifles echoed over the frozen Flanders fields—all ghosts, but living close to him. After some anguished hesitation, he removed shoes and socks in the kitchen and in bare feet crept up the back stairs to Lucy's small room. He felt his way slowly to her bedside, and whispered her name, and knew by the silence that she was asleep. After standing still for more than a minute, he moved to the bed-head and reaching down, softly stroked her head.

"It is I, Phillip."

"Is anything the matter?" her voice from the darkness said.

"No," he replied, and knelt by the bed, laying his cheek on the edge of her pillow, his forehead touching her cheek. A hand came from under the bedclothes and sought and held his.

"I've been for a long walk, Lulu."

"How lovely! I thought I heard you closing the gate."

"I've been thinking."

"What about, darling?"

He hesitated. "*Am* I your darling?"

"Of course you are. Don't you know it?"

"You must think me an awful washout."

"Of course you're not!"

"But I am *really*, you know. I'm not a bit like I seem! There's a hard, critical person inside me. I've tried to alter it for years, but it won't be suppressed."

"Only when silly people upset you. People *are* silly! I won't let them upset you any more, see?"

"Pa doesn't like Dick Sheppard, does he?"

"Oh that! He doesn't know anything about him! It's only what that silly paper said! Why, if Pa knew him, I'm sure they'd be friends at once. Don't take any notice of what Pa says."

"I admire Pa very much, really, you know."

"Yes, he's a dear, isn't he? He and Mother were inseparable. Poor dear, when she died I think he felt his life was over. But look at him now! Reading his boys' stories, just like Donkin in your book! It *is* such a lovely book."

"Do you *really* think so?"

"Of course I do. Don't you know it?"

"I wasn't sure."

"Well, don't ever think it isn't, for it is! Don't worry any more, will you, darling? One day we'll be alone, just we two, won't we, with Billy? Then we won't let people worry us, will we?" Her arms softly drew his head to her, she held him close, smoothing his hair with one hand, while murmuring as to a child. So they kissed goodnight, and he went outside to the chalet on a lawn crisp with frost; and undressing swiftly, got into bed and lay back thinking of the beauty of the morning star over the battlefield, years ago.

Some time later he was aware of footfalls on the gravel path. Looking up he saw the outline of Tim.

"Hullo," he said, "how goes it?"

Tim came into the chalet. "I thought you might be asleep, Phil. I say, I wonder if I might ask you a question?"

"Of course, dear boy. How is Pansy?"

This was the name of a girl Tim went to see in the only shop in the hamlet, kept by the widow of a sea-captain and her elder daughter. Phillip had been told by Lucy that she was Tim's first love.

"I was wondering, Phil, if I dare ask Pa if I might invite Pansy and her young sister to supper tomorrow night. It's her sister's last day, and I thought it might be a good opportunity to introduce Pansy to Pa. She's been too nervous hitherto to come by herself. What do you think?"

"Have you asked Lucy?"

"Oh yes, she says it would be quite all right. Only Pa, as you may have noticed, is a bit old-fashioned—not that I wish to imply the slightest criticism of him, or anyone else for that matter."

By 'anyone else' Tim meant 'Mister' and Mrs. à Court Smith. He had confided in 'Mister', with the result that Mrs. à Court Smith had invited him to dinner the following night, and talked to him about it, advising him not to let his friendship with the girl become serious. Tim had been too shy to tell her that he *was* serious.

'Mister' had confided Tim's confidence to Phillip, taking the line that he ought to warn young Tim not to make an ass of himself.

"Oil and water won't mix in this world, there's no use denying that fact!"

"But human beings aren't internal combustion engines, 'Mister'."

"You can make a joke of it, but I've known men marrying beneath them before, and it jolly well doesn't work, old chap! I know what I'm talking about!"

"Ah!" said Phillip, noncommittally.

Tim had a secret admiration for Phillip, not only because he was so understanding, but he had fought in the war which to Tim seemed a truly terrible thing, of attacks night and day without ceasing in mud and blood, machine-guns going all the time, bombs bursting, scout planes falling in flames, little to eat and nowhere to sleep for four and a quarter years. How Phillip or anyone else had lived through it all Tim could not understand.

"Well, if Lucy says ask them up, why not ask them up? I'm sure they would enjoy themselves. What's the sister like?"

"She's quite different from Pansy, who is very shy. Her name's Marigold, by the way," breathed Tim, as though he were afraid of his own voice. "She's a short-hand typist in Dorchester, and, Pansy says, has some experience of office work. We'll want someone to keep the books, of course, when the Works are built."

"When do you think you'll get going?"

"Oh, in the spring. We'll be able to employ several girls as well; we'll have five thousand square feet of floor space, you know, half in the machine shop, the other half in the loft upstairs. We're having a bench put along all one wall, with almost continuous windows to let in light. The whole place will be wired for electricity, of course. We'll have our own batteries and engine, and by the way, the Misses Jardine in the house up the lane want electric light, too, but say they can't afford to have a plant installed. So Ernest and I are considering a cable from our battery house, to be laid under the lane, if we can get permission to dig it up, and then under the Jardines' garden and orchard to their house."

"Won't an underground cable cost a lot?"

"I haven't yet gone into the matter deeply, but to be on the safe side we think we ought to get an inch and a quarter submarine cable, which will come to close on a hundred pounds. I hope they won't find that prohibitive, for the two sisters weren't left too much money when Colonel Jardine died, so I understand." Tim was almost inaudible with sympathy for the two elderly spinsters, daughters of the late Colonel.

"Why not two overhead wires, on posts? After all, it won't be much of a voltage from your batteries."

"We did suggest that," said Tim, "But they are dead against it, for their father's sake. He loathed everything modern, I understand. In India they used to have a great many native servants, and nothing mechanical. Even two natives to work one spade, they said, one to push it into the ground, the other to pull the handle down by a string. It was a question of the caste system, I think."

"To share out the food, I suppose, in a land of semi-starvation and over-population. I never thought of it that way before, Tim."

"Nor did I, now I come to think of it."

"Then we'll be seeing the two girls tomorrow night?"

"Yes, I'll go down first thing in the morning and tell them the good news. I am awfully grateful to you for your advice, most truly I am. Are you quite comfortable in that bed? I meant to rewire the mattress, I hope it's all right?"

"Oh yes, I've got a coal-scuttle under the middle, which supports the sagging bit. I know now how a cuckoo feels in a wren's nest."

The two girls arrived before supper. Pansy was small and shy, her sister taller and apparently confident. The sister perched herself upon the edge of the table, while they were waiting for Pa to come down, swinging one long leg under a skirt which barely covered the other knee, and remained thus when Pa came in, holding out a hand to him when Tim introduced his father.

They sat at table. Pa held up carving knife and fork, and with a genial expression said, "Pansy, there's rabbit pie, or brawn. Which do you prefer?"

Pansy, who had scarcely spoke so far, replied almost inaudibly, "I don't mind what I have."

Knife and fork still poised, Pa said, "Well, I don't mind either! It's for you to say."

Perceiving her nervousness Phillip said, "Plump for rabbit pie, Rusty wants the bones afterwards!"

"Rabbit pie it is," said Pa, after which he turned to the other guest. The name of Marigold seemed to be too much for him, so he said, "And you?" disguising his fear with a quizzical glance.

"I'll try the brawn, if it's all the same to you," she replied, with a wink at Phillip, which he amiably ignored.

Three slices were meticulously detached from the mould, and handed on a cracked Wedgwood plate of terracotta and gold with the Copleston crest on the rim.

Phillip had bought a bottle of claret. "Ha! I'm in luck! Pansy, you must come to supper every night!" declared Pa.

Ernest and Fiennes ate without a word. Afterwards Lucy and the girls washed up. Tim looked happy, and the five of them went for a walk by the river. The next day, as Tim was scraping the dining-room wall—the temporary office—Phillip sitting in the next room heard Pa go to him and say, "Tim, I shall have no objection to your engagement to Pansy."

"Oo-aa," Phillip heard Tim reply from the top of the ladder.

Pa went away into the garden; Tim got down from the ladder and looking round the doorway said, "Am I disturbing you, Phil!" When Phillip said not at all, Tim went on, "If you can spare a moment to come with me to The Point, I have something to impart."

They went together past the workshop to a small triangular parcel of semi-waste land which once had been a garden.

Tim, expressing himself joyfully, then continued in a style and manner acquired from reading nondescript humorous fiction.

"You see, lying before you, my dear Phil, The Point. I ask you to regard it as it is now. I think you will agree that it is a mass of weeds, and, as you will perceive if you look closely, cankered apple trees, standing among what can only be described as entirely useless blackcurrant bushes. On one side of The Point lies this lane, on the other, that deep railway cutting. From my early years this has been known as The Point; but the point about The Point is this, my dear Phil: there is every likelihood of The Point in the near future being cleared, and a new building of fabulous dimensions and floor-space arising on it!"

"I see. But—won't it require a certain amount of capital, Tim?"

"Ah, that, my dear sir, is precisely to the point! Or should I say, The Scheme! It's all rather wonderful, in a way, Phil. You see, one day we shall have a certain amount of money; and bearing this in mind, and moreover the pressing fact that treadle-lathe work at any time is dashed tiring, and most particularly so at night, as I know to my cost—do I not!—well, to cut a long story short, we have long considered that the sum of two hundred pounds, advanced against our future inheritance, would buy sundry long-felt wants, to wit, an oil engine and an extra lathe capable of taking much bigger work than the much-esteemed treadle lathe, of somewhat ancient pattern, let me add!"

"Very good idea, Tim, but what's this leading up to?"

"Ah, but that is the point, my dear Phil! You see, we originally argued this way. Two hundred pounds would allow us to take more contract work for sac-machines for little men to make batteries. So we hied us to the town and went to see a certain legal luminary who has recently arrived in Shakesbury from, I am told, South Devon. The said legal luminary at once said he would make enquiries on our behalf. And lo and behold, likewise hey-presto! we learned that we could obtain much more than the sum we originally contemplated asking for! So you see, my dear future brother-in-law, Ernest, Fiennes and I have been scheming schemes, and one of them is now about to materialise, to wit, the erection of a Works at The Point, where the wheels of industry will turn upon several thousand square feet floor-space, both up and down! There is no end to the possibilities of such a scheme, my dear Phil! Such as, in addition to the aforesaid oil engine and power lathe, the very latest pattern of milling machine, an extra *three-inch* lathe for garage work, besides other machines absolutely necessary for the firm of Copleston Brothers. A first-floor storey will of course have benches, where later on girls can make batteries. Why indeed should *we* not make batteries, as well as the sac-machines for the manufacture thereof? The whole, of course, to be lit by our own electric light, which will be extended to the house!"

"But will you have enough work, out here in the country?"

"We have considered that deeply, I do assure you! We propose no less than a monthly *standing* advertisement in *The Model Engineer*, in lieu of merely one casual insertion, to attract budding genii and others of that ilk to send their models to be made by the Copleston Brothers. Ernest, I do assure you, is a man of remarkable skill and ingenuity; he can make absolutely anything from any blueprint ever drawn! Then we are considering the idea of a forge to be attached to the Works, and a smithy, for there is absolutely no one near to shoe horses, both farm and hunting, and of course a forge is absolutely indispensable to any engineering shop!"

"It seems pretty good to me, Tim. Whose idea is it?"

"Chiefly Ernest's, with a few suggestions from me. We both have long wanted such a lay-out, Phil, but until now the wherewithal has been most conspicuously absent. But hear me to the end. I'm not boring you, am I?"

"No, of course not! I think it's a very fine scheme. But it will cost a good bit, won't it? What else do you propose to have here?"

"We think one of the new petrol pumps, also a proper well, which will of course supply the house, and so dispense with that truly beastly and horrible rain-water tank which collects soot from the railway engines, and also a great many leaves, not to mention an occasional sparrow. There is one small snag, however, which I must mention. We propose to have windows facing both east and west, and having gone deeply into the matter with Mr. Thistlethwaite, the aforesaid legal luminary, we find that we will have to pay a rent to the railway company, for use of their light over the cutting. The railway, you see, claims what are called Ancient Lights."

"Thistlethwaite? I knew a solicitor at Queensbridge named Thistlethwaite!"

"Yes, he mentioned that he knew you, and had indeed acted for you. So we considered that we could safely place our affairs in his hands."

"Well, I don't know very much about him, you know. By the way, reverting to Ancient Lights, must you pay for the engine smoke which drifts over your garden and into the rooms of your house? Why put up with the railway's rights to provide ancient darkness?"

"Well, you see, the railway was here before the house was built! But to continue. We plan nothing less than the complete redecoration of our abode! We shall wire it ourselves for both light and power-points. We shall provide irons for ironing, kettles for tea and coffee—to be drunk, let it be understood, in rooms with walls freshly distempered and painted! And last, but by no means least, my very dear Phil, Pa can now have the latest edition of *The Encyclopaedia Britannica,* to help him in some of the particularly thorny problems in the crossword puzzles of *The Morning Post.*"

So far Phillip had been asked no questions about his family; nor had he spoken about his parents, even to Lucy. He had told only his mother about her during his visit to London before Christmas, dreading possible criticism, particularly from his sister Elizabeth, that he had forgotten Barley so soon after her death. Now he thought to break the ice by taking Lucy to meet his Uncle John at Rookhurst; he was easily the nicest of his relations. So he wrote to Fawley House, and had a reply inviting him to go over at any time, with two days' notice.

It was a happy occasion. Phillip felt free with Uncle John, who repeated, while Lucy was upstairs with the housekeeper-cook, that he had left everything to him in his will.

"Not very much, I am afraid, old chap, as I am living on a purchased annuity.'

He went on to ask Phillip what he thought of Uncle Hilary's proposal that he should come to Rookhurst and learn to farm.

"I think I would like to very much, Uncle John, thank you."

"That is splendid news, my dear boy! I shall write and tell Hilary, with your permission, at once! I expect you know that he has recently bought Skirr Farm, which I think you once visited with Willie, a year or so before the war? Oh yes, Frank Temperley gave up—he had a pretty hard time in the war to keep going, what with most of his young labourers joining the Forces. How fortunate that you have come just now, Phillip! Hilary, I understand, is going to have the farmhouse made more comfortable inside, and was proposing to let it off."

"Do you think he would let it to Lucy and me, Uncle John?"

"I am certain he would! It was his idea that you should go there in the first place, but he wasn't sure what you wanted to do with your life."

Phillip wrote that evening to tell his father that he was going to be married to Lucy Copleston, 'who knows Uncle John', but gave no particulars. He felt shaky and disturbed that his life had changed so suddenly. Had he been rash in agreeing to the farming idea? What about his writing? Would Hilary expect him to give it up? He couldn't give it up—it was his only purpose in living.

In the period that followed, as Phillip went to and from his cottage, a three-hour journey, the Boys' plans seemed to be materialising. Tim had already spoken enthusiastically of what he called 'a little man who calls himself a builder'; and one afternoon, arriving from North Devon, Phillip saw him talking with Tim; literally a little man, short and thick, with round head, broad Dorset accent and a face partly hidden by long drooping moustaches under a bowler hat. Mr. Pidler had been recommended by someone Tim had met in the cooked-ham-and-beef-shop in Castle Street, Shakesbury.

Soon single walls of red-brick were arising among the weeds. A week later these walls were twelve feet high. There was a southwest gale one night, and lying in the chalet, Phillip heard a crash. Exploring with a torch, he saw that the walls had collapsed. By noon of the next day they were going up again. Another gale blew them down once more. Up they went, Mr. Pidler having explained to Tim that when the roof frame was on, it would hold the walls up proper.

Tim and Phillip surveyed the resurrection under a calm sky. Rusty, sniffing about, cocked his leg at the base.

"Stop!" cried Phillip. "One Pidler is enough. And the roof isn't on yet."

Tim explained that it was to be a corrugated iron roof, with steel girders. The central H-section would be strong enough to support, on an endless chain with wheels and rachet, the heaviest type of motor-car.

"But do you think you will ever want to hoist up a motor-car, Tim?"

"The alternative was a pit, and Fiennes objected to a pit. He once fell down an open hatch, you see, on board ship."

"Now about these walls. I did, as a matter of fact, wonder about their strength when I saw they were of a single-brick thickness for so high a building, but I suppose the builder knows what he is doing, Tim?"

"Pidler assured me that it would be quite all right, as matter of fact."

"Didn't you get an architect?"

"Pidler said it wasn't necessary, and would save us expense."

At that moment 'Mister' arrived on The Onion. He wore a crinkled oversize flying-helmet on his head, several mufflers round his neck, two overcoats, woollen gloves under leather gauntlets, trousers concealed under water-proof leggings. He had his asthma back, he explained, and couldn't afford to take risks with the beastly complaint. He beckoned Tim aside, and the two moved away into the house; and passing through, Phillip saw 'Mister' putting a cheque into his pocket-book.

'Mister' then asked for a word with Phillip, and taking his arm led him away.

"I say, old chap, have you any idea of what the Boys are spending on this building?"

"I haven't, 'Mister'."

"They've no experience of money, you know. Between you and me, I don't like the look of that builder feller. My gardener has heard things in Shakesbury, you know. Also they say that that new lawyer, Thistlethwaite, is a pretty sharp customer. Oh yes, people in a district like this soon get to know about everyone's business, you can be sure of that. I haven't interfered of course—it's none of my business—but you seem to have your head screwed on the right way, so couldn't you find out what they've done about their reversions of the Marriage Settlement? Only keep me out of it— you understand—I'll rely on your discretion entirely, I know I can do that."

"I'll be as discreet as you, 'Mister', count upon it!"

"Thanks, old chap. Well, how is life going with you? I'm under the weather most of the time, you know." He sighed. "The Onion needs new piston rings as well as a new piston, new bearings, and probably a new cylinder into the bargain, confound it. I hope Ernest will be able to put it right for me. I've got to go to Salisbury next week to see Ness. Surely I told you about her? Keep it dark, old chap, but Ness is what I suppose nowadays would be called my *belle amie*. I've known her over thirty years, so it's no flash in the pan, I do assure you."

The broken sofa and Pa's armchair went away to be re-uphol-stered. Half-hundredweight tins of distemper stood about, open to the March rains. Paint-brushes lay in pots and by window sills. New carpets arrived. Puddings of pink plaster lay about the rooms, solidified. Wires trailed in passages. A corrugated-iron roof hid externally the girders, spans, and principals of the Works. New woodwork staircases and panelling of tongued-and-grooved planks lined the interior upper brickwork. Two lavatories and a couple of washing basins were connected to the old septic tank, which was found to be choked. Phillip set to work to clear it out, distributing pails of black compost upon that area of the garden he had cleared of docks, thistles, nettles, and rusty tins.

Commercial travellers began to arrive. Following their visits, packets, cartons, and wooden crates were delivered by the Railway horse-drawn dray. The packets, cartons, and crates lay about, opened, their contents half-removed. Heavy machinery arrived by lorries. They were driven through tall double doors upon the new floor of the works, and unloaded by means of the endless chain with a breaking strain of twenty tons. Every new arrival was greeted by Tim with immense enthusiasm. Discussions followed with Ernest about where exactly the three-inch lathe, the milling machine, the power hacksaw, power drill and power grindstone and buffer should stand.

"Confound it," muttered Ernest. "We forgot to leave holes."

Tim set to work cheerfully to chip holes in the new concrete floor. It was a great moment when the oil engine arrived; followed by carboys of acid and crates containing batteries. Then the anvils and smiths' tools for the forge, with boxes of horse-shoes and nails, packages of screws, nuts, bolts; a gross of assorted pincers, ditto of spanners; dozens of cartons containing electric-light bulbs; a gross of sparking plugs of various makes, all of them surplus Disposal Board war-time aero-engine plugs which fitted no known lorry, car, or motorbike engine; a gross of tins of anti-grease paste for cleaning hands. A till was set up in the new office to be managed by Fiennes, who locked the door when he went out and hid the key. Tim got through one of the Ancient Light windows to fill the till with petty cash, ready for the change of Sales.

Nobody came to buy anything, so in the days that followed the ready cash was convenient for small purchases in the town such as cigarettes and cooked ham or beef—beef browner than mahogany, over-cooked and tasteless in the usual country manner—when sudden hunger told the Boys, in Tim's words, "that the inner man must not be neglected."

The food was fetched from the town in a Trojan motor-car acquired for the Works' business. It was a year-old model, but to Tim the salesman of the Shakesbury Motor Company had explained that it was a demonstration model, and as such a very fine motor-car indeed, and well worth the full price he was asking for it; in fact he had intended to buy it for himself, but he would as a favour let them have it. Tim had thanked him for this kind act, and Fiennes wrote out a cheque for the full amount of a new car.

The signing of the cheque gave Fiennes an idea. As office manager, he would need a new motor-bicycle; so he ordered a model he had admired in *The Motorcycle*. It arrived one day and was much admired. Now, stove-enamelled black, and nickel-plated, it stood in the Works, far too good to be used on the road. It had a new kind of sleeve-valve engine, and electric lights. 'Mister' asked to be allowed to ride it, was given permission and a shove off; a wobble followed; a cry.

"Too powerful for me, Fiennes old chap. To tell you the truth, I don't feel I could manage it. I'm used to The Onion's ways, don't you know. It lost all compression on the way over, and there's a noise I don't very much like in the crankcase."

There followed a long conversation by telephone to Salisbury, after which 'Mister' mooned about unhappily before going back to stare at the motionless Onion.

Phillip found Fiennes hard to talk to. When he asked him if any work had come in, Fiennes replied, "That's my affair," before locking the office door and going in to Shakesbury to have his hair cut. The telephone receiver was left off, so that no calls could be taken while he was away. The telephone was a bore, said Fiennes.

Another bore, according to Fiennes, was the loose, tall, prematurely bald young man who had bought a small house above the river, with a few grazing meadows. He had paid them a visit, asking questions about what the Works were for, and trying to be friendly in a gauche manner. He was, declared Fiennes, an idiot. That became his nickname, and whenever 'The Idiot' turned up for a talk Fiennes turned his back on him, and walked away, unheeding his remarks. Even when 'The Idiot' wanted petrol, at the new pump, he wasn't served. Anyway, said Fiennes, the damned tank was half full of water.

Chapter 16

FOOD AND THOUGHT

Hetty wrote to Phillip saying that she hoped she would be allowed to meet Lucy before he was married. He replied that he had no idea when he would be married. For one thing, it was a question of money. Twenty-five pounds, he wrote, was due from Hollins when the new book was delivered to them; but it had taken rather longer than he had expected.

In fact, the novel had been abandoned more than three months now, ever since the vain attempt in the past winter to write in Pa's study.

During the dark months, in his cottage, he had written several short stories about birds and animals, but these had not been accepted by magazine editors in London; nor had anything been printed in America since the flying start of four years previously. Anders Norse had written to tell him that his style appeared to have changed: a little too realistic, he said. Could not he rewrite them, or better still write new stories in his old, romantic manner?

Phillip's style had changed since reading some of cousin Willie's books, including Barbusse's *Le Feu*, and other literature with a revolutionary basis or theme. One of the writers who had influenced him was H. M. Tomlinson, whose long essay *The Nobodies*, written with irony and grief for the fate and circumstances of the common soldiers of the war, had affected him deeply; and thus Tomlinson's radical views were woven into his life. Often to himself Phillip repeated a paragraph from Tomlinson's essay on Kipling:

> Kipling has an uncanny gift of sight. It prompts no divination in him, but its curiosity misses nothing that is superficial. If he had watched the Crucifixion, and been its sole recorder, we should have had a perfect representation of the soldiers, the crowds, the weather, the smells, the colours, and the three uplifted figures; so lively a record, that it would be immortal for the fidelity and commonness of its recorded experience. But we should never have known more about the central figure than that he was a cool and courageous rebel.

Phillip knew very little about Kipling, beyond an earlier admiration for *Plain Tales from the Hills,* and *Actions and Reactions*. Then on another occasion, looking at a poem containing an invocation to the Lord God of Hosts he had read no further, linking this phrase in his mind with the civilian outlook during the Great War, particularly that of self-righteous clergymen preaching from pulpits. Kipling was dismissed as a fireside-patriot until Lucy's grandmother, during a visit there, had told him that Kipling's poem *Recessional* had been written as a warning against false pride during the year of the Queen's Jubilee of 1897.

"I think I am right in saying, dear Phil, that Mr. Kipling foresaw what would happen if the growing euphoria of the age of industrial expansion brought with it a feeling of false pride and even of arrogance, which would in its turn bring ruin to all the hopes of those who had dedicated their lives to the service of the many peoples of the Empire."

"I see, Grannie."

"I think it was the idea of Money, as an end in itself, almost a be-all and end-all, as they say, which would bring a lowering of standards, leading to corruption and eventual ruin, that Mr. Kipling was worried about."

Mrs. Chychester went on to say that she had spent many years in India with the Regiment which her husband had commanded then, and saw for herself that the ideas of eventual self-rule were being encouraged before their time by opportunists, which, if they had their way, would lead to a general massacre between those of different religious beliefs.

After this he decided to rewrite some of his short stories, taking out the critical slant which he had absorbed from reading Tomlinson and another essay on Kipling in Arnold Bennett's *Books and Persons*. It was with relief that he recast them clear of his own personal complications. What did birds and animals know of the human tragic scene? For them life and death were elemental with air, water, light, heat, and food. Life was a borrowing from the elements, death a returning. And the spirit permeating the elements was that of form, of precision, of harmony. That was God! In this revision he rewrote story after story; but when he came to human beings, he found little or no exaltation. The mess they made of the elements, of God, and of themselves! Having typed the stories, he took them to Anders' office one morning.

From the Adelphi he went to see cousin Arthur in the square, dingy brick building off High Holborn which was the Firm, with its several floors of machinery working and hundreds of men in aprons and women in dull cloth caps and aprons. It was a sight from which he escaped as soon as he could, taking Arthur out to lunch at the Cheshire Cheese, where a red-and-grey African parrot had been trained, in answer to the question *What about the Kaiser?* to reply with three terse words, two of which were *the Kaiser*.

"I don't think it's funny," said Arthur. "I don't like vulgarity."

"Nor do I, Arthur. But that's how most men regard sex, which isn't love, only its base. By the way, I must insure my life—do you, by any chance, know what company gives the best terms for an endowment policy?"

Arthur said he would find out and let him know.

"Thanks, old chap. When are you coming down to spend another holiday with me? I'll be leaving Devon some time this year. Strictly between ourselves, I'm going to live at my father's old home, at Rookhurst."

"Yes, Aunt Hetty told me."

"What else has she told you?"

"Only that you're going to be married again. May I offer my congratulations?"

"Many thanks. By the way, will you be my groomsman?"

"What's wrong with 'best man', Phillip?"

"Oh, it's the older term, I suppose."

"Does it matter?"

"Does what matter?"

"Calling it 'best man'?"

"Not at all."

"Then why mention it?"

"You mentioned it, surely?"

"Let's agree to differ, shall we? By the way, if ever you decide to sell the Norton, will you give me first refusal? I mean, I can fix you up with a new model, through commission agents, suitable for a sidecar."

"A sidecar! No fear! When I start farming I won't want anything except the Norton. Besides a hunter, and a pony and trap for Lucy and Billy."

He took Arthur to Cross Aulton on the motor-bike. It rained, the belt slipped. A new chain-driven model was the thing. As they lay in bed, side by side, listening to dance music on headphones, he said, "I can see that I'll have to get a chain-driven bike, with a three-speed gear-box. Could you arrange to get me one on the Easy Payment System?"

"I could arrange it for you any time, Phillip, and give you a good discount."

The next day Phillip agreed to let Arthur have the old Norton for twenty pounds. They shook hands on the bargain, and Phillip motored back to his cottage.

A week later the arrival of a letter from Anders Norse caused such excitement that he set off for London without waiting for breakfast. At Exeter he stopped only to send a telegram to Arthur at his office. *Will collect new Norton today paying cash.* Then on to Dorchester, Ringwood, and Farnham, where he stopped for a pint of ale and to read Anders' letter once again.

                        Adelphi Terrace
                            London
My dear Phillip
    John MacCourage wants to publish all your books. He has offered
$500 immediate payment for an option, this sum to be taken into
account as an advance against royalties when the agreement is signed.
He cables that he will be in London at the beginning of next month
and will want to meet you.
    Will you let me know meanwhile if you will accept his offer, which
I consider a fair one.
                        Ever Yours,
                        Anders Norse.

    For the last time he rode LW 82, touching nearly seventy across
the Hog's Back, and left it with Arthur in Surrey; then on to town
by train, keen with the vision of a resplendent new model at the
agents. There it stood, electric lamps, three-speed gear-box, chain-
driven, in the window of the Great Portland Street agents. Anders
Norse had advanced him £100; Phillip paid in £5 notes, and telephoned his cousin that he was leaving London immediately.
    The new bus was so different in weight and balance from the old
one that he was nervous of driving into the kerb, or a taxi; while
to have to change gear from second to top seemed a fearful ordeal.
Would he strip the gears, or worse, shoot forward and knock someone over? His first ride on the old Connaught two-stroke in 1915
had been diagonally across a road and into a lamp-post.
    He sent a telegram to Lucy, and started off with determin-
ation to go slowly in London traffic. He drove sedately, threading
in and out of solid-tyred omnibuses, horse drays and electric trams,
gradually gaining confidence. The engine was not run in, and for
a thousand miles or more he must go at a steady thirty to thirty-
five miles an hour.
    The afternoon was fine, soon he was at Staines, and on the
Great West Road to Andover. The goal of Lucy was fixed in his
head, so he did not stop for food. At twilight he ran free-wheel,
with engine silent down the lane to her house, stopped by the iron
gate, set the machine on its stand, took off goggles, and walked
round to the kitchen. He felt no emotion now that the long ride
of more than three hundred miles was ended.
    Lucy had been waiting for some hours to greet him. After
reading the telegram she had put off going on her bicycle to

Ruddle Stones for dinner. Knowing how keen he was on a new bike, the first thing she said when she saw him was, "Hurray! Where is it?"

"Outside the gate."

"Do show it to me. Oh, it's got foot-rests! How perfectly and *absolutely* lovely! We can go miles and miles without my getting tired!"

"Did you get very tired before?"

"Only sometimes."

"What a selfish fool I was, not to realise it."

"Oh, it wasn't much," she said. "Won't you come in?"

"I think I ought to be getting back to my cottage."

"Must you?"

"Well, my work is far behind. Also, I've got to return to London soon, to meet an American publisher. Where are the Boys?"

"Gone to Shakesbury to see Charlie Chaplin." She added, "I was just off to Ruddle Stones for supper, when I got your telegram."

"I'm sorry I deprived you of a good meal. I'll take you there."

She wondered if his remote manner was due to thoughts about his work. "Will you? How lovely! Just a moment, I'll get a cushion."

While he waited there, void with fatigue, Pa came out in his slippers and after the least greeting gave him a small parcel wrapped in brown paper, saying, "This is a bestial book. I have had to keep it hidden from my children," and without further words he went back into the house.

Lucy returned. In silence they arrived at 'Mister's'. By the glass door he stopped. "I'll say goodbye now."

"Won't you come in?"

"Sorry, but I can't face Mrs. Smith."

"Oh, she's quite harmless."

They went in.

'Mister' was sitting in a chair within, bent of back, twiddling his thumbs, varying this symptom of an empty life by sometimes tapping his nails on a Chinese lacquer table beside his chair. On the table was *The Radio Times* and a pair of headphones, for he tried to relieve marital boredom by listening to singing, gramophone records, and talks from 2LO.

By a lamp, sewing in another chair, was Mrs. à Court Smith, a squat figure with blackberry eyes beneath feathery eyebrows that emphasised a heavy face under a pile of grey hair.

On a sofa in another part of the room sat a man and a woman, obviously not at ease, and looking what they indeed were, two new paying guests who had come to enjoy a holiday in the country.

"By Jove, hullo, hullo!" cried 'Mister', half pulling himself out of the chair on to his long bent legs. The effort seemed too much, he compromised by slewing himself round. "If it isn't Lucy! Well, well, well, and how are both you good people tonight? Come on in, and make yourselves at home!"

After shaking hands with Mrs. à Court Smith, Phillip was asked if he knew the paying guests. The couple rose hesitantly and awkwardly, saying that they were very well thank you in reply to an enquiry as to how did they do. Mrs. à Court Smith gave Phillip a significant glance, but he pretended not to see it, and she resumed her sewing, to enquire of Lucy, "How are Pa and the Boys?" at the same moment that Phillip said to 'Mister', "How's the Onion?"

"Oh, the beastly thing's gone wrong again," complained 'Mister'. "Magneto this time, I think. I wanted Ernest to come over and look at it, and sent him a telegram, but he was too busy this afternoon, I gather. So I'm stuck here, you see, old fellow." He drummed his fingernails on the Chinese table. "Well, what's your latest news?"

"We're all motor-bike fiends here," said Phillip to the paying guests.

"Go on!"

"I see you've got a new Norton," said 'Mister'. "Wish I had!"

"It's such a beauty," said Lucy happily.

"Lucy", said Mrs. à Court Smith, equably, "tell me, are you going to announce your engagement in *The Morning Post*?"

Lucy looked at Phillip.

"Well," he said, "we weren't going to, for the present."

"I think you ought to, you know, old chap," said 'Mister'. "It's the thing, don't you know."

Phillip felt utterly exhausted. He made no reply until 'Mister' repeated his advice, then he said distinctly, "I'm not awfully keen on advertising."

"It's no joking matter, I assure you, my dear fellow."

"But why *The Morning Post?*"

Mrs. à Court Smith laid down her work as she prepared to say, also distinctly, "Well, you see, after all, Lucy comes of a rather good family."

A silence followed. The paying guests began a conversation in low voices, to show that they knew it was not the thing to eavesdrop.

'Mister' rattled finger-nails on the table. "I used to ride a penny-farthing bike, you know," he said to Phillip. "I must say it was more reliable than the beastly Onion."

"We thought a quiet wedding, just a few friends," said Lucy.

"By Jove, the time signal ought to be soon," exclaimed 'Mister', fastening the headphones over his large ears. He sat expectantly, lying back in the chair on the base of his spine while gazing at the ceiling, finger-tips placed together, long knees in apogee.

"I've just been reading Martin Beausire's latest," said Mrs. à Court Smith to Phillip, with an unexpected change of tone to the affable. "You know him, don't you?"

"Yes."

"What do you think of his book."

"I'm really no critic."

"I much prefer his early schoolboy books to his novels. His characters are always rushin' about so. Perfectly charmin', his first book about schoolboys, I thought. You met him once, didn't you, Lucy?"

"Yes, when I was 'Guiding'."

"I see he uses the names of real places—Barnstaple and Speering Folliot—isn't that your village, Phillip? His hero, or should it be villain, is a writer, too. I thought it rather a coincidence that he made his character live in the same village as yourself." She pulled her ball of wool nearer, and went on, "Of course, I know nothin' about writin', but to me his novel appeared to be somethin' of a hotch-potch."

"Just a moment!" exclaimed 'Mister'. He whipped out a watch. Pips sounded in the headphones. "Two seconds late tonight, not so bad!" He listened, then removed the headphones. "Same old news, I heard it at six o'clock. More beastly rain."

"What are you writin' now?" enquired Mrs. à Court Smith.
"Nothing at the moment."

"Lucy tells me it is about an otter. That ought to go well round here."

"I went otter-huntin' once," said 'Mister'. "Ernest took me in the Tamp. I must say all my sympathies were with the otter. Although we didn't see one, it was a blank day. Like most of my days," he sighed, putting on the headphones again.

"I expected you to dinner, Lucy. Did you forget?"

"No, Mrs. Smith. I meant to telephone, but Fiennes had taken the office key by mistake."

"Have you had anything to eat?"

She blushed. "I don't usually eat much supper."

"What about you?" Mrs. Smith said to Phillip.

"I'm not really hungry, thank you."

"But you must be starvin', all the way from London! When did you go up? This mornin', and from Devon! Lucy dear, tell me the truth, has he had any dinner?"

"Oh dear," said Lucy. "I quite forgot to ask you when you arrived, and all that long way, too!"

"No, really, thank you, I'm not hungry," he insisted.

"Come and show me the new bike," said 'Mister', taking off the headphones.

It began to rain while they were outside, and at 'Mister's' suggestion Phillip wheeled the Norton into the garage, where it stood beside the oily little Alldays & Onion vehicle with its narrow tyres, bullock's-horn handlebars, and push-bike brakes.

"A beastly thing," lamented 'Mister'. "Either it won't spark, or the mixture is wrong and it spits through the carburettor, or it over-heats, or the chain breaks. I'm sick of it, I can tell you. I've asked the Boys to look out for something better, though I doubt if they'll succeed. The trouble is lack of money, don't you know." He began to sibilate tunelessly; then, turning to the younger man, he said, "You know, old chap, it isn't cricket to go about with Lucy as you do, with no formal engagement announcement. I know you Bohemians, but dash it all, there's her people to think of. As for Pa, he's too easygoin' for words. His wife wouldn't have died of consumption if he'd looked after her. Tim, you know, arrived only eleven months after Lucy, and Margaret was pretty well knocked up with it, I can tell you! Pa allowed her to visit a cottage where the woman had consumption, and she caught it there. He's far too easy-goin' about everything. Well, old chap, I think you ought to do the decent thing, and put the engagement in *The Morning Post.*"

'Mister' pulled sadly at one half of his ragged moustache. "Between you and me and the gate-post," he continued, kicking the smooth back tyre of The Onion with his foot, "I'm not too well. This beastly asthma gets me down. That reminds me, I must get The Onion repaired, so that I can go and see Ness at Salisbury. I've been trying to get there a long time now, you know, but whenever I've got ready to go either The Onion breaks down or this beastly asthma gets me first. I'd like you to meet Ness one day, and tell me what you think of her. We've been great friends for over thirty years, did I tell you? It only goes to show you how deep it is!"

'Mister' sighed, and mistaking the other's silence for sympathy, continued his confessions. "You mustn't think, you know, that because a man has passed sixty he ceases to feel hope, or loses any of the feelings he had as a youngster! Not by a long chalk! I feel just the same now as I did when I was your age, don't you know, the only trouble is one wears out, like The Onion." He regarded it with a sigh. "We've had some times together, The Onion and I. I'm quite attached to it in a way, we've had some fine rides in our time. I'd hate to get rid of it, even if I could. Who's got your old bike?"

"A cousin of mine."

"That was a fine machine, you know. Well, I must have one with a clutch and gears, my heart won't stand paddlin' off any more. This rain will make the roads slippery, be careful as you go home, won't you? We'd both be most unhappy if Lucy took a toss. By the bye, I hate to ask you, old chap, but could you manage a loan of a fiver?"

"I'm awfully sorry, 'Mister', but I've only got ten bob on me."

"A cheque will do, old fellow. I'd really be most frightfully grateful, don't you know. But not here." He glanced around. "I'll be comin' over to the Boys tomorrow. You'll be stayin' there, I expect? You don't know how lucky you are, you've got your life before you; I've got most of mine behind." And taking Phillip's arm in a friendly way, 'Mister' led him into the house.

As they entered the drawing-room Phillip observed that Mrs. à Court Smith hid a black book under a copy of *The Lady* on the table beside her.

It was now raining steadily. Mrs. Smith said they could spend the night there if they wished, there was plenty of room, but Lucy said she ought to go home, as there was a lot of work to be done; and after goodnights they set off in the darkness.

Phillip returned by another way, a lane more tortuous than the route they had come by, but nearer. He went slowly, anxious about skids, and was turning a corner about a mile from the house when the back-wheel slid away from under him, the handlebars turned askew, they were falling. The lights went out as they struck the stony road.

The engine was racing and he wondered if it would catch fire. He got up stiffly and went to where it was gyrating in the darkness, the back wheel spinning; and groping for the handlebars, managed to lift the valve-lifter and stop the engine. His right knee hurt, his right hand was bleeding. He stood there, overcome by a sense of disaster.

Lucy was getting up from the road near him. "It's the machine that matters."

"Are you hurt?" she asked.

If he had really loved her, would he not have hastened to find out if she were hurt?

"Are you hurt?" she repeated anxiously.

"Lucy, I think you ought to realise why I sent you those articles in *The Daily Crusader* by Arnold Bennett's wife, revealing what a fastidious, nervy person he was. All writers are fearful egoists, that's why they start as writers! They can't compete with the world on the world's terms, so they invent their own, and credulous, kind people like you accept them on those terms—sometimes! But the sensible ones regard them, and quite rightly, as Pa does *The Brothers Karamazov* which he gave back to me when you went for a cushion. It's a great book that strives to find the truth about human nature, and so find clarity."

"Oh, Pa wouldn't understand a book like that!"

The rain fell gently, the clouds were passing. A star shone in a space above. He went to look at the machine. It was lying in the long grass, half hidden by umbelliferous plants at the side of the lane. He tried to lift it up; it was much heavier than the old

Norton. The handlebars were askew. One foot-rest was bent. He lugged it up, and turned off the leaking petrol.

"Is it all right, Phillip?"

"I don't know."

He managed to pull it back on the stand. Lucy, waiting in the dimness, said, "Don't be unhappy. Your lovely new Norton! And your hand is bleeding. I think we ought to go back to 'Mister's', so that I can wash and dress it."

"I couldn't face them again. Why don't you go back, you mustn't get wet. I'll stay here, and repair it."

"I rather like the rain. It's my fault, too, it was me on the back that made it skid. I'm so sorry, dear. And please don't worry about Mrs. Smith, or Pa. What they say or think doesn't matter in the least."

"But it does! Cousin Willie was right! Dick Sheppard knows, too, but he won't live long! He's nervously exhausted, seeing all the human world disintegrating into another war just as Willie said——" He turned away; returned to say desperately, "Lucy, I must tell you the truth! I am not a pleasant person at all. I can't really *bear* what most people think, and say. I *pretend* to be tolerant, at times, because I don't want to hurt their feelings, also I know I am like them. *But,* after Barley's death, I realized that it is wrong to stifle one's intuitions—especially when things are obviously going wrong, out of a pose of good manners—which in my case is only a veneer."

But he knew he was not being really truthful: he was diverting his real thoughts, afraid to hurt her feelings. Barley *understood*: Lucy gave all her sympathy, but did she *understand*? Even to himself he could not face the answer.

When she did not reply he got astride the machine, and managed to jerk the handlebars round to normal. Turning on the petrol, he flooded the carburettor, and kicked the starter. The engine fired after a few kicks. He opened the throttle, the engine raced; closed it, the engine ticked over. But the lights would not switch on. He let in the clutch and moved forward. The machine seemed all right. He put it on the stand again.

"There now, it isn't so bad after all, is it?" she said. "It might have been worse, but you are a careful driver."

"But are *you* hurt, Lucy?"

"No, I fell on the grass, where it was soft. But your hand——"

"Only a scratch. What luck, the Norton may be all right, after all! You must think me a miserable, selfish creature!"

"Of course I do not," she said. "I know exactly how you've been looking forward to your lovely new bike. I am sure that Ernest or Tim will be able to put the lights right in the morning."

The half-moon was now clear, and after he had washed his hands in running water, they started off, slowly in bottom gear, then in second, while confidence came back with steady progress, and they got home without further mishap, to find that the others had gone to bed. She put on a kettle for tea, and while it was heating she bathed his right hand and put iodine on the broken skin, and a bandage, while he sat in Pa's chair and held *The Morning Post* with his good hand, and sipped milky, sugary tea. The effect was relaxing.

"I'll send in an announcement after submitting it for Pa's approval."

"I am sure it would please him," replied Lucy happily, as she went into the kitchen to cook eggs and bacon with fried bread.

While she was there Tim came in, sniffing eagerly. "Well, well, well! Do my eyes deceive me, or do I behold the delectable sight of eggs and bacon? Will I have some, do you ask? Will I not!"

"You shall, Tim, you shall!" cried Lucy. "There's enough for all."

The three sat down together.

"By Jove, this food is good!" exclaimed Phillip, after the meal. "Lucy, I must tell you that I do understand, really, why Pa thought as he did about *The Brothers Karamazov*! All life is an idea, and ideas change with time. The great thing is to see life calmly, like Tourgenieff. I say, the Savoy Bands are on now—let's listen!" He put on a pair of headphones, and lay back in Pa's chair, stretching out his legs.

"Quick, Lucy, quick! The nightingale is singing!"

In the drawing-room at Ruddle Stones, 'Mister' was also lying back in his chair, headphones adjusted to hear the Stock Exchange prices. For the past quarter of an hour he had been reading the black book which his wife had hidden when Phillip had returned from showing him the new Norton. The paying guests had, thank goodness, gone to bed. Now at last they could talk freely.

"What do you think of it for Lucy?" asked Mrs. à Court Smith, pointing at the black book on the reading stand beside her husband.

That gentleman, with a weary gesture of patience extended so far that no resilience was left to him, lifted an earphone to catch her words. Mrs. Smith repeated the question.

"I'll tell you in a minute, I want to hear if my Rio Chakko-stumer Tin Mines are quoted in the Stock Exchange Prices."

'Mister' still lived in the hope of one day hearing that these mines, shares in which he had bought in 1903, and from which no dividend had been paid since 1904, were to be reopened. They had, in fact, never been dug, but 'Mister' did not know this. His wife's business training in a solicitor's office had, however, given her a more realistic attitude towards human activities.

"Of course they won't be! They've been derelict for more than twenty years now. Why don't you do what I ask you, and read that book?"

Mrs. à Court Smith, realising Lucy's inexperience, her lack of social life beyond a few Christmas dances in neighbouring houses, had endeavoured to fill the gap as far as she could without direct words of advice regarding the realities of marriage. Recalling her own inexperience as a bride, she had answered an advertisement in one of her weekly papers; and in due course a stout black book had arrived from a Ludgate Hill publisher in the advertised plain cover.

The author had a number of letters after his name which seemed impressive: but she had regarded doubtfully his photograph opposite the title page.

"Nothing about Rio Chakko-stumer," muttered 'Mister', taking off the headphones.

"What do you think of his photograph?" asked Mrs. à Court Smith, pointing at the book.

"He looks a bit of a vampire to me, Lal, old girl."

'Lal old girl' was a survival from 'Lallafanny', pre-marital nickname in a period of pseudo-bliss before 'Mister' had discovered, as he put it to himself, her true nature. After marriage the endearment had become abbreviated with his moods to 'Lally', followed by 'Lal', after which the diminutive remained. At times even 'Lal' was too much.

He had first seen 'Lallafanny' in the office of his solicitor in London. She had then seemed, with her short but comely figure, to be good enough for second-best (he had never dared to propose to Ness). She spoke the Queen's English, and knew more or less how to conduct herself.

"Now read those pages I've marked with a marker."

'Mister' turned to a chapter with the caption *The Pitfalls of Marriage*, and began searching for titivating details, but without success, since the pages were inspired by intense moral indignation.

"He's been bitten himself, if you ask me," he pronounced moodily.

"How has he been bitten? Are you at the right place, I wonder? It concerns the bride, not the groom. Yes, that place where I've put in a bit of paper for a marker."

'Mister' read half aloud, half to himself:

"'On the hymenal night, which should be an exhibition of good-breeding, and high-toned affectionate joy, too often is the bridegroom driven insensate by a brutal lust of conquest. Deep down in man's nature is a streak of atavism, a survival from the steaming swamps and murderous jungles of his prehistoric ancestors. Such traits, when a virginal wife becomes his prey, too often rise uppermost in his unholy nature, and he yields himself to the brutal lusts of the flesh, causing his bride to recoil in horror from his bestiality.'"

'Mister' laid down the book. "Going a bit far, isn't it?"

"It could have been expressed better, I agree," said Mrs. à Court Smith. "But then he's an American. I saw it advertised in *The Lady*, and thought it would be just the thing for Lucy to read. The author *is* a qualified doctor, I suppose? That rigmarole sounds pretty foreign. You can never trust foreigners."

'Mister' turned to the title page.

"Doctor Sylvanus O. Saloman, Associate of Little Rock Academy of Therapeutic Medicine, Arkansas—Associate of Nebraska Homeopathic Institute—G.L.O.B.—whatever that means, of Talahassee—wherever that may be—Founder of Kappa Beta Phi Medicine Hat Ethical and Philosophical Society. It looks a bit odd to me, but then as you say, he's an American."

"They're nearly all quacks over there, I've heard," remarked Mrs. Smith.

'Mister' sat up. "I say, you're not really going to put this into Lucy's hands, are you, Lal old gel?"

"It can't do any harm."

"I don't know so much. It would me, if I were a young gel, don't you know. What did it cost?"

"Never you mind."

"I don't like any of it," he said, and put on the headphones. Mrs. à Court Smith stared at him with the unwinking stare of a toad about to fix a fly. Whatever her own hymenal experiences had been, she certainly was not afraid of 'Mister' now.

"Why bother to read it if it upsets you? But everything upsets you nowadays. Why don't you do what Lucy's Pa does, go and dig in the garden? Your liver needs a bigger shaking up than sitting on The Onion can give you."

A cry came from the fly. "I'm trying to listen to the nightingale!"

"It's too late now. You should have listened earlier on."

"I wanted to, but you made me read this beastly book!"

Moodily 'Mister' removed the headphones as the distorted tones of Big Ben came vibratingly through the diaphragm.

"My battery's run down again, that's the trouble," he muttered.

Part Five

LUCY

'If I leave all for thee, wilt thou exchange
And be all to me?'

Sonnets from the Portuguese
by Elizabeth Barrett Browning.

Chapter 17

FORMALITIES

In the early morning sunshine his doubts of the night before seemed worthless; and later, sitting at Pa's desk, by invitation, he wrote an announcement for *The Morning Post*. In this spirit he wrote another notice and put it up in the bathroom.

Invariably after a tub at Down Close the plug was merely pulled up, and the next bather was confronted by an increased high-water mark on the new paint on the bath. At least a dozen lines denoting an equal number of previous immersions were registered there when Phillip, in the spirit of Shakespeare, pinned up his *Advertisement*.

> THERE IS A TIDE IN THE ABLUTIONARY AFFAIRS OF MAN WHICH RELICT AT THE EBB REVEALS ITS JETSAM.

"Ha!" exclaimed Tim. "By Jove, that's rather good!"

"Do you think Pa will tear it down?"

"I doubt very much if he will see it."

"It's rather cheek, don't you think?"

"Oh no, please leave it up. I think it's jolly good! You're perfectly right! People should leave the place clean, after a tub."

The *Advertisement* remained for some days, while only Lucy and Tim took heed of it. The next time Pa had a tub, his tide-line remained near the top of the bath. Phillip used Zog, a tin of which he had placed under the bath, and took down the notice.

"I'll tell you what," said Tim. "The sooner we connect the Works' tank to the house tank, the better. All our bath-water, as well as that for the loo, comes from the rain-water tank on the roof. And every dashed train that passes in the cutting below the garden sends up a shower of soot which falls on the water. Our own smoke, too, makes it dirty. The tank should be covered. By Jove, you've given me an idea! We must do it without further delay!"

"I'll help you."

Phillip went up to examine the tank. It was nearly empty, with six inches of black slime on the bottom. He saw an immense black beetle, with fearsome jaws, swimming about in the mud. He put it in a matchbox, not an easy job, and took it with him to the luncheon table, while it seemed that the beetle was about to tear its way out of the flimsy prison.

"Ha!" exclaimed Pa, when he saw the box on the cloth, and the head of the beetle nearly through it. His eyes lit up. "One of the *Hydradephaga*!"

"Look at those jaws, sir, like secateurs!"

"One of those beggars once cracked a pane of glass in my hot-house, Phillip, at any rate I found him dead in the gutter the next morning."

Ernest came into the room, and saw the beetle crawling on his empty plate. With his usual immobility of expression, Ernest said "Ha!" and sat down, as though prepared to eat the beetle should nothing else appear on his plate. Then Tim came in, and ejaculated, "By Jove! How absolutely incredible!"

The beetle opened its black shards of horn, thrust out its wings, and in deep droning flight sailed around the room, bumping into the ceiling and falling to the table again.

"*Hydradephaga* all right," said Pa, peering with satisfaction. "Sub-species *Dyticidae*. Our fellow is *Dyticus marginalis*, I fancy."

He went to his study, returning with *Insects at Home* by the Rev. J. G. Wood. It had many engravings, some of them hand-coloured.

"Here's the fellow, I fancy," he said, pointing to a wood-cut. "Yes, it's *marginalis* right enough. The beggar flies from pond to pond by moonlight, and when it decides to come down, closes its wings above the water and drops in. That's how one of my panes of glass was broken, I fancy. It mistook it in the moonlight for water."

"I want lunch!" said Ernest, distinctly, staring at his empty plate.

"You shall, Ernest, you shall!" cried Lucy.

"Mind that brute!" said Pa to Tim, who was about to pick up the beetle. "It's got an appendage from its metasternum which is like a forked dagger. If you don't want it," to Phillip, "I'll have it in my water-garden. Useful little brute to watch."

Phillip offered to put it in the sunken tub, where grew various water-plants, but Pa said it was no bother. With a spoon he lifted the insect into a tumbler, and bore it outside to its new home.

"I'll finish the tank after lunch," Phillip said to Tim. "It's full of excellent compost, mainly soot and dead leaves. I imagine that the railway company won't want it added to their ancient lights." This joke having fallen flat, he tried another subject. "If anyone wants to insure his life, I'm the man. I have applied for an agency of the Millennium Life Assurance Company, in order to get commission for my own proposed life policy, and they have appointed me. All commission, of course, will go to anyone who wants to insure."

"Oo ah!" said Tim. "I must consider the matter."

Lucy arrived with a genuine subject for conversation of sorts— a dish of sausages and mashed potatoes. Noises of approval arose. Pa came back, saying the glass was dropping, and a change in the weather was coming if he wasn't mistaken. Bukbuk got in her usual place beside Lucy, to await scraps to be placed on the edge of the table. She now had kittens, her duties were shared by Moggy in a bee-skep in the workshop.

Hardly had silent munching started when the bell in the kitchen, one of several in a row under the ceiling, began to jangle.

"Oh damn."

"Who the deuce is it?"

"Dashed nuisance."

"H'm, who's that likely to be, I wonder."

"Probably 'The Idiot'."

"I'll go." Lucy had already risen.

The men sat still. Phillip offered to serve second helpings. This interfered with an awaited Odd Man Out, and found no response.

Lucy came back, smiling, telegram in hand.

"For you," she said to Phillip.

"Oh lor', what does this mean?"

"Open it and see," said Fiennes, putting a sausage into his mouth.

"By all means, we don't stand on ceremony here."

"Thank you, sir."

AMERICAN   PUBLISHER   LONDON   TWO   DAYS
LONGER   URGENTLY   WANTS   SEE   YOU   INVITA-
TION   DINNER   TOMORROW   2   MAY   7   P.M.
REPLY   MACOURAGE   ALBERT   HOTEL   NORTH-
UMBERLAND AVENUE LONDON.

He laid it down.

"I ought to get the tank cleared as soon as possible, if rain is coming. I must go to London first thing tomorrow."

"Ah," said Tim.

"An American publisher wants to see me urgently."

"By Jove!" from Tim.

"It looks as though he wants to publish my books, Tim," while the other men were intent on their food.

"I say, that's good news! I'm awfully glad, really I am."

Under the table Phillip squeezed Lucy's hand.

"So I must get the tank cleaned right away!"

"Oh, I shouldn't bother," said Pa. "It's been like that some years now, and will probably be like it for a good many more to come."

But Phillip had plans to clean out the loo as well. He had bought a tin of Whizzitoff, a chemical which dissolved everything.

"If you'll forgive me, I'll go and get ready, sir."

The journey would give him an opportunity to get a morning suit and topper; also Pa had asked him to get his father to send him the name and address of his solicitors, for the matter of a marriage settlement. "It's not my suggestion, but some interfering relations have written to me about the matter."

Whenever Phillip had thought of *that*, his stomach had seemed to go hard inside. Now he could, purely formally, give the message to Father when he got to London.

While the Boys went back to the Workshop, he got on with the cleaning of loo and water-tank. It did not take long to mop up the black residue on the bottom of the tank, and carry it in a pail to Pa's compost heap. Then to flush everything out, with gallons brought from the well. Lucy had washed up when the job was done, and they went for a walk beside the river.

It was an afternoon of blue skies and blowing white clouds, with lower dark clouds from which rain sprinkled, soon to blow over. The sun shone hot and bright once more. He lay con-

tentedly on the bank of a pool, and watched the trout rising to a
hatch of olive duns. Lucy sat near, knitting the last of a grey and
yellow pullover which he was supposed not to look at, since it
was to be a present for him. Then below the bank he saw an eel
burrowing into a hole. Creeping down he scooped it up and
flung it on the grass. The very thing for Pa's water-garden!

He made a carrier of his wet handkerchief, and when they
returned put the eel in the sunken water-tub beside the rock-
garden. He told Pa at tea that he had put the eel there, and to
his surprise the old man got up and left the room, muttering
about interference, and that he didn't want the beastly thing in
his water-garden. After tea Phillip got the scullery pail, meaning
to remove the eel to return it to the river. As he went round the
corner he heard Pa say to Ernest, "Maddison's an interfering ass
in my opinion."

It rained all through the journey to Surrey. He called at his
Uncle Joseph's house cold and stiff, with sodden gloves, helmet,
coat, breeches and pack. His boots too were wet, for he had
foolishly wound his puttees cavalry-fashion, with the tapes round
the ankles, so that the rain spilling off tank and coat had soaked
down, and not off, the coils. He arrived in the late afternoon;
Arthur had just come down from his office in London.

There was no fire in the sitting-room. As he sat there he wondered if his mood had affected Arthur, for his cousin was subdued.
Phillip told him that the new bus went very well, and that if it
had been the old belt-driven model, he would never have arrived
that day. How did Arthur like his purchase? Running well?
This was a hint about payment: he needed the £20 to pay part
of his first premium of the £1,000 endowment policy.

"As a matter of fact," stammered Arthur, avoiding Phillip's face
while smoothing his hair rapidly with one hand, "I wanted to see
you about that Norton."

"Well, here I am, old boy. Get it off your chest."

"You see, I—I was relying on my commission from your life
assurance to pay half of what I owe you."

"But you didn't tell me that when you bought the bus, did
you?" When Arthur made no reply, he repeated, "Did you?"

"I didn't think it necessary. I thought you were a fellow who
played the game."

"What game? Your secret game? Naturally, having worked in an insurance office, I knew there was a considerable commission on the first payment of a life insurance policy, and so as a matter of course I applied for an agency."

"That's the point. You didn't tell me. You see, I fixed up with a man to get half commission, when I found out the company which would give you the best terms, as you asked me. I consider you have not been straight with me."

"But does that absolve you from the fact that you owe for the Norton?"

"I think it does."

"But surely the two things are separate? Now if you'd told me that you expected to place the insurance for me, on the terms you've now revealed, it would have been a different matter. And in law, isn't an arrangement for secret commission illegal?"

When Arthur did not reply, Phillip said quietly, "Aren't you going to pay for the bus?"

"Frankly, I don't think I am called upon to pay you anything."

Was this his friend speaking, the man who was to be the best man at the wedding, the rather dreamy youth who liked poetry, and who ran the local branch of the Poetry Association? Arthur, who was, in theory, in revolt against the money-materialism of the middle classes; the soullessness of the City money-grubber? Was another friendship to go west because of money, as with Desmond Neville, to whom he had lent money whenever he had asked for it, on over seventy occasions during the war? Desmond had come into several thousand pounds in 1919, but had never offered to pay back the comparatively small sums totalling £39 10s. which he had borrowed.

"Very well, I'll take the Norton back, Arthur. I can sell it quite easily."

"Just a minute. There is another point I would like to mention. You told me the bus was in good order. Actually I've had a lot of trouble and expense over it. For one thing, you didn't tell me that the magneto was dud when you brought it here."

"But I'd just driven it two hundred miles! It was all right when I left it with you. It had been remagnetised, and over-hauled, only three months before, at the C.A.V. Works in North London."

"Well, I don't agree that the magneto was in sound order when I received it. I had to have it sent away almost at once. And the bill isn't paid yet."

"Very well, I'll pay the bill! Will that satisfy you? And I'll take back the bike. Where is it?"

"As a matter of fact, it's in a garage near here," replied Arthur, avoiding his cousin's eyes.

"I'll arrange to sell it. Will you give me the name of the garage? Well, why don't you answer?"

"I've already sold it to them," Arthur said at last.

Phillip got up.

"Goodbye, Arthur. I'm sorry our friendship had to end like this. The rain's stopped, so I think I'll go on now."

He had only half-a-crown in his pocket, and must reach Anders Norse's office before it closed. The way to London lay through lanes and fields spattered with brick houses to tramlines which gleamed ahead for several more miles of thickening commercial traffic to East Croydon; thence to the Crystal Palace and along wet cobble-stones past motorbuses, vans and other vehicles; past a fishmonger's where several hundredweight of black eels writhed desperately on a wooden counter; past shops hung with portions of slaughtered animals; and halls advertising exotic female forms and primary-coloured muscular heroes (*Ben Hur*, catharsis for ten million repressed factory and shop serfs); past pubs and gin palaces, tea shops and skating rinks—all becoming more and more drab until he came to Vauxhall Bridge and the Embankment, to turn up Northumberland Avenue with puttees, breeches, and coat spattered by the thin black mud of London streets. Thence to the Adelphi, wondering if Anders would be in his one-room office in the basement of the corner house of the terrace. The light was on! With relief he ran down the steps, to be greeted by a smiling red face.

"I was just signing a letter to you!" Anders exclaimed. "You've come up to see MacCourage, of course? He wants to be your American publisher all right! And I've other good news for you! This afternoon I received a cable from New York telling me that *The Pictorial Review* has accepted one of your animal stories, paying five hundred dollars. That's a hundred and eight pounds for you at the present rate of exchange.

"That clears the hundred pounds you lent me. Good!"

They went for a drink to the bar of the Adelphi hotel. Anders let him have five pounds. "More tomorrow, when my bank opens!" Phillip explained his dilemma—wet clothes, and nowhere to sleep.

"Then why not book a room here?"

Why not, indeed? How very simple after all! He had forgotten that there were such things as hotels.

"There's a garage under the Arches. By the way, have you seen a copy of Martin Beausire's new novel? I was told about it, and got a copy. Later I'd like to hear your comments on it—put it in your pocket. Now I'll take you down to the garage."

"I say, Anders, where can I send a telegram? I'd like to ask my fiancée to come up—I can telegraph money, can't I?"

"Certainly."

Together they went across to the Strand post office where Phillip telegraphed two pounds to Lucy, asking her to come up as soon as she conveniently could. And then, Norton safely under cover, back to the hotel bedroom, puttees and boots removed, dry stockings and shoes on, breeches drying at the knees before a gas fire; to shave and wash, and with high heart walk round to Northumberland Avenue to his dinner engagement with *his* New York publisher!

A short elderly man with greying beard and deprecatory, almost shy manner came to meet him as he waited at the reception desk in the warm light of the foyer. At first it was not easy to talk with him. Mr. MacCourage did not seem able to get his words out easily, he used his hands to help him, while nodding many times and smiling at what he said, nodding almost before he had made the point of what he was saying, so that Phillip wasn't altogether sure what he was talking about.

Then Mr. MacCourage called a waiter, and still nodding, ordered two large scotch whiskies and soda, or would Phillip like ginger ale with his? Phillip had already had one double whisky, and was uncertain about another; as he hesitated, Mr. Mac-Courage smiled and said in his husky tones, "Do you good, boy, I said, do you good! Bring two, waiter, bring two large scotch whiskies and soda, and waiter, don't forget the ice. You're tired," he said to Phillip, moving his hands less now to help his meaning. "You're tired, you've come a long way, the whisky will do you good. I guess that Britain has come a long way, too, but Britain is still very strong, yes sir! To read some British writers is to be told that the Britishers are finished." He shook his head gravely, and looked at Phillip with the gentle eyes of a deer. "Britain is still immensely strong, yes sir! Now drink your whisky, boy, then we'll have some dinner, and you shall tell me about your books. But if you don't want to talk, boy, just relax—I know you already from your writings. Yes, sir!"

The mellow whisky certainly did Phillip good, and he was glad that he had not given way to a feeling of resistance that he was being given a drink against his will. The older man, as though reading his thoughts, went on, "You'll pardon me ordering whisky for you, but I guess I know you from your book, which I want to publish, and a little whisky at the right time is a very sound investment for tired muscles."

Phillip felt a sudden liking for him. Had not W. H. Hudson called him Honest John? The two had been friends in Cornwall, just as he was now becoming friends.

He saw the dinner as a splendid kindness of one man to another. He rejoiced in the bright lights and the happy faces of the diners, in the music and the food. O, why was not Lucy already with him? He imagined her in the kitchen cutting sandwiches of bloater paste for supper. She should be sharing these *hors d'œuvres*, these myriad dishes in red, green, and yellow—smoked salmon, sardines, anchovies, salted herrings, prawns, eggs, tomatoes—the waiter bending over her while she chose. Then sea-trout and mayonnaise sauce with finest slices of cucumber, and his American publisher, *his* American publisher, asking him if he could drink a sparkling Burgundy?

"By Jove, yes, thanks very much!"

Secretly he drank to the Boys, to Pa, to Lucy, to his Mother, to—to—steady now, this is the present, this is today, this is a full life *now*. Chicken and fried potatoes, green peas, salad, yes please, everything! Would he like another bottle? With memories of hectic guest-nights the answer is, Every time! but steady on, there is no death any more up the line, and besides, if you get tight you know you'll be beastly ill.

"No thank you, sir! But may I have another strawberry ice-cream?"

A bowl of delicious sweets, marzipan, crystallised rose petals, chocolates. Dare he eat rolled fried bacon wrapped around mushrooms?

Indigestion be damned! Brandy? Thank you! Puffing a cigar, he left the dining-room with Honest John, feeling that life was pretty good, and there was no reason why a poet, or any man, need be unhappy on the earth if he used his brains. There didn't seem anything more to talk about, and after coffee and brandy he could hardly conceal his yawns.

"You want to go to bed, boy, you need a good night's sleep, I guess." Honest John shook his hand several times, smiling and beaming. "I'll be seeing you, I said! Write me that book about the search for your tame otter. I have lost a dear wife, boy, I guess I know your thoughts. I could never love another woman, but you are young, boy. So write your pilgrimage story, and how it led you to Miss Lucy."

"I will, certainly! When Lucy and I are married we plan to spend the first part of our honeymoon on Exmoor, exploring the rivers. Then we thought of touring the battlefields, for my other book."

Honest John looked at Phillip for a moment with unguarded eyes, and thought that a part of the boy before him was dead beyond resurrection. "What I am looking forward to reading is that book on your tame otter," his quiet, grave voice was saying.

Lying in bed in his hotel bedroom Phillip looked through Martin's novel and found it all a tremendous joke. It appeared to follow Martin's own ragged life, but everything had been changed. The hero, Fitzroy d'Egville, left London with Flora Bosanquet for Devon, feeling as though they were in the half-world of *Outward Bound*. They were met at the railway station by a tall, thin young man with a lantern jaw and lugubrious expression who manifested no enthusiasm on seeing them. Rollo Gangin had engaged a rattling, draughty open car; and when Fitzroy asked if it were the only car available, Rollo replied in an off-hand manner, "You're lucky to get this one," before relapsing into sullen silence. He was surly, casual and rude, sitting down at table with unwashed hands and unbrushed hair. He ate noisily with his mouth open, and belched loudly.

At this point, remembering Martin's own belchings, Philip shook with laughter. Then he read on. During walks above the sea Rollo asked innumerable townee questions, boring Fitzroy nearly to tears, and when Flora, in desperation, said, "*Have we got* to have him with us *all* the time?" Fitzroy replied, "I am protecting your good name by taking him with us." Fitzroy had a separate lodging, in the village gravedigger's cottage. Rollo took them to see his girl, Lydia, whom he snubbed in order to enjoy her suffering while he had an open affair with the village postman's red-headed daughter, Bathsheba. The gravedigger spent his time listening, during meal-times, to their conversation, trying to find out if Rollo intended to marry Lydia, who worked in the Speering Folliot basket-factory. The food provided was horrible: brown Windsor soup (out of a packet) and cold pork and prunes were the only dishes provided. All attempts to get a fire lighted in the only sitting-room were foiled by the avaricious and bigoted landlady. Rollo was suspected of dope-taking habits; he wrote stories about deer, buzzards, herons, and ravens, which he insisted in reading to them at night in a monotonous voice, driving Fitzroy to near frenzy and Flora to desperation. Rollo allowed his cringing mangy spaniel to clean up his plate—after he had kicked it—while his cat, which might have belonged to one of the witches out of *Macbeth*, hissed and spat whenever Flora attempted to stroke it. It brought in live birds while Rollo gloated over their sufferings in the intervals of talking about the money earned by Dikran Michaelis, H. de Vere Stacpoole, Ethel M. Dell, and F. Scott Fitzgerald.

During the morning walks, when Flora wished to be left alone, bare-headed and sylph-like, Rollo's voice grated on her ear with questions about fashionable people whose names he knew only from *The Tatler*, old copies of which he stole regularly from dentists' waiting rooms.

The story moved away from Devon to Sussex and Phillip fell asleep.

Hetty took to Lucy at once, as he had known would happen; but he dreaded what his father would say about the marriage settlement. Nevertheless, he must ask him out of courtesy to Mr Copleston, who had said, "Some busybodies in the family have got on to me about it. I've got nothing to offer, but perhaps you will be good enough to let me have the name of your family solicitors." Phillip spoke first to his mother, asking her if he could give the name of her solicitors, Leppitt & Co. She showed him a letter, which cheered him.

"Good, they also have an address in Lincoln's Inn! I'll give that address to Pa, and explain that I want to make over my life policy to Lucy, and all my copyrights, which Anders Norse says will be valuable one day."

"I think you had better mention the matter to your father first, Phillip. He may feel hurt if he is left out of it."

"But you know how he behaves when he is 'hurt', as you say!"

How would Father respond? Would he think he was trying to get him to support him? He wanted nothing from anyone, alive or dead, and if any money ever came to him, he would at once give it to a hospital, he went on to tell his mother.

"You won't tell Father that, will you, Phillip?"

"Hardly! I've learned just a little bit of tact, you know."

He was much relieved when Father got on well with Lucy; and happy that Father showed the same charm of manner as when Barley had come to stay. All the same, he could not help wishing that Father would not put his tin of Samson Salts, which he usually took with his tea—'Enough to cover a sixpence'—on the table beside his cup and saucer.

Observing his son's glance, Richard said playfully, "I suppose you're not old enough, old chap, to appreciate the 'little daily dose'?"

"By the way, Father, it must be splendid exercise flying kites. Are you going to fly yours this coming summer, as you did before the war? I miss the kites above the Hill!"

"I must tell you, Lucy," said Richard, playfully, "that Phillip has inherited his grandfather's sensitive liver——"

"Oh, Father, really!"

"—with his grandfather's love of nature. Now when the time comes that the cares of family life impinge on that seat of sensibility, always remember——!" And he held up the little tin of Samson Salts.

Then seeing the expression on his son's face that he was being criticised by that, at times, superior young fellow, he went on, "Well, we can't *all* afford to go fox-hunting three days a week in winter, and follow the otter-hounds in summer, to keep ourselves fit, you know, old chap!"

"I do quite a lot of sedentary work, too, you know, Father. Anyway, my foxhunting days are over."

"Of course they are," remarked Hetty, encouragingly.

"Henceforward you'll have to dig in your garden, old chap! Does your father like gardening?" Richard said, turning to Lucy.

"Oh, yes! He spends nearly all his time with his rockery and green-house. Pa would be lost without his potting-shed, and plants to bed out!"

Phillip returned to the deviating subject of kites. "Father, do you think that if one flew a six-foot double-box kite over the sea, from the shore, one could catch fish by a line let down from a pulley?"

"But I thought you already caught fish by means of a tame cormorant, with a ring round its neck to prevent it from swallowing fish, as you described in your story, old chap!"

He turned again to Lucy. "Of course, if that was a fiction, you might train Phillip to dive from a boat, with a ring round his neck!"

When his mother and Lucy had cleared away the tea-things, Phillip breathed deeply before plunging in about the marriage settlement.

"Of course," he began hurriedly, "I realize it is merely a formality, as Mr. Copleston told me that he had nothing to put in, so I feel, with respect to him, that I ought to ask you, as I said, merely as a matter of form——"

"What are you talking about?"

"I was wondering, Father, if anything is due to me in the natural order of things, in which case I suppose it should be settled on our children. There is the family plate, I suppose, and for all I know something in your grandfather's will, part of that hundred and forty thousand pounds he left on trust——"

"So you've been representing yourself down in Devon as a man of means, have you?"

"No, Father! It is a purely formal request, by Mr. Copleston, who said, as I mentioned just now, that he, anyway, had nothing to offer——"

"Now look here, my boy! I am a poor man, and have always been a poor man! There was a family trust made by my great-grandfather, but that has long ago been determined, anyway it only applied to the Aunts. I would have you know that the greater proportion of that hundred and forty thousand pounds came to my own father, who squandered it. Is that clear?"

"Yes, Father. Thank you for telling me."

"As for my own will, everything I possess is left to your mother! 'Marriage settlement', indeed! What have you been pretending to this girl's family, pray?"

"As I said, Father, it is merely a formal question."

"It looks to me to be very much like a case of misrepresentation—if not of fraud! What have you been telling Mr. Copleston about your means, I should like to know?"

"Well, I did mention that in a few years' time I shall have several thousands a year, Father."

"*What?* You had the effrontery to tell Mr. Copleston that?"

"Please give me a hearing, Father! My literary agent told me that in a few years' time my books would be earning several thousands a year——"

"Oh-ho, so that's it, is it? Here are you, a young fellow proposing to get married again and take on the responsibilities of another family when you have no steady job—and now you talk of a marriage settlement to shore up your pretensions! How much money have you saved up, may I ask?"

"I am about to take out an endowment policy for £1,000, and now I think of it, I might as well take out another for the same sum."

Richard stared at his son before crying out, "Have you taken leave of your senses? How can you afford to keep up the premiums, without a regular income? Now may I ask for a reply to my question! How much money have you managed to save during the past four years?"

"Well, Father, to be truthful, nothing. But when I arrived in London three days ago——"

"Nothing saved up? What in heaven's name is this foolishness in getting married again then? Or is it worse than that——" Richard broke off, trying to control rising agitation; but immediately gave way to the fixed idea about his son.

"Ah, I recognise the same old pattern of your character! I can see what you have been doing! Now let me tell you this——"

Phillip tried vainly to quieten him down, for surely the raised voice would be audible in the front room where Lucy and his mother were sitting together. "*Please*, Father, will you listen?"

"No, I will *not* listen! You will listen to *me*! I am telling you that it is a case of my own father over again! He had extravagant tastes similar to your own! Salmon beats in Scotland, a partner in shoots he could not afford, fox-hunting—just like you, my boy——" Richard turned away in his distress. "Good God, it's unbelievable! Here you are, without money and in with a fox-hunting set, wasting the best years of your life, and now you propose to get married on the flimsiest and most precarious basis of future expectations from writing books."

Phillip felt an acid burning at the bottom of his throat. Unhappily he compared this reception of his confidences with Pa's off hand remark that it saved a lot of bother having nothing for the settlement.

"Father, *please* will you listen?"

"By all means! But I must ask you to stick to facts. And there's another thing I have to ask you about." He went to a table and picked up the copy of Martin Beausire's novel. "What do you know about this?"

"Martin Beausire is a friend of mine."

"Oh is he! Well, it's none of my business, you are, after all, of age, but I would call your attention to the fact that the so-called poet, or writer, in this novel lives at Speering Folliot like yourself, and makes his living by writing stories about birds and animals for the magazines. To some people it might very easily occur that the character is based on you!"

"It isn't based on me, Father. I told him about Julian Warbeck, who has red hair, and Beausire's concocted a character from that, I imagine. Anyway, it's all a joke, written in the train, to and from Fleet Street. I read it, and thought bits of it very funny."

"Oh, that's what modern literature is, is it, 'all a joke'. Well, all I can say is I don't pretend to understand modern literature!"

He went into the garden, where cats dug up his straight lines of lettuce and carrot seeds; no sooner had he got rid of slugs by traps of the peel of half-oranges when beetles or flies came along. Sparrows tore his lettuces, mice exhumed and ate his peas; now they were talking of building in the Backfield behind the garden fence. He would retire before long, and dreamed of a cottage in the country, perhaps in his native Wiltshire—but Hetty's having re-bought the house next door, to be with those two daughters of hers, had put a stop to that.

"Father, the day before yesterday I received over one hundred pounds for four days' writing! At the same time I signed a contract with an American publisher for my next three books. I receive at once fifty pounds advance against royalties of the first book. On the day of publication I get a further fifty. That is for the U.S.A. For the English market I also receive advances, though not so high, for the same books from my English publisher——"

"Then what was all that about having no money in the bank?"

"I haven't put it in the bank yet, for it hasn't arrived. You see, my money comes in lump sums. Then there are the short stories. It takes me one day to write a short story, working very hard and close, of course; about three days to rewrite it, and shift it about to get the proper dramatic flow. For such a story I get about twenty guineas in an English magazine, and something over a hundred pounds in an American magazine. That isn't very much, as things go. Top writers of short stories, such as Irving Cobb, get as much as five hundred pounds a story over in America. And I have two or three dozen stories in my head, ready to be written."

"Then why didn't you say that at the beginning, instead of that misleading remark about nothing in the bank?"

"You asked me for facts, and I told you the correct answer about my bank balance, Father."

"I don't think it's at all fair of you to convey a wrong impression, anyway! You see, in the past I have had cause to feel not very sure of you, Phillip—oh well, we won't talk any more about that."

"I'm sorry I told inessential details first, and so upset you, Father. I've been a bit nervous, to tell the truth. I wrote my news stories like that when I first worked in Monks' House, until a sub-editor told me to put the gist of the story on top, to give the reader the point of it at once, then to tell how it happened."

"Well, I am relieved to hear it. I hope it will continue to be so. You are very lucky, you know, to have all these chances. And, if I may say so, to have found such a very ladylike young woman as Lucy. Now mind that you look after her!"

Why did most old people say that sort of thing, he wondered, especially those who had made a muck of their own marriages? And get quite sentimental over small children? He would treat Billy quite differently from the way most fathers used to treat their sons.

As though receiving this thought, Richard added, "You wait,

old chap, until you have the responsibilities of a family! Oh, by the way, I almost forgot to tell you: I had a visit from your Uncle Hilary this morning, and he asked me how long you were up for. He wants to see you particularly, I gather. He asked me to tell you to ring him up at his club, and leave a message when you would be free to dine with him one evening. You know his club, I fancy, the Voyagers?"

"Yes, Father, I had lunch with him there once, soon after I had left school." Phillip had not forgotten the occasion, or how he had run away afterwards. "I didn't bring my dinner jacket with me."

"Well, perhaps it would be simpler to ask Hilary down here. He tells me that Aunt Dora is staying in London just now—would you like me to ask them down to supper one evening?"

Richard was now feeling buoyant; it had been his youthful dream to farm land; now his son would succeed where he had failed. He thought of a flint cottage, with a large garden, his pension arriving regularly every half-quarter, and a life of peace, under the hills of his boyhood.

Sir Hilary Maddison, K.B.E., C.M.G., Captain (retd.) R.N.R., who had bought most of the land at Rookhurst which had belonged to his grandfather and father, had also been imagining a not unsuccessful conclusion to his life in that he would be able to put back, if not the clock, at least a generation of his family upon the land he had seen, as a boy, come to nothing. Once he had hoped to have a son of his own, but his marriage had failed. His worry since the war had been, Who is to succeed me after my death? Of the heirs male bearing the name there was only Phillip.

Whenever he thought of that young man, he was chilled by doubt. There was something in his nephew which he couldn't stomach, as he put it to himself. As a boy he had been cowardly and deceitful; as a youth he had shown himself to be evasive, and at times had done very stupid things. What the cause of this behaviour was—apart from pure cussedness—Hilary had no idea. No one had been more surprised than he to read in *The Times*' list of *Decorations and Awards*, one day in the summer of 1918, his nephew's name. Then, after the Armistice, Phillip had reverted to his old form of playing the ass, getting himself involved in a case of arson while the worse for liquor, and to find himself cooling his heels in prison.

How far was this instability congenital, how much due to a young fellow kicking over the traces? How much did he owe to his Turney blood—look at that fellow Hugh Turney, a bounder if ever there had been one, incapable of any real work, a profligate *dilletante*. Phillip was in some ways like him: he had stuck his job for only three months in Fleet Street—after writing amateurish articles on the light-car—and then had chucked journalism to write novels—rotten novels, according to his sister Viccy—while living in a labourer's cottage in South Devon and growing a beard—wasting his life, in other words.

No: to put Master Phillip into farming would be chucking money down the drain.

And then, one day after golf, at Bournemouth—where his sister Victoria Lemon kept house for him—'Valentine', an author of romantic novels, told him that his nephew was writing 'brilliant' short stories in American magazines. Hilary was impressed to hear that for such stories anything up to two or three hundred pounds was usually paid.

"Your nephew has a real streak of genius, in my opinion, Captain."

Hilary told his sister Viccy this welcome news. She remembered that as a boy Phillip had always been keen on birds and nature; indeed, she told him that she had given Phillip, when he was nine years old, a copy of *Our Bird Friends*, by Richard and Cherry Kearton.

"Our father, you know, Hilary, was also very keen on all things to do with the country."

This remark set another course for Hilary's imagination: the boy took after his grandfather, after all. However, while writing led to nowhere, the fact that the cobbler had stuck to his last for several years, and had some monetary success with it, did tend to show that he had it in him, if he liked, to put his shoulder to the wheel. 'Valentine', the *nom de plume* of the golfing acquaintance, said that writing, to be successful, needed concentration and the will to keep going; he had seemed a sensible sort of chap himself; and, after weighing the matter in his mind, as he put it, the 52-year-old Hilary, having heard from his brother John good reports of Phillip and his new wife-to-be, had decided to propose to him that he become the tenant of Skirr farm as a pupil under his land-steward for one year, with an annual allowance, to be paid to Lucy, of £250. After that, if all went satisfactorily, he would become an improver for another year. At the end of that time they could review the situation, with the prospect of Phillip becoming the tenant of the Skirr holding, under a trust to be set up. This trust would include the estate of 1,200 acres in a ring fence, of which, after his death, his nephew would be tenant-for-life, subject to certain annuities to his sisters Belle, Viccy and Dora during their life-time. After that, it would be the turn of Phillip's son, or sons.

Sitting round the mahogany table covered by a white cloth and set with family plate from the brass-bound oak box—these silver objects seen only once before by Phillip, at the end of July 1914, when Willie had come to live in Wakenham to work in the City—he thought that Uncle Hilary was agreeable but rather too fat, while Aunt Dora looked far too thin. She ate nothing, but sipped lemon juice and water; she explained that she had been fasting for a fortnight, to cure herself of chronic dyspepsia.

It was, for Phillip, an easy occasion. Neither of his sisters was present, both were still forbidden the house by Father; despite this, Mother looked fairly happy. Lucy, across the table, next to Uncle Hilary, was talking freely as he had never known her to talk before, although she had put her hand over the glass when he had gone round with the Burgundy (Australian variety, from Phillip, *via* the Victoria Wine Company in the High Street). Father was jovial, often laughing; while Aunt Dora was sympathetic and understanding.

It was a simple meal—Richard had decided not to rely upon Hetty's cooking in that wretched gas-oven—of ham, tongue, salad with French dressing prepared by Phillip from a recipe learned in a Soho restaurant where he had lunched with Anders Norse, and mashed potatoes; followed by compôte-de-fruit and three kinds of cheese with brown bread, butter, and Thin Captain biscuits. Phillip noticed that Uncle Hilary had not drunk his glass of Australian Burgundy, although he had owned a fruit farm in Australia; Father likewise had refused a second glass, pleading that his interior economy would not stand it; so he had put away most of the flagon bottle by himself. By God, he was enjoying life! As old Julian used to say, *It's a poor heart that never rejoices!*

"Leave a little for the toasts, old man," said Richard, as his son prepared to help himself to the last glass.

"Phillip will, I am sure," said Hetty.

"Sure thing, I guess," replied Phillip, with an American accent.

"Well," announced Richard, from the head of the table. "I propose the health and long life of Lucy coupled with the names of Phillip, and of young William the heir!"

"Oh, I wish the baby could have been here!" said Hetty. "Well, your health, Lucy! And yours, my dear son, and your little son's, too!"

"Thank you," replied Phillip, remaining seated with Lucy as the others arose.

"Now you must respond, old man," declared Richard.

Phillip got up. "Father and Mother, Uncle Hilary and Aunt Theodora, on behalf of Lucy, together with myself, I thank you for all your kindness and care shown us tonight. And, if I may say it, always in the past. Since I became a father myself, I know one thing—that a child is seldom, if ever, out of its parents' thoughts."

He stopped, to be sure that his voice was steady.

"I think, with cousin Willie—for whom I always had the greatest respect—that the future of the world lies in the coming generation. I wish that all children could be brought back to Nature, to absorb, in the impressionable years, the beauty of the countryside. I think that farming is the ideal life for a man. Father, in the old days of our Sunday walks into Kent—or Kent that was—used to tell us children about his old home, and the downland country in which his father's family was brought up. So in a way this has always been 'the real country' to me."

Hilary was surprised: this was a new Phillip to him.

"My fear is that I may not be worthy of such a position, which, of course, should have been cousin Willie's. Now I propose to drink the health of my parents, with that of Uncle Hilary and Uncle John, Aunt Belle, Aunt Dora, and also Aunt Victoria. Lucy joins me in this. By the way, it is just as well that you cannot drink your own healths, by custom, because the bottle is empty!" He raised his glass, held it towards Lucy, emptied it and sat down.

"Well spoken, Boy!" said Dora.

When the women had gone into the other room Richard said, "Well, I must see how my plants are getting on," and opening the french windows, gave Hilary an opportunity to talk to Phillip alone.

Hilary waited for Phillip to broach the subject. He had written a letter to his nephew, but had had no reply. The wine had given Phillip a certain confidence, so that the usual feeling of being partly suppressed when in the company of Uncle Hilary was, for the moment, gone.

"It's jolly good of you, Uncle, to give me this chance. I hope you will forgive me for not replying at once—— By the way, I wonder why in some of Shakespeare's plays they used the word 'Nuncle'? Was it a sort of joke?"

"What makes you ask the question?"

"Well, I read Shakespeare quite a lot, and all that, you know. Yes, 'nuncle' is a sort of happy greeting, usually by the Fool."

"Oh. Well, you won't be able to give a lot of time to reading when you're farming, you know, Phillip. It's about the hardest and most demanding work there is. The daily paper for half an hour or so before bed, just to get the news, is about all the average farmer can expend on reading. By the way, what newspaper do you usually take?"

"*The Daily Crusader.*"

"Well, at least it's better than *The Herald*, but even so, its news is not reliable."

"Little so-called news is, I suppose, really—except perhaps in *The Times.*"

"Why do you take the *Crusader*, anyway? It's a rag."

"I know the Literary Editor, Brex. He gave me a guinea and a half a week for a couple of months, for a small weekly piece about the country. That kept me going when first I went down to Devon."

"But as a newspaper it's not reliable, Phillip. I happened to see a copy one morning, and it gave as the main item of news for the day what the *Trident* gave only a small space to. And that was on an inside page."

"But only on occasions of really big news do newspapers happen to have the same 'splash', Uncle. Such as the outbreak of war, or the death of a king or someone equally prominent."

"Well, I don't want to argue, Phillip. I was merely giving reasons why *The Daily Trident* is a more reliable medium for news than the sensation-mongering *Crusader*."

"What was the *Crusader* 'splash', can you remember?"

"I remember very well. C. B. Cochran was proposing to mix coloured players with white players on the stage, and there was naturally some opposition. So he gave a supper party for his coloured players, and invited various actors and actresses—'Bea' Lillie and Tallulah Bankhead, I remember, were among them. *The Crusader* made a fuss about the two parties sitting at different tables."

"But the country edition of the *Crusader* also had only a 'stick', uncle. I remember it. The London edition is printed in the small hours of the morning, the country editions much earlier."

"Well, it's not my idea of how a newspaper should be conducted." Hilary's tone until then had been persuasive; now he looked at his watch.

"Before I go, I would like to make certain that you really *do* want to spend your life as a farmer!"

"Yes, Uncle, I think I would."

"To make a proper go of it, you'll have to chuck this writing, you know! At least for a few years."

"Couldn't I write at night?"

"If you do, you'll fall between two stools. It's fatal to try and do two jobs at once, of different natures. I know what I'm talking about. I had to give up either the sea or my Australian farming interests, and so sold my land there."

"But Rider Haggard wrote and farmed——"

"Yes, and incidentally lost a lot of capital in the process! Now look here, Phillip! During the first years you'll have to put your back into it! You'll have to break yourself in to muck-carting and spreading, to hoeing roots, to cutting and carting hay, to corn-carrying—ploughing—cultivating—making a rick—everything! You can't expect to know how much a man can do and how he should do it unless you've first learned to do it yourself."

"I understand that, of course."

"Good. Well, now you know my terms. I am prepared to pay into your bank twenty-one pounds a month for the first year. You will live rent free, and have your own milk and butter. If you keep a pig you'll have your own bacon and hams. You'll shoot as my guest, and also fish by invitation. But you'll have to put your back into it, and make it your life. When the year is up, we can decide on the next step. Now what I want from you is the answer to one question—Are you prepared to accept my offer, and all it entails?"

"Yes, Uncle. And thank you very much."

"You've discussed it with Lucy, of course?"

"Yes. She likes the idea."

"I am glad, Phillip. I wish you success—which can come only through your own efforts, remember!" They shook hands. "Skirr farmhouse will be ready for you at midsummer. That will give you time to settle in before the corn harvest."

"Will it matter if we come at Michaelmas, Uncle?"

"Any particular reason for the delay? The sooner you get your teeth into it the better, you know. Also, you'll be starting during the easiest part of the year, between haysel and harvest. Well, why do you demur? Better to speak out now, you know, than later on!"

"Lucy and I thought we would like one summer by the sea, in Devon."

"Very well; but if you should want to change your mind, let me know." He gave Phillip a frank look. "You want to feed up, you're much too thin, you know. How's your general health?"

"Oh, I'm quite fit now, thanks."

"By the way, I've got the option on another five hundred acres from Tofield, the fellow who bought the land from your grandfather. His only son's a bit of a waster, I hear. When you go to Rookhurst, keep clear of him—after the initial courtesy calls, of course. When do you intend to return to Devon?"

"In two days' time, Uncle."

"I might run down and see you."

"Do. You know my address—Speering Folliot?"

"Yes. Now I must give thanks to your mother——"

When Hilary had left, it was Dora's turn with her nephew. After repeating more or less what her brother had told Phillip, she said, "What do you *really* want to do with your life, Boy?"

She looked with sympathy at one, to her, hardly more than a child, who still bore the traces of having been the unhappiest small boy she had ever known. Could one ever outgrow the effects of such a marked childhood? Would the strains of farming—and with markets fallen as they had—be too much for him? He was still exhausted from the war, she thought. Too much had been asked of his generation; the survivors still bore the mental weight of what it had gone through. He looked frail; and the way he had drunk the wine, nearly a whole bottle, so quickly, had grieved her. Would he have done that if the love of his life had not died? Lucy was a dear girl, tender and kind; but had she the strength which that other had possessed in her own right? Was she imaginative enough to cope with *un poète manqué*, as Phillip appeared to be? How would Phillip get on with Hilary? The two were worlds apart. A dear brother, yes, simple and straight-forward, but congenitally unable to understand ideas outside his own scope, and so tending to dismiss what he did not understand as having no reality. Whereas the true world was the world of the Imagination, as Keats declared.

"If you have a nervous tummy still, Boy, you should try fasting for a couple of weeks. I have found fasting to be of great value in the past; now, with my Babies constantly to look after, I can seldom undertake that way of purification. Do you remember my Babies? The blind one is now partly paralysed, while her sister has delusions, and thinks sometimes that I am trying to poison both her and her sister."

"How old are they, Aunt Dora?"

"One is turned seventy-eight, and her sister is a year younger, Boy. You must bring Lucy to Lynmouth to see them, when you are settled in your new life. I am afraid I shall not be able to put you up. Now tell me, what are you writing at the moment?"

"Nothing, Aunt Dora."

Phillip felt that he would not be able to pay the high prices of his war-time tailor, Mr. Kerr of Cundit Street, so he went to a tailor in the City to be measured for his 'glad rags', thinking that they would be about half the price of a West-end tailor. It was not done, of course, to ask about prices of one's tailor. He was measured, and arranged to come up later on for a fitting. There was no time to go to a hatter's, as he was to meet Lucy for lunch and then take her to a matinée in the Strand. The next day they were returning to Dorset, staying for the night with some of her relations in Hampshire, Aunt and Uncle Kimmy, said Lucy.

Chapter 18

PHOENIX

They arrived after a seventy-mile journey at what turned out to be a country house. Lucy's aunt, after greeting them, enquired in a voice holding incredulity as she looked at the motor-bicycle, "But is this *all* you have come on?" as though inferring surprise that such a vehicle could have any existence.

A maid showed Phillip to his bedroom. "Her ladyship will be in the garden, sir."

When he was alone with Lucy he said, "You didn't tell me that your aunt was Lady Kilmeston. I called her Mrs.! Is your uncle a knight, like Hilary?"

Lucy flushed with shame. "I'm awfully sorry, dear, but I forgot to tell you. He's Lord Kilmeston. We've always called her Aunt Kimmy, she's Pa's youngest sister."

"Are we supposed to dress for dinner?"

"Oh no, they don't bother!"

In the garden he met Uncle Kimmy wearing a Norfolk jacket and knickerbockers. At dinner it was black trousers and velvet smoking jacket, while the women wore evening frocks and long white kid gloves to the elbow. Phillip thought this glove-business rather strange. It was a simple meal, the men ate asparagus with the fingers, while the ladies, still wearing gloves—Lucy had been lent a pair—ate with forks. This was followed by grilled trout with mayonnaise, *and* new potatoes and peas—an odd mixture, he thought. There were no fish knives, they ate with a fork, with a piece of bread used as a pusher.

Bridge for threepence a hundred followed in the drawing-room.

In the morning he was wondering whether he, as guest, was expected to help Lucy and himself to breakfast from the dishes on the sideboard, for the others stood there, when a sudden entry of servants in rapid step passed them, to form up along one side of the table and kneel down. He had read of this happening in books, and so knew what was coming. The family knelt down on the opposite side, while his Lordship read prayers, followed by a text for the day from the Bible. On rising the servants curtsied or bowed, the women, picking up their long skirts to leave immediately, while the two footmen removed covers of silver dishes above spirit-stoves on the sideboard, revealing eggs scrambled and poached, grilled kidneys, tomatoes, fried mushrooms and bacon.

It was, like dinner the previous night, a reserved meal. One of Lucy's cousins was a tall girl with intellectual face who had been at Girton, where she had read the Russian language. He spoke to her about Dostoevski and Tourgenieff but made no headway. It was a relief to be on the open road once more, making for the Dorset hills along the south coast to Dorchester, and so to Lyme Regis and the coast road through Seaton to Sidmouth, where they were to stay the night with other cousins who were to be the bridesmaids, whose mother—"Aunt Dolly married Mother's younger brother, Matty"—was to help in the choosing and fitting of the bridal gown made locally by her "little woman".

These cousins were as open and jolly as the others had been reserved; delightful creatures, he thought, one eighteen and the other still at school. They were fairly poor, Lucy had told him.; after a supper of kippers and cocoa, when he helped to clear the plates into the kitchen, he saw Mrs. Matthew Chychester picking pieces of half-eaten kipper and putting them on a saucer—not for a cat, as he supposed, but to help make bloater paste.

"Where's your Uncle Matty?" he asked Lucy; regretting that he had shown curiosity when she replied, "Oh, he went away long ago, after being sent to prison. He was so nice, too!"

"I shouldn't have asked!"

"Why not? You're almost one of the family now!"

The girls prepared coffee after the washing up, and Lucy's Aunt Dolly said to Phillip, in a tone of voice suggesting the intimacy of an established friendship, "Shall we smoke a cigarette in the sitting-room, and you can tell me what Lucy's brothers are up to!" with the air of one who was only too ready to enjoy a real gossip.

"Coffee will be here in a moment, now tell me all about Tim! I hear that he is engaged to a gel in the shop where they buy their cigarettes?"

"Yes, I think he is, Mrs. Chychester."

"Do you think it will come to anything?"

"I really don't know!"

"Rather a pity, don't you think, that Adrian shuts himself up so? How can the boys meet anyone of their own kind, with a recluse for a father? Now tell me what this gel is like!" she said winningly.

"Oh, she's quite a nice sort of gel, quiet and rather shy. Tim seems to be quietly happy with her—but then I've only seen them together on one occasion."

"But a shop gel——!"

"Well—I suppose that Tim, as a working engineer, will sooner or later need a wife, to fit in with that sort of—er, work, don't you know." He felt like 'Mister' for a moment, and tried to shake off the imposture.

"What about Ernest and Fiennes?"

"Oh, Ernest is a very clever draughtsman, as well as a sound engineer. Fiennes, on the other hand, is in charge of the office of the—of the Dogstar Works——"

"Dogstar Works? What an odd name? Where did they get that from?"

"Well, as a matter of fact, it was my suggestion, Mrs. Chychester—a trade mark for the flash-lamp batteries they're going to make when they get everything going."

"How clever of you to think of a name like that! Now tell me, what is a dog-star?"

"It's a heavenly body, in the constellation of Orion, a big flashing winter star, technically known as Sirius."

"How jolly! I shall buy one when it comes out. Ah, here are the gels with the coffee! It's only 'Bivouac', I'm afraid. Do you mind?"

Was ever a walk in the twilight so beautiful with the darkening hues of the sea along the promenade shattered by a great storm of the previous winter, when it had been feared that the entire length of water-front houses would be swept away by the waves? All was peaceful now, like his life among these pleasant people. Lamplight on table, a game of rummy, cocoa and bread-and-butter before going to bed; and on the morrow a journey to North Devon to see the rector of Speering Folliot about reading the banns. The only cloud on the horizon was cousin Arthur; would he reply to the letter almost begging him to see that the misunder-standing had arisen over the old Norton because Arthur had conceived an unmentioned, one-sided, and therefore fancied arrangement which did not exist other than in his own mind? It was doubtful. Ah well, he was like his father, a little man after all.

Who else might he ask to be groomsman? All his other cousins had been killed in the war.

The next day Phillip prepared to set off alone, to leave Lucy to be fitted for the wedding dress with her cousins—delightful creatures, he thought as he kissed them on the cheek before pushing off and turning to wave his hand; then up the hills to the north-east, through narrow village streets and winding lanes to Exeter and the road to the north, and so to Speering Folliot, and the inevitable buzzing questions of the Mules'.

Some days later he returned to take Lucy home. Then they went to see Billy; and while she was helping Zillah to give him his bath, he beckoned Mrs. Mules into the closed post-office room and confided to her the news of his forthcoming marriage.

"You are one of my good friends, Mrs. Mules, with John and Zillah, so you shall be the first in the village to be told."

Mrs. Mules threw up her hands. "My dear zoul, us knowed what was comin' along months agone! Yew can't tell us nought about that! And what about they banns? And you nivver go to church! Supposin' pass'n won't allow they banns? What wull 'ee dew then, hey?"

"Do you think he'll refuse?"

"Tidden nought to do wi' me, better go and tell'n now, and ask him to read'm out for 'ee. And you'd better be in church when 'a readeth they banns just in case there be objections!"

"Mrs Mules, how can anyone possibly object?"

"Well you never knaw what might happen, now that they'm all talking about Mr. Beausire's buke!"

"I thought no one read books in Speering Folliot!"

"Git out! Us'v all read'n, of course us have!" Mrs. Mules was beginning to be short of breath. "Whativver be you about, allowin' such a man to come yurrabouts and tell all they lies about us yurr in the parish! And with that young woman he pretended to be his wife! Mules be proper upset, I can tell 'ee, how Mr. Beausire has put him in th' buke! Tidden true, you know. Tidden true about they cold prunes, neither! 'Twas only because us nivver knowed when 'a was comin'! And you'm made out to be a proper ole moucher, I can tell'ee, a proper rough man you'm made out to be! And you can tell Mr. Beausire from me that if 'a cometh yurr again, I'll tell he what I think about'm to's face, I wull!"

"Tes all lies in the book!" cried Zillah, coming into the room. "Come now, Mis'r Mass'n, tell the truth and shame the devil!"

"Oh, he doesn't get much chance, with all his work in Fleet Street, to write any other kind of book."

"I don't think it's very nice for you either, Miss Copleston! I suppose you've seen the book, haven't you?"

"Well, parts of it," replied Lucy. "I don't think Mr. Beausire meant it to be taken seriously."

"Us will miss Billy, you know, when you'm gone away!"

"Oh, but Phillip is keeping on the cottage. Mayn't we still come and see you? Billy is so fond of you all, I am sure."

"Aiy," murmured the grave-digger, coming in on rubber-tipped heels, removed from an old pair of the parson's shoes saved from the heap of rubbish for burning in the crypt furnace. "Aiy, that be so. Dear li'l babby. Dear li'l babby he be. A proper boy he be, as proper a li'l boy as ever trod ground," as Billy tried to stand upright, but sat down again immediately.

Calling at the Rectory, Phillip learned to his dismay that a copy of his birth certificate was required before the rector could publish the banns of marriage on three consecutive Sundays. Also he would require assurance that Phillip had been baptised, and thereby show qualification for membership of the Church of England.

After taking Lucy home Phillip went on to London to get the copy, and be fitted for morning coat, vest, and trousers. On the way up he wondered if he could ask Anders Norse to be his grooms-man? Or should he write to give him a chance to refuse without embarrassment? Would Anders want to come all the way to Dorset? The sky was clear and the wind from the west as he fled along smoothly at fifty miles an hour, the engine almost inaudible, so sweet was its power now that it was run-in.

After the fitting he called at his agent's office, to be told by an alert new secretary that Anders was seeing a publisher in York Buildings, in the lower Adelphi. Thither Phillip went, and while waiting in the dingy little office, with its window view of a smoke-bricked wall rising to the unseen sky, he heard in an upper room a voice protesting loudly, and footfalls passing to and fro on a boarded floor. Could that be Anders? No, said the very young girl clerk in the next room, that was the Office of *The New Horizon*, and it sounded like Mr. Wallington Christie arguing with one of his contributors, whom she called 'Kot'.

"They're always arguing about something or other!"

"Wallington Christie? I've always hoped to meet him, ever since reading his essays in the old days—particularly those on Charles Sorley, and Wilfred Owen! Do you think he would see me?"

"You can but try!"

Phillip had sent to *The New Horizon* an essay on *Wild Birds in London*: it had been returned with a note saying that the editor would like to use it, but unfortunately he had not the space. He wrote a letter back to say that there was plenty of space if only the pages were not filled by analyses of God instead of poetry. He thought of sending to Christie a copy of Willie's *The German Concentration Graveyard at Le Labyrinthe in Artois*, but dread of having it returned had stilled the impulse. Then he had wondered if he should send it to Austin Harrison for *The English Review*. Had not John Masefield filled an entire number with *The Everlasting Mercy* in 1911?

But the letter was not posted. He put it with the essay by Willie back in the drawer with other relicts of his dead cousin which Uncle John had handed over to him.

In the pages of *The New Horizon* at that time were appearing essays by H. M. Tomlinson, far and away more quickening than anything else in its pages: shimmering descriptions of sun and wind upon the wave-beaten shore of the Two Rivers estuary, Crow Spit, the Santon Burrows, the port of Appledore, the summer mirage along the sands to Down End. There were essays by D. H. Lawrence, too, but they had not the clarity of Tomlinson, though under the strain and the bars of brass that bound him, there was genius in Lawrence. Christie had been good, too, before his wife had died.

Now, as Phillip hesitated outside the office door, the old feeling of diffidence possessed him. Christie might think him pretentious, Christie who was the friend of the great—of Proust, Hardy, Bridges,

Bennett, Shaw, Lawrence, and other famous writers. What visible authority had he to claim for Willie entry into the circle of the elect? In twenty years' time, perhaps, when coffin and frame had slept away in the chalk of Rookhurst——

But there was a deeper reason for Phillip's hesitation to declare himself: deeper than his former desire to see *The German Concentration Graveyard* printed in *The New Horizon*. The reason was inherent in one of the old essays reprinted in Christie's *Insights of Literature*, called *The Phoenix*. He had read Christie's essay in *The New Horizon* in the public library in Wakenham, soon after the war, and immediately had thought to himself, I shall write the book which Christie foretells: I am that phoenix, and through me my generation shall arise into life again. After that tremendous self-assumption he had not dared to think more about it, much less confide it to anyone, even to Aunt Dora.

Tremulously he went up the stairs to declare himself; he knocked on the door, was told to come in. Christie sat at a table, reading galley proofs. He was a slight, dark man with large brown eyes filled with a look of perpetual search and hope. He saw a tall young man hesitating at the half-open door. "Come in," he said.

"I—I—I'll come back another time. Forgive me. Goodbye."

"Goodbye," said Christie, in a soft, friendly voice.

On the ground floor Anders Norse was talking to a tall young man with a face of fascinating eagerness. "Do you know Roy Inverary?" said Anders. "You should know one another. Inverary—Maddison."

The two looked at each other, feeling a warmth of friendship passing between them. "We must foregather," said Phillip. "I have read your great poetry."

"Thank you," replied Inverary, with a South African intonation. "I don't know your work, but I shall! We'll meet again! Just now I have an appointment to throw a man out of a window in Soho." He disappeared.

"Walk with me to my office," said Anders. "Then we'll have lunch together, if you're not going elsewhere."

"Thank you, Anders. I want to ask you—perhaps I should have written a letter and not have confronted you with it—don't be afraid to say no—but will you be my best man at the wedding next month?"

Anders replied at once that he would love to, provided he would be able to get away, as he thought he might, the wedding being in the last week of May.

"I'll come anyway! Have you thought about that book on your wanderings in search of the otter, which MacCourage asked you to write?"

"Yes, I'm always thinking about it."

"When will you do it, Phillip?"

"I plan to start after I'm married, Anders."

"Good for you! I have a feeling that that book will bring you fame and fortune!"

They had lunch together, and afterwards Phillip went to see his mother. She told him that both she and the two girls were looking forward to coming down for the wedding.

"Oh."

"Don't you want your sisters to come, Phillip?"

"Well, as it's going to be a very small wedding, it's hardly worth Doris and Elizabeth coming so far."

"Oh, but I'm sure they will want to be at their only brother's wedding, dear."

"Yes, of course. By the way, will Father be coming? We're not sending out any formal invitations. It's to be a specially quiet, small wedding."

"Father would expect to be asked, even if he couldn't come, you know."

"Do you think he might come?"

"I don't expect he will. But you won't forget to ask your uncles John and Hilary, and Aunt Dora, will you? They will be hurt if they are not invited, I think."

"Yes, of course, Mother. I'll ask Father, too, when he returns from the City." He felt weak, and went for a walk on the Hill, but soon returned. It was now an alien place.

"Lucy asked me to say she hoped you would come to our wedding, Father."

Having prepared himself for the ordeal, he was disappointed by the reply, as well as relieved.

"Weddings are not in my line, old man. There's a board meeting on your happy day, and as the Registrar I'm afraid I shall have to be in attendance."

"I see. I suppose you're in the Mezzanine Room now?"

"Yes, it's still the same poky little place you once knew. By the way, is Master Arthur to be the groomsman?" enquired Richard, lightly.

"No, Father."

"Ah, I did wonder, after hearing something about an accident when Arthur was riding your old motor-bicycle."

"I heard that he went round a corner too fast, and banged into a wall, Father. One reason he gave me was that the magneto was dud!"

"H'm," said Richard. Feeling that he had an ally, Phillip went on, "Do try and come to our wedding. I can fix you up with the sexton."

"Did you hear that, Hetty? Phillip wants to get rid of us even quicker than I thought!"

Laughing at his own joke, Richard went away to tidy up his garden tools, which were already standing, meticulously clean and aligned, in a row in his tool-shed.

"Now about a little matter, dear," said Hetty. "We want to give you something useful for your cottage, so the girls and I have decided to give you an armchair, specially made to keep your back from the draughts. It should arrive any day at your cottage now. I do hope you will like it."

"Thank you, Mother," he said, while suppressing a feeling of disquiet. Why did she have things specially made for him, without telling him first? If the chair was anything like the shirts she had had made for him some years back, cut to the pattern of one that had shrunk until he could hardly wear it, or the curtains that he did not want to hang beside his windows—oh dear, Mother was so anxious to please, so well-meaning: but did she *really* put other people's feelings before her own? She felt intensely for others—but only with her own personal feelings. The truth was that she had never *registered*. Her shells were fired with the best of good intentions into the air—to fall wide of the target.

If only he could stop criticising her——

It was seven o'clock. No wind, high clouds, the glass in the hall set fair: he must go back with the copy of his birth certificate, or he would miss the banns being read in time. He must begin the otter story. He must be with Lucy. Lucy was detached, she did not cling, or smother, or reveal quivering concern. He was safe with Lucy. Feeling suddenly free at the thought, he kissed his mother,

and the constriction gone, went into the garden to be with Father,
to talk to him, seeing him as he saw himself.

"You've made a fine garden, Father!"

Richard showing him round his beds, each made of soil carefully sifted and raked level; then the squared compost heap he was
making. He told Phillip how good was hop manure, and how he
suspected that chemical manures harmed the soil by injuring the
benevolent bacilli in the humus. Had Phillip a good garden with
his cottage?

"But I have forgotten that you will soon be at Rookhurst, where
the loamy soil has an entirely different character from your red
sandstone."

He spoke of the country of his boyhood—the walks on the downs,
with their early summer scent of wild thyme—his father's tame
partridges, which settled round his boots in the library—boots
recognised as protectors, since the covey had never known their
real parents.

"There's a story for you, old chap! You ask Uncle John to tell
you about them. And give him my kind regards, won't you?"

Phillip felt he had progressed: he had got away from his personal feelings and so had been able to enter the feelings of his
father. "Are you sure you can't come to the wedding?"

"I'm afraid not, old chap. But I'll be thinking about you on
the day."

An hour later, after an omelette, Phillip left for Dorset, through
Streatham and Mitcham; and once over Thames, thrusting up
goggles, he settled himself for the long ride into the sunset with the
moon soon to arise behind him, like the yellow Chinese lantern
Father once bought at Staines for a bicycle lamp on his way from
a West Country holiday to Cross Aulton, to see Mother secretly
in the garden of Maybury Lodge.

As he sped along he thought in pictures of the origins of his
father's malaise with his mother's family, the Turneys. He tried to
fit together the pictures in his mind, from stray words and remarks
of his parents, uncles, and aunts, heard in boyhood. Soon, soon he
must begin the great novel of his life—fearful thought, like having
to live on the dark side of the moon.

Wallington Christie in *The New Horizon*—what did he want?
What did he mean by 'a wisdom that came not of years of experience?' Was that mere rhetoric? 'Some strange presentiment, it

may have been, of the bitter years in store, in memory an in-
effaceable, irrevocable beauty, a visible seal on the forehead of a
generation.' Was Christie a sort of medium, too—but without
power to express the feeling in words? Miss Romer Wilson's strange
book, *If All These Young Men* had a glimpse of the 'presentiment'.

When he had read the book, Phillip had seen Christie as the
prototype of the strange, restless hero, possessed by fears and
visions, while in London, during the March, 1918, attack by the
Germans on the Somme. O, why hadn't he talked to Christie?
And why wasn't he writing his book at that very moment, instead
of getting married, with all the fuss it involved?

He thought of the cheering, idealistic crowds outside Bucking-
ham Palace, seen with Willie on the night of Tuesday, August the
third, 1914; of the young volunteers marching away, cheer after
cheer: the same in Germany, schoolboys with flowers in forage caps
and *pickelhauben*: the bearded B.E.F. in France with tunics stripped
of buttons given to civilians lining the routes to the canvas camps
on the chalk downs above Boulogne. It was still the spirit of
Rupert Brooke, of the inexperienced. Wilfred Owen's 'poetry is
in the pity' was not known, not felt, in 1914. Then the poetry
was in the spirit of men untried by war, each man a hero in his
nation's eyes, but seldom in his own. Would Christie have written
that 1919 essay if he had been an infantry soldier? Was he thinking of his own youth and that of his friends in the splendid sun of
those pre-war summers? Before the sun swelled the dead?

Should he stop, and turn round, and go back to seek out
Christie?

No: it was too late now.

But he must begin the book as soon as he got back to Devon.

What *really* caused the war, in which all sides had believed
themselves to be fighting for freedom, home, beauty, and civilisation? Could the causes of war be found in any one family in
Europe, as germs seen under a microscope? Was it, as Tom
Cundall, his old schoolfellow had told him, when they had met on
Blackheath during his last visit home, a capitalists' war? What
was a capitalist—every small shopkeeper? If it was a capitalists'
war, the shopkeepers died in their own war. Was it, as Willie had
declared, an attitude of mind, that must be changed before war
came again? How far was an attitude of mind deriving from the
economic situation in any country?

Novels of propaganda soon dated. What then? One small family unit, with all the attitudes of a family coming to disharmony? His own family, as an example?

As he passed by Stonehenge in the moonlight he told himself that he must always avoid what Conrad had called 'the terrible tyranny of a fixed idea'. Was there a way to free human beings, including himself, from personal constriction: so that the true self would shine before all men, arising above the obscurity of the petty self? Could this come only through social revolution, as Willie had declared? Or was it a personal matter of self-discipline and self-training as Jesus had indicated?

There were no lights in the windows when he reached Down Close. As usual, the doors were unlocked. All were gone to bed. He undressed in the chalet, put on his dressing-gown, went into the scullery to wash, and then stole up the back stairs into Lucy's bedroom.

He heard her whisper to him in the dark. Without speaking he got into bed beside her, marvelling at the warm softness of her body against his own. He longed for her to put her arms round him, to hold him secure; he longed to tell her, while thus held, that all was well with him, that there was harmony at last, that the love of his mother was flowing out of him once more through herself; that the breach of the war was healing; that the future would be clear where before it had been obscured; but she lay still. A feeling that he had shocked her came upon him, and as personal hope grew smaller, so did thoughts of the war and the tragedy of mankind increase. Doubt arose; she was not Barley; he must follow his life backwards into time, to live as it were in memory, instead of in the present; be apart from other people forever.

"Good-night," he said and went down the stairs, and through the kitchen, and round the path to the lawn and the chalet, while the innocent moon, companion of the night journey, seemed to have meaning no longer.

Chapter 19

THE PROMISE

A dark green Delage two-seater, its driver avoiding a heap of
earth, stones, and uprooted thorns, drew up before a notice
board, freshly painted to judge by the odd fly feebly moving upon
its surface.

COPLESTON BROS
Dogstar Works

ENGINEERS & CONTRACTORS

Battery Manufacturers, Wireless Sets,
Electric Light Installations & Wiring.

MODELS MADE TO SCALE

Every kind of Contract Undertaken

HORSES shod in a Modern FORGE

Petrol, Oil & Motor Cars SUPPLIED

Tel. 75 Shakesbury

Turning away from this ambitious effort Hilary Maddison
walked towards the roof of a house visible beyond the white-
washed Works. By the big double doors, painted the same colour
as the corrugated iron roof—a reddish brown lead-based paint—
he examined a cyclecar with rusting two-cylinder V-engine standing below the large eastern window. Nettles were growing through
the floor-boards. The long rubber belt from engine pulley to rear-

wheel axle was beginning to crack. It looked as though it had stood there since the previous summer—as it had.

Opposite, behind a new fence—already beginning to split, he noticed, as green wood had been used—stood four empty carboys, each in an iron cage beginning to rust. He looked at the label on the nearest—the date of despatch from the vitriol factory at Bristol was over a month old: and £5 allowed on each carboy upon return.

Looking through the window, he saw new machinery, with balata belting to each machine taken off the pulley of a six-horse-power oil engine. He estimated that £600 had been laid out inside. Whatever did Lucy's brothers think they were going to do with that workshop right out in the wilds?

Walking on towards the back premises of the house, he passed, with disapproval, a large heap of ashes mixed with garbage piled against a stone wall of what looked to be a blacksmith's shop. How long had the heap been accumulating? Several years, by the look of it.

On the other side of the yard was a bed of nettles strangling a flowering currant bush; and beyond, a wooden work-shop raised on a sill of bricks. The windows were laced on the inside by spider-webs. The putty holding the glass panes to the casements was cracked, and in some places fallen. Long-standing neglect there!

He went to the door of the workshop and knocked. There was no movement within; but water gushing into a drain led him to the kitchen door at the end of a rough concrete path. Beside the door was an untidy row of pails, some part-filled with distemper, others solidified with cement. He noticed that all the paint-pot lids were imperfectly secured; some were torn at the edge as though pliers had been used to remove the lids. Beside an enamel bowl full of either chicken or rabbit bones lay a large silver tureen spoon with an encrustation like solder in its bowl. He picked it up and saw that it had been used for melting lead which had part fused with the silver. The hall-mark on the back of the crested handle revealed its period to be George the First. So this was the family his young nephew was about to marry into!

The scullery door opened and Phillip looked out, pen in hand. He had been writing in the kitchen.

"Hullo, Uncle Hilary! I was just going to write to you. We're not sending out wedding invitations, Lucy and I, but asking people to come on the twenty-seventh."

"I see. What's this, d'you know?" He held out the heavy spoon with its curved handle.

"I think Tim used it when trying to melt lead to sweat on a cracked water-pipe."

"But it's a fine piece of family silver! It should not be used for such purposes. Hasn't their father anything to say about this sort of thing?"

"Oh, he leaves the Boys alone. After all, they're grown up."

"Oh." A feeling of remote heaviness passed through him. Recovering, he went on, "How are they proposing to get work here, miles away from anywhere?"

"I'll show you the water-wheel for the grist mill they're making."

He led Hilary round the path into the garden. On the lawn beside the chalet stood a wooden wheel about ten feet in diameter, bolted to a cast-iron frame. At regular intervals new elm-wood troughs formed the perimeter. "They catch the weights of falling water which turn the wheel."

"My dear fellow, I've seen a water-wheel before this, you know!" Hilary examined it closely. "Good workmanship!" he remarked, pointing at the copper nails which secured the troughs. "It must have taken some time to bore the holes for these nails."

"Ernest, the eldest brother, is a very careful craftsman."

"How are they going to get this to the mill? How far away is it?"

"About six miles. They'll have to hire a lorry, I suppose."

"Won't that add to the cost? Such things are usually built on the site, you know. How much did they estimate for this job? D'you know?"

"There wasn't an agreed price. They told the miller they would charge for the wood and their carpenter's time only."

"They employ a carpenter, then?"

"They took one on to make the cupboards and benches in the new workshop. At the moment he's helping Pa to repair the benches in the church."

"Who pays for that?"

"Nobody. It's a present for Pa."

"But somebody must pay!"

"Oh yes, they'll pay the carpenter!"

Hilary decided that his nephew's complacent attitude would have to alter if he was to succeed as a business man.

"What other work have they got?"

Phillip led his uncle to another part of the garden.

"They're going to lay this cable from their new battery house, near the notice-board, to a house up the lane."

"But this is a submarine cable! It must have cost a small fortune!"

"About a hundred pounds."

"Why not two overhead wires? That would carry the small load from the batteries quite well—and at one tenth of the cost!"

"Well, you see, the people who want the electricity won't have overhead cables."

"Do they know that this cable costs about five pounds a fathom?"

"It's not really my affair, Uncle."

"What happens if the power plant fails? A contract is a contract, you know! They might claim damages in the form of a complete battery set and engine to be installed!"

"Oh, they're two maiden ladies, I expect they'll light their oil lamps, should the engine conk at any time."

Hilary looked around. "Where is Lucy?"

"She's gone otter-hunting with Pa and the Boys."

"Why haven't you gone?"

"I'm trying to write."

"I see. Any other jobs in prospect for Copleston Brothers?"

"They intend to hire girls to make flash-lamp batteries, later on. Meanwhile they're making sac machines, and also putting a roof on the extension building of the Shakesbury Gas Works."

"Did they tender for that?"

"Oh yes. They were £100 cheaper than the nearest tender."

"Have they any experience of how to estimate for such work?"

"Not really."

"What does that mean, 'not really'? Either they have experience or they haven't, surely?"

"They're doing these first jobs cheaply to advertise the Dogstar Works, Uncle, and to gain experience."

"Where did they get that name from? It sounds odd to me. It's also capable of being parodied!"

"I thought it would be a striking 'style and title', Uncle. *You* noticed it, you see!"

Phillip explained that, further to advertise the firm, he had been drafting a new style of advertisements for the Boys in the local paper.

"They intend to make a really first-class battery, equal to the famous Hellesen battery, Uncle. Just a moment, I'll get you a copy of *The Shakesbury Herald*, and show you."

As Sirius, the Dog-star, is the strongest flashing star in the winter heavens, so the Copleston Bros. forthcoming Dogstar Battery will provide the finest light for every kind of torch, flash-lamp, and Dogstar Wireless Set, so listen-in with an improved pattern of Dogstar Head-phones.

"Are these things in production?"

"Not yet."

"Whatever is the purpose of spending money on advertising goods that aren't yet on the market? It's money chucked away!"

"I hadn't thought of it like that!"

"What sort of a roof is it they're putting on?"

His nephew explained that the Gas Works roof had been ten-dered for at a price which allowed only for what it would cost Copleston Bros.—the estimated wages of the smith, cost of H and T steel girders, galvanised iron sheets, bolts, nuts, lead paint, and a ventilating louvre.

"They must have a lot of money to throw away on all this so-called advertising!"

"No, they haven't."

"I don't understand all this. What have they allowed for contingencies?"

Phillip looked blank.

"If the job should take longer than estimated, they'll lose money on the extra time taken, which means extra labour costs. Then there is the penalty clause for not finishing to time. It might be, for such a job, so much as ten pounds or more a day. Where is this Gas Works? Have you seen what they're doing?"

"Yes. As I said, they're doing it as cheaply as possible to advertise their name."

"They'll advertise their name into the bankruptcy court in no time at all if they continue like that! And you tell me they've gone otter-hunting while in the middle of a contract job! As for those would-be comic advertisements in the local paper, you should stop them at once."

"Yes, I agree. And as it was my idea, I'll pay for them. It costs only two pounds a week for six inches single column."

"*Only* two pounds a week! How long has this been going on?"

"For a month, or so. I'll stop it right away."

"What's in here?" asked Hilary, by the tall red-brown doors.

"The Works."

"Of course it's the works! But what's inside?"

The office door was unlocked. Hilary saw that the receiver of the telephone had been left off the hook.

"Pretty careless, isn't it?"

Phillip explained that it was Fiennes' idea to leave it off, so that they would not be disturbed.

"Good God! They advertise for sales of goods they haven't made, and they fix the telephone to avoid listening to inquiries!"

"I know, Uncle, I know! You needn't think I can't see what's wrong here! But it's also to discourage 'Mister' from ringing up."

"'Mister'? Mr. Who?"

"Mr. à Court Smith. He's an old friend of the family, and a bit of a bore, as well as a sponger. Anyway, another reason—a cracked one, I'll admit—put forward for keeping the receiver off is that, if anyone rings up and can't get through, the 'line engaged' will give an idea of the Works being extremely busy."

"Busy on what? Dogstar batteries and wireless sets?"

"Well, that's Fiennes' idea, not mine. I'm not responsible!"

"But the operator knows whether the receiver is off or not!"

"It's nothing to do with me, Uncle. I am merely reporting facts!"

"Do you spend a lot of time here? I mean, with the affairs of Lucy's brothers?"

"I thought I would help them until they get going. They're rather innocent people, you see, with no business experience."

Hilary resolved to say no more; but it was too exasperating to remain silent.

"Now look here, you're marrying Lucy, not her family! The Boys, as you call these young men, are obviously going to lose all their capital. I don't want you to be involved. If you try to alter them, which is what help would mean in this case, eventually you'll meet with nothing but ingratitude. I've seen it again and again in my life. I've even tried to alter people's ways myself, in the past! Your job is to learn to farm, not to get messed up with cranks of any kind! The sooner you realize that the better. Hullo, here's Lucy! How are you, my dear?"

The next morning a furniture van arrived at the Works to deliver a massive War Surplus Disposals Board desk. This was with difficulty lifted out by five men—Tim, Fiennes, Phillip and the two who had come with the van. It was not easy to get the heavy object into the office, for the passage between the wall of the east side of the building and the wooden partition of the office was found to be too narrow for entry. Eventually part of the partition had to be taken down, together with the office door. It was then seen that the roll-top desk would take up more than half the office space.

"This must have been designed by Whitehall during the war to stop German tanks from entry into No. 10 Downing Street," remarked Phillip. "Why did you buy it?"

"Because I wanted to," replied Fiennes, shortly.

"He saw an advertisement somewhere," said Tim later, "and wrote off for it without telling us."

"But don't you three, as partners, discuss what you are going to do before you do it?"

"Ernest and I do, but Fiennes likes to act on his own."

That evening the insurance surveyor had an appointment with Tim. After he had gone Phillip saw Tim standing by the new double-gates at the Works' entrance—gates which dragged after being hung there less than a month—and looking unhappy.

"Anything the matter, Tim?"

"Oh, I've been thinking about things, that's all, Phil."

"Anything I can do to help? Only say the word."

"Well, I don't want to bother you, but the fact is, we are all somewhat appalled by the cost of this building."

"Didn't you have an agreed price? I mean, a contract with the builder?"

"Unfortunately we didn't. You see, Pidler told us it would be a bit awkward for him to estimate, with all the contingencies liable to arise."

"Such as a gale blowing down his jerry-built walls?"

With a dry laugh Tim replied, "Yes, no doubt there is something in what you say."

"Pidler should have shored up the walls, especially as they're only a single course of brickwork. How much is the bill, if you don't mind my asking?"

"Frankly, I hardly dare say!"

"Eight hundred pounds?"

"Actually it's sixteen hundred," said Tim, in a low voice.

"Sixteen hundred? Walls one-brick thick, and on end? Four-and-a-half inches thick? The woodwork already warping upstairs? And that plastering, which looks as though kids have been having fun with a whitewash brush, already cracking!"

"I know," said Tim, his voice nearly inaudible. "And that's not the worst of it, I fear. You see, the insurance surveyor said we can insure the buildings for sixteen hundred if we like, but in the event of a total loss by fire, his company will only pay replacement value, which he puts at six hundred."

"Overcharged one thousand pounds! Surely you won't pay the bill?"

"Unfortunately Fiennes has already paid it, without telling either Ernest or me. He's in charge of the office, as you know, and says it's none of our business what he does. Oh well, it's done now. Dashed poor job, though, in my opinion."

The next day 'Mister' arrived with a story he had heard of Pidler the builder in the town having hired a horse-cab in order to visit, with a barrel of beer, various friends and relations to celebrate his good fortune.

"It's a jolly shame, I can tell you," said 'Mister'. "The trouble is, old chap," as he turned to Tim, "if you don't mind my saying so, you are too kind-hearted. By the way, before I forget, I've a message from my wife. May I have a private word with you?"

He moved, arm linked with Tim's, towards the Works, now congested with other purchases from the War Disposals Surplus Board at Slough—file cabinets, typewriter, fire-extinguishers, swivel desk chair, oil-stove, etc. When he came out again, Phillip thought that he looked just like one of the illustrations of Old Mister Rat in a story in *Little Folks Annual*.

"By Jove!' cried 'Mister'. "How time flies, Phillip! In little more than no time I'll be playing Mendelssohn's *Wedding*

March on that rotten damp organ for you and Lucy! Well, I must be gettin' back, I suppose. Why, I don't know, but there it is, old chap! Give me a push off, will you? I've got this confounded asthma, now the hawthorn's out in blossom. Can't stand the smell of flowers, you know. The Onion's a bit more racketty than usual, I fancy—needs a rebore badly. I'll be glad, I can tell you, when the Works get goin', and Ernest can do the job for me. Right—push away—keep goin'—she'll fire soon, I hope—don't stop, whatever you do!—keep her goin'—any moment now she'll fire—don't stop——"

Phillip had to stop, with thumping heart. After bending down to recover, he said, "Did you turn the petrol on?"

"No, dash it all, I forgot to! She'll go now, I've flooded the carburettor—Ready?"

Another fifty yards, and Phillip stopped again.

"I expect I flooded the dashed thing too much, don't you know. The plug is probably wet. That's very good of you, old chap!"— as Phillip prepared to remove the plug. He dried it by setting fire to the petrol on it.

"I say, look out, old chap. The Onion isn't insured, you know!"

Phillip dropped the flaming plug on the ground beside the rubble by the hedge where the new petrol pump and tank had been installed, and sucked his burnt finger.

"Any damage?" enquired 'Mister', as Phillip picked up the plug.

"None at all. This should give you a quick start." He refitted the plug. "Ready?"

"You seem to want to get rid of me in a hurry, old chap."

"I thought you wanted to go back to Ruddle Stones, 'Mister'."

"Not on your life, old chap. Between you and me and the gatepost, I've no desire at all to get back."

He looked around him, the straps of his leather helmet hanging below his ears. "I can't see any profit from this petrol pump, you know. They had to plank down fifty pounds and guarantee to pay off the balance for the pump within twelve months, and all they get is twopence for every gallon sold. That means they'll have to sell close on five thousand gallons during the next year. I doubt if they'll do it. Now Ernest is thinking of installing a cigarette machine beside the pump, to help matters. But I can't see how it will work. There's only a few cottagers here, and the men smoke cheaper cigarettes. Besides, the packets will get damp very quickly, you know. Ah well, it will all be the same in a hundred years' time."

"Perhaps someone will light a cigarette and set fire to the pump, then they'll get the insurance money!"

"It's all very well to joke, old chap——"

The hot plug did the trick. The engine fired, the Onion disappeared, wheezing irritably. Phillip sought Tim. He found him in the narrow annexe built beyond the office, one side of which was a showcase for electric bulbs, car-polishing wax, rubber sponges, goggles, and hand-tools sold to Fiennes by visiting travellers. One row was taken up by a great variety of 1916–18 aeroplane plugs, also from the War Surplus Disposals Board.

"Aren't you going to try and sell the Tamp, Tim?" said Phillip kicking one of the flat tyres.

"The trouble is, no one seems to want it."

"Haven't you advertised it?"

"Now I come to consider the matter, I don't think we have."

"Is all this stock you've got here paid for?"

"Dashed if I know. Fiennes is in charge of the accounts."

"Is the machinery in the Works paid for?"

"Well, some of it is. But we have a month's credit, of course, for what isn't paid for."

"Tim, forgive my interfering: but how much of the money from selling your reversions to Mr. Thistlethwaite is left?"

"I don't really know, Phil. We sold our three shares, of what we would have coming to us when Pa died, for a thousand pounds the share."

"What was the marriage settlement worth?"

"Eighteen thousand, I think was the sum."

"And how old is Pa?"

"Getting on for seventy-four."

He went on another line, away from Mr. Thistlethwaite. "And you don't know how much you have spent, in all?"

"I'm afraid not. But we plan to live on the fifty pounds or so a month coming in for the sac-machines."

"Is that profit?"

"Oh, yes. It's the amount of the cheque, you see."

"But the sac-machine material must cost something?"

"East Anglia sends us all materials, except the phosphor bronze castings, which we get made in Shakesbury, and pay for ourselves."

"And you're always behind with delivery?"

"Well, yes we are, as a matter of fact. But when we get the Works really going, we should be all right."

"Has the Gas Works paid you anything on account?"

"Well, no."

"You'll have to meet the bills for all the materials, won't you?"

"Yes, I suppose we shall."

"How's the job going?"

"Well, we have struck a snag, as it happens. You see, the blueprint included a louvre in the roof, to ventilate fumes, but did not specify of what it should be made. So Joe, our blacksmith, made it of one-eighth-inch sheet-iron. Then, during the lunch hour a week or two ago, someone from the Gas Office came out and looked at our louvre, and expressed the opinion that it wasn't substantial enough. It would corrode quickly in the sulphurous fumes, he said. Ernest and I deeply considered the matter, and came to the conclusion that the louvre should be made of cast iron, to withstand the corrosion. So Ernest worked all night and the next day making a wooden pattern for the mould, and we sent it off to a foundry at Bristol and had it cast. As a matter of fact, it was delivered at the Gas Works only this morning, and to our horror it weighed nearly ten hundredweight. When the manager saw it, he said it would cause the entire roof to sag. We didn't agree, having worked out the stress on the main trusses of the roof, which are of six-inch T-section mild steel, but he said he wouldn't accept the new louvre. With the result that the original louvre is to go up. The cast-iron louvre cost sixty pounds, I'm afraid."

"But why didn't you specify sheet iron before you signed the contract?"

"It didn't seem necessary then. Joe told us that all louvres were of sheet iron."

"Who told you it wouldn't do?"

"As a matter of fact, it was the Gas Works junior clerk, who had only been there a fortnight, as it turned out. We told the manager, who questioned the clerk, who denied all reference to the matter."

"I expect he was afraid of losing his job. Now, Tim, I know I'm an interfering bore, but did 'Mister' borrow any money from you?"

"Well yes, as a matter of fact he did."

"You must stop that, Tim! Or you'll go bankrupt!"

The next day Phillip went to the bank in Shakesbury to ask the manager how the Boys' account stood. The Manager said he could not tell him without a written authorisation.

"I would be relieved," he said, "to discuss matters with you, in that event."

Phillip called on Mrs. Chychester at Belville Cottage. When she asked how her grandsons were getting on he said, "They are very keen, and work hard, they know the mechanics of the jobs they do, and they are competent as engineers, Grannie. But they need a business adviser."

"I was afraid that that would be the trouble, dear Phil. Of course, what you have told me shall be entirely between us. Now do not let it worry you—you who have an entirely new career before you, which will take all your strength, you know." Her wrinkled hand touched his. "My grandsons have grown up a little wild, perhaps, lacking a mother's care. Adrian, their father, is hopeless. But there, he was my dear Margaret's choice."

"Lucy told me that they were ideally happy."

"Yes, I suppose they were. But happiness, as you know, should not come before duty." She sighed inaudibly. "Adrian was forty, when he first saw Margaret, and somewhat stilted in manner. They were first cousins. His mother was one of the Oxfordshire Chychesters."

Phillip had already noted that she pronounced 'aunt' as 'ant', just as Pa did; while referring to the insect as an aunt. He had made up a doggerel rhyme about some of the strange (to him) terms of this family. The raised wall of the garden, where it bordered the meadow to the south, with a vallum below, was called a ha-ha wall; the lavatory a loo; while the small, broken-down summerhouse was a hoo.

> The Loo and the Hoo and the Ha-ha
> Are Victorian words used by Pa-pa
> But ants that are aunts
> And aunts that are ants
> Is regressing a little too far-far!

"You are smiling, dear Phil!" She took his hand, and looking into his eyes, said, "And now you are to be married to Lucy! I was so glad to see your Uncle, Sir Hilary, the other day, he has great hopes for you, you know! And when you are married, you will bring your little son to see me, will you not? Lucy tells me he is the dearest boy, and she is already most attached to him."

Her voice quavered almost imperceptibly as she leaned forward to pat the hand she held.

"Phillip, you will look after my dear Margaret's children for me when I am gone, won't you? You are so wise, in many ways, for so young a man! I am sure, from what you tell me, that a word of advice now and again will be just what the Boys need for success."

He saw Mrs. Rawlings hovering outside the door, and got up to go. "I promise you I will do my best for them, Grannie."

"Dear Phillip!" She kissed him on the cheek. "But you must not allow yourself to forget your own work, you know!"

Chapter 20

WEDDING

Phillip made up his mind to finish the story of his search for Lutra before he was married. He returned the next day to North Devon and shut himself in his cottage, sitting at the table upstairs through much of the day and night; coming down to eat food brought over by Zillah, and then up again; possessed by what he thought of as the luminous fume of the mind, in simple words, by his imagination.

The countryside was in flower, the nights becoming shorter; and when the village lights in cottage window and inn were out, he wandered over the fields and beside the estuary, trying to believe that the spirit of Barley was with him, trying to believe that the source of all life was the Imagination, that God was the Image Maker, that the species were but images which must pursue their ends to perfect God's purpose, which was to create beauty in form, sound, colour, and scent: from the co-ordination of which came the higher love which was above and beyond the personal image.

Opposed to God, or the Image Maker, were forces of destruction, nihilism, darkness, all exploiting the lower feelings by which individual life was maintained, but which if not transmuted into greater love, by their release in individuals, would frustrate the purpose of the Image Maker.

With fear he realised that, when he thought of Lucy, this idea became brittle, a mere personal wish: an illusion arising from fatigue and consequent inability to face the truth of competitive living on the earth—which meant his own personal weakness and failure as a human being. And yet——

During three days and nights, with intervals for walking and sleeping, he wrote nearly 50,000 words; and was about to lie down one morning as the clock struck seven times when Zillah knocked at the door, opened it, and called up the stairs.

"Mis'r Mass'n, please listen! You told us that you wanted a top hat, and asked me to remind you to buy one. Well, have you done so?"

"God's teeth, no! It quite slipped my mind! Did my morning suit come this morning?"

"I don't know. Father doesn't take round parcels until second post, you know that, they arrive about eleven by the van every morning. You had better look what you are about! This is Tuesday, and you told us your wedding day is Friday——"

He rolled off the bed, and went down the stairs in his bare feet. "I'd forgotten it was so near, Zillah. I must get a move on!"

"Look at you, Mis'r Mass'n! Are you going to the altar with Miss Copleston in a beard? And that hair over your ears? You look a proper old mommet, you do!"

"I must stop writing. It's no good, anyway. When can I have breakfast? I must go into town and see about things. Send off telegrams. Get measured for the hat. How does one take measurements for a hat?"

"Try one on, of course!"

"But men don't wear them any more, there aren't any for sale locally. I'll have to measure my head on a piece of paper and send it off to a London hatter. Right! I'll wash and change, and be along soon for breakfast."

"Don't forget to shave, will you? Mother says you look just like some old moucher!"

"My razor's blunt, I'll get a shave and haircut in town. I'll be over soon."

He lay across the table and made a list.

Silk hat from Lincoln, Bennett, London.
To be sent by passenger train.
Morning suit, etc., also.
Clean Cottage for A. N.'s arrival.
Engage motorcar (large) for Shakesbury.
Write Mrs. Tidball for lodgings at West Farm near Dunkery.
Collect ring from jewellers.
Get distemper, paint, and brushes to do-up cottage. 8 walls, 3 ceilings.
Wire Anders for £50 advance against otter book to be completed on honeymoon.
Telephone Shakesbury 75 to order side-car for Norton.
Write for Passport form for self, Lucy and Billy. Arrange photos for same.

The list appalled him. He lay in the armchair, heavy with fatigue; and then prayed without words, ending with three words, *Help me, Barley.*

Footfalls of Mules came to the door. There was a telegram among the envelopes.

HAPPY TO TELL YOU COLLIERS HAVE ACCEPTED TWO STORIES PAYING FIVE HUNDRED DOLLARS FOR EACH STOP LOOKING FORWARD SEEING YOU THURSDAY ANDERS

He must be resolute and open the letters later. He put them on the chimney shelf. Now for a wash and breakfast. £200!!

The scene in the Mules' kitchen afterwards was almost farcical. Phillip's idea of getting his head measured was not by means of a tape around the 'ade, as Mrs. Mules suggested, but by diagram.

"What's the good of saying my head is so many inches round? It's the shape that counts! The perimeter is what a hatter requires for fitting by post! Now here's a piece of paper. Take this pencil

—you do it, Zillah—and when I bend over the table, hold the pencil as near parallel as you can to the sides of my head and draw the outline."

"What be you about, be 'ee goin' vor stand on your 'ade on th' table?" cried Mrs. Mules, as Phillip bent over one end.

"Go on, Zillah. There isn't any time to lose!"

He had to kneel on the table, and with bowed head down on the wood, told Zillah to draw its shape; while Mules giggled and bobbed, saying softly, "What times us be livin' in, my dear zoul, I nivver zeed anything like it!"

"Now I know what King Charles felt like before his head was knocked off, Muley," he replied, looking up.

"Keep your head down, how can I draw the line if you keep bobbing about, Mis'r Mass'n?"

At last it was done. The shape looked rather large, but there was no time to be wasted; it must be sent off marked *Special Delivery* with a letter and cheque for £5, the difference if any to be credited to his account.

"Tie up Rusty, will you, until I am clear of the village? I don't want him haring after me."

So to the town, a shave and haircut; letters dispatched; to jewellers for the ring, engraved with initials as ordered. Good. Now to buy brushes, paints—white and gold for lining out—and distemper for walls and ceiling.

He had forgotten to ask for the certificate of baptism! The banns had been read (he should have gone to church to hear them) the copy of his birth certificate was in his pocket book. Pack on back, holding pots and brushes, he called at the vicarage.

"I must aplogise for not coming to church, Vicar. My only excuse is that I have been writing about my escaped otter, which is also, in a way I suppose, a search for God."

"The search was concluded a long time ago, you know! There is no need for man to make his own search. But I understand your problem, as I think I understood that of your cousin William. Now you will want your certificate. Come into my study, my dear boy!" said the smiling priest.

On the birth certificate Richard's occupation was described as *Banker's clerk.*

"My father is now the Registrar of an Insurance Company, Vicar."

"He was a banker when you were born, I see, so I will put down *Banker* in my certificate." He completed the form and said, "I suppose Mary will be going to the wedding?"

"Do you know, sir, I really don't know! I suppose Lucy will have invited her. But the Copleston's are a bit vague, so perhaps I'd better ask her. There aren't any formal invitations being sent out, I do know that. It's to be a small, very quiet wedding. Do you think I should ask Mary?"

"I think she would like to go. She is very fond of her cousin, I fancy. I shall look forward to seeing you and your wife when you come to live here."

"Yes, of course. Only—for a while at least—we may not be here. My uncle is starting us off on a farm near Lucy's home, but we shall be here in the holidays, of course."

Phillip went to Wildernesse, and asked Mary to come to the wedding. He could give her a lift there, and she could return in the same motor. She thanked him, and said that her mother was not very well, and in bed, so she must decline his most kind offer.

"I'll write to Lucy, of course, and explain; but you'll give her my love, won't you? Dear Phillip," she said, and kissed him on the cheek. "You both deserve every happiness, my dear." She smiled, and he knew she was thinking of Willie. "Look after Lucy, she is made for you, I think. Be gentle with her, Phillip, and don't try and do too much. She adores Billy, as we all do! I often go and see him when I'm in the village. Now I mustn't keep you, you will have so much to do just now."

Pots and brushes were ranged neatly on the table. First the rooms must be cleared of junk. He began, tremulously, conscious of the rushing of time, to fill a sack with his old shoes, boots, threadbare jacket, shapeless trousers, worn socks, newspapers, and tipped them in the centre of the garden. Should he burn her shoes, too? In two minds about this, he set them aside, thinking that he would take them, with her clothes in the trunk, to the Infirmary, for poor people. Or should he burn them, give them 'the honour and purity of fire', in Warbeck's words?

His idea for the best part of a year in Willie's old cottage had been that nothing must be disturbed; all must be left as when Willie had lived there. The barest room; the simplest furniture; the grandfather clock which had never been wound up since

Willie had gone; no food whatsoever in the larder; no curtains over the windows; on the wall a solitary picture of Queen Victoria presenting a Bible to a kneeling Indian Prince; the Prince Consort standing behind her, and the quotation below, *This is the Secret of England's Greatness, England's Glory*—the picture Julian Warbeck had scoffed at during that evening before Willie had been drowned.

He took out two worn rubber tyres and started the bonfire. As the rubber began to frizzle and thick black smoke to unwind itself into the air the large, pale face of his neighbour at the end cottage of the row looked over her garden wall and cried out that the thatch would catch fire, whatever was he thinking about, he would burn them all out of house and home, it was dangerous, it was making an awful smell too, couldn't he put it out?

"Sorry, it's rubber, and can't be put out!"

The flames were becoming fearsome, with the dark red flaring of the rubber; and in alarm he ran upstairs, pulled the clothes off the bed with Moggy asleep with her kittens, and began to heave and shove the lumpy old mattress through the narrow casement window. It fell at last, and he leapt downstairs to haul it on the fire, hoping it would smother the flames. White smoke was soon pouring from its four corners, joining the black smoke of the rubber.

Mrs. Mules, passing down the lane, cried out, "What hivver be the man about now, what hivver is it you be up to, what hivver be you a-doing?"

"Burning this old crennelated mattress!" he yelled through the smoke.

"Aw, there be no sense in what you'm doin'!"

"I was saying Mr. Maddison will burn us all in our beds, Mrs. Mules," ejaculated the neighbour still watching anxiously over the top of her wall. She was the widow of a small retired shopkeeper, and considered herself to be an educated person, above the rest of the village.

"Then I suggest, with great respect, that you don't go back to your beds for the time being," said Phillip.

"A proper mazed man!" cried Mrs. Mules. "I allus told'n 'e was mazed as a brish! How be 'ee gettin' on?"—to Phillip—"You won't vinnish that yurr place by tonight you know, not likely! Better if you'd let me and Zillah tidy'n up for 'ee, and gived that old mattress to Mules to rat (rot) down for his raspberry canes! 'Tidden right that you should be bringing your best man to thaccy ould place, you know! You can't go on living like a moucher now you'm about to be a married man once more!"

"That's right!" said the neighbour. "My friends all say to me, 'What, that man an author! If he is, why does he go about in such old clothes?'"

"Only my characters can afford to wear 'faultless Lincoln and Bennetts', Burberries, shoes by Lobb, and eat caviare on toast for every meal," said Phillip. "Someone's got to pay for that, you know!"

"I don't understand what you're saying, and I don't suppose you do either, Mr. Maddison!"

"And you didden ait your breakfast, only a mouthful! What sort of weddin' groom will 'ee be like, and your wife zaying us starved 'ee! 'Tidden sense, you know, goin' on the way you'm goin' on, 'tidden no sense at all! You'm got to settle down now, no more midnight rinnin' about the viels, or sittin' by a candle all night 'till cockcrow!"

When the lady and Mrs. Mules had shut up, Phillip went into his cottage and opened his letters. One from his mother said that Elizabeth was unwell, and would not be able to come to the wedding. His relief at this news changed to doubt when he read that his cousins, May and Topsy, had said they would like to come. May was on her honeymoon at Swanage, and Topsy was spending her holiday there, too; and since they were not far by train from Shakesbury they would find their own way to the church, so there was nothing for him to worry about, wrote Hetty.

So May had married Herbert! Supposing Herbert came to the wedding with May and Topsy? Nothing to worry about——? Why did the weak always destroy the strong?

Phillip's first thought was to send a telegram to his mother asking her to send a telegram to cousin May advising her that the wedding had been postponed for a fortnight, by which time Herbert Hukin would be safely back at his Nonconformist printing shop. He drafted several messages, then threw them on the fire in despair and started to scrape the upstairs ceiling. He soon gave this up as hopeless and tried washing off the thick layers of lime-wash. The water ran down his arm; he had covered less than two square yards in a little over half an hour when he gave it up: the loose flakes came off all right, but the firm patches were too hard. He tried with a knife, making shallow ruts and scratches which made the ceiling look worse than ever, before abandoning the idea.

As the hours tolled from the church tower he drove himself to work faster. He was now on the walls; the ceilings were done. White splashes were all over the beds, on his hair, face, and clothes. His right arm was white to the elbow. At two o'clock Zillah came over to ask him whenever was he coming to lunch.

"Mother's put it back in the oven, it'll be all zamzawed, then you'll complain it's all her fault, like when she washed your breeches for you, remember?"

"Zillah, I honestly haven't any time to eat anything!"

"Why didn't you let Mother and me come to help you? Look at you! A proper sight you look! Come on now and have your lunch, you were up most of the night, too. Aggie over the way saw your light from her bedroom window go on and off and on again all night, she told me. Come along, won't you?"

She was concerned for him; he yielded, and said, "I'll come when I've washed off this muck! You're a kind girl, Zillah. You'll make a fine wife for someone, one day."

"Niver 'appen!" she cried, sharply, turning her back and walking away.

Mrs. Mules and Zillah set to work to sweep and swab the upper floor, while Phillip covered the kitchen floor with old newspapers before tackling the downstairs ceiling and walls. In the middle of this work the carrier stopped outside. He said he had a heavy package to deliver. Whatever was it, asked Zillah out of an upper window, as the two men carried it into the kitchen.

Phillip ripped off the hessian to reveal a round and dumpy armchair upholstered in thick tapestry. It had very short legs, and when he sat in it the top of the back and sides, about ten inches thick, came only to the middle of his back. He remembered telling his mother once that he liked the shape of the old-fashioned cock-fighting chairs; this was apparently a local upholsterer's idea of one.

It was so heavy that the two men with Zillah's help failed to get it up the stairs, Mrs. Mules calling down from above that the stairs were hardly so wide for take down a coffin. Mules came from the graveyard to help. The chair, shaped like an enormous dough-nut, got wedged at the turn of the risers, and they had to get it down again into the kitchen, where it was lifted against one wall—the castors were too small for the weight—and left there, covered by newspapers.

Later Rusty climbed upon it and settled down amidst old *Times Literary Supplement, Manchester Guardian* and *Westminster Gazette* weekly editions, and Brex's new *Sunday Crusader*. Moggy joined him, and the two slept peacefully together.

Phillip was dipping the brush in the pail of distemper, about to start on the boarded ceiling, when the railway van arrived with three packages, also sewn in hessian. They were the table and supporting drawer-sets of a mahogany knee-hole desk which had once belonged to Thomas Turney, his grandfather. A card pinned inside the main drawer below the desk said, in Hetty's handwriting, *For Phillip from his loving sisters Elizabeth and Doris. The chair is from me, I hope it will keep off the draughts.*

He turned out the animals and sat in the chair again. It fitted so tightly around his back that no draughts would ever be able to get near him, he thought, either inside or outside the cottage. The trouble would be, when he wore thick clothes in winter, to get out of it. He would have to walk about like a snail. The fancy made him laugh, and Zillah upstairs asked what he was up to.

"'Life is a comedy to those who think, a tragedy to those who feel'," he said as he lifted Moggy and Rusty into the chair.

"There you go again!"

"It means that it is better to laugh when things go wrong, rather than to cry."

"My dear soul, what be the matter now?" called down Mrs. Mules in her panting voice.

"I think I know what it feels like to be a snail."

"Aw, you'm mazed as a brish! 'Tidden no sense what you do say!"

At five o'clock his helpers went home to get 'Feyther's tea'. Phillip went over at five-thirty and returned after ten minutes to work on until with feelings near to panic he realized that the sun was going down. Swifts were whistling around the church tower, a golden haze hung over the cottage roofs. The church clock struck nine. He got the tubby armchair upstairs by careful movements and sat before the knee-hole desk, in a kindly light from the open casements reflected upon wet walls and ceiling. What a fine character he would make out of Thos. W. Turney one day, and a sympathetic, otherwise true, one at that. The old mahogany knee-hole desk was kind and thoughtful: there was a spirit in the worn green leather top, in the hand-polished nobs, even in the dust in the corners of the drawers. The artist must always think steadily why people were as they were. He must live alone in the wilderness; or be lost to truth.

Below in the garden the bonfire was still smouldering. He went to throw earth on it.

"About time, too, I must say," remarked a voice from a bed-room window.

"That old mattress was full of worry, pain, and fear. Its sufferings are nearly over. Thank you for watching over its last hours!"

He finished painting the upstairs woodwork by candlelight about half-past one in the morning. He lay on the wire-mattress in his clothes, so to be sure of getting up early, and fell asleep at once. When he awoke he examined his painting. It had looked even and shiny by candlelight, now it was seen to be uneven and dribbly. He had until four p.m. to finish painting downstairs. But before that he must go to the station to see if hat and morning suit had arrived. It was Y/Z day. Tomorrow he was to be married. Mother, Doris, and Anders Norse were arriving that afternoon. He had eight hours.

He felt Barley's wedding ring, tied round his neck. At one time he had wondered if it would fit Lucy's finger, but had recoiled from the thought.

"Do you mind my wearing it round my neck?"

"No, of course not."

"I shall give it to Billy when he's bigger."

"Poor Billy, never to have known a real mother." Soft voice, eyes downheld, a genuine feeling. He recalled to himself what Conrad had written: that a writer should write as though he saw things for the first time—'as a child sees them—or an idiot'.

Dostoevski's *Idiot*.

Wondering what he should do if the wedding uniform wasn't

at the station he found, to his relief, that the two packages had arrived with the first train.

The hat brim touched his chin, having first pulled down his ears, which had apparently flapped back in the roomy space under this 'tile'. He folded several bandages of newsprint and fitted them inside the leather band, as stuffing. Four were required to fill the gap between his skull and silk-lined cork interior. Even so, the damned thing wobbled as he rehearsed a slow walk down an imaginary aisle. But relief came as he thought that one did not wear a hat in church. He would not need to wear it at all; he could carry it in his hand when he got out of the hired motor taking them to Shakesbury.

The suit fitted. This was pleasing, unlike the bill, which was lying in the box. £12/12/- for the coat; £4/4/- for the vest; £2/2/- for pair of white spats; £1/1/- for white slip; £4/4/- for a pair of striped trousers. It was a swizzle! The lining of both coat and vest was ordinary cheap cotton fabric—white with blue stripes for the vest, black for the coat. Both should have been of silk for that price. He would send them back after the wedding, plus the hat.

He finished painting by one p.m. All was done, not very well, but there was a new look about the place. Now he would put the blue ribbon guarding the ring into the Bible-box for Billy one day. Having placed it there, feeling light of heart, he closed and locked the oaken box with the big hand-made key; and broke into tears, for something seemed to be crying remotely from the darkness of the box, it was so final. He took out the ring at once, and placed it round his neck.

The new ring was also of red gold, engraved inside with his initials and Lucy's. He gave it to Anders for safe keeping. After dinner of roast lamb, and a bottle of burgundy, Anders said they ought to go to bed early. They said goodnight to Hetty and Doris at ten p.m. He was glad that the calm, sensitive Anders was with him in the adjoining bedroom of the cottage.

They went for a walk in the morning, and bathed in the sea. Anders said, "Don't keep looking at your watch. You've looked at it a dozen times since breakfast. Leave everything to me." At last came the moment to dress.

His hands trembled as he pushed gold cuff-links through stiff starched linen. The tie got stuck in the collar: pulling it round to even the ends, it burst collar from stud. He fitted a new collar. Anders fitted the tie. It remained at an angle. "It doesn't matter, Phillip."

Phillip tried again. It ended up as before, with one end of the collar bent. "You've got the wrong collar on."

"But this kind is the latest fashion, Anders."

"Haven't you got a wing collar? Yes, here's one. Try it."

"It's an evening collar."

"What does that matter?"

At last, feeling slim and natty in tail-coat, vest with white slip, striped trousers, and white spats over boots feeling to be thin after nailed brogues, he got gingerly, on account of his wobbly hat, into the hired Daimler landaulette, to sit opposite his mother and sister in an atmosphere of trepidant unreality.

"We'll stop on the way there," said Anders, "and buy ourselves each a red carnation."

"Doesn't the groom wear a white one, Anders?"

"Right, wear a white carnation. It's up to you."

They stopped in Taunton High Street; and coming out of the shop, Phillip noticed his mother's hat for the first time. It was of dark blue stiff cloth, and adorned by sprays of small artificial flowers, like those seen growing in Switzerland, where she had spent a holiday with Elizabeth. She saw Phillip looking at her hat, and smiled at him, while anxiety came upon her for the remote look in his eyes. Had she, after all, bought the wrong sort of hat? The assistant in Dickins and Jones had assured her that it would be the very thing for a country wedding.

Phillip was thinking of the burning sun of Spain over the Col d'Aubisque, of gentians in bloom where the snow had melted; he was hearing a voice saying *I am all your friends*. He smiled at his mother, and looked into her eyes, thinking that she, too, needed all her friends.

"That's a pretty hat, Hetty!"

"Oh, I'm so glad you like it, Phillip!"

It was sad that so little could make such happiness. If only she did not depend on him, but on impersonal things like poetry— art. But could he? Did he? Before he had known Barley?

Hetty said gaily, "Aren't the wayside flowers lovely? Oh, I almost feel I might be back in Cross Aulton!"

Phillip suggested that they play a game of naming flowers pointed out by each in turn.

"Your go first, Anders!"

"What is that one?" asked Anders, pointing to the feathery green plumes of a plant growing out of the rocky outcrop above the hedge of a bend in the road.

No one knew.

"Can you tell us, Phillip?"

"Well, I can, but it isn't fair, really. You see, Lucy told me one day as we passed on the Norton. It's used for making a sauce with mackerel. Fennel."

"Of course, how silly of me to forget! Of course, it smells of aniseed. Oh, how well I remember it growing in the herb fields around Cross Aulton when I was a girl!"

Pink campion; honeysuckle; sow-thistle; traveller's joy climbing the stay-wire of a telegraph pole; ferns, royal, hart's-tongue, unknown; then trees—beech, ash, holly, elm, white and black thorn, oak, furze, pine, sycamore. Round corners and over bridges, and in no time in the distance they saw the downs.

The sun over Dorset was warm, the day was bright—almost too bright. Would there be rain later?

"I can smell the south-west wind from the Atlantic," said Phillip as they approached Shakesbury.

"There's forty minutes to go before we need get to the church, Phillip. So I am going to give you a glass of champagne, with some ham sandwiches. Will you mind, Mrs. Maddison, if I take Phillip into this hotel? Perhaps you would care to join us?"

Phillip concealed his feeling that it was hardly the thing to be seen drinking together before the wedding of Mrs. Chychester of Tarrant's grand-daughter; but it would be worse if they left Mother and Doris outside, sitting in the car, like trippers waiting for their men to come out. He had a relieving idea: Would they like some coffee in the hotel?

"Mother, you know that coffee doesn't agree with you," said Doris.

"Just for once, dear, it won't matter."

They entered the Palm Court of the Chychester Arms, Phillip concealing the loose layers of paper stuffing inside his 9½-size hat.

"Don't worry about us, Phillip, we'll look after ourselves," said Hetty, going to the drawing-room.

When seated in white cane armchairs, Anders ordered a bottle of Veuve Cliquot, 1917 vintage, with sandwiches. The waiter returned and said they had only Moët, or Heidsiek.

"Which would you prefer, Phillip?"

"Oh, Moët!" as though that was the only possible brand.

Anders asked for a bottle in a bucket of ice. The waiter said there was no ice. When the bottle was brought Phillip swallowed a glass without enthusiasm, but the ham sandwiches induced optimism, whereupon the bottle was soon emptied.

"It's a poor heart that never rejoices, Anders!"

"I agree. Where are you going for your honeymoon?"

"On Exmoor."

"Any idea how you will get there?"

"Tim, one of Lucy's brothers, is going to take us in the Trojan."

"Then you'll come back part of the way we've come?"

"Yes."

"Then why not use our car? They always charge for the return journey, so it would be no extra expense."

"Well, we've made the arrangements already, but thanks for the idea. I did hope to have a sidecar for the motor-bike, but it won't come until next week. So we may walk back from Exmoor, to train for walking over the battlefields."

"I see." Anders looked at his watch. "We'll have to be moving!"

At two-fifteen o'clock they approached the church where he was to be married. Fifteen minutes to go. He began to feel liquescent, and by the time they arrived outside the small church with its shingled tower holding a single bell, and saw the gathering of people there, his hat seemed to be monstrously black and hollow. Quickly he removed the paper bands—supposing one fell out in the church?

"Remember to tell me never to put on my hat, Anders."

But the feeling of anxiety passed; and he felt happy to see so many friendly faces as he got out of the car.

"I'm Lucy's Uncle Francis, how do you do!"

"How do you do. May I present you to my mother? Mother, this is Mr. Francis Copleston! My sister Doris! Mr. Norse——"

Francis Copleston was quite different from Pa. He took Phillip aside. He beamed. "You haven't forgotten the certificate from your village parson that the banns have been read, have you,

Phillip?" He looked as though if Phillip had forgotten them, he would have roared with laughter.

"I put it in my tail-pocket as soon as it arrived from London." He fumbled. "Thank goodness, it's still here."

"May I take it? A mere formality, of course—ha! ha! ha!"

"Hullo, Tim! This is Anders——"

"Mother, this is Tim—Ernest—Fiennes."

"Hullo, May! So glad you could come. Topsy! I say, you both look jolly nice!"

May saw him looking for her whisker-curls. "I've pushed them up for the occasion, dearest Phillip."

Both girls were dressed in coats and skirts, May in blue serge and Topsy in black, which suited her tall, slim figure and grey eyes. Her fair hair was coiled thickly under a small straw hat with a plain grey riband.

"You both look topping! Have you met the Boys?"

"Oh yes," said Tim, adding, "I'll go and tell Pa that you've arrived."

Phillip said in a low voice to Topsy, "Is Herbert here?"

"No. He went fishing for mackerel in the sea."

"In a boat? Was the sea rough?"

"A bit. Why?"

"'Herbert Hukin started Fishin'
Herbert Fishin' ended Pukin'. I'm tight!"

Tim laughed gently. "Well, well, well! The happy day!"

"You're taking us in the Trodge, aren't you? Is it in good order?"

"I absolutely guarantee to get you there, my dear brother-in-law-soon-to-be!"

"I say, Tim, before you go. Is it usual for everyone to wait outside the church for the groom? I mean—is it a Dorset custom?"

"Dashed if I know, now you come to mention it. There are a few people inside already. I say, may I show you to your seat?"

The Master of otter-hounds, copper-horn hidden in pocket, approached up the path through the tomb-stones. Phillip saw with some surprise that this retired Eton house-master was wearing a bowler hat with a frock-coat, a green tie with stick-up collar, and brown shoes. And he had worried lest Father wear his antiquated top hat and frock-coat! How right Mother was. *It is what a man is himself, Phillip, that matters.*

"I really must congratulate you on the literary style of those advertisements appearing in the *Shakesbury Gazette*, for the new Works and the Dogstar batteries! Absolute genius, I consider!"

"Thank you, Master!"

"You haven't found your tame otter, I suppose?"

"No, I haven't."

"We're looking out for him and will let you know, if we spoor him, where he is lying."

The Master went into the church.

The open Delage arrived with Uncle John and Uncle Hilary. Both wore dark tail-less coats, and bowler hats with curly brims. Lucy's Uncle Francis was shaking them by the hand. He felt that he belonged to these people—he was one of them. Anders said they'd better wait until the car bringing the bride was in sight. Tim came back. He was hatless, wearing a ready-made grey lounge suit.

"We'll go in now," said Anders.

Harmonium playing; a hardly recognisable 'Mister' in a surplice, thin hair brushed flat, pedalling away amidst an escape of wind from the bellows—a mouse had gnawn a way in, the hole had been stuffed with paper. 'Mister' was playing *The Voice that Breathed O'er Eden*, or parts of it, for some notes were mute and others wavery with harmonics consequent on irregularity of nodes and antinodes in the pipes. Phillip had a wild impulse to laugh, and got rid of it by holding himself limp. Then suddenly he felt entirely detached, completely at ease now it was happening.

The Voice began to breathe, or rather wheeze anew. It ended abruptly. Phillip heard a susurration as villagers' heads turned. The bride had arrived. He decided that it would be gracious to stand half-facing the altar in order to receive his bride. Then doubts came: was it the parson's place to do this, as the vicar of Christ?

His face assumed an impersonal smile of welcome for pale, unsmiling Lucy who had not seen him, for her eyes were downheld; Lucy in white with veil of family Honiton lace, orange blossom in dark hair, Lucy holding the arm of a very serious Pa with grey beard and moustaches combed, wearing stiff white collar and short black vicuna coat. What was Pa thinking behind those hollow eyes downheld: of Margaret lying under the rough grasses outside the northern wall, her grave marked only by a bush of flowering currant? He saw the old man plain, felt love for him.

Now Lucy had seen him, her eyes were grave; he inclined his head and turned to face the altar: conscious of what Pa must be feeling: dead Margaret's daughter beside him with eyes downcast, her voice so quiet in her responses to the Catechism of the visiting priest, a Copleston uncle from the Chapter of Winchester, a tall, soldierly man with a quiet voice. Was Lucy nervous? He felt himself to be completely detached, everything to be happening outside himself as he answered clearly, "I do."

Now Anders was offering him the ring. Then the Wykehamist parson was giving advice in his quiet voice. Phillip heard nothing as he stood there with the beautiful spirits of the dead, coming, it seemed in fancy, from the very stone fabric of the church, with their far-beyond-serene quietude. He was kneeling down to pray. What words could be used to God? The barrack square made the soldier resolute against his nature. So with prayer. Let me be a better man, less nervy, help me to be calm and steady on all occasions: help me to be kind to the living, as to the dead.

So soon the vestry! Beyond the oak door the harmonium was playing; around him the Sidmouth bridesmaids laughing gaily, Mother smilingly signing the book.

O God, was it the wine, or was he psychic? He shivered, his eyes brimmed, he felt that Barley was just above him, in the air, calm, detached, seeing all, serene, the soul, the very germ of Barley. Did she know that Lucy came to him because of the baby, as a falcon flying to the aid of a tiercel with eyesses, whose mate had been shot? Mother was looking at him gently, and he knew she *knew*.

He was walking beside Lucy down the aisle, her hand lightly on his arm, slowly—wondering how to keep in step with the notes of organ stuttering, amidst harmonic squeaks, Grieg's *Wedding March*.

There was a swallow flying wildly, swiftly about the church from its nest under the porch: surely an omen! *Phil-lip! Phil-lip!*

Outside a double line of small girls in blue tunics and blue hats, Lucy's Guides smiling away.

"Good luck, miss!"

"Bant 'er lovely!" Showers of confetti nearly in their faces; then they were in a motor and going down the lane, passing thatched cottages and the communal rusty water-tank on wooden posts—smiling village faces, hands waving for Miss Lucy. So to the main road and quickly, it seemed, the new red-brick Works came into sight, and beyond the white iron gate newly painted in the wall where grew hundreds of small lizard-like ferns—maidenhair spleenwort—for one of which, exactly similar, Pa had recently paid five shillings, post free from a Rock Garden nurseryman in Southampton. Passing to and from church, Pa had never noticed the same ferns on his own wall, from where, possibly, the nurseryman's agent had originally dug his collection.

How ordinary now seemed the perennial lace of spiders' webs on glass, the old faded brolly, the worm-eaten sticks in drainpipe stand—how ordinary, and *small*, the dining-room freshly distempered, with coarse rough brush marks showing, the unpolished, deal-parquet flooring—as he stood beside Lucy to receive congratulations from two score or so of guests.

Then to move among people talking and pretending to eat bloater-paste sandwiches, sipping lemonade made with powder, or claret cup, while some were eyeing the strangers as though casually.

"Let me get you a drink, Phillip. You need it."

He drank whisky and water given him by Anders, who saw to it that his glass was kept filled.

Anders Norse thought that whisky was a food, by which he helped to overcome what he saw to be a mood of exhaustion in the man he thought of as a genius. He had seen tears come into Phillip's eyes again and again during the service; he knew that Phillip's sister was subject to fits, which was the reason why Mrs. Maddison had not brought her to the wedding; that there was some constriction in the family which, he considered, had helped to produce the genius in Phillip. During the service he was prepared to act, should Phillip collapse, by first thrusting a handkerchief between his teeth, lest the tongue be bitten in a paroxysm, followed by hand pummelling of the body as a counter to the seizure.

Anders Norse believed that evil spirits did exist, that they strove to possess certain rare spirits, and that, in the initial stage of possession, they must be expelled by vigorous action.

The whisky appeared to have the effect he hoped for: so that when the photographer moved to them to ask if he might be allowed to take photographs in the garden, Phillip, his face alert and smiling, led his bride by the hand on to the lawn. There, standing on the horse-skin lugged out from the floor of the chalet where it had lain ever since Phillip had brought it over from his cottage, several exposures were made of smiling bride beside happy groom whose hands were thrust deep into his trouser pockets with an air of relaxation and a wide grin upon his face.

Then bride, groom, parents, groomsman and bridesmaids were grouped on the skin, against the background of hollow rectangular hut. Once more bride and groom were taken, this time amidst a dumpling of Brownies ranging against the open chalet.

Anders came to him about twenty minutes later and said, "Are there to be any toasts proposed, do you know?"

"I don't suppose it has occurred to the Boys. Anyway, Anders, you know what they say in the Gats' Home next door to the Battersea Dogs' Home?"

"What do they say?"

"'Don't for heaven's sake mention it'. I'll be back in a minute."

He went to the lavatory in the Workshop. On the way there by the half-open gate, hovered Tim's girl, Pansy. She had a small brown-papered package in her gloved hands.

"Why didn't you come to the reception before?"

"Oh, I wasn't invited. But I did come to the church."

"I know how you feel. I've just escaped, in case I have to make a speech. Be a kind girl and come in with me, and talk to Lucy, give her a kiss, I'm sure it will buck her up."

"By Jove," exclaimed Tim, "I was wondering where you'd got to, Pansy. I'm *awfully* glad to see you! I was afraid you weren't coming."

Half an hour later Phillip was sitting, coat and vest and collar removed, on Tim's bed beside Anders, while rain from the south-west beat on the window.

"I must send the hat back, also the coat and trousers. I must find cardboard boxes for both. There are some in the Workshop, up on the beams."

"Never mind that now. I'll shove them in the car. You can send them off tomorrow. Get changed now," Anders ordered.

But Phillip had set his mind on getting rid of them; the hat for exchange, the coat and vest to be lined with silk, as befitted the price charged. He went through the rain to the Workshop for

box, paper and string, and returned to make a rough parcel of
the clothes; the hat-box was old and dusty—labelled *White,
Piccadilly*—but it would do. He must ask Tim to put them in the
car. That job done, he put on his new Donegal tweed suit and
went downstairs with Anders to rejoin Lucy looking a little unreal
in new coat and skirt of similar Donegal tweed. Then a word with
Tim about the parcels; and goodbye—goodbye—goodbye!

The Master of Hounds was holding his copper horn. The hired
car was waiting, white ribbons had been strung upon it—awful!
No matter, goodbye all round, jump in out of the rain. The Master
was blowing the *Gone Away*, an old boot of Tim's bobbling on the
string behind the rear number plate; it was OVER. The day
was a blank grey. He had no feeling beyond subdued exaspera-
tion because he had forgotten to go round and talk to all the
guests in turn. He wished he had talked with Lucy's Uncle
Francis, a most delightful fellow, unexpectedly alert and bright,
free and easy, not at all like a younger brother of Pa. Oh damn,
he had missed all the fun; seen nothing; talked sensibly to no one;
merely strutted on the blasted horse-skin. Why hadn't he remembered to remain calm and urbane. It had all passed in a
haze of unreality, like nearly everything in his life to do with
people.

Phillip had arranged for the hired motor to stop half a mile
away by a certain field-gate. The plan was for them to get out
there with Lucy, pay off the driver, hide behind the hedge,
and await the arrival of Fiennes with the Trudge. Fiennes was
to leave after the last guest had gone, and then come to take
them back to Down Close to pick up Anders, his mother, sister,
and cousins.

"Bad staff work on my part, Lucy. Mother and the girls could
very easily have gone with the driver to the teashop in Shakesbury,
and waited for us there. I'm completely inefficient,"

"Oh, it will turn out all right, don't you worry."

Wearing identical mackintoshes, they waited behind the hedge,
listening to the motors going past. After a long interval of silence,
except for the drip and patter of rain from the tree overhead,
Fiennes arrived.

"They've all gone, thank God!" he announced; and then
reversing the Trudge with grinding friction plates giving out a

cloud of smoke, he took them back to the house. There five women fitted themselves into the back in two layers, after which Phillip hauled himself in to sit on Anders's knees beside the driver.

"Go carefully," said Ernest. "The mudguards are scraping on the wheels."

The rectangular steel box, hood up and celluloid side-curtains rattling in a gale of wind and rain, the springs laid, narrow solid tyres humming against the mudguards and slipping on the wet macadam surface of the road, arrived at the station. There Phillip said goodbye to Anders, after insisting that he accept the price of his return ticket to London.

"I wish in a way you were coming with Lucy and me. I think honeymoons are hell. In Italy they have a party going on night and day for the best part of a week."

"Yes, and they also have the Mafia. But I know how you feel. I felt exactly the same when I was married. Every wedding is a strain, you know. But the main problem is, Will you be able to reach Exmoor through this storm?"

"I've been thinking the same thing. Ages ago there was only one bolt holding the engine to the chassis. I told Tim about it, and he said he would see to it."

The London train came in.

"Goodbye! Goodbye!" He felt desolate.

Then goodbye to May and Topsy in the waiting room, after kissing them both, and a return to the Trojan through skits of water blown from the station roof, gushings from gutters green with sprouting grass, the seeds of which appeared to have come from the numerous sparrow-nests in the wooden louvres on the roof ridge.

Now for the second phase of the plan. Fiennes was to return to the house and hand over the car to Tim who was to join them at the teashop, take Phillip's mother and sister to the station to catch a later train; then on to Exmoor.

So began a long wait, while the tea in the pot grew colder, and no Tim. What had happened? Had the single bolt holding the engine sheered off?

"If he doesn't come soon, I'll hire a taxi to take you and Doris to the station, Mother, then Lucy and I can stay here and go to the pictures." There was a bill on the wall, advertising the local programme. "Oh no! It's *The Phantom of the Opera*—milksop stuff. That would be the last straw, as the cow said before jumping over the moon. No, don't laugh, Mother."

Where was Tim? He should have been back an hour ago. Nondescript people drifted in, sat down, picked up worn *Tatlers* and *Bystanders,* dropped them again to be waited on, to eat muffins and toast and cakes, to sit about, to ask for the bill, to get up and go out again. Others came to sit at the same tables while the *débris* was cleared and fresh trays were brought.

"This place closes soon, you know."

"He'll be here, don't worry, dear."

Tim arrived.

"I say, I'm most frightfully sorry! This confounded rain has once more got into the tank of the petrol pump. We had to syphon out the last lot, too. I distinctly remember telling the builder that he was putting it in too far below ground level."

"Perhaps he piddled into it for luck," said Phillip. "How about the three missing engine bolts? Have they been put in?"

"Well, no, I'm afraid they haven't, now you come to mention it. As a matter of fact, Ernest simply hasn't had time to turn up two mild steel bolts. But he did remove the existing bolt and bored it to take a split pin, so I can absolutely guarantee that the bolt won't fall out like the others!"

Outside the street was prickled with rain as they got in under the hood. The engine started at the first pull of the lever; and so to the post office to send off the parcels. He could not speak until he had seen his mother and sister to the train.

And when they were gone he grieved; and could say nothing to Lucy.

Chapter 21

SUMMER WEATHER

So the long drive into the north-west gale began, up and down hills, round spurs and escarpments while the light of day was dulled by rain; and passing through Taunton, at last they were climbing up to a land of poor grazing seen through gate-gaps in the beechen hedges as they ground in low gear, feeling colder and wetter. The narrow, solid tyres slewed up and down rocky lanes, as stony as they were steep; the engine smelt of hot oil as it pulled slower and duller until, compression gone, it stopped.

"Dash it all, this is a demonstration model," muttered Tim.

"It was worn out when you bought it for the price of a new one."

"There may be something in what you say, now I come to think of it."

On both sides of the lane there was visible, through celluloid curtains, a torment of threshing beech branches. New leaves, pale green and tender, stuck on the windscreen. Water bubbled in with cold jets of wind. Lucy sought to hold the hand inert beside hers as the hailstones began to strum on the roof and clatter on the bonnet with such force that it looked as though the windscreen might be shattered. The hand was withdrawn.

"Do you think we should turn round and go back?" she asked.

"You mean push it to the top first?"

There was silence until Tim said, "It's my considered opinion that the carbon on the cylinder heads was red-hot, causing pre-ignition."

"Is it very far, to the farm I mean?" asked Lucy, as the rain changed to sleet.

"About ten miles. I must apologise for having chosen such a dud place to come to."

"But you couldn't help the weather, could you?"

"If it's any consolation, I can guarantee that this weather won't last for long," said Tim, over his shoulder. "After all, it is very nearly summer."

"A pity the wind isn't the other way, then we might get there without the engine."

"I promise you that it *will* get us there, Phil, the engine I mean. I am only waiting to let the pistons shrink in the cylinders."

The windscreen was now clogged by snow. Minutes passed.

"I'll just turn the engine a few times before I switch on. That should allow a film of oil to lie between the rings and the cylinder walls, which ought to restore compression. I assure you both that unless the ignition has failed owing to wet, the result will soon be felt."

Tim pulled over the engine half a dozen times to fill the crank case with gas.

"Here goes! Cross your fingers!"

He pulled the lever. The engine fired. They crawled on up the rocky lane, splashing through rivulets gushing down from beyond the thousand-foot contour. The engine began to smell again and to lose power when they met the full force of the wind across the Brendon hills.

"Change gear, you fool!"

"All right, all right! I was just about to, when your words startled me," said Tim, as the engine stalled.

"It looks as though the bolt holding down the engine has sheared. I ought to have seen to the damned thing myself!"

"If that mild steel bolt has sheared, I'll not only eat my hat, but my boots as well!" replied Tim. "Do you realise, my dear sir, that that bolt has a tensile strength equal to two tons direct pressure? I absolutely guarantee that it will not shear!"

Tim got out and wiped the two plugs with his handkerchief. The engine picked up afterwards. Rain sloshed away most of the sleet on the windscreen.

At last they were bumping and sliding crabwise down a long hill.

"It's half-way up the next hill, Tim."

"Oh, good! I'm awfully sorry to have taken so long, I do assure you."

Out of the mist appeared a plantation of fir trees.

"This is the place, Tim!"

They got out and stamped their feet. Tim pulled their bags from the back of the car and set them side by side on the grass.

"Are you sure you'll be able to find your way back, Tim? Here's two pounds for emergencies. Have a good dinner on the way."

"Are you sure you can spare it?"

"Au revoir, Tim dear," said Lucy. "Thank you for bringing us safely here."

"Yes, jolly kind of you," said Phillip. "Don't heed my damnable back-seat driver's remarks!"

When Tim had gone he carried the three cases into the plan-

tation, and then leaned against a larch tree. Lucy stood beside
another tree, waiting patiently for him to make a move. He knew
it, and was irritated by her patience. A narrow track exposing
yellow clay lead down the coombe to Tidball's Farm.

"The weather will clear up soon. Don't worry any more,
dear," she said at last.

"I didn't know that there was any yellow clay on Exmoor." He
stuck his heel into it. "It rained like this at Third Ypres. My
God, I don't know how we stuck it out! And for what? Waste of
life, waste of treasure, waste of hope!"

She was wearied out herself, she remained silent. They
were both half-starved. Neither realised it. He became more
querulous.

"Look at this ghastly bag I bought!" He kicked the pig-
skin suitcase. "Why did I allow that shopkeeper to sell it to
me?"

He half hoped she would come to him, but knew that she was
affected by his self-strangling mood. O, he must abandon the
otter book, and begin his war-book! Yellow shell-craters on the
Frezenberg ridge, the mournful rising and falling of strombos horns
as gas stole across the watery wastes: the tremendous glitter and
flame of the guns, making an immense volcano of the night;
'Spectre' West wounded, the hot and sweating rush to get his
message to West Cappelle . . . *'Spectre's' book should have been written
by now.*

He looked at pale, silent Lucy. *Be good to my dear Margaret's
Lucy, dear Phil.* The living, too, were ghosts. He picked up the
bags and saying, "I'm sorry, I didn't mean to be beastly just now,"
started off down the slippery foot-track to the farmhouse, followed
by Lucy.

If Mrs. à Court Smith had had ideas to help Lucy in her new
relationship, so had Phillip. Everything must be plain and natural,
without shame, as Barley had been on her wedding night. Barley
had stood before him naked, making no attempt to cover
herself.

"Now that we're married we needn't shut any doors." Lucy,
who was about to shut the bathroom door, looked startled. Her
face became serious, plain, without light. He had made a mistake.
Why was he behaving like that? To escape from the swaddling

stale air of the room, with its heavy bed and elephantine bag of a
mattress containing a loose conglomeration of feathers—like one
of those horrors carried on carts by refugees passing through
Albert on the twenty-sixth of March, 1918—he opened the casement window and resisted an impulse to jump out. He faced
blackness and the glint of falling rain.

"I expect you will be hungry. Supper will be ready now, I
think." They went downstairs. No fire in the grate. How well
he understood Martin Beausire's feelings, on his honeymoon with
Fiona, after the long cold train journey! Cold pork and prunes for
supper? Not so: a small hard end-section of what appeared to be
leg of ram, a tureen of watery cabbage in which a caterpillar lay
embalmed, another of watery potatoes boiled to burst skins, a
loaf of bread, a jug of water, and thou.

"Ah tea—tea!" said Lucy, as Mrs. Tidball came in with a tea-
pot of strong brown tea.

"I hope you'll enjoy your supper. Are you brother and sister?
You look like it, I must say," she said, hoping for a good talk
about the wickedness of the rising generation.

"I hope the weather isn't going to last like this, Mrs. Tidball.
I came here with my cousin in the summer, but I expect you have
many visitors."

"One or two, now and then," she replied, looking at them
mournfully.

When she went out of the room Lucy tried to carve the knuckle
of ram. It resisted the knife.

"I'm terribly sorry about this," said Phillip. "I asked for *lamb*,
but my writing isn't too good. Perhaps Mrs. Tidball thought I
signed my name Abraham, and got the idea of sacrificing a ram.
Oh, what a dreadful joke!"

"I think it's rather funny, Pip! Let me give you some
vegetables, with some of this gravy. I'm afraid I can't cut this
meat."

He examined the gravy. "It's Beefo! Dear old Mulesian Beefo!
Out of a cube. Still, this is a dry billet! We've at least got a roof
over us! Why didn't I bring a bottle of whisky? Ever drunk
whisky? It makes you feel so frisky."

Mrs. Tidball came in with paper, sticks, and a pail of coal.

"Are you enjoying your supper, Mr, Maddison?"

"Oh, yes, rather! You haven't got any cyder, I suppose?"

"Father never held with strong liquor, Mr. Maddison! There's none of that in this house!" She pointed to an enlargement of a photograph of a bearded man, in cloth coat and low tight collar, on the wall. "Father was chapel through and through."

Filled with Beefo and vegetables, cheese and bread and saffron cake, they went up to the bedroom. He sat on the bed while she opened her new Revelation suitcase, present of groom to bride. He saw a childlike smile upon her face as she lifted out, so carefully, her new clothes.

"Do you know, I've *always* wanted a 'Revelation'! How *did* you know? It's a lovely present!"

She began to lift out folded clothes. She put her only pair of black silk stockings on the bed. Then a black book, which she hid under a pile of folded linen. At first he thought it was a Bible, but the manifold gilt scroll and lettering on the spine revealed it to be something else.

"What's the book?"

"Oh, only something Mrs. Smith gave me to read. I haven't had time to look at it yet."

She replaced it at the bottom of the suitcase, and taking out a plain gown put it over her head.

"What's that, a new sort of tent?"

"I believe it's called a cover."

Under the cover she began to remove her clothes; and having done this, pulled a nightdress over her head and wriggled out of the cover. "I've never used one like it before," she said. "So it's a bit awkward."

"I must apologise for not having brought mine!"

"Oh, I expect you'll manage!" she laughed.

"Why didn't I bring a bottle of whisky? It really does annul the dark and the rain."

He saw spots of confetti on the carpet, and went down on hands and knees to pick up all he could see, to hide them in a matchbox. Then pointing at the small single bed in the corner of the room, "I wonder if the old woman put it in here because she thinks we *are* brother and sister! She said so when we arrived, if you remember."

"Yes, Mrs. Smith said the same thing when she first saw us together."

"D'you know, I said that Barley and I were the same kind to Dr. MacNab when I asked him to draw my blood for a transfusion for her? I still think that there might have been a chance to save her, if he hadn't taken so long over the test. I knew the moment I saw her, sitting up in bed with the baby, her face pale and drained, that she was dying. There was only one chance to save her—my blood—but he wouldn't listen."

Her face, less pale now, regarded him with concealed compassion. She sat on the bed beside him, and took his hand.

"He had his reputation to consider, I realized that, of course. So he insisted on a routine taking of her blood, what was left of it, to separate the serum. By the time he had mixed that on a watchglass with my drop, fifteen minutes were lost. During that time she died."

She wanted to comfort him, but his manner discouraged her. He went on, as though casually, "Oh, it was entirely *my* fault! I knew he was careless, and forgetful; but I *did* nothing about it! I have the mind to see these things quickly, but I don't *act* on my intuitions! My *only* hope is to be a writer, quite apart from ordinary life."

"Oh, it's easy to say afterwards what should have happened!" she replied, with sudden animation. "Why, if Pa had known that Mrs. Orchard had galloping consumption, Mother might not have gone to see her, but I expect Mother knew all the time! And if she hadn't caught it there, she might have caught it somewhere else. So don't worry your poor head any longer, dear. You're shivering, let's get warm, shall we?"

He felt easier with her when she spoke like that, and undressing, got into bed, but lay apart from her. After awhile she put out a hand to stroke his head. It felt hot.

"Don't worry, dear. I know how you are feeling. It's been rather a tiresome time, hasn't it?"

He moved to put his head against her bosom, lying awhile in her arms, but without the imagined delight of the warmth of soft *flesh*. He could not yield to her, so he gave in to mental lust of a sort and without any preliminary fondling set about achieving his self-will. She was not ready for him. At her words begging him to stop he leapt out of bed and returned to the open window, while she lay still, wishing that she had had time to read the book Mrs. Smith had given her.

Through the darkness he heard her voice saying, "Don't worry, dear."

Later, after the hypocrisy—as he thought—of acting the little boy, he accepted her tenderness, and things were easier. They fell asleep back to back, one reassuring the other sometimes by touch of hand or foot. When he awoke the storm had passed, the sun was shining in the window.

Seeing that he was awake, Lucy gave him a little kiss on the forehead.

After breakfast they must explore the stream which ran down the valley. Carrying ash-sticks cut from the hedge, they followed its course, looking on the scours of mud and sand for the footprints of otters, particularly for the three-toed seal of Lutra. The stream, or runner as the moor-folk spoke of it, was in places overgrown with crooked oaks and other trees; there were gaps in the shadow where the sun revealed every stone and frond of moss growing on the rocky bed. Here was the home of the water colley, the sturdy black-and-white bird which waded underwater, searching for caddis grubs and freshwater shrimps.

The stream ran fast and shallow, the water was clear, amber from the peat of the moor. It was a tributary of the Exe; salmon in the late autumn had swum up the smallest runnels of water to shed their eggs. Now the fry were everywhere upon the gravel in glass-clear places. The parent fish, while spawning, had been stabbed with a dung fork and heaved out on the banks by the eldest son of the farm, to be fed to pigs.

Lucy as a child had sought for birds' nests, and kept a diary; so had Phillip. That was the basis of their coming-together, and so it seemed natural that they should spend several hours every day looking for nests. They both loved wild places; for that reason they had come to one of the wildest places in the West for their honeymoon. The next day they went farther down the valley, Lucy wearing the pair of breeches he had suggested she have made for the honeymoon, with stockings, shin-high boots, and woollen polo jersey. He wore similar boots, the pair of cotton drill breeches which had been boiled by Mrs. Mules (new buckskin strappings to replace the shrivelled ones) and woollen polo jersey. Thus equipped, they found over a score of nests of the water colley in five miles of river. The nests were all built of moss, with a hole in the side, and were lined with oak-leaves. All had young, ready to fly. Some indeed flopped out of the nest and, after splashing in, swam downstream underwater.

Apart from birds, what was there to talk about? He sat beside her, feeling the inanity of his new life. Sometimes he was sharp with her—exasperated—she did not understand—he felt lonely as they wandered through the heather, or toiled to the top of a hill to look at an ancient tumulus.

On the third day he found her reading *The Psychology and Practice of Successful Marriage*, and saw the sentence

> Most pre-marital sex-knowledge on a casual basis is worthless, for it merely augments the primal male selfishness which is devoid of tenderness.

"Not bad! Where did you get it?" He read the passage which 'Mister', an inveterate commentator of library books with the aid of a pencil, had side-lined.

"It seems to me that the author had in mind to appease the puritans of the Victorian age. Don't you think that the wording is more violent than the thing itself? Do you want this wedding present?"

"Not really!"

He ripped up the book and burned it page by page in the hearth. "You see, I am exactly like Pa! At least he didn't burn someone else's book! You can plead *The Married Woman's Property Act*, Lucy! I'll plead *guilty* now, and give you a set of my first editions as compensation!"

"I have a set already, you know! Don't worry any more—I know that you want to write so badly—we won't be here much longer, anyway——"

"You *do* understand! You are really a very kind and unselfish girl! Please don't take any notice of my stupid 'moods'!"

They walked for miles every day across the moor, sometimes climbing to Dunkery Beacon, whence the hills of Wales were visible across the Severn Sea; while in other directions lay valley after valley until all was melted in mist. At evening they returned, foot-weary, sun-burned, and hungry for dinner.

At the end of the first week came the bill, a bit of a shock: four guineas a week for the use of the rooms and attendance in addition to the cost of the food, which the farm widow bought for them. The knuckle of ram dressed as mutton had reappeared on the table for the first three days, finally to disappear with the terrier dog, Spot, who trotted away over the moor to bury it.

"I know—she thinks we're rich, because of that picture paper!"

On the third morning the landlady had come into the sitting-room with a copy of a picture paper in her hand, to point at a photograph in 'Mr. London's' column—dear old Martin Beausire.

"So you left the church in a barrage of rose-leaves," said Mrs. Tidball. "It must have been a lovely sight, they roses!" There they were, holding hands, *Peeress's Niece Marries Author.*

She went on to talk about the great grief of her life. Her husband had been a well-known local preacher, "chapel through and through", she said.

"And now my youngest has become a Roman. There's none of them sort in heaven," she said dolefully, while a tear stood in her eye.

"It killed Father, aye, it did! He died in your bedroom last March did Father!"

Phillip listened to her with apparent sympathy, while hoping that the unhealthy-faced woman in black widow's weeds would not remain too long at the open door, since the eggs-and-bacon were getting cold.

There were three sons of the house. As soon as he and Lucy arrived Phillip had noticed pelts of deer lying on the floors, and knew they must have been shot; but it was a surprise to learn that the middle son objected to deer-hunting on the grounds of 'privilege for the rich' in one breath, and in the next breath told them how he got compensation for damage done to root-crops, while also snaring and shooting deer. Phillip could understand shooting the deer that did the damage, and claiming for the damage, but not the 'ethical', as the ranting farmer sometimes called it.

He was a pale-faced young man who described himself as an atheist. The veins stood out on his forehead when he argued, his thin lips curled with scorn, his voice often exploded with derision.

The youngest boy, the Roman Catholic convert, was smiling, red-faced, and pleasant in manner. He took life easily and worked hard. His mother's frequent sighs and doleful head-shakings about 'them Romans' left him serene and smiling as before.

One evening after supper they were invited into the kitchen, a low room with a smoke-dark ceiling crossed by a rough-hewn oaken beam. There was an open hearth where the cooking was done on split lengths of beech wood. A black iron kettle hung beside a black cauldron. The three sons were there; the eldest had come up from the village garage where he worked. The reason for the invitation was soon clear. A day or two before Phillip had remarked an old and rusty flint-lock gun in the passage, which idly he had said might have been used by the robber Doones, well knowing they were but characters in a novel. They had not been long in the kitchen when the eldest son, who claimed the gun, asked Phillip if he would like to buy it.

"Yes, I think I would."

"What will you bid for it?"

"You tell me what you value it at."

"Oh no, you tell me what you'll bid for it."

It seemed clear to Phillip that the owner wanted to ask too much, but was reluctant to reveal his greed; while he himself, not wanting to pay more than ten shillings was reluctant to expose himself to a suggestion of meanness. He started cautiously.

"But if you have offered it for sale, you know what you want for it, surely?"

"Maybe, but you said you'd buy'n, zo you must make me a bid. That's fair!"

"I don't see that fairness comes into it. I don't know the value of the gun, and you do. But if you want to bring in fairness, I suggest it would be fair to tell me the value."

"But if you want 'n, you ought to know how much you are prepared to pay for 'n."

"Well, you tell me your price, you're willing to sell, you say. If I come into your garage for a gallon of petrol, wouldn't you tell me the price?"

"But this ban't petrol, noomye! It be a val'able ole gun, what London museums 'ud pay a great deal of money for!"

"Well, I doubt that, with all due respect; for most museums exist on presentations."

For the best part of their stay in the kitchen this wretched situation continued, with long pauses and sometimes changes in the conversation. The youngest boy, sitting apart near Lucy, told her how baskets were made out of brambles from which the talons had been stripped, then the bramble split. Phillip spoke of badgers on the moor, and ravens; of chars-à-banes that were increasing every year, of the bad situation in the coal mines—then back to the gun. But the one would not make an offer, while the other would not name his price. At last Phillip mentioned ten shillings, to which the owner responded as he had forethought, with a mixture of anger, contempt, and derision.

"I be an ethical man, I be! And no man wull cheat me by trying to get this gun from me, not for ten pound!"

"Very well, coming from the ethical to the financial, tell us what you paid for it, at the auction where you said you had bought it!"

"Ah, wouldn't you like to knaw? But I ban't tellin', see?"

Phillip kept up his journal, and one evening gave it to Lucy to read. "Tell me, truthfully, what you think of it. I shan't mind if you agree with my self-criticisms!" She read the entries, sometimes laughing, at other times serious.

"I think you are far too severe on yourself," she said. "You are usually a pleasant companion, and although you may not believe me, I *am* enjoying our holiday here very much! Anyway, I always remember the happy things of life and tend to forget the unhappy moments."

Owls called beyond the open window.

"Anyway, don't forget to put in the lovely walks we had with Spot, and how you insisted on carrying me nearly a mile because I had a blistered heel. And you have become quite gay as the time to leave approaches, and get on well with the land-lady, who is really quite a nice woman, as you have said in your diary."

The widow had taught Lucy how to make butter: first scalding the hand to remove every bit of natural grease from the skin; then turning, almost flipping, the cream in the earthenware bowl with the hand until the cream set; then squeezing out the butter milk, and working it up in platters of beechwood, with a little salt.

"Yes, she is a nice woman. So is everyone under their defensive crust."

"Isn't it a pity she is so unhappy, about her son being a Catholic, I mean. It made him happy, and that is all that matters, I can't help thinking."

The summer holiday season was beginning, with the great inroll of coloured monsters, now called motor-coaches, to the West Country. The visitors' book in the church of Oare was renewed for its annual seven thousand signatures. They walked there on their last afternoon, and had a 'Lorna Doone' 1s.6d. tea in a barn at a long trestle table which, had it not been well made, would certainly have groaned, as a Victorian novelist would have written, with its load of bowls of scald cream—fifteen inches across, with the yellow crust hiding the thick liquid—the ham, the stewed fruit, the cake. Everyone to help themselves.

Afterwards the idea of a return walk across the moor seemed formidable, for it had taken them all day to walk there. They had said they would sleep in the heather, and watch the moon rising over the Forest: but here was a coach, about to start, which would be passing the cross-roads only a mile or so from the farm. Should they? Would it not be a betrayal if they succumbed to the monster? Was it, after all, worse than the Norton, which some artist on the moor, painting in yellow, purples and emerald greens, might have cursed as its pale-blue exhaust flames stabbed the twilight by Brendon Two-gates?

"Come on, it will be fun to ride in it!" said Lucy.

They rode home side by side, while he began to feel a content come upon life, and with it a memory of the bull and the cow grazing together near Farbus village below the Vimy Ridge, during his pilgrimage of a year ago. Their return was greeted with yelps of joy from the terrier who had accompanied them on all their walks except this one. They were his new friends, said Lucy, who patted him, spoke to him, and invited him into the sitting room.

"Poor Spot, he doesn't seem to have any other friends but us."

After she had given him the leg of ram, which Spot had buried, the terrier had become their faithful friend.

On the morrow, when the Trojan rattled to a standstill in the lane, with Fiennes and Tim come to fetch them home, the terrier whined and barked when through the window he saw his friends going away with their bags. He managed to escape and came rushing over to leap into the car and press himself low on Phillip's lap, eyes looking back at the pale atheist coming to remove him by the scruff of the neck. Spot gave a low sobbing howl as they drove off, and the last they saw of him was walking dejectedly, tail between legs, behind his master.

After a day or two learning to steer with the Norton shackled to a cumbrous sidecar, Phillip felt confident to proceed to Devon with Lucy, where they picked up Billy, Rusty, and Moggy, and made for Rookhurst. In the morning, leaving dog and cat with Uncle John, they went on with the sun in their faces, stopping for midday rest on a high grassy hill overlooking Portsmouth with its gantries and ships and smoke faintly diluting the summer colours of the sky. Should they stop the night at Worthing, and call on Martin Beausire and Fiona? Or go on through Brighton, making for Folkestone, to get the early boat to Boulogne?

"Just as you like," said Lucy. "But is there any great hurry?"

"Not really. I quite like old Martin, you know. Let's call on them. No hurry, Martin won't be home until about seven."

They lay upon the grass of Portsdown hill, while the hours went by.

"Won't it be fun when we're in Skirr Farm?" said Lucy. "I do so love it. And those white owls nesting in the roof! Billy loves them, too, don't you, darling?" She smiled uncertainly at the child crawling naked in the grasses, then glanced tenderly towards Phillip, who lay on the sward with his face to the sun.

She sat there so happily, touching the grasses, picking up the empty shell of a small banded hill-snail to show Billy, while blue butterflies and red flying beetles passed in the sunshine. Phillip, eyes closed against the bright sky, was re-living his first visit to the farmhouse one starry night with Willie, in that time now gone for ever. Perhaps it was right that the place was being altered: a new bathroom added, a new water-system put in, the tank in the loft to be filled by a ram fixed beside the stream, and a water-softening plant. The new outside boiler was to be fired by coke. Captain Arkell, the estate agent, had shown him the plans. It was a queer feeling, that he, a nobody, was now almost a country gentleman. Could he play the part? He was a little afraid of it all, regarding what he considered to be luxury as almost hostile to the simple surroundings needed for writing.

But need one change? A farmer was an ordinary person, trout in the brook were but trout in a brook. He saw himself, after the day's work, lying beside long bines of water-crowsfoot in the gravelly channels kept clear of weed by chain-scythes.

They called on the Beausires. Martin greeted them with enthusiasm, both he and Fiona insisting that they stay the night.

"How do you like my new house?" asked Fiona.

"It's lovely."

"What did you think of Martin's novel?"

"I felt honoured to have been chosen to sit for my portrait by a great *litterateur*, one of the *cognoscenti*!" he said with a straight face.

Fiona looked pleased. "Of course, it wasn't *all* true," she said. "But K. G. Wiggs wrote Martin a letter, saying it was a very good study of a genius."

"The book, you mean, or the author?"

"Which author?"

"Well, both you and Poogs, of course!"

After a 7 a.m. bathe on the shingle they enjoyed an excellent breakfast and left just before noon for Brighton, where they had lunch in Sam Isaacs' fish-shop; then up and over the downs, bumping upon a flinty road past a formless scatter of bungalows and suburban-type houses and empty wilderness plots of the housing estate formed on war-time slogans; and leaving behind this scene of his mother's investment which had so exasperated his father, they ran down to Eastbourne and on to Hastings, where they had another bathe, declaring as they lay on the shingle afterwards that it was as good a day as that one on the Burrows when they had begun to know one another.

At sunset they stopped at an inn by a little village on a hill overlooking a coast of silted and lost little ports, with its associations with Henry James, Conrad, and other writers; and a poem on Night, read in *The Oxford Book of Verse* by a lady who bore the romantic name of the place where they were now staying. The inn had wisteria in full bloom growing over its front. Such quietness, such peace as the sun went down in an aquamarine sky.

"We're only an hour's run from Folkestone," he said, at dinner. "I wonder if they have rebuilt the basilica at Albert, with the Golden Virgin on top. I meant to visit the Ancre valley last year, but somehow we never went that way."

He looks lost, my poor boy, thought Lucy. She remembered how Pa had looked after Mother's death, and wondered if she dare ask him to go for a walk with her, it was such a lovely evening.

"I'll tell the maid to keep an eye on Billy, now and again."

Leaving the child asleep in the bedroom they walked through the fields. Lucy took off her shoes and stockings in the dewy grasses, and he saw for the first time that she had feet like Barley's; the two toes of each foot, being slightly longer than the big toe, made them broad-splayed. Their beauty drew his glance again and again as they returned in the twilight, she going on upstairs barefooted, holding shoes and stockings in her hand, lest she wake the child.

"The darling," she whispered, leaning over the cot.

"I believe you love Billy as though he were your own son!"

"I do. Didn't you know?"

"I thought once that you might not really like a step-son."

"I would like him to have a little brother to play with," she said, lowering her eyes before him.

"You don't mind my still thinking about Barley?"

"No, of course not!" She added with a blush, "You see, I am not really conventional!"

Winchelsea—beautiful name, in harmony with the stars of the dusky summer night—Antares low on the horizon, cuckoo calling afar over the marshes, moths fluttering in the open window by which he stood, absorbed in the calm peace of the night. While he stood by the open window, watching the rim of the rising moon, a nightingale's notes rang with startling clearness, as though the bird were in the room. It was singing in the garden immediately below. In the pause of the deep throbbing notes, *tereu, tereu, tereu,* another answered in the distance, and soon a third had joined in the singing, and a fourth far away across the fields. He thought of Keats, of Stravinsky nights in the Doves' Nest above the gallery at Covent Garden; he thought of the poem *Heraclitus* in *The Oxford Book of English Verse*; he thought of Willie, and the spring nights of the vanished world while the guns were flashing and 'thy nightingales awake' in the valley of Croiselles before the Hindenburg Line; he thought of 'Spectre' West; and of other faces in that hopeful June before the Somme; and it seemed as though his heart had opened to all life through the friends he had known in the war.

Then to his side in the warm twilight a form moved, seeming strangely shorter; primitive with dark hair loose over dusky shoulders and breasts. The smooth-brushed head touched his tweed coat, leaning there a moment before his arm was taken above the elbow to enclose the head pressed against his ribs, as though for shelter, as though for claim upon his being. He leaned his cheek upon the dark head, his arm enclosed the warm shoulders, he held her there while her face was hidden in his jacket.

In silence she led him past garments lying on the floor—and Lucy usually so tidy—to draw him beside her on the bed.

Gould this gipsy be the modest and passive girl all of whose being he had thought to have discovered already? With tremulous anticipation he took off his jacket and hung it on a chair-back; then his other clothes, folding them calmly and neatly for the first time in his life, laying them on the seat of the chair the while a warm satisfaction of life spread through his being by which all thought was quelled. It was as though his blood knew what was wanted, beyond the antics of the brain, and was quickening with its own purpose. Without speaking he went to where she was lying, waving a foot in the air, and felt himself to be one with the night and the singing, and the stars beyond the window.

In the morning they walked upon the Romney Marsh, and he said they would go on to Folkestone on the morrow. They stayed that night at Rye, and the next at Lydd after wandering over the Denge Marsh. Then to Folkestone—where, avoiding the places he had known during and after the war, he said suddenly, "I want to go home."

"Yes, dear, I'm quite willing. Do you mean to Speering Folliot?"

"Oh, no."

"Well then, to Wakenham?"

He shook his head.

"Bless the boy, where then?"

"To Down Close. Perhaps the Boys are in a muddle."

"Bother the Boys," said Lucy. "Why can't they look after themselves?"

"Young soldiers can't, you know. I'll tell you what—let's go to Rookhurst and camp out on the meadow beside the brook until Midsummer! Then we'll start farming, as Hilary wants us to!"

"How lovely!"

They went through the flat country of dykes and sea-walls to Dungeness, and lay about on the shingle by the coastguard station, idly listening to the piping of ring plover and the fragile breaking of summer waves on the shore.

He sat apart, watching the gentle girl playing with his son. When Billy put his arms round her neck and said "Billy's mummy, Billy's mummy," he looked down at the pebbles for a few moments, before moving close, with head averted, to put his arms round them both.

Journalized: *Artois—Somme, 1924–1925*
Drafted: *Florida, 1934*
Recast and rewritten: *Devon, March 1961—July 1962*

Printed in Great Britain
by Amazon